STARSHIP OF THE ANCIENTS: BOOK 1

STRANDED

A K DUBOFF

This is a work of fiction lovingly crafted by a human. Names, characters, organizations, places, events, and incidents are either the products of the author's imagination or are used fictitiously.

www.akduboff.com

Published by Epic Realms Press
Cover by Robert Rajszczak

ISBN-10: 1965614000
ISBN-13: 978-1965614006
Copyright Registration: TXu002466398

0 9 8 7 6 5 4 3 2 1

Produced in the United States of America

TABLE OF CONTENTS

PROLOGUE

EACH COMMUNICATION WAS a risk, but such were the realities of war when sending sensitive information over interstellar relays.

The voice on the other end of the call knew the danger every time they spoke. "Well?"

"The ship is ready to embark. Everyone is on board."

"And the sample?"

"Secured and packaged with the equipment needed for synthesis." Years of preparation were about to come to fruition. Soon, they'd have everything in place to reclaim what had been lost. Colony ships always represented the promise of a new beginning, but this one stood at a pivotal crossroads for humanity. Its successful mission would be a beacon of hope for a brighter future.

"That's good news. Why do you sound concerned?"

"There was another development—a last-minute addition to the roster. It came from high-up."

"An enemy operative?"

"Maybe. Their profile is… complicated. It's not someone I'd want on board, but there's nothing we can do without tipping our hand."

"A challenge of working in the shadows. We've built in as many redundancies and contingencies as we can. If this new addition proves to be a problem, we'll adapt, just as we have before."

"I'll forward everything we've found on him." Disaggregating files and sending them piecemeal took time, but it was the only secure way to relay critical intelligence. The colony ship's manifest had been set for months, so a change so close to launch was highly suspicious and couldn't be ignored. Too much hinged on this mission. The expedition to Aethos had already been delayed by over a year, and they couldn't afford additional setbacks to getting their people and supplies to the planet.

"I appreciate everything you've done for our cause."

"I'd do it again, even knowing how difficult it would be."

"If any of this were easy, we wouldn't have needed to go to such great lengths."

"It'll all be worth it once you have the key."

1

ATMOSPHERE STREAKED BY outside the viewport as Evan's landing pod plummeted toward Aethos' surface. Red warnings flashed across the front control screen, casting an eerie glow inside the cramped space.

What the hell went wrong? He scanned over the readouts, desperate for a clue.

The screen showed other pods in the vicinity, also in uncontrolled descents. Something must have happened to communications with the main colony ship.

Straining against his harness, he reached out to the comm unit with the intent of calling for help. With his hand only centimeters shy of the controls, the pod violently lurched, sending his arm flailing to the side. The concussive force on the hull indicated that the pod had collided with something midair, though there was no sign of what it may have been.

Another jolt rocked the craft, followed by a piece of flaming debris streaking by the viewport.

What the...? Evan stared with horror at the flight map. The orbital location where the colony ship had been just minutes before was now a blank space on the readout. With a sickening twist of his stomach, he realized the pieces of debris impacting the pod were the remains of the once magnificent vessel.

Rather than becoming a new home, the planet might instead be their tomb.

As the reality of his plight set in, he started to chuckle. Aethos was supposed to be his escape, a chance to start over. Even though joining the colony expedition hadn't been his choice, at least it had offered an opportunity to rebuild a life of his own design. The fact that all would go up in flames due to a botched landing had enough poetic irony that he had to laugh.

Proximity warnings lit up the main control screen, strobing in angry red. Alarms blared.

At least it will be quick, Evan told himself. Given the torturous death he'd escaped back on Constella, this was a mercy. He closed his eyes and let out a slow breath, ready to accept his fate.

The landing pod bucked unexpectedly. Its spinning slowed.

"Emergency stabilizers activated," the computer's friendly female voice announced. "Warning, guidance system offline."

The altitude countdown was racing toward zero. Evan braced for impact.

The pod collided with the ground, jostling him against his restraints. His cushioned seat absorbed most of the impact, but the harness dug into his shoulders and waist. A shower of dirt smeared across the viewport. Though it blocked his visibility outside, dirt meant he was on the ground in one piece.

Everything was still and quiet compared to the rattling from moments before. The warnings vanished from the screen, replaced with a readout showing an exterior atmosphere analysis, errors where there should have been a map, and an indicator that power reserves were at thirty-two percent. Make that thirty-one and dropping rapidly.

Maybe this won't be a quick death, after all. He had no illusions that surviving the crash unharmed meant he was out of danger. If the colony ship had been destroyed, the struggle to survive had just begun.

He released his harness, causing a new set of controls to appear on the front panel. *All right, let's see what we're dealing with.*

Evan checked the readouts displaying the detailed exterior environmental scan data. The air was a breathable oxygen-nitrogen mixture with no identified pathogens. Temperature was within temperate range. All in all, the place was as livable as the expedition commanders had said it would be.

He next checked the communications system. There were errors across the board, indicating that the antenna had probably been damaged in one of the impacts.

The rest of the pod's controls were useless at this stage, so Evan powered down the craft to conserve its remaining power. Anxious to check for other survivors, he released the hatch lock. It opened with a hiss.

Evan grabbed a handhold and dragged himself out. He squinted in the sudden light outdoors, bringing one hand up to shield his eyes.

A warm breeze carried the scent of burnt metal, mixed with the aroma of damp soil and grass that reminded Evan of his youth—strange scents after spending most of his life in space. Other pods were scattered around the field where he'd landed. Small fires smoldered near several of the landing sites, casting a smokey haze across the landscape. Bits of wreckage were interspersed with the craft; it was unclear at first glance if the remains belonged to pods or the colony ship. Several of the pods appeared to be shattered, having had the misfortune of crashing down onto rock rather than the soft field. Evan thanked the stars for his safe landing site on grass.

Other people had started to emerge from their pods. Their expressions were full of fear—eyes darting and brows knitted as they took in the wreckage. Many of their faces had become streaked with dark smudges as they dug through burning scrap to check for survivors.

A woman screamed somewhere behind Evan, followed by indistinct shouts from several other men and women.

Evan dove back into the pod to grab his travel pack from a storage bin. He quickly slung it over his shoulder before running in the direction of the shouts.

Coming around the back side of his pod, he saw a man trapped under a piece of wreckage. Based on the awful angle of his leg and the blood pooling on the ground, he wasn't going to make it through the night without serious medical attention. Three people were trying to lift a fallen metal beam off him, groaning and swearing more than making genuine progress.

"Stop!" Evan shouted, running up. "The pressure is keeping him from bleeding out faster. We need a treatment plan before getting him out."

The trapped man was barely conscious, but his eyes widened with concern at the statement, followed by a pained grimace.

Evan didn't want to be the one to say it, but the man was most likely a goner no matter what they did. If a full medical facility were close at hand, he may well survive. But here, with no surgeon evident and an apparent lack of supplies, he'd bleed out or succumb to infection.

"He's right, we need to slow that bleeding!" a young woman said, elbowing her way to the patient. Her dark hair was pulled back into a sloppy ponytail, mussed bangs framing her pretty face. Her movements had the confidence of someone who was experienced responding to trauma, though her petite frame made her look young and innocent at first glance. "I need something to use as a tourniquet."

One of the assisting men unclasped his belt and handed it to her. She deftly wrapped it around the patient's thigh and tightened it. The trapped man cried out in pain as the belt cinched tight.

"I'm going to get you out of here," the woman told him.

Evan noted that she hadn't said "you're going to be okay" or any of the other platitudes a doctor often said to their patient. She had promised that he wouldn't die while trapped under the wreckage. It was a fair statement, and Evan immediately respected her for it.

"Hey, what's your name?" the woman asked, looking up at him from where she was crouched next to the patient.

"Evan."

"All right, Evan. I'm Anya." She wiped the back of one hand across her forehead, smearing the soot sticking to her perspiration. "I could use some help here."

"Sure." He knelt down next to her. While no stranger to blood, he didn't like it. At least Anya seemed to be taking it well. "Are you a doctor?" he asked her.

She shook her head. "Just field medic training. I didn't see anyone else jumping in, so..."

He nodded. "I've had a little myself."

"Good. So, you know what we have to do." She met his gaze, silently communicating that she understood there was nothing they could do for the injured man aside from make him more comfortable.

"I do."

"The rest of you, give us a hand," Anya instructed,

motioning to the three people who'd been trying to assist. "Find a pry bar."

The man who'd offered up his belt located a length of round metal that may have once been a railing. "Will this work?"

"Good enough. Wedge it under this beam and raise it on my mark," Anya told him.

The man stuck the lever in place, and the other helpers got in position to assist with the lift.

For his part, Evan crouched down by the trapped man's shoulders, ready to drag him out as soon as the metal wreckage was elevated.

Anya positioned herself by his wounded leg, prepared to stem the bleeding. "All right, everyone ready? Three… two… one!"

The helpers pried up the piece of debris. With a firm tug, Evan pulled the man away from the wreckage. Anya moved with him, immediately applying pressure to the mangled leg with a balled-up shirt. As soon as they were clear, the others lowered the gnarled metal back to the ground.

"There, we've got you." Anya kept both hands firmly pressed against the man's leg, blood seeping out around the cloth.

Mercifully, the man lost consciousness, though he still trembled from the shock of the ordeal.

"I wish we had a med bay," Anya murmured.

Evan stood up. "There are a lot of things that would be nice to have right now." Knowing there was nothing else he could do, he stepped away from the injured man and wiped off his hands on the grass. "Have you seen any of the mission commanders among the survivors?"

"No. I don't recognize anyone here."

A countdown had started, and there wasn't time to waste. They needed to take inventory of their limited resources and come up with a plan. The colonists were never meant to survive on the planet with only what was contained in the escape pods. The colony ship had all their supplies, and that had been destroyed. Now, it was a matter of how they were all going to die, and how quickly.

In an attempt to keep his thoughts from going into a doom spiral, Evan took his first good look at the surroundings. The crash site appeared to be halfway down the slope leading to a massive basin. In the distance, rolling hills transitioned into towering mountains. Below, at the base of the valley, a lush jungle spread for kilometers. Between the crash site and jungle, the landscape alternated between trees and open fields. There was clear ground in the immediate vicinity to the crash site, so at least they'd have eyes on potential approaching threats from three sides. The forest to the west was the one blind spot. However, the trees offered potential shelter and building supplies, so it was a worthwhile tradeoff.

"You know how to stay cool in a crisis," Anya said behind him.

He turned back to face her. "So do you."

"I don't know about that." With the injured man still unconscious, she stood up and adjusted her ponytail. "I just do what needs to be done."

"That's all it takes."

She studied him with inquisitive, copper-colored eyes. "Were you military?"

He simply nodded, not wanting to delve into a more complicated explanation at the moment. "You?"

She laughed. "Not even close. I'm actually a biologist."

"A biologist who moonlights as a medic?"

"A xenobiologist who's scouted enough rough terrain on alien worlds to know how to field dress injuries."

"Ah."

Anya placed her hands on her hips and gazed up at the sky. "What do you think happened?"

"Clearly, there was an explosion, but that happened after the 'abandon ship' order had already been given. Your guess is as good as mine about what prompted the emergency evac. And then something messed with the pods' guidance systems." Evan doubted that everyone had made it off the ship to escape pods, but he kept that part to himself.

Anya glanced around to confirm that no one was within earshot. "Can I level with you?"

"Sure, why not?"

She took a step closer and dropped her voice to a whisper. "I helped select the colony site, and," she looked around meaningfully, "this hillside isn't it."

"How screwed are we?"

She looked him over again from head to toe. "With a military background, you know how to… handle yourself. Is that an accurate assessment?"

"I've been around, yeah."

Anya nodded solemnly. "Well, shit's going to be real around here come nightfall. We need a plan. *Now.*"

"What brand of shit are we dealing with?"

"The kind that eats you before you know you're being hunted."

He stared at her. "That wasn't in the colony brochure."

"Because it was a non-issue for the specified site. We spotted some… creatures during the preliminary survey. They're only down in the lowlands, and we were supposed to be up on the plateau." She pointed uphill. Unfortunately, there was a sheer cliff face between their present location and level ground above.

"So, there are only happy bunnies up there, but instead we're stuck down here with the monsters?"

"Something like that. I know we're only several kilometers from the target site, but the elevation difference is significant. I can't tell you exactly *what* the predator is, but it's big and vicious. Took out a Ranger-R like it was a plaything."

From what Evan had heard, Ranger-Rs were a version of the automated scout units used by the military, enhanced with additional sensors. Fast, armored, and perfect for difficult terrain. By all accounts, they were supposed to be near-indestructible.

Evan sucked on his teeth. "And we're in this creature's hunting grounds?"

"If we're lucky, we landed up high enough. The Ranger-R went missing down in the jungle in a valley somewhere around here. But I don't exactly have a nice chart of its territory, and the crash definitely made enough noise to draw attention."

"Well, sounds like we need to get to higher ground as soon as possible."

Anya looked over at the colonists, many of them injured. "A lot of these people won't be able to travel."

"I hate to break it to you, but we're going to have to make difficult decisions here. If you say the plateau is the place to be, then every able-bodied person should get up there as fast as possible—maximize chances for survival. Everyone else can dig in here for now."

"No, we have to stick together if we're going to get through this."

Evan evaluated the people rummaging through the wreckage. They had survived the crash, but most of them didn't look like they'd make it a week on the planet, let alone long-term. He'd learned a long time ago that it was a terrible idea to go down with a failing ship; there was nothing noble about that. Yet, as much as logic told him to walk away and fend for himself, the reality was that trying to go it alone on an alien planet wasn't likely to end well. Extra hands—even if they belonged to an inexperienced person—were a helpful resource. Perhaps, working together, they *could* stand a better chance.

Reluctantly, he sighed and nodded. "Okay."

"Glad we're on the same page."

"You know the tenets of survival. Secure shelter, find water, find food."

"And establish communication to call for help," she added.

"Immediate physical safety is the priority. That means establishing a base camp."

"We can use the debris to fill in the gaps between the pods and the boulders to make a perimeter fence. Staying here is temporary, but it will give us time to triage the injured. We'll need to conduct a survey of the area and figure out precisely where we are."

Evan judged the route up to the plateau. Though the cliff was nearly vertical, the rock had plenty of texture to make it climbable. "We need to scope out the plateau in case other pods landed up there. That higher ground will also give a better vantage on potential resources in the area."

"Agreed. I'm also hoping our military escort is en route."

Evan didn't have the heart to tell her what he'd seen through the viewport while his pod was ejecting. It was only a glimpse, so he wasn't certain, but it had looked like the military cruiser had sustained damage from an attack. If that was the case, crash-landing on the planet was only the start of their problems. "Best to assume we're on our own for now."

She nodded grimly. “Us against the world, right?”

“That’s right. Let’s go tell the others our plan.”

2

EVAN HAD LOW expectations for the colonists, but they still managed to disappoint.

"But won't they send help when we don't check in?" someone called out after Anya finished explaining her plan to turn the wreckage into a perimeter fence.

"Any help is potentially months away," Anya explained, circling back to the question for the third time. "Think about how long it took us to get here—it's no faster for them. We planned on making this place home, and that hasn't changed."

"Who put you in charge, anyway?" a man called out.

Anya stood her ground. "The official mission commanders are either dead or landed elsewhere. I was on the team that established the colonization profile for this planet. That means of those of us here, I know more about it than anyone else. If you'd rather have someone in charge who can't tell you what plants will kill you and what won't, go for it."

The protestor fell silent and no one else raised an objection.

"Good," Anya continued. "Now, it's mid-morning, so the good news is that we have most of the day to get organized. We need to go through all the pods to pull out emergency rations, medkits, and anything else that may be useful. Let's delegate team leads for each task."

After a needlessly contentious discussion, four delegates were selected by the group of forty-seven survivors. One was responsible for overseeing the collection and inventory of food. Another was assigned to collect and catalog other useful materials, such as medical supplies and personal items scavenged from the wreckage. A third was tasked with securing the perimeter of the crash site. The remaining delegate would tend to the injured and coordinate shelter.

While the delegates worked out the members of their team, Anya pulled Evan aside.

"Up for a hike?" she asked.

"I thought you'd never ask."

"Peter over there," she nodded toward a dark-skinned, middle-aged man, "seems to have leadership experience and can keep an eye on things here. I figure the two of us are best equipped to get up to high ground and see what we're up against."

"Works for me."

Evan went through the preliminary collection of supplies to grab an empty bag, which he filled with a couple of water bottles, two packs of emergency rations, a medkit, and some scrap cables that could be used as rope in a pinch. As prepared as they were going to get under the circumstances, Evan and Anya headed up the hill.

The hike started out easily enough, with a shallow incline and knee-high grass. It'd been years since Evan had spent any meaningful amount of time on a planet. Though the gravity simulated on ships was close to that of this world, everything from the strange scents in the air to the sensation of sun on his back reminded him that he was a spacefarer, not a colonist. He was never supposed to be here, and now it may be the last place he'd ever see.

"We got lucky, all things considered," Anya said, breaking the silence.

"How so?"

"Aside from being alive, we didn't land in the middle of a forest. Getting impaled by a branch would be a nasty way to go. We also could have lost a lot more pods on those rocks."

"True."

"Where did you serve? Any planetary assignments?"

"Not really."

She glanced over at him. "You know, talking about yourself isn't a crime."

"It could be in my world."

Anya raised an eyebrow. "And what world was that?"

He chuckled. "I see what you did there."

"Us scientist types ask a lot of questions. Can't help it."

Evan had spent so many years hiding his true self that evasion was his default. It'd take time to learn another way. "I spent some time working a job where asking questions was a quick way to get yourself killed."

"What were you doing?"

"Probably best if I don't talk about it."

She nodded slowly. "So, military and then… had plans to start over on a new colony to reinvent yourself?"

Evan let out a long breath. "A lot happened in between. But coming here was never part of my plans. How that disaster precipitated is a story for another time."

"We have plenty now."

"I'll need a drink or two in me before diving into that mess."

"Fine. Suit yourself."

"What about you?" he asked. "How'd you find yourself running surveys for new settlements?"

She laughed. "Funny, about that—I wasn't supposed to be here, either."

"No kidding?"

"What are the odds, right?" She threw her arms wide. "Guess I was too good at my job and they decided they needed a specialist for the boots-on-the-ground colonization work. That's what I get for actually *traveling* rather than strictly being a desk jockey like most of my co-workers."

"But hey, never would have gotten that field medic experience."

She turned solemn. "That guy's not going to make it through the night."

"Better than suffering. I'm most concerned about the two people with broken legs. Not fatal, but also unable to travel."

"Especially not this route." Anya looked ahead.

The terrain was becoming steeper. Expansive meadow grasses were now transitioning to patches of rock as they neared the cliffs.

Their conversation died out as the travel got more strenuous. The combination of a steeper angle and less stable ground made Evan work for each step. A fall here would mean a long tumble down the hillside, so he was deliberate with his footing.

The further up they went, the more treacherous the scree terrain became. The incline was soon steep enough that he needed to use his hands to pull himself up. Only a few meters ahead, the cliff face towered above.

Anya scowled at the rock wall. "This is a lot bigger than it looked in the distance."

Evan looked behind them at the crash site of the surviving

colonists. They could return to the group, but hope would fade the moment others realized they were trapped and there was no hope. They *had* to make it up the wall to the plateau. If they didn't, they may as well give up on any future right now.

Wordlessly, Evan's eyes met Anya's, and she nodded with understanding. They'd have to climb, no matter the risk.

"I'll go first," Anya stated.

"Are you sure? I can scout ahead," Evan offered.

"I'm lighter. Better if I'm up top."

He couldn't argue with that. Firstly, he may have a chance of catching her if she fell, but the same wouldn't work in reverse. And secondly, if he wasn't able to catch her, at least there'd be less chance of her knocking him off the wall.

With that in mind, he gave her a two-body-length lead before beginning his climb. Despite the grand scale of the rock wall, it had plenty of cracks and ledges to make it easy to find secure hand- and footholds. The initial seven meters were a relatively easy climb, but then Anya reached a more sheer section.

As she climbed up, several chunks of stone she'd used as grip points broke free. Evan pressed himself against the rockface to avoid being struck as they fell.

"Sorry!" she called down to him. "It's brittle through here." She climbed up another two meters. "Getting better again. There's a big ledge up here." With a few more moves, she pulled herself over the lip.

"You good?" he asked.

"Yeah, this is a big enough spot for both of us to rest."

Now, he just had to get up there. The newly broken sections would make his climb more difficult.

"I'm on my way," Evan said to encourage himself forward. He was up high enough now that his head swam when he looked down, so getting to a secure resting place sounded delightful.

He carefully found grip points to work toward the ledge. Nearly to the destination, he stretched up, his fingers barely brushing the stone ledge. The only way to grab it fully was to jump. He made the leap. As his feet pressed down with more force for the move, the rock underfoot gave way.

There was just enough spring from the jump to propel him upward, and he hooked the ledge. Desperate now, he clung on and managed to swing up his other arm to get a better hold. He hauled himself up, using his feet where he could get traction on the wall.

Once over the lip, he took a moment to catch his breath. *I really need to get in better shape.*

Anya stood at the back of the natural platform, looking down at him with hands on her hips. "What took you so long?" she asked jokingly.

"You busted out all the good handholds, thank you."

Her smug demeanor faded. "Oh. Sorry about that."

He took another deep breath and got to his feet. "All good. But we're going to need to find a different route down."

"I think it might actually be possible to go through the forest." She pointed to the trees running along the far side of the crash site.

From the ground, it had looked like the forest terminated at the same rockface they were now scaling. However, from the higher vantage point, it was now clear that a band of trees continued all the way up to the plateau, and the ground was more gradually sloped heading up to that level.

"Good eye," Evan told Anya. "We might even be able to get injured people up that way. We can scope it out on the way back."

Anya smiled. “We may have a chance yet. Come on, we’re almost to the top.” She took hold of the rock behind her and continued the ascent.

Unlike the section they’d just traversed, the next portion was distinctly sloped, so it was closer to crawling than climbing. In short order, they’d ascended the final fifty meters and were coming up on level ground.

The plateau wasn’t nearly as flat as Evan had anticipated. Though there was a sizeable wide open and level area, there were also additional hills. A ridge ran perpendicular to the valley where they’d crashed, and its base was about a kilometer from their present location.

“We should get up there,” Evan said. “If we can see over the other side, we’ll have a much better idea about what we’re dealing with.”

“Agreed.”

They took a brisk pace up the hill, eager to reach the crest and see what was on the other side.

Near the top, Evan got his first unobstructed view of their surroundings. Below, the landing pods were scattered around the hillside. However, they weren’t confined to the meadow where Evan’s had touched down. Some were scattered even further down the hill, and others beyond the tree line. The white pods stood out as bright dots against the green landscape, but he couldn’t make out the smaller forms of people from that distance.

“All right, so we might have more numbers than we thought,” Anya said.

“We can send messengers to them if they haven’t already connected with our group by the time we’re back.”

He finished hiking the remaining distance to the crest of the ridge. Getting his first look at the other side, his heart sank.

A column of smoke was rising in the distance—far too large to be from landing pods. It could only be one thing.

Anya also caught sight of the smoke. “What’s that?”

“Our military escort.”

3

ANYA RESISTED THE urge to shout a string of expletives and storm away down the hillside. She hadn't even wanted to go on this colony expedition, let alone find herself in a leadership role. Her only hope for salvation in the challenging situation was the prospect of being able to hand over control to the military escort once they'd landed, but now it seemed like they might be even worse off than the colonists.

"That's a lot of smoke," she said after taking a moment to gather herself. "Do you think the ship is intact?"

"I don't know." Evan seemed like he was holding something back. He'd been frustratingly evasive, and it was making Anya slow to trust him. She considered herself much better at reading plants than people, but Evan's expressive green eyes told a deeper story than his few words.

"What aren't you telling me?"

He sighed. "I wasn't sure before, so I didn't want to say anything. But I thought I saw damage to the ship as my pod was ejecting while we were in orbit."

"Damage to the guard ship?" Anya's brows furrowed. "But how?"

"All part of the mystery about what caused us to evacuate,

I imagine."

She crossed her arms. The evacuation order had come out of nowhere.

The plan had been to remain in orbit for a month while landing parties went down to Aethos' surface to survey settlement sites. They'd explored everything with probes and automated ground survey units before ever sending the colony ship, but it was important to confirm all findings before sending settlers down to the surface. However, they had only been two days into that verification process when the emergency evacuation order had been given. Within fifteen minutes, they'd been in pods heading down.

None of those pods were part of the actual colonization kit. Prefab habitation structures, food stores, agricultural supplies—all those modules had been lost when the main ship was destroyed, as far as Anya knew. If the military escort cruiser had crashed, as well, they were either facing a terrible freak accident, or it was all very intentional.

"I'm starting to get the impression that someone didn't want us to settle this world," Anya murmured.

Evan nodded slowly. "I didn't want to be the one to say it."

"But why? It's a *massive* expense to send out a colony expedition. If we weren't wanted here, then why not stop the mission before we left?"

"It doesn't make sense. So, maybe an unforeseen environmental factor took out both the ships. Uncharted solar activity, or something?"

"Maybe." Anya shrugged. "The reason doesn't matter right now. We need to focus on our survival."

"I'd love to get a look at that escort ship's crash site. We'd have a lot better chance of salvaging something useful from the ship than anything we'll find in the pods."

"Do you think there were any survivors?"

"I can't begin to guess without knowing why we all crashed in the first place. We won't find out by sitting here."

"You're not suggesting hiking all the way over there, are you?" Anya asked incredulously. She appreciated when someone was willing to take action, but knowing what she did about the planet, wandering into the wilderness without proper gear very well may be a death sentence.

"I'm not one to just give up and sit around waiting to die."

"That's a long trek for a potential dead end—in more ways than one."

"Our only hope is sending out a distress message about our situation. Our pods don't have anything close to an interstellar comm array, but that escort ship does. Even if it's damaged, there's hope where we have none now."

"Yes, but—"

"But nothing. We can't make it on this world without support. You've said as much yourself."

"Part of that was the shock talking. People have lived off the land for years."

"On other planets where they have ancestral knowledge. Can you cite one colony where people were dropped off with next to zero gear on an alien planet and lived to talk about it?"

"No. But that's because that never happens."

"Not never, apparently."

She let out a long breath. "I can't argue that our best chance to make it on this world would be to get access to a comm relay."

"The notable problem being that there are the… whatever horrible monstrosities in the lowlands between our current location and the crash site."

"Which has been my objection from the start. We're not

equipped to take those on."

Evan stood in contemplative silence for a minute. "Let's head back to camp and mull it over. There has to be a way."

"Sounds good. Let's try to find a route through that forest."

Having a specific problem to solve gave Anya much-needed grounding. She had no clue how they might be able to safely get to the crash site many kilometers away over rough terrain with unknown creatures lurking in the trees, but solving that challenge gave her a tangible goal to work toward. Under normal circumstances, she thrived on that kind of problem-solving. Selecting settlement sites for new colonies was nothing but finding creative solutions. This project, though, had gotten way too personal.

Did I miss something in the original survey? Is it my fault we're in this mess? She knew better than to believe one person could bear singular responsibility for a project of that massive scale, but guilt began to gnaw at the back of her mind all the same. Ultimately, she'd given her approval for settling this planet, despite knowing its risks. Now, those dangers she'd told everyone wouldn't be an issue might lead to her own end.

"No," she muttered to herself in an attempt to expel the dark storm of thoughts.

"Sorry, what?" Evan asked.

"Nothing. Just reminding myself that this isn't over."

"Not going to lie—I know we're in a tough spot. I don't intend to go down without a fight, though."

"Me either."

He glanced over his shoulder in the direction of the smoke, already hidden from view again as they descended the hill. "How much should we share about what we discovered here?"

"I don't know. I never intended to be a leader, deciding what information to share or what everyone should do."

"Well, if we tell the whole group everything, half the people are bound to want to go with us and the rest will either give up because they think the situation is hopeless, or they'll get violent as they compete for supplies."

"Those are all bad outcomes. A better approach would be for a small group to go investigate the site while everyone else joins together to establish a base camp."

"Agreed. But scared people don't think rationally."

"Are *we* even thinking clearly?"

"Better than most of the people here, I'd wager. We've had a whole lot more survival training than most."

"True." She drew a long breath and let it out slowly. "Thank you for being a voice of reason."

"It's out of pure selfishness, but you're welcome."

She eyed him. "I don't think you're nearly as selfish as you'd like me to think."

— — —

Evan wouldn't admit it, but Anya was shaping up to be more perceptive than he'd like. He had, genuinely, intended for his new life in the colony settlement to be focused on him and his own needs, setting aside the pressure and expectations around serving others for the first time in his life. For as long as he could remember, he'd put other people first—even when it was to his own detriment. For years, he'd been okay with that. But after his last assignment, he'd been unwilling to continue with that lifestyle.

Now, he was faced with other people needing help on a scale he'd never imagined. While he wouldn't consider himself to be a survival expert, there was no denying he had more skills than most. There weren't likely to be other people with military training among the surviving colonists, given the selection process for candidates, so he was singularly equipped to offer the kind of insights afforded by his experience.

"I don't want to be in charge, Anya," Evan said after a time.

She raised an eyebrow. "Who said anything about that?"

"I'm just jumping to the punchline."

"A little full of yourself, aren't you?" She crossed her arms.

"You don't know my background."

"Probably because you refuse to say much of anything about yourself."

"I have my reasons." He let out a long breath. "I hope you can grow to trust me."

"That will come over time if your actions match your statements."

"Fair enough. I'll start by solving the mystery about what happened to us."

"Wow, okay." She let out a little laugh. "I was expecting something little, like showing up on time. But you're going straight for the big one. Bold move."

"Any other goal is meaningless. We need to understand what happened so we know what we're up against. Is there an environmental threat? Was it sabotage? Just a freak accident?"

She nodded. "You're right. Even if we find a way to call for help, some of those scenarios might complicate getting assistance."

"Colony ships can be fragile, but military ships are designed for toughness. The likelihood of an accident is…"

"Slim, yeah." Anya sighed. "Like it or not, we're in this together. I fully intend to give you the benefit of the doubt. I don't see anyone else who stepped up."

"Which is going to be a problem."

"In what way?"

"When we head out on our scouting mission to that crash site, who's going to run things here at camp?"

"Peter seemed to have no problem delegating."

"I hope he's up to the challenge."

They continued to the west toward the slope where the forest transitioned to the plateau. The grassland made for fairly easy walking, though there were plenty of small rocks posing a tripping hazard. Seeing the location up close, Anya was pleased to verify that it perfectly matched her assessment from her previous survey. Had they not crash-landed on the planet instead of following the staged landing—

"Holy shit, Evan! We *don't* have 'nothing'!" she exclaimed.

"Wait, what?"

"We hadn't sent down any people from the colony ship, but right after we arrived, there was an automated supply drop of some basic survey equipment. At least, there should have been."

He didn't allow himself to get too excited. "And you're just remembering this *now*?"

She flourished her arms. "Sorry, there've been a few other things on my mind!"

"Okay, fair." He looked around. "Where would the drop have been made, assuming it happened?"

Anya placed her hands on her hips. From their current position, there weren't a lot of landmarks to pinpoint their location. "Best guess, about two kilometers that way-ish." She pointed further into the plateau.

"I didn't see anything from the hilltop."

"We also weren't looking very hard in this direction. The supply drops aren't bright-white like the pods. It would blend in with the landscape."

"Meant to be found with a tracking beacon, not by sight."

“You’ve got it. Which will make our job more difficult, but if it’s there…”

“First step toward salvation.” He nodded. “We have to look.”

“Good. I was hoping I wouldn’t have to convince you.”

“That resource possibility is well worth the extra hike. I don’t suppose it’s too much to hope that the drop would contain a long-range comm unit?”

“Not likely.”

“Well, I’ll take whatever we can get. We still have enough daylight for a detour. Let’s scout it out.”

4

THEY HIKED ACROSS the plain, keeping a watchful eye for any sign of the supply drop. Despite the horror of the crash and the fear of uncertainty, Anya found herself energized. Aethos was a singularly beautiful world, with the clearest skies and freshest air she'd ever experienced. She'd spent much of her career admiring planets from afar, and it was always a treat to perform physical surveys of new worlds. Many of the places she'd visited fell into the zone of 'barely habitable', but this world was truly a paradise.

"Are you… smiling?" Evan asked, glancing over as he walked alongside her.

"You have to admit, setting aside the 'we're screwed' part of this disaster, the landscape really is spectacular."

He chuckled. "You did pick a good one."

"I'm sorry we botched the landing."

"I suspect it wasn't your fault. But I do want to have a word with your supervisor and request a refund."

"Sorry, no refunds. I guess you didn't read the fine print."

"Skipped right over it. Darn."

"That's how they get you. Every time."

Evan's brows raised. "Hey, I think I see something up ahead!"

Being a little shorter, Anya didn't yet have it in her sightline. She spotted a knee-high rock nearby and hopped up on it. Following the line of Evan's outstretched arm, there was, indeed, an object that didn't blend in with the rest of the landscape. She couldn't be sure it was the supply cache or part of the ship, but it was worth investigating.

With renewed urgency, they continued in the direction of the object. As they got closer, the form of a crate came into view. It was partially covered in a black parachute, which is what had made it difficult to identify from a distance.

"I still have a lot of issues with the service, but the early supply drop policy is a keeper," Evan said with a grin. "This very well may save us."

"Don't get too excited. It might all be useless."

"One way to find out."

They worked together to haul the parachute off the crate, setting it aside to salvage for materials. The fabric would make an excellent shelter covering, and the cord could be used for all manner of projects. The crate itself was about nine meters long and three wide and tall.

Anya gripped the release hatch and gave it a tug. It didn't budge. "Hey, give me a hand."

Evan gripped the lever next to her, and they pulled again together. With an angry groan of the metal, it came free. A hiss of air rushed out with the release of the pressurized seal.

"Good sign," Evan said.

Anya swung the large door open. A wall of crates blocked the view deeper inside. The crates were marked with the NovaTech emblem, signifying that they were supplies issued by the colony's planning team. No other indicators for the contents of each crate were immediately evident.

"They sure make it easy to find what you need," Evan

muttered with heavy sarcasm.

"There should be an electronic inventory on each crate." Anya reached for the nearest crate and started to pull it down. It was heavier than she'd anticipated, and it slipped out of her grasp.

Evan lunged forward to help her catch it.

"Thanks," Anya said as they lowered it the rest of the way to the ground.

Now that the crate was fully visible, there was, indeed, a touch-interface on the top side of the crate. Anya tapped it, bringing the screen to life. The first words to appear on the screen were 'Survey Equipment', followed by an itemized list. While all valuable items for their intended use, none of the materials would be particularly helpful for their immediate survival needs.

Anya and Evan worked together to lower the remaining crates. They checked each, in turn, with similar disappointment. Finally, the fifth showed promise: 'Water Purifier'.

Anya smiled. "Now we're getting somewhere."

"Do you think this container will have all the materials for a base camp?" Evan asked as they resumed pulling down crates.

"Habitation modules are a separate drop, which hadn't happened yet for our colony, as far as I know. But this should have a few infrastructure components, like water and power."

"A generator would be huge for us."

"I'm not certain there will be one. Packing these drop shipments isn't my department."

"We've got a water purifier now, so that alone was worth this detour."

The next crate of interest was labeled 'Scouting Gear'. Evan flipped through the inventory list. "Hey, looks like this has binoculars, compass, and the like. That could be useful for our expedition."

"For sure. That'll be one to go through."

They set the crate aside for now, wanting to finish going through the stack before prioritizing the items to investigate further. The deeper into the container they got, the less enthusiastic Anya became. It was clear the inventory had been designed strictly for scientific study rather than to support a person living without any other resources. Having the materials was certainly better than nothing, but it was far from a golden ticket to easy living.

"Yeah, I'd been hoping for more," Evan said, seeming to pick up on her disappointment. His tone wasn't as upbeat as when they'd started.

"Hey, I'm happy with the water purifier."

"Yes, that is a big one, provided we can find a water source. I don't suppose there could be a well-driller packed in here?"

"Very doubtful. But I recall seeing a stream on the survey data for this area. And," she gestured to the screen for the latest crate they'd uncovered, "tubing. Not meant for use as a water line, but a hose is a hose. We've got five hundred meters here, which will go a long way for running a line to camp if we can find water uphill."

Evan nodded. "We can scout on our way back."

They moved the next layer of crates, which unveiled a void behind them. As Anya's eyes adjusted to the darkness, she noticed the outline of what looked like a vehicle. "Oh, this is great!"

— — —

As Evan assessed the vehicle, he couldn't share Anya's

enthusiasm. It was a bare-bones rover that looked like it'd be ripped to shreds if a branch hit it the wrong way. While it'd be fine out on the open plateau, its usefulness would rapidly diminish in more extreme terrain. "I know what you're thinking, but no."

"Why not?" she asked. "It could go far enough, fast enough to make it to the crash site in one day."

"It's a glorified aluminum can on wheels."

"I think you're underestimating its capabilities."

"Have you ever been in one?"

"No," she admitted.

"Well, I have. Or at least one like it. They're not stable on rough terrain, and the battery is about half of what the specs state."

"It looks like this one has a solar charger." She pointed to a collector on the roof.

"A lot of good that will do us under trees. Not to mention it's not enough to keep the vehicle going over sustained use."

"Then what's the point?"

"They sent it here for surveying, right?" Evan motioned toward the door. "We're on a flat-ish plateau with no trees. Surveying is a lot of starting and stopping. A vehicle like this is perfect for that. But trying to make it to that crash?" He shook his head.

"Are we better off walking the whole way, then?"

"No."

She raised an eyebrow. "So…"

He sighed. "It *is* better than nothing," he clarified. "But there's no way it's making it the whole way there and back. We could use it to give ourselves a head start, but we'll have to abandon it wherever it breaks or runs out of juice."

Anya thought it over for a few moments and then nodded.

"All right, I'm game." She looked over the rest of the equipment. "We need to tell the others about this stash."

"They might not want us taking the rover, knowing it's a one-way trip for it."

"You're right. I don't really want to keep secrets from the group, but sharing everything is likely to cause more problems."

"We could move it out of here and hide it somewhere in the woods," Evan suggested.

"As long as it's far enough from the route back up here, that should work."

"Only other option is to drop it on the other side of the ridge, but that would be a lot of extra time walking today and when we set out again."

"Woods it is," she agreed.

They went through the potentially useful crates they'd set aside and gathered up the most critical items to bring back with them now. Other things that would be most useful for their journey, they loaded into the rover to store with it overnight.

Once everything was packed, Evan drove the rover outside and they sealed up the container.

"We'll give the others instructions about where to find this," Anya said. "We can be long gone in the rover by the time they get here."

"And, hopefully, by the next time we see them we'll have good enough news to make them forget we hid anything from them."

"It's for the greater good." Anya sounded like she was trying to convince herself.

"I hate that expression."

"Well, it applies here."

"Hey, I wouldn't be here now if I didn't think it was the

right thing to do," Evan told her. He was determined—or perhaps just crazy enough—to trek to the ship crash site on the small chance that they might find an intact radio or other help. That journey was a hope for salvation for not just him, but for the group. Whatever gave them the best chance at success in that mission needed to be their priority.

She stopped outside the rover. "Wait, a radio isn't the only form of communication."

"True, but—"

"We've been focused on getting a message offworld, and that is important, but what about getting in touch with other potential survivors? We could see the crash site because we have the high ground here, but there are no hills near them. They'd never see us."

"Assuming anyone else lived."

"They might be saying the same thing about us."

"What do you have in mind?"

"Go low-tech. A signal fire."

"Smoke signals?" he asked.

She nodded. "Why not? It would have been better from the top of the ridge, but I'm not walking back up there now. This plateau is still high ground compared to where we crashed."

"A flare gun would be a lot easier. We have them in the pods."

"And that also lasts for, what, thirty seconds? Fire gives a more sustained alert."

"Agreed, but we're running low on daylight now, and I don't want to get stuck in the forest at night."

"All right, it can wait until tomorrow," she agreed. "We can instruct whoever comes to retrieve this crate that they can set one and tend it while inventorying."

"That's good. It will also give us a reference point while

we're traveling."

"Win-win." She flashed a smile as she climbed into the rover. "Let's go."

5

EVAN DROVE THE rover back toward the valley where they'd crashed. They covered ground quickly with the vehicle, and he was pleased to see its light build didn't leave significant tracks on the scrubby grass. Since they hadn't erased the vehicle from the cargo crate's inventory, its existence wouldn't be a secret once others started going through the container. Nonetheless, it was better to not aggravate the situation further by leaving tracks all the way across the plateau.

"I really hope this has enough power to get us most of the way there," Anya commented from the passenger seat.

"I'm not holding my breath, but I'm with you."

To his surprise, he'd been on the same page as Anya with most of their key decisions thus far. Having worked alone for much of his recent career, he liked being able to set a plan and execute without needing to get buy-in from others. Nonetheless, it was better to have someone to watch his back as they ventured into the unknown situation. As long as she remained as objective as she had been, he expected they'd get along fine. It also didn't hurt that she was easy on the eyes. All in all, he could think of a lot worse travel companions.

When the edge of the plateau came into view ahead, Evan

cut to the north. He kept a heading parallel to the cliffs, looking for any signs of trees. Finally, after nearly two kilometers, he spotted a place where the cliff transitioned into a downward slope covered in young trees and shrubs.

"I think this might be our spot," he said, slowing the rover and going closer to get a better look at the landscape.

Unlike the terrain further south, there was a smooth transition between the hillside and plateau edge, in contrast to the rocky cliffs they'd climbed up. This section had been completely blocked from view by the forest from their vantage below. From up top, however, it appeared they'd have access to at least a kilometer-long stretch of forest. That would leave them plenty of territory to scout and mark a pathway up for the other survivors and also find a convenient place to stash the rover overnight.

With that plan in mind, Evan continued along the forest's edge. About half a kilometer away, he spotted a thicket with brush tall enough to hide the rover and drove it in.

"I can't imagine any colonists wandering this far before we get back to it," Anya said.

Evan powered down the vehicle. "I'll lock the controls just in case." He made the necessary precautionary entries. "You know, as convenient as this hillside is for us, it also means that there's a way for your mystery monster to get up here."

"I thought about that, too. But its territory seems more tied to elevation than terrain—staying in the lowlands." Anya shrugged. "I mean, I don't know where it *might* go, but there've been no signs beyond the valley jungle. Besides, there's minimal cover here on the plateau. If it did venture up, at least we'd be able to see it coming."

"That's a good enough reason to get everyone moved up here."

They grabbed their packs filled with the items that they'd deemed most critical to bring back to camp. Though encumbered now, at least the trek would be mostly downhill. However, they were facing unknown terrain going through the forest.

"I really hope this is a nice, easy walk," Anya said as they set out. Her new pack was making her walk with a slight lean forward.

"Are there any other forest monsters I should know about?" Evan asked.

"Nothing that showed up on the survey at this elevation. But it's not like people have been hiking around here before. Our assessment was only a best guess."

"You've been slowly eroding my faith in scientific investigation."

"Oh, like you'd be able to do a better assessment from multiple light years away."

"Not saying I could. It's just eye-opening to realize that our civilization's operation is more precarious than most people realize."

"Sometimes I think we survive by sheer stubbornness alone."

"I don't doubt it."

They hiked south to find the best access point for their path back to camp. Shrubs marked the outer boundaries of the forest, transitioning into taller trees further down the slope.

"How about we cut in here?" Evan suggested. There was a natural break in the foliage, and a large boulder offered a great signpost for the entry.

"Perfect," Anya agreed.

They headed down the slope and into the forest. The trees were larger in person than Evan had realized from a distance;

a few of the trunks would be a stretch for him and Anya to reach their arms around together. Looking through dappled light on the smooth, light-gray bark trunks and broad leaves reminded Evan of something out of a tourism brochure for a nature preserve. Birds sang, unseen in the upper branches, and they passed by several small animals reminiscent of squirrels rummaging on the ground. It was a vibrant ecosystem, and the wildlife seemed wholly unafraid of their human presence.

"It's beautiful," Anya commented as she took in the surroundings. Her eyes were bright with wonder and appreciation.

"This must be a xenobiologist's dream."

"It's true. Nothing beats putting boots on a new world."

"Hopefully, that doesn't involve getting eaten by an unidentified forest monster."

"I mean, what else can go wrong, right? It's not like things can get much worse for us."

"Don't jinx it."

There was surprisingly little underbrush on the forest floor, making for comfortable walking. Visibility was limited due to the large tree trunks, however, so navigating in a straight line was difficult.

The ground took a sharp decline a hundred meters into the trees. Soft ground made it more of a slide than a hike down the first segment. Despite her heavy pack, Anya handled the slope confidently and wasn't afraid to get her backside dirty to control her descent. Evan, likewise, found himself sitting on several occasions when the soft ground was too unstable for him to stand upright.

Dirty but intact, they eventually made it to a more gently sloping section. The density of trees had also diminished, allowing for better visibility. They enjoyed walking through the dappled light for half a kilometer before a white form came into view—definitely not a natural part of the environment.

"Hey, is that a pod?" Anya pointed toward the white object partially obscured by the trees.

Evan repositioned to get a better look. "I think it is!" He headed in that direction.

Once they were a couple dozen meters from the crashed pod, it was clear there were no signs of movement around it. It'd been hours since the crash, so it wasn't a good sign that the pod's occupant had yet to emerge. Evan slowed his approach.

The pod was still sealed. Despite having crashed through the trees, the exterior appeared to be intact, albeit dirty and scuffed. Its landing had brought down several trees, leaving a path of destruction twenty meters long up to its resting place.

Evan walked around to the hatch on the side of the craft. The exterior display was flashing red, indicating distress. Power levels were critically low.

"We've got to get this open," he said, hopping up on a fallen tree trunk to get up to the hatch's level. He activated the depressurization sequence.

The pod's hatch opened with a hiss.

They peered inside. A passenger was strapped to the seat, unmoving.

"Hey, we're here to help!" Anya called out.

There was no point. Blood was splattered around the cabin, with the greatest concentration on the person's clothes. Based on the darkened stains, they were long since dead.

Anya brought a hand up over her mouth. "Wow, that's a lot of blood."

"Too much." Evan climbed halfway into the pod to get a better look. The splattering around the walls must have happened during an uncontrolled, erratic fall, similar to his own landing on the planet. However, that didn't explain what kind of injury had resulted in that amount of blood loss in the first place.

Suppressing the queasiness in his stomach from the gruesome sight, he crawled the rest of the way inside. From there, he spotted bloody handprints and drag marks leading from the hatch to the seat. Similar smears covered the harness. The narrative came into focus when Evan spotted a bullet wound in the passenger's stomach.

"Anya, you know how we were joking that things couldn't get much worse?"

She nodded hesitantly. "Yeah..."

"Well, they just did."

— — —

"What do you mean?" Anya asked, her voice quavering. She'd been trying to keep her cool, but a person could only take so much.

"This man was shot before he entered the pod," Evan stated, pointing to a bloody patch on the man's chest.

From her vantage point at the hatch opening, Anya couldn't make out the details of a wound. "Could a piece of debris have pierced the pod on the way down?"

"It was pressurized when we opened the hatch. No breach."

"Right, good point." The thought had been wishful thinking. She took a steadying breath, tasting iron in the air. "So, in other words, he was murdered slightly before, or during, the emergency incident that forced the colony ship's evacuation."

"That's my guess."

"And brings us to the next logical question... Why?"

"Precisely." Evan frowned at the body. "Wrong place, wrong time? Or is he a clue to what happened?"

Anya tentatively stepped down onto the bloody floor. "Let's see if we can find some ID."

Trying to use the objective, scientific part of her brain that had been trained to conduct animal autopsies, she began patting down the man's body to see if he was carrying any identifying documents. Holding her breath, she slid her hand underneath the body to check. Her fingers met the smooth edge of an ID badge. She pulled it free.

"Got something." Anya looked it over. The badge displayed the man's picture—at least, she thought it was him, though it was tough to tell through the blood—as well as the issuing organization. It was access credentials for NovaTech. "Oh… oh, no." She shook her head, her eyes going wide with alarm as she made the mental connections.

"What?"

"He…" She faded out, laughing a little to ease the growing tension in her chest. "This was a corporate liaison, for lack of a better term. His job was to understand the details of this colony expedition and coordinate between NovaTech, the government, the military, and all other stakeholders."

"So, the person who would have been on this end of the comm when they called to check up on us?"

"Yep."

"And the person who would have been first to realize something was wrong when we arrived here?"

"Exactly."

"Meaning, he was silenced so that whatever happened to our ship could play out."

She nodded. "I don't like this one bit."

"Well, it's the reality we're facing, so we need to confront the facts."

"The big thing that keeps coming to the forefront for me is that someone wanted us all dead."

"Or, at the very least, stranded and out of communication."

Anya crossed her arms. "But *why*? I still can't think of a viable reason for any of this."

"Because we don't have all the pieces yet." Evan's brows were knitted in thought. He kept glancing between the body and the pod's control panel as though there was some other clue he was missing.

"I don't think the answers are in here," she said. "It's more important than ever that we get to the escort ship. Its flight recorder is our best shot to find out what happened in the minutes leading up to the crash."

"Agreed."

"Let's grab the pod's emergency kit and then get back to camp. We're going to have a busy day tomorrow."

6

EVAN HAD SEEN enough in his storied life to sense a conspiracy when he stumbled into one. However, nothing he'd faced to date was on the scale of disrupting the colonization of a new world.

Drug running. Weapons dealers. He understood how to navigate the criminal underbelly of society. But corporate espionage and politics… that was another beast entirely. And he suspected that it could be just as dark and dangerous—or more—than black market business dealings.

He and Anya didn't say much on the rest of their hike back to the crash site. Seeing a dead body, especially a murder victim, had a way of souring the mood. However, the realization that their situation was more complicated than he'd originally anticipated had ignited a new sense of urgency in Evan to solve the mystery. As much as he'd tried to set aside his old life, he'd been trained to think like an investigator. Now that a case was before him, he needed answers.

They marked a path using spray paint—one of the survey supplies they'd taken from the supply crate. The route was significantly easier than the cliff-climbing on the way up and would make for a decent pathway for the other survivors to use up to the plateau.

Finding the right place to exit the trees was the tricky part. They guessed how far down the slope they'd need to be to make it past the rocky spots and started angling over. When they reached the tree line, the makeshift camp was visible about half a kilometer down the slope.

Anya smiled. "Hey, couldn't have planned that much better!"

"At least *something* has gone right today," Evan replied with a smile back.

In reality, there'd been a lot more good fortune than that. Both of them easily could have been killed in the crash. They also might not have located nearly as many supplies. All in all, for being in the middle of a disaster, they were pretty well off.

After their trek across the grassy slope, they were greeted by excited chatter around the campsite.

When Peter spotted them approaching, he ran over, sporting a broad grin. "Good, you're back! What did you see?"

"No other signs of survivors up on the plateau, but we did see pods scattered around this hillside," Evan replied truthfully, but leaving out the details for now in the way they'd discussed. "Sending out some scouts tomorrow might be a good idea."

"We can do that." Peter nodded, his brows drawing together, but he still seemed upbeat. Considering that he'd been left behind in a leadership role, things had to be in order.

"The scavenging must have gone well for you to be smiling like that," Anya said, echoing Evan's thoughts.

"Did it ever!" Peter exclaimed. "An emergency supply pod."

Evan's spirits lifted. "And it's intact?"

"It got a little busted up, but there were some amazing

things inside. We're still going through it."

Anya smiled, joining in the excitement of the discovery. "Where is it?"

"About a kilometer that way." He motioned to the southeast. "Hey, Cora, are you heading over to the supply pod?"

"Yeah," a young blonde woman called back. "Why?"

"Take these two with you. They can help with the inventory." Peter motioned to them. "What about you? See anything else noteworthy?"

"We can talk about that later," Anya replied. "Let's just say that it's best to keep assuming we're on our own."

He nodded his understanding. "All right, we'll keep at it." He returned to his work.

Evan and Anya followed Cora down the hill. As they approached the crash site for the supply pod, they realized that they'd spotted it from the hilltop but had mistaken it for being a normal escape pod like the others. It wasn't nearly as large or boxy as the survey equipment crate they'd recovered, but actual survival equipment would likely be more useful.

Three people were currently working at the site, moving crates from inside and arranging them into groups on the grass.

"Anything useful?" Anya asked.

"*Everything* is useful right now," a middle-aged man replied. "But yes—many things are going to be especially helpful." He straightened and knuckled his back. "Over there, we've got some MealPaks. A handful of tents and blankets in that pile. But the real gem of it all is still in there." He pointed toward the crate.

The label on its side was bold and unmistakable: 'HABITATION SHELTER – Capacity 50'. With forty-seven survivors currently in the camp, it couldn't be much more perfect.

"This is amazing!" Anya grinned. "I can see why Peter was so excited."

"I'm more excited to have food. Between the MealPaks here and the emergency kits from the pods, we're set up for about a week, as long as we keep it to two meals a day."

"A week will give us time to get a handle on hunting and foraging. I can show you lots of plants around here that are edible," Anya replied.

And when is she planning to give this instruction? Evan wondered, since they'd decided to set out first thing in the morning. That was for her to figure out.

Anya's eyes suddenly lit up, and she grabbed one of the crates. "I'll start with this one." She carried it away.

Evan set his mind to helping the other survivors empty and inventory the cargo pod so they could unpack the habitation shelter. The remaining dozen crates held additional practical gear like flashlights, canteens, and fire starters. It was enough to give them a fighting chance.

Once the gear had been relocated away from the pod, the team was faced with a bigger challenge.

"How are we supposed to move this thing?" Cora asked on behalf of the group.

While it was an amazing boon, the habitation shelter weighed nearly a thousand kilograms, based on the specs printed on its side, and it required a reasonably flat twenty-by-twenty-meter space to deploy. They wouldn't be able to approach 'flat' anywhere on the slope, which meant transporting the heavy shelter through the forest up to the plateau.

"That's going to have to be a tomorrow problem," Evan

said. "It's too late in the day to get it set up for tonight, so let's leave it here and get the rest of these supplies to camp."

— — —

Hauling heavy crates up a steep hillside reminded Anya that she had been spending too much time at a desk in recent years. She'd handled the initial hike without too much trouble, but carrying around heavy items when she was already tired quickly sapped her reserves.

By the time the group made it back to the main campsite with the salvaged items, she was ready to curl up on a bedroll and take a nap. However, there were still important conversations to be had.

Evan pulled Anya aside as soon as they'd dropped off the crates. "When do you want to talk to Peter?"

"We should probably do it now. Are you sure we shouldn't mention the rover?"

"Depends on if you want to walk the whole way to the crash site," he replied. "They'll look at it as the best solution to get the hab up to the plateau."

"Maybe it is."

"No way it can move something that heavy. Sure, it could *help*, but they'd be more likely to break the rover than have it save much work in the end."

She nodded. "Then we focus on our mission."

Hiding information went against her nature. It seemed easier for Evan, which pestered the back of her mind about what that might mean about him keeping things from her. Some of his comments made it sound like he might have been involved in some pretty shady dealings, which called into question his reliability in the long run. Regardless, she needed him for now. Especially after finding out that the expedition liaison had been murdered, all hopes now rested on finding communications equipment in the crashed military cruiser.

A dark thought flitted by. *What if Evan is the killer?*

He didn't seem like a cold-blooded murderer, but sociopaths and trained assassins could often pass as perfectly pleasant people. He had seemed genuinely surprised to come across the body. However, that surprise could have been from realizing they'd inadvertently stumbled across evidence that should have burned up in the atmosphere.

"Hey, you okay?" Evan asked from next to her.

Anya realized that she'd frozen in place and had been staring into space while her thoughts spiraled. "Uh, yeah. Just thinking through what to say."

"Are you having second thoughts about us going out?"

"No. Maybe." She took a step back from him.

Understandably, he tilted his head and narrowed his eyes with confusion at her sudden change in demeanor. "Let's talk." He motioned for her to follow him behind one of the crashed pods, as private a place as could be had in the campsite. "What's wrong?"

Anya kept her voice to a whisper. "There's a murder victim up there in the woods. The killer could be here. It could be *you*." She stared at him pointedly, searching for any cracks in his expression.

Evan chuckled and shook his head. "It's not me, I promise."

"That's what the killer would say."

"Sure. And if you want to believe that about me, then there won't be anything I can say or do to change your mind."

Her cheeks flushed. "I'm sorry, you're right. And if you'd wanted me dead, there are a lot of ways you could have done it today."

He cracked a smile. “I very much would like for you to stay alive.”

“How reassuring.”

“For what it’s worth, I don’t think whoever killed him is here.”

“What makes you say that?” Anya asked.

“Everyone has been too shocked about what happened. Anyone who could shoot another person at close range like that would be too cold and calculating to blend in with the crowd.”

She had to agree with Evan’s logic on that front. And for that matter, she recognized that Evan’s calmness under pressure was trained poise. He certainly didn’t give off creepy killer vibes. “I want to trust you.”

“But you’re finding it difficult because I won’t talk about myself?”

“Something like that.”

He let out a long breath. “I learned my survival skills in the UPDF. I’ve done a lot of things since then.”

“Yeah, I figured.” The United Planetary Defense Force was one of the few places where a person could learn to work with their hands without the need for fancy tech, but most UPDF soldiers she knew were more blunt instruments than refined tools in their work.

Evan shook his head. “Oh, you're one of those?”

“A what?”

“Someone who thinks anyone who was in the UPDF was a meat-head soldier.”

Anya’s cheeks burned, not realizing her thoughts had been that easy to read on her face. “I don’t think that at all.” It was half-true. While she did feel that way about other people she’d met in the past, Evan wasn’t anything like them.

“Then why the tone?”

“I didn’t mean any offense—just putting some pieces together in my head. But that past isn’t anything to keep secret.”

“After I got out, I joined the UPA Security Corps.”

“Ah, a cop!”

“My work with them was a little more… sensitive.”

She nodded thoughtfully. “That explains it.”

“I hope that hasn’t dispelled all my mystique. Can’t give everything away at once.” He flashed a charming smile.

“Well, good to know you were using your skills for the good guys.”

“From this perspective, at least.” His warm smile faded. There was definitely something darker beneath the surface.

Anya studied him, weighing whether or not to press the topic. Just because he’d allegedly been a Security Corp officer, that didn’t mean he’d been an honest dealer. “I’m not going to get any more than that right now, am I?”

He shook his head. “Sorry, Anya. It’s complicated, and this has been a hell of a day. I don’t have the energy to get into it right now. Let’s take care of business, and we’ll have plenty of time to talk on our expedition.”

“Oh, ‘expedition’, huh?”

“Makes it sound a little less desperate and insane than it is.”

“Agreed.” While she hadn’t actually gotten much more information, the conversation had helped set her at ease for the present. She was a long way from putting her full faith in him, but the fact that he’d looked her squarely in the eyes and finally answered some of her questions was a step in the right direction.

Shouts rang out from the other side of camp.

Anya snapped to attention. "What was that?"

"No clue." Evan ran in the direction of the shouting.

The voices were pitched with distress, though the words had been indistinct at that distance. Anya braced for the worst.

She jogged through the wreckage. Coming around one of the centrally located pods in the encampment, she spotted the area that had been set aside as a medbay for the injured. Several people were standing over one of the patients, and it was clear from their expressions that the situation wasn't good.

Anya slowed her pace as she approached them. "What's going on?"

One of the women was standing with a hand over her mouth. She only shook her head in response.

An older woman next to her found her voice. "He didn't make it." She pulled back a blanket, which had been placed over a body.

A quick glance was enough for Anya to recognize the man she'd helped free from the wreckage right after the crash. Her gut lurched with a twinge of sadness, followed immediately by relief. She'd feared that he might suffer for days from his injuries. Passing so quickly was a mercy.

"What do we do with… the body?" the older woman asked tentatively.

Evan came up behind Anya. She glanced back at him, to get his input.

"It's dangerous to keep it in the camp, given the unknown scavenger animal situation," he replied to her unspoken question. "But I think one of the crates we brought up today would be large enough. We could put it in that overnight outside the perimeter. Bury tomorrow."

Anya nodded. "Unless anyone has a better suggestion, that seems like the best way to handle it."

No one spoke up.

They set about the somewhat gruesome task of checking the dead man's clothes for any potentially useful items in his pockets. His clothes were too bloodied from his injuries to be worth salvaging, but they removed his shoes. He also had a datapad in his jacket, which they added to the bin of other potentially useful things that had been gathered from the wreckage; the device itself was locked, but its components could be repurposed.

Anya hated how emotionally detached she was becoming from the whole ordeal. Seeing such a tragic death should have been a gut punch, but instead she found herself going through motions without any weight to the action.

Evan, likewise, was the picture of cool professionalism. Perhaps it was his calming influence that helped her get through contorting the corpse into a crate, or maybe she was simply too overwhelmed to process the events. In either case, she was grateful to get through it without having a breakdown.

Once they'd dragged the sealed crate a hundred meters from the camp's perimeter, Anya returned her mind to the other business. She tracked down Peter.

The older man was helping to set up the remaining section of perimeter wall for the night. With the sun now below the horizon, they were finishing just in time.

"Peter, a word?" Anya requested.

He nodded his assent and followed her to a private setting behind one of the pods. "How did it go today?"

"Can you keep what I'm about to tell you to yourself?"

"Why?"

"Because we don't have a good grasp on everyone's personality here yet, and it's best we avoid panic. I think we should keep certain details need to know among people who've shown they can keep a level head."

"I can agree to that, but not complete silence. Cora, Don, and Amelia have been essential, and I don't want to keep anything from them."

"Sure, loop them in," Anya assented. "For starters, we were able to get up to high ground and get a look at our surroundings. The good news is that there's a back way up to the plateau through the woods. It'll be a lot safer up there than on this slope, so you can start relocating everyone up there. We marked a trail."

"What about you?"

"There's something else I need to do. We spotted another crash site many kilometers from here. We think it's the military escort ship."

"Shit, that's…"

"If we're right, then help isn't coming—at least not anytime soon. Our best chance is to get to that ship and see if we can salvage the communications array."

He frowned. "That's a longshot."

"I know, but that's all we've got. Evan and I want to head out for it in the morning."

"And the rest of us?"

"Make camp on the plateau. The supplies we brought back today were from a survey equipment supply pod that's up there. It doesn't have nearly as many useful survival items as the other pod you found, but there are a few more things that were too big for us to carry back here. I marked its location for you." Anya handed him a crude map she'd drawn on a white shirt she'd found, with notations of notable landmarks, the forest path, and the supply crate. "Set a signal fire up there when you make it. It'll let us know you're okay, and it will alert any other survivors your scouts don't locate."

"We'll find our way there," Peter acknowledged.

"I also showed Cora some edible plants while we were working this afternoon, and I saw plenty of them up on the plateau. Any animals you may be able to snare in the forest will be safe to eat, too. It won't be easy, but it's possible to carve out a life here even without all the equipment we were supposed to have." She was grateful that they had that basic environmental information from their preliminary planetary survey to fall back on; knowing they'd have ample food and water made all the difference for their survival prospects.

Peter nodded. "I spoke to someone with farming experience today, and a rancher. There's a lot of spirit in the group. We'll make it work."

Anya placed her hand on his arm. "Thank you for stepping up."

He smiled. "I raised five boys. I know what it means to lead by example."

"Well, everyone here will be better off for it."

"You're a real go-getter, yourself. It's brave to venture out there."

"Someone has to do it."

Peter beamed. "We'll have a proper homestead set up by the time you're back. You'll see."

"I have no doubt." Anya wished she believed the words, but she'd seen too much that day to share his optimism. "Before I go, there are a few other things you should know."

7

IT TOOK A few minutes for Evan to realize that Anya had disappeared from view. Through no intentional decision, they'd all but been joined at the hip since the crash landing. Her partnership had become a comfort in their uncertain circumstances, despite his loner tendencies.

Don't be ridiculous, he told himself. *You don't need to track her every move.*

Still, he was curious where she'd gone. Looking around, he realized that Peter was also nowhere to be seen. Most likely, Anya had pulled him aside to discuss what they'd discovered.

"You hungry?" a woman asked from behind Evan.

He turned around to face her. Though he recognized her from around camp, they hadn't spoken before. "Ravenous."

"We're rationing so you won't be able to eat your fill, but hopefully this will take the edge off." She handed him a MealPak.

It was labeled 'Meat Stew', and he knew from experience that the contents were as ambiguous as the name. "Thanks."

Evan found a crate and sat down to prepare the packaged food. It'd been years since he'd last consumed one of the packets, but he went through the self-heating steps with muscle memory.

"Hey, how did you do that?" a man perched on a nearby crate asked. His MealPak was somewhat mangled.

"You need to break the seal down there." Evan set down his packet and went to help the man. He manipulated the package to get the chemical heating process started and handed it back.

"Wow, thanks! I never would have figured that out."

Evan resisted the urge to point out the large-print instructions and visual diagram printed on the package. It'd been a long day for everyone. "They can be tricky." Warming complete, he ripped open the top of his own packet and dug in. Just as mediocre as he remembered.

By the time he was finishing the last morsels, Anya returned to the center of camp with Peter, confirming Evan's hunch. Neither of them looked particularly happy.

Evan went over to Anya. "How'd it go?"

"Could have been better."

"Anything I should know?"

"We'll talk later."

The rest of the camp was getting settled for the night. Most people had their bedrolls on the ground out in the open since the sky was clear and rain was unlikely. Evan opted for a spot next to one of the emergency pods at the outskirts of camp, which would make for an easy exit in the morning.

Fifteen minutes later, Anya came over with her own bedroll. "Mind if I join you?"

"Sure. We still on for tomorrow?"

She nodded. "I gave Peter a heads up about the other supply pod and the gear we took."

"Even the…?"

"I hadn't planned on getting into that part, but when he asked how we were planning to carry all the other things, it came out. Things were going well up to that point."

"Was he mad?"

"More frustrated. But he ultimately agreed that trying to get the ship's communications array is the top priority. He has a few other people he wants to bring into the fold, and they'll work together to get everything in order here while we try to get answers." She paused. "I also told him about the body."

"Anya…"

"I couldn't leave here without telling someone. What if the killer *is* here?"

Evan nodded reluctantly. "Hopefully, they won't tear each other apart with false accusations while we're away."

"Better than the alternative."

Evan wasn't sure about that, but he didn't want to argue. Instead, he rolled over and adjusted his backpack that was serving as a pillow. "We should get some sleep."

—

Evan snapped awake. There was no sign of light on the horizon. But something had abruptly awoken him. He lay still, listening.

Snuffling and scraping sounded in the distance. The sounds were definitely coming from the direction of where they'd left the dead man's body in the crate.

Anya roused next to him. She blinked with confusion in the dim light and then froze, eyes wide, when she heard the creature moving.

Evan held his finger to his lips. Slowly and silently, he got up and began creeping toward the makeshift perimeter wall.

The scraping sounds grew louder. Evan's heart pounded in his chest with anticipation. They might get their first look at the mysterious monster Anya's team had spotted during the survey.

Either we're going to die quickly if it spots us, or we'll get lucky and see what we're up against. Given the odds against them, a quick death at the hands of a monster wouldn't be the worst way to go.

Peeking around a metal plate serving as a wall, Evan couldn't make out many details in the dim night beyond, despite Aethos' three moons hanging in the sky. His eyes strained against the darkness, searching for the crate and whatever was determined to get inside.

After twenty tense seconds, he glimpsed a shadow moving against the grassy hillside.

The creature stood at least as tall as a man, alternating between its hind legs and all fours as it twisted around the crate and pawed from all angles. Its texture was impossible to make out in the dark from that distance, but the indistinctness of its shape suggested it might be covered in hair or feathers that softened its outline. The clacks and scrapes of its movements indicated claws or talons.

Anya watched it from Evan's left, keeping her body hidden behind the fencing. Her breath was shallow and quavered slightly.

A loud crack of snapping plastic filled the night, followed by rapid scuffling. After more snaps and cracks came rhythmic, wet crunching.

Evan winced. The creature had clearly found its way inside the crate and was enjoying a hearty meal. *I guess we won't have to dig a grave.*

They remained nearly motionless while the creature finished eating. Now that it had a taste for humans, there was no telling if it might go after them as a live prey.

If this is the same thing that took out the Ranger-R, we are absolutely screwed. A pit grew in Evan's stomach as he played through the possible scenarios for their planned expedition in his mind. It was sounding more and more like a one-way mission.

Eventually, the chomping sounds ceased. The creature stood on its hind legs and sniffed the air. It swiveled its head to stare directly at Evan and Anya's location.

He instinctively held his breath, not that it would make any difference. The creature snuffled and then slinked downhill into the black. Evan and Anya remained silent and unmoving.

When he was certain it was long gone, Evan let out a long breath and relaxed against the wall. "What was that thing?"

"It doesn't have a name yet. I'm thinking it should have 'killer' or 'death' in there."

"What would stop that thing from coming up onto the plateau?"

"Nothing," she admitted. "Maybe we just missed it in the survey. Or maybe it just didn't have prey up there."

"Until our camp relocates and gives it a reason."

She breathed out slowly through her nose. "I can't begin to speculate about it based on what little I could see in the dark. It wasn't that large, so it might not be the same type of creature that attacked the Ranger-R."

"Great, so there might be something even worse than that thing out there."

"I thought we knew more about this place than we actually do."

Evan pinched the bridge of his nose. "The trek to the other crash site was already going to be iffy, but now it's downright crazy to go out there without weapons."

"About that..."

He eyed her. "Is there some secret weapons cache you've been keeping to yourself?"

"Got lucky." She showed him a pulse handgun tucked underneath her jacket at the back of her waistband. Such energy weapons were more common than kinetic rounds, mostly because of their variable intensity—from stun to deadly.

"Where did you get that?" Evan asked.

"You know that crate I grabbed when we got down to the supply pod with Cora? I saw that it was marked 'Tactical' and knew what that was code for."

"Were there other weapons?"

"Yes. Three more handguns and two rifles."

"Better tell Peter you have it, or people might tear the camp apart wondering who stole it when they check the inventory."

"Already done. And the others are secure."

Evan eyed the pistol. He didn't want to sound patronizing by asking if she knew how to use it. But even if she'd had basic shooting lessons, there was no way she'd had as much training as him, given their difference in professions. "Do you want me to hold onto that?"

"I'm good." Anya hid the pistol from view again.

"Well, I'd feel a lot better if I had a rifle."

"Peter wasn't willing to give any up. We're already taking the only functional transportation and more than our share of food."

"None of that matters if we're attacked and eaten."

"This one handgun was all I could negotiate. There are almost fifty other people here to think about."

Evan crossed his arms. "Well, sounds like you have it all under control."

"No, not at all. Just taking it one thing at a time."

“What we’re facing is too dangerous to not have a plan. Or better weapons.”

“We do have a plan. Get to the ship and call for help.”

“That’s really not a plan,” Evan countered. “It’s an ambition. And I don’t like the idea of going about it unarmed.”

“You were ready to go without *any* gun yesterday.”

Frustration was building in Evan’s chest; he’d been hoping that she would come around on her own. He had half a mind to end the debate by grabbing the weapon out of her hands and then raid the rest of the armory.

But even though the soldier in him wanted to take control of the situation by force, his more recent experiences had emphasized the importance of building relationships with people. Working with Anya was far more analogous to his time undercover than on a battlefield. From that perspective, he needed to get her to trust him; that way, she’d be on his side when it really mattered. Right now, her holding the weapon was what she needed to feel secure. If it came down to a dangerous situation, he could disarm her and do what needed to be done in a matter of seconds. So, for the sake of building a stable relationship, he didn’t want to press the issue for fear of undermining the rapport they’d already started to build. Having an intelligent, capable ally was ultimately more critical to his survival than a pistol.

Nonetheless, a debate over who had possession of a handgun was a minor quibble in their current plight. He’d been in many situations where he didn’t have a lot of control, but at least he’d always had an exit plan. This was different. Not only was he trapped, but everyone around him was equally stuck. Worse, any action they took would be based on guesses. All of his training told him that guesswork was a recipe for disaster. One needed to be prepared for contingencies, and not even knowing the basics of a situation meant that Plan A might be doomed from the start.

Still, doing nothing was unlikely to improve their situation. Getting to the other ship remained their best chance to make contact off-world; that was the only way to improve their long-term prospects. And Evan stood a better chance of making it there with Anya than alone.

He rubbed his eyes. "I don't see any way around it, but I can't shake the feeling that venturing away from camp has 'giant mistake' written all over it."

"The only mistake here was assuming the colony ever had a chance. We're here now, so we either roll over and die or we try to make the best of what we have."

There was no arguing with that. "We should try to get back to sleep so we can get an early start." They returned to their bedrolls and tried to relax. Despite his best efforts, Evan's mind remained on the creature. *What else are we going to encounter out there?*

8

ANYA STIRRED AT the first hint of light on her eyelids. The sun had yet to crest the distant hills, but the sky already had a pink tinge along the horizon.

Next to her, Evan startled awake. He stretched his arms and rubbed his eyes. "It's morning already?"

She rubbed sleep from her own eyes. "Yeah. It took me a while to settle down again after seeing that thing."

"Same here."

Tired or not, they needed to get moving.

As agreed, they slipped out of camp before the other survivors had gotten up for the day. They'd no doubt be peppered with questions or ill-informed suggestions if they stuck around, and trying to explain how the corpse had been eaten last night wasn't how she wanted to start the day. Still, she had questions of her own.

With packs slung on their backs, Anya and Evan swung by the now-empty crate as their first stop after leaving camp. As expected, the container was covered in deep scratches, the walls were cracked in several places, and the hinges had been broken. Based on the spacing of the scratches, the creature appeared to have feet the size of an adult human's head with three prominent claws. There was nothing left of the dead man, aside from a few bloody smears on the crate and some shredded strips of fabric scattered around the area.

Evan crouched down in the grass, examining something. "I think there's a print here."

Anya went to see.

Squatting down next to Evan, she spotted large imprints in the ground. The grass was matted, and outlines of the foot were visible in dried pools of blood. The print was the length of her elbow to fingertips, indicating that the creature was even larger than she'd thought from a distance.

As a xenobiologist, she'd directly studied all manner of creatures on multiple planets, and she'd read about thousands of others in school. No matter the planet, certain traits were universal across predators, and this creature was no exception. The positioning of the claws was set up to attack, and the power of these particular limbs seemed to be enough to tear through any potential protection that the colonists presently had.

"What do you think—hunter or scavenger?" Evan asked.

She was certain it was predatory, but she also didn't want to dissuade Evan from their mission. "Can't know for certain, but we should assume it will stalk us."

"We're going to need something more substantial than a handgun. I really want one of those rifles."

Just because she had to work with Evan, that didn't mean she fully trusted him yet. Maintaining control of the sole weapon would be her insurance until she could better evaluate him. "The perimeter walls won't offer much protection, so the community will need every other gun to defend the camp," she deflected. "Besides, the escort ship will have a well-stocked armory we can scavenge."

"First, we have to make it that far."

She glanced at the camp. "If we head back now to demand a rifle, we're never getting out of here. I'm going to find that cruiser." Without waiting for a response, she headed up the hill.

"Alone?" he called after her.

"Not if you come with me."

— — —

Seeing the carnage from the creature's midnight snack had left Evan even more uncertain about their upcoming journey.

If he'd had body armor, a rifle, and plenty of extra rounds in hand, his concerns would have been a cautionary nag at the back of his mind. But given their only weaponry was a single pulse handgun—currently in Anya's possession—he may as well have been standing in the middle of the forest naked.

Even so, he wasn't about to let her venture out by herself. But with each step further from the camp, he regretted not pushing harder to get better armaments.

As they began heading toward the path that would take them up to the plateau, Evan's hand instinctively reached for a nonexistent weapon at his hip. The monster had appeared to head down the hill into the valley, but there was no telling if it had looped back to the forest or if there were others of its kind nearby. Just because they hadn't encountered any on their hike yesterday didn't mean they were safe.

Anya also appeared to be on edge. She kept a swift pace, which Evan was happy to match to get them to the rover that much sooner.

The path they'd marked on the way down the previous afternoon made it easy to find their way through the trees. They added extra directions in a few places to aid the other survivors.

Eventually, they made it to the top of the incline where the trees gave way to open grassland on the plateau. The sun was well above the horizon and the chill of the night air had given way to a pleasant warmth.

"Any idea what season it is now?" Evan asked while they walked along the tree line toward where they'd stashed the rover.

"End of summer, approaching autumn, I think," Anya replied.

"Are the winters cold?"

"Not overly in this area, but it will get wet. That's a future challenge."

One step at a time, Evan reminded himself. He couldn't help the inclination to plan ten steps ahead. Having long-term plans and contingencies was how to avoid getting caught unprepared… not that such thinking had done him any favors with this surprise crash scenario.

He sighed. This situation was thoroughly and truly out of his control, and stressing about unknown variables wouldn't help. He resolved to take each scenario as it came. Adaptability was the way.

Keeping his mind on the present, Evan walked alongside Anya to the rover's hiding place. Together, they cleared away the brush concealing its location.

Evan placed his hand on the rover's door. "Are we really doing this?"

"Yep." Anya opened her own door and climbed in.

Evan joined her in the cab. The controls were barebones but should get the job done. "I must again state that I'm not sure this bucket will get us there and back in one piece."

"I'd still rather take this than walk."

Resolute, Evan turned on the rover and backed it out from the trees. As soon as he was on the open grass, he steered the vehicle on a diagonal path across the plateau toward the military ship's crash site.

The large tires made for a smooth ride at speed. They quickly covered the six kilometers across the plateau. He slowed as they approached a downslope.

"Let's hope there isn't a sheer cliff where we're headed," he said.

"There isn't. I remember it from the survey—we'll have a slope down," Anya replied.

True to her memory, the level ground transitioned to a moderate grade. While mostly covered in grass, there were sporadic shrubs and rocks.

Evan kept a slow pace, unsure of the vehicle's traction. When turning to avoid rocks, the tires would occasionally slip and spin.

"I'll admit, you were right about the rover being great for flat ground and not so much for this," Anya said after their fourth slip.

"It's still better than walking the whole way. We'll see how far we can get in it."

That declaration was about to be put to the test as they reached the bottom of the first slope. Though relatively flat, the ground in the immediate vicinity was covered in rocks. The stone rubble varied from little pebbles to boulders the size of the rover. Only a few meters in and it was already clear that finding a path would be a challenge.

"We may have to get out and walk," Evan warned.

"Can't give up yet. The rocks would be a lot harder on our ankles than the tires."

To her point, the vehicle's tires were an interlaced metal

mesh that shaped itself to any landscape and could never go flat. While that made for reliable travel even on challenging terrain, it wouldn't do them any good if they were penned in by boulders too big to drive over.

Nonetheless, Evan forged ahead along the best course he could see at each decision point. There were a couple of close calls, but the boulders eventually diminished and they were left driving over small stones and gravel.

"Well done," Anya told him with a smile. "Seems like you've done this before."

"A bit."

"Military deployment?"

"Among other things. The spatial awareness from docking a shuttle comes in handy in lots of other ways."

"Oh, you fly?"

He nodded. "I haven't been able to do it as much recently, but I really enjoy it."

"Space travel makes me a little queasy. I love *being* on a new world, but the getting there part is sketchy."

"What, you don't like being light years away from breathable air aside from what's on your ship?"

She side-eyed him. "You could put it that way."

"I know, it's strange. Humans are very ill-suited for space travel, but now the future of our species is dependent on seeking out new worlds amongst the stars."

"We're an enigma. And that's coming from a xenobiologist who's studied some weirdo lifeforms. No species other than humans is so determined to modify our environment and carve out life in seemingly unlivable places."

"That we've encountered yet, anyway."

"True. I have no doubt that there's other advanced life out there. It's only a matter of time before we meet each other."

"That'll either be the end of us or the start of a whole new era."

As the rover bumped along over the rocky landscape, a warm breeze smelling like pine and sage ruffled Evan's hair. The humidity was higher down here at the lower elevation, leaving his skin sticky.

Evan kept his sights on a distant mountain peak that reminded him of a jagged tooth. It was the only landmark tall enough to offer orientation in their present position. The smoke from the day before had dissipated, so he only had a vague idea of the correct direction.

Anya had shifted her attention to the sky. "Hey, Evan… they may have left something else out of the travel brochure."

"What?" He glanced upward, not seeing anything out of the ordinary. A few clouds had rolled in.

"Back to the thing about us picking the plateau—the other reason is because it was high ground."

"Right. Defensible, away from the monster thing—"

"And also out of the floodplain."

He looked over at her. "Meaning…?"

"There was some evidence that the weather can shift pretty rapidly around here. Like, torrential rains kind of thing."

"And why are you mentioning that now?"

"These clouds don't look happy. And they're rolling in fast."

Evan leaned forward to get a better upward look out through the rover's windshield. The spotty clouds he'd noticed straight ahead were the leading edge of a much larger front behind them. "That does not look good."

"It might be fine." Anya's tone suggested otherwise.

They were completely exposed in their current position. Being at the base of the tall slope, they'd be in the direct path of water shedding off the plateau. The little rover wouldn't stand a chance against a torrent.

Keeping an eye on their intended destination, Evan altered course slightly to head toward a small rise. While not ideal, it would at least prevent them from being in the low-ground path of a potential flood.

"I like the way you think," Anya said when she realized his intentions.

"We'll have to backtrack a little, but—" He cut off as the first raindrops hit the windshield. They sent a sizeable splatter across the dusty surface.

Anya tightened her seatbelt. "Maybe it will pass over us."

More drops fell, growing in frequency. Evan found controls for the front wipers and activated the blades. Soon, even at the wipers' top speed, the splatters were obscuring his view as quickly as they could be cleared away.

Unable to see more than a few meters, he slowed the rover. The ground was getting soggy, and the wheels began to slip on the wet grass and mud.

"We might need to wait it out," Evan said. He hated the idea of stopping so soon into their journey, but crashing would be worse.

"Maybe near those rocks?" Anya pointed to a group of boulders several dozen meters ahead.

Evan coaxed the rover to the rocks, crawling along by the end. He pulled as close as he could to the boulders and set it in park. Not wanting to waste their limited power, he turned off the engine.

Anya let out a long breath and slouched down in her seat. "Not off to a great start."

"I had no illusions that this would be smooth travels."

"Neither did I, but I didn't have 'flash flood' on my list of potential issues."

Evan gazed up at the heavy drops pelting the vehicle. "It really did come out of nowhere. Things can't be good back at camp."

Anya's brows knitted. "We can't do anything." Her tone had taken on the same flat affect as when she'd tended to the fatally injured man right after the crash.

Evan appreciated her mission-focused attitude and ability to remain objective. He'd found that to be a rare trait, especially outside the military. She had surprising fortitude for someone who had spent most of her career in a research lab—almost suspiciously so. "You don't get ruffled easily."

She shrugged. "No point getting upset about things I can't control."

"Have you always felt that way, or did something happen?"

"Oh, so you expect me to answer questions about myself when you won't tell me anything about you?"

"I've said a lot more than 'nothing'."

"Barely."

"Lead by example?"

Anya let out a sarcastic scoff. "You're impossible." She sighed. "We moved to a new city when I was ten, and I started mid-term at a school with a bunch of entitled kids who'd never been taught proper manners. I got picked on as the newbie, so I had to get a thick skin. My dad would tell me that there's no sense getting upset over what's happening around you because you can only control how you react to it."

"That must have been tough to hear as a kid."

"But it was good advice. Maybe there are times I turn off my feelings *too* much, but it's better than the alternative."

"You would have made a good soldier."

"No, I don't like killing things."

"All the more reason you would be. Don't want someone who's too eager to pull the trigger."

"True—" Anya cut off as the rover jolted. "What was that?"

Evan braced his hand against the side wall as the vehicle shook again. He couldn't see well outside through the rain streaming down the windows. The entire vehicle was shaking now. "Oh, shit. I think we're sliding."

Anya's eyes went wide. "While parked? But—"

Evan strained to see through the water. He could barely make out the nearby boulders... which were now inching further away. "No, no, no." He pressed the ignition.

The interior lights sprang to life, casting a glare that made it impossible to see outside. He found the headlights and flicked them on. Bright, blue-tinted beams appeared out front, highlighting the constant onslaught of rain. Worse, it cast the first look at a river forming underneath them, which had already pushed the rover from its original parking place.

"We need to get out of here!" Anya's tone was sharp with panic.

"Where do we go?" Evan couldn't spot a clear path.

The hill above was an absolute no-go with the water rushing down. Going horizontal on their current elevation might work, but they'd be fighting the current. They could go with the flow of water and head downhill, but they had no idea what awaited them at the valley floor. Trying to maintain their current position was the best option.

He gave a little power to the accelerator and angled the rover toward the up-slope. The vehicle crawled forward on a roughly parallel path as the over-corrected steering compensated for the push of the water.

"I'm sorry I got you into this," Anya said, her voice faint and tight through her tension. She had a white-knuckle grip on the grab bar above her door.

"Nothing about this is your fault. I probably would have hiked out into the forest on my own, and then where would I be?"

"Probably still up on the plateau rather than caught in this runoff."

Evan let out a bitter chuckle at her matter-of-fact response to what he'd meant as a rhetorical question. She was right about the timing; without the rover, someone on foot would not yet have made it off the plateau, which was likely a much better place to be in the storm. "And miss all this excitement?"

Anya smiled slightly through her nerves. "Just keep going, slow and steady."

Evan was doing his best to keep the vehicle on track, but even with the over-steering, they were creeping further toward the steeper slope below them.

Ahead, though, there were trees. It was the first significant foliage they'd encountered since descending the hill, and it would offer at least a little shelter compared to being out in the open. Evan kept a deliberate path toward the tree line, intending to wedge the rover between some trunks to keep it from sliding around.

They were almost to the trees—only a few meters to go.

"Those two trunks look like a good brace," Anya said, pointing to a pair of multi-trunk, white-barked trees.

"Yeah, if I can just—"

The wheels slipped, sending the rover careening sideways.

Evan turned the wheel into the skid, but it was no use. The tires had zero traction on the soaked ground. The rover continued sliding sideways, but it was still heading in the direction of the trees. He braced for impact.

9

THE FRONT OF the rover slammed into a small tree trunk at the outside of the grove, which further spun the vehicle's rear end down the slope.

"We have to jump out!" Evan shouted, unbuckling his seatbelt.

"But—"

"Now, Anya!" Evan opened his door and leaped out, hoping Anya was right behind him.

He landed hard on the muddy ground, the warm rain obscuring his vision. Water flowed around him, pushing him toward the steeper slope below.

Evan crawled toward the trees. Each step was a struggle, digging in his toes to prevent himself from getting washed away.

When he reached a tree, he looped his arm around its trunk and tried to spot Anya. She was nowhere to be seen.

"Anya!" he shouted over the drumming rain. He could barely see through the sheets of water. "Where are you?"

No response.

The rover was teetering at the top of the slope. He could only watch, helpless, as it tumbled over the edge. He winced as it flipped end-over-end before disappearing into the trees below. All of their gear and provisions were inside. They'd have to track it down.

"Anya!"

"Evan!" a reply finally came through the roar of pounding rain and rushing water.

His chest lifted with relief. She sounded close. "Are you at the trees?"

"Yes, holding on for dear life!" she shouted back.

"Stay put. I'm coming to you." Evan pushed off his tree toward another downhill, working his way toward the sound of her voice.

After two tree transfers, he spotted her. She had both arms wrapped around a trunk the width of her shoulders.

"Is the rover...?" she began before fading out.

"At the bottom of the ravine now. We'll find it when this lets up." He grabbed ahold of the tree next to her. "Are you okay?"

"Yeah." Anya adjusted her grip on the tree trunk. "This is a nightmare."

"We're going to get through this."

"It's not looking great right now."

"I've been through worse."

She groaned. "We knew there were challenges with this planet. There always are. We'd planned for ways to cope, but without that—"

"Anything else you haven't told me?" Evan asked. At this point, he wouldn't be surprised if she were to reveal that they were on top of an active volcano.

"Forest monster, weather..." she started to list off. "Those were two of the biggest ones. There were also some strange energy readings, but who knows what that might be?"

"Fantastic."

They fell silent for a few minutes, getting pelted by rain while muddy water flowed over their feet. The one saving grace was that the temperature and rain were warm enough to not make it chilly. Hopefully, being early in the day, they'd have time to dry before the sun set. Of course, it would have to stop raining first.

Evan peered deeper into the trees. Water was dripping down everywhere, but the tree canopy was definitely breaking the worst of the downpour.

"Hey, why don't we try to find a drier spot?" he suggested. "I don't like the idea of standing here indefinitely."

"Agreed. Since we'll need to head downslope to get the rover, anyway, may as well head that direction."

"Over there might be good." Evan pointed to a large tree fifty meters downslope and slightly to their left. It had several other smaller trees grouped around it, and the combined foliage appeared to offer a reasonably dry shelter.

The two of them carefully worked their way toward the refuge, sliding from tree to tree so they could use the trunks for support. Evan's feet were caked with mud, weighing down each step. Between the mud and slick leaves underfoot, he wouldn't have been able to remain upright without the tree handholds—and even then, he fell on his backside twice.

When they finally made it to their destination, Evan was relieved to see that it was, indeed, much drier. The occasional raindrop made it through, but the ground was simply damp rather than soaked.

Anya picked at the sleeves of her shirt clinging to her skin, trying to air them out so they'd dry faster. "I really hope it lets up soon."

"At this point, we should plan to camp overnight. There's

no way we'll make it to the crash site after this delay."

"If the rover is shot, it might take a few days."

He nodded. "Despite what I'd said, I did think we'd get farther than this before having to go on foot."

"Me too. I also thought there would be more warning signs of an approaching storm."

"The sunrise was awfully red. I wasn't sure if this planet might be an exception, but looks like the old wisdom holds."

"What are you talking about?"

"Something they told us when I was in the service. 'Red sky at night, delight. Red sky in morn, take warning.' Something passed down from Old Earth, I think. But, I guess there's truth in it with any atmosphere we humans find pleasant."

"Hmm." She braced her back against the largest tree's trunk.

"I'm surprised you never heard the adage."

"I'm a xenobiologist, not a climatologist."

"Well, I'm just a non-degreed ex-soldier."

She chuckled. "Practical skills are a lot more useful than book smarts at a time like this."

"Fortunately, it seems you have some of both."

"I'm useless with weather, apparently, but I can tell you that spikey plant over there will hurt you if you touch it," she said with a completely straight face.

Evan wasn't sure if she'd meant it sarcastically or not. "Such wisdom."

"What can I say, I'm a fountain of knowledge." Despite her deadpan delivery, there was a playful sparkle to her copper eyes, which he now noticed had a hint of gold at their center.

"Thank you for finding the humor in our dismal situation."

"It's either laugh or cry."

"I feel more like breaking something."

She motioned down the hill. "You did a number on that poor rover."

"I blame that mishap on a shoddy weather report."

"You should definitely fire the person who said this would be a pleasant place to set up a colony."

"If we ever get our hands on that communications array, the NovaTech customer service department won't know what hit them."

— — —

Anya plopped down on the ground, not caring that she'd get even more covered in mud than she already was. There was no telling how long they might need to wait out the storm, and she may as well get comfortable.

Some people had a calm, reassuring presence, and Anya found Evan to be one of those individuals. Her natural snarkiness came out when she was stressed, and he'd been playing off that rather than becoming confrontational, like some people she'd worked with in the past. All in all, he was turning out to be a pleasant person to be stuck with in the wilderness, and it was making her more comfortable with him despite his initial reticence.

A half-hour passed with them making smalltalk before the rain decreased to a light drizzle.

"We should try to recover the rover," Evan suggested. "We'll find other shelter if the rain starts up again."

Anya got to her feet. Her clothing had half-dried during their break, and the muddy spots on her pants crunched slightly as she moved. "It should be a straight shot down the hill."

“Stay close,” Evan called over his shoulder as he led the way.

Following a similar technique to their earlier descent, they slid from tree to tree, using trunks as handholds and to brace their feet. The air had a crisp sweetness to it, intermingled with the earthy aroma of freshly churned soil. Every scent and sound jumped out at her as she soaked in the experience of being surrounded by so much life. In spite of the rough start to their journey, there was no denying that the planet was beautiful, and the storm they’d just endured was a way of life for the local flora and fauna.

Evan abruptly skidded to a stop and held up a fist. Anya recognized the gesture to mean ‘stop’, and she froze in place, remaining silent. Evan stood motionless, watching and listening. From Anya’s position behind him, it was unclear what had put him on edge.

After a tense minute, Evan dropped his hand to his side and relaxed. “I thought I’d heard something following us.”

Anya’s pulse spiked, the horrifying images of the creature tearing apart the deceased colonist still fresh in her mind. “Are you sure it’s gone?”

“No, but it had ample opportunity to attack us while we were standing still.”

There are real dangers out here. Evan has given me no reason to doubt him. Her hand went to the pulse pistol strapped at her waist. She released the buckle. “I think you should be the one to carry this.” She handed him the holster and pistol.

“Why the change of heart?”

“Because you noticed a potential threat when I didn’t. You could have fired before I’d even have known something was wrong.”

He took the offered weapon. “Good to hear all that time

and money spent training that situational awareness into me paid off."

"I'm not oblivious, but I'm out of my depth here. I'll follow your lead."

"I've got your back, don't worry." He met her gaze with calm assurance.

Though it went against her nature to rely on others, the tension in her chest eased. After their experiences over the last hour, she had no doubts that he was committed to keeping both of them safe while accomplishing their mission. There was no point letting pride get in the way of their shared goal, and trust had to start somewhere.

Evan angled their path toward the tree line of the open hillside where the rover had tumbled down. The temporary waterfall had ceased, though a few small streams still snaked their way down the matted grass. All signs of the rover's path had been erased by the water.

"Everything is soaked, so I doubt the other team will be able to get a signal fire going anytime soon," Evan commented as they continued their downward slide.

"Yeah. I hope they're okay." Anya glanced back toward the plateau above, but it was impossible to see anything beyond the hillside. *We need to focus on us and our mission.*

Evan slipped on a muddy patch, barely catching himself. "I still can't believe how much rain dropped that quickly."

Anya sidestepped the hazard. "I wasn't expecting weather that extreme. But it seems that there's a *lot* about this planet that we didn't get right."

"It doesn't help that our ship was destroyed before we could get proper equipment down here."

The ache of worry returned to her chest. "I don't know what to do if we can't find a working comm array."

"We've got the hab shelter, a water purifier, and there's clearly plenty of wildlife, so food shouldn't be a problem. It won't be the modern settlement we'd planned, but I think we could get comfortable here."

"Old school, low-tech agrarian—like the early settlers." Anya smiled at the thought of forming a peaceful little community of farmers.

"We could hunt with bows and spears. All we need is a cave and some loin cloths."

"I'm not sure 'fur bikini' is really my style aesthetic."

He glanced back over his shoulder at her. "You could pull it off."

Her cheeks burned, but thankfully he'd already turned away to watch his footing. "Well, I'm going to put that at Plan Z. We have a lot of avenues to explore before then."

"Speaking of which…" Evan broke into a jog, nimbly stepping over fallen logs and out into the open.

Anya followed at a slower pace. When she reached the forest's edge, she spotted the rover wedged against a cluster of fallen tree trunks. Remarkably, it had landed upright. Aside from being caked in mud and covered in several dents, it appeared to be intact.

"The universe doesn't completely hate us," Evan said through a grin.

Anya smiled back, a tingle of hope spreading through her. "I'll take the win!"

"Let's see how lucky we are." Evan popped open the driver's side door. It stuck a little due to a dented panel.

The rover's interior appeared unharmed. Evan tried the ignition. The vehicle hummed to life.

"All right!" Anya ran around the far side of the rover to get into the passenger seat. When she climbed in, Evan was frowning. "What's wrong?"

He motioned to the front display screen. It was reading a 'check power connection' error.

"Do you know what that means?" Anya asked.

"I think the solar panels were dislodged, which makes sense. Whatever battery charge we have left might be all we'll get."

"Looks like it must have auto-shutoff when we bailed out."

"We do have that going for us. Let's not waste the charge." He strapped on his seatbelt.

A few careful maneuvers and mud sprays later, Evan had successfully backed the vehicle away from the logs and set them on a new path across the valley.

The terrain at the bottom of the slope was mostly flat and covered with widely spaced trees. Reedy grasses stood as tall as the rover's windshield, making it difficult to see too far ahead. The mountain they'd selected as a visual guidepost was one of the few landmarks Anya could make out, but, ultimately, it was the only one that mattered right now. They were headed in the right direction, and they needed to cover maximum ground as quickly as possible.

The terrain and vegetation were not going to work to their advantage for long. Ahead, the trees were growing closer together and underbrush obscured the ground. Navigating the labyrinth of trunks would push the rover to its limit.

Evan's jaw was set and his eyes were focused on the path ahead. Not wanting to break his concentration, Anya remained quiet and took in their surroundings to look for further clues about the environment.

The coarse, chest-height grasses were vibrant green, and the trees all had the top section of their roots exposed, forming twisting archways around the landscape. There were no smaller bushes to be seen.

"Evan, we need to turn back and find another path," Anya stated as the clues came together.

He glanced over at her. "Why?"

"All that water flowing down the hill had to go somewhere, right? Look at these trees! This is a floodplain. A marsh. The ground could get soft and bog us down without any warning."

Evan stopped the rover. "What other way are we supposed to go? We can't drive through that forest above. Crossing this valley is the only way to get where we need to go."

"I know. But it's not worth risking the rover and all our gear. We should find a secure place to park it and continue on foot."

He released a frustrated sigh, flexing his fingers on the steering wheel. "Is your thinking that the vehicle is more likely to sink because it's heavier?"

She nodded. "And if it got stuck or started to go under, we'd have no way to get it out. It doesn't have a winch."

Evan stared at the denser trees in front of them. "We were just about to run out of maneuvering room, anyway. All right, let's gather up what we can carry."

10

THE EXPEDITION COULDN'T be off to much worse of a start. Evan's training had prepared him to take setbacks in stride, but everything about his time on Aethos was testing the limits of his tolerance.

As they sorted through the equipment in the rover and decided what was worth bringing in backpacks, Evan tried to ignore the growing pit in his stomach. Surrounded by buzzing insects with only wind and distant bird calls to break up the utter silence, he was reminded that they were the only two humans for kilometers, and there were only a few dozen people on this entire planet. If they got hurt or trapped, no one was coming. Sticking together back at the crash site would have been far safer.

"I know I've said it before, but again, I'm sorry I talked you into this," Anya said as she loaded her pack.

"Don't be. I would have been too antsy sitting around with the other survivors."

"We had the supply crate. We could have gotten by."

"For a while," he agreed. "Making it to the other crash to look for a radio is still the only long-term play. I would have done this without you."

"Same. But I'm really glad you're here with me," she said, glancing over at him but not meeting his gaze.

"It was the right thing to do."

"A lot of people wouldn't care about being decent under these circumstances. Just look at the way some people were trying to hoard supplies back at camp."

"People are happy to work together until there's real competition. Doesn't take long for it to turn into every person for themselves."

"A flaw of humanity, I guess."

He shrugged. "One of many."

A rustle sounded in the shadowed foliage to Evan's right—low to the ground, so likely a small foraging animal.

Anya had heard it, too. She was tense and focused on the bush nearest the source of the sound.

"Probably a rabbit, or whatever these local equivalents are called," he said.

"They really should just be called 'rabbits', right? Or maybe 'Aethos rabbits'. It's silly how we feel the need to come up with new names for everything when we colonize a new planet." Based on her pinched brows and the flush to her cheeks, the naming conventions were a sore subject.

"Doesn't it make sense to give distinct creatures different names?"

"Oh, sure. But if the zoology notes are 'a deer-like creature', just call the darn thing a deer." She paused her packing to throw up one hand. "Slap whatever scientific name on it for the galactic encyclopedia, but will any local actually care about the difference between the deer on one planet or another if they look roughly the same and serve similar roles in the ecosystem? No, of course not. We'd be much better served to come up with general *classifications* of wildlife following practical nomenclature and leave the sciencing to scientists. Don't get all bent out of shape if a colonist just says 'deer' rather than 'Elosian red-shouldered forest deer'."

Evan clenched his jaw, trying to keep from laughing at her animated rant. "Exactly. I totally agree."

She sighed. "Sorry, it's been a 'thing' in the xenobiology community."

"I think I can guess your position on the issue."

"Yeah, the *right* one."

He laughed.

"It's the only commonsense solution when examining the biomes of dozens—or hundreds—of worlds," she continued. "And don't get me started on the researchers who want to name new discoveries after themselves!"

The bushes rustled again—louder and closer this time. And whatever had disturbed the branches sounded much larger.

Evan reached for the handgun on his hip. "I don't suppose that's a deer."

She stood still. "The only ones here are crepuscular."

"What?"

"They're only active at dawn and dusk. It's midday."

He drew the handgun, ready for action. The forest around them had gone eerily quiet.

Anya was gripping her pack, glancing around the trees. "What do we do?"

"This rover looks like a big target, which is probably keeping whatever that is at a distance. As soon as we walk away, we'll look a lot less threatening."

"It might just be curious and not after a meal." Even Anya didn't sound convinced by her own words. The midnight snack they'd witnessed had not left a friendly impression of the wildlife.

"Suggestions?"

"We could try making some noise. Loud. Try to scare it off."

Evan had heard a similar suggestion on one of his deployments where there were bothersome scavenger creatures stalking the camp. Those had only been knee-high and were harmless, but the same principle might work now with something bigger and meaner—at least temporarily. "The other option is to draw it out and kill it."

Anya frowned. "I don't like the idea of killing things without knowing they're actually a threat."

"We're strangers here. How long do you want to give these creatures to decide if we're an easy meal?"

Anya grabbed something from the back of the rover. She hurled it into the trees and covered her ears.

Not waiting for an explanation, Evan quickly covered his ears as well as he could without holstering the pistol.

Three seconds later, a concussive *bang* echoed through the landscape. The pressure of it reverberated in his chest, and his pulse spiked. As the echoes faded, he lowered his hands.

Something big was crashing away from them. He followed a wave of movement through the reeds until it disappeared into the trees. Birds were crying out with angry caws and flapping their wings.

"What was that?" Evan asked.

"A little something I picked up from the survey supplies. Concussive charge for sonic analysis of ground composition. It was too heavy to bring with us on foot, so why not use it now?"

Evan nodded, impressed. "Well, I think that did scare it off, but everything within two kilometers now knows something interesting happened here. We should get a move on before anything else comes to investigate."

They shouldered their packs. Evan's was heavier than he would have liked for a long trek, but he hadn't brought anything that he'd regret having. Aside from food, water, and a medkit, he also had a compact tent, a bedroll, flashlight, and rope. Anya had her own provisions, bedroll, and she'd insisted on bringing her bioanalyzer so they could locate new edible plants to supplement the MealPaks. While it wasn't his top pick for filling limited pack space, he wasn't about to turn down fresh greens.

Before leaving the rover, Evan activated its emergency locator beacon. Though they didn't have any reader to pick up the signal at present, they might locate something in the military ship.

Evan took the lead as they trekked through the forest. He headed for slightly higher ground with the hope of skirting around the marshlands. Given the recent rains, the last thing he wanted was to get stuck in boggy ground.

Anya kept up with his brisk pace, likely spurred by the knowledge that potential predators might be nearby. He was happy to cover ground without worry of her slowing them down. Nonetheless, it was obvious they wouldn't make it anywhere close to the other crash site by nightfall.

They kept a decent pace for another two hours before breaking for a snack. To conserve their rations, they shared one of the MealPaks and supplemented it with berries Anya deemed safe using her bioanalyzer. Though Evan had initially been skeptical of the device's worth, it earned its space in her pack with the first taste of the fruit.

"Being stuck here might not be so bad if there's more food like this," he said while happily munching on a handful of purple berries.

"Beats the stuff they grow on space stations, doesn't it?"

Anya popped another berry in her mouth. "My favorite part of expeditions is trying out the local produce. Can't beat right off the vine."

"I could definitely get used to this."

With a new appreciation for what the planet may have to offer, Evan resumed the hike after they'd finished the meal. He took a slightly slower pace than the first push, covering another three kilometers of gentle downward slopes before the landscape started to change again. The trees grew larger and denser, and the reedy grasses gave way to leafy bushes and vines. He wasn't sure if he was just warm from exertion, but it seemed like the temperature and humidity had also increased.

Anya wiped her brow with the back of her sleeve. "Wow, it got muggy really quickly."

"Must be some extreme microclimates."

"The rain didn't help." She looked around while rolling up her sleeves to her elbows. "Based on the plants, it looks like it's always wetter around here. It's more jungle than forest."

"What's the difference?"

"Vegetation density, mostly. Bad news for us is that jungle means dense, which will make for slow going."

Evan found himself wishing that they were back on the open plain of the plateau. Hopefully, the other crash survivors had been able to move the main camp up there and were safe. That way, there'd at least be someone to tell the story about what had happened to the colony expedition. *But we need to call for help so there will be someone to tell.*

Evan picked up a meter-long stick to use for beating aside vines hanging in his path. A long blade would have really come in handy.

"Are you sure we're going in the right direction?" Anya asked after a few minutes of silence.

Truthfully, he wasn't positive. In the denser, taller trees, he'd lost sight of the mountain they'd been using as a reference. And even if the other team had been able to light a signal fire back on the plateau, it'd be impossible to see through the vegetation. "A compass would be great."

"Magnetic guidance is wonky on this planet—one of its many quirks. But we do have good, old-fashioned sunlight."

"Go on."

"We know where the sun sets, and we know what time of day it is, so we have the position in the sky. We might not be able to see the horizon right now, but we can see the shadows. A little triangulation and we can orient."

"Okay, so we can work out shadow angle for different times, and as long as we keep track of the hour, we should be going in roughly the right direction."

"It's not like we can go in a precisely straight line, anyway. As long as we're not going too off-course, we can correct when we get closer to the crash."

He nodded. "Good thinking. There's more to you than just a biologist."

"*Xeno*biologist. And there's no 'just' about my profession. We're full of surprises." She grinned.

"I bet you've always stood out from your colleagues."

"No comment."

"No need to be modest."

She sighed. "Okay, fine. At least half of them were idiots."

"That half that wanted to name new discoveries after themselves?"

"How did you know?" She laughed. "And how'd your colleagues measure up?"

"Mixed bag. I've always tended to be more of a loner."

"I never would have guessed." Despite her walking behind

him, he could sense her eyeroll.

"Don't worry, I meant it when I said we're in this together."

"Good, because I'd hate to have to feed you to that monster."

He broke stride to turn around to stare back at her. "Wow, your mind makes very unexpected leaps."

"I'm an enigma, what can I say?"

Without the crunching and rustling of their own footsteps over fallen leaves, Evan noticed movement in the nearby underbrush.

Anya tensed. "What was that?" Her eyes darted as she searched for the source of the sound.

To Evan's ear, it had been only the standard rustling that was expected in a jungle. There was life in the place, no doubt about it.

"Relax," he said. "Probably just a bird."

A twig snapped nearby. There were no swaying branches or any other sign of movement to indicate the size of the creature. However, he realized that everything else had abruptly gone quiet.

"Over here," he said softly, motioning her closer. Perhaps by standing together, they'd look like a bigger—and more difficult—target.

"There's something hunting us, isn't there?"

— — —

Anya's heart pounded in her ears. Being tired and hungry was one thing, but she hadn't counted on genuine concerns about being eaten herself.

"We never should have come here," she murmured.

Evan held up his finger over his mouth to indicate for her

to be quiet. She nodded her understanding and searched for signs of the creature.

The rustling had stopped. Its last location was thick brush and mostly obscured in shadow, so anything could be lurking inside.

Evan had drawn the pistol and was holding it in both hands, elbows bent. His eyes scanned the trees.

Anya silently turned around in place so she could keep watch behind him. The dappled light made it difficult to make out distinct shapes.

But then she saw the eyes.

Her breath caught in her throat. She averted her gaze slightly, watching the creature from the corner of her eyes. Though she couldn't make out more than its eyes and the top of its head, it was clearly large.

Anya slowly reached out her hand to tap Evan's back. He initially startled under her touch but then turned to follow her sightline. His breathing deepened when he spotted the creature.

"I'm going to take the shot," he whispered, his lips barely moving.

"What if it doesn't take it down?"

"Be ready to run." He pulled the trigger.

The blast was louder than she'd anticipated for a pulse weapon, making her jump. The energy discharge electrified the air and made her fine hairs stand on end.

A rippling energy pulse struck the creature squarely in its face. It reared backward and promptly fell over.

Anya stood in stunned silence for a couple of seconds before gathering herself. "Is it dead?"

Evan lowered the weapon but kept it at the ready. "I don't know." He took a cautious step toward it. "Still breathing."

"Kill it!" Anya urged.

The creature jumped to its feet just as Evan fired again. The shot passed over its back and sent up a spray of dirt and leaves behind it.

"Run!" Evan shouted. He bolted.

Anya raced after him. Her vision focused on the ground directly in front of her. She reflexively dodged branches and vines as she ran, not even feeling the heavy pack that moments before had been digging into her shoulders.

At the distant edges of herself, she knew her lungs were burning and her legs ached. Yet she couldn't slow down. Even a moment's hesitation might mean the end of her life.

Evan skidded to a halt steps ahead of her. He grabbed her pack to stop her short as she was about to careen past him.

She fought for her footing. The ground dropped away in a steep slope—really, more of a cliff. They were trapped.

A deep growl sounded behind her. Over her shoulder, Anya spotted the creature emerging from the trees. It moved with the grace of a big cat, with broad shoulders and piercing eyes, which were presently fixed on Anya and Evan.

Evan fired another shot at the advancing animal. The energy pulse struck it center mass, but the charge rippled harmlessly over its fur and dissipated.

"What the—?!" He cut himself off. "We have to jump!"

Anya glanced between the creature and the cliff. "Oh, no freaking way!"

"Jump!" He didn't wait for a reply. With a bounding step, he launched himself over the edge.

11

A SHRIEK AND string of curses following closely behind Evan confirmed that Anya had taken the leap, too.

A blur of greenery raced by, and then he landed on the steep hillside. The grass didn't offer as much cushioning as he'd hoped. He took most of the initial impact on his right hip, and then he started to slide.

He skidded on the slope, tearing up clumps of grass and shrubs on his uncontrolled descent. He grabbed at the larger bushes as he sped by, trying to control the angle and speed. Though the goal was to get to the bottom quickly, breaking bones or impaling on a branch on the way down would be counterproductive.

Eventually, he was able to reposition to his back and use his pack as a makeshift sled. Momentum carried him down the hillside until the ground started to level out. He dug in his heels to slow to a stop.

Anya came to rest a few meters above him. "Ow." From her tone, she sounded more sore than injured.

"Ditto." Evan remained sprawled on the ground, panting. Slowly, he moved each limb. While bruised, nothing seemed to be broken or sprained. He coughed and it turned into a laugh.

"That was quite a ride!"

"You're insane." Anya groaned and propped herself up on her elbows. "I'm never doing that again."

He looked up the hill. There was no sign of pursuit. "We had to get out of there."

"How was it unfazed by that blast?"

"You're the xenobiologist."

"It was like it… adapted."

Evan shook his head. "I don't want to think about that possibility."

"We'll need to figure out another way to deter it if it comes back. She dusted herself off and began picking out the twigs and leaves that had become tangled in her clothes and hair. "What now?"

"We need to reorient." Evan got to his feet and looked for the direction of his shadow. Before the interruption, it had been extending at a slight upward angle from his right shoulder. He turned until he matched the correct orientation. "Looks like we need to go that way." He extended his arm to point toward their destination.

Anya squinted her eyes. "Is that the tip of the mountain?"

Sure enough, without the trees blocking their view, the top of the peak was visible—and precisely in the direction Evan had pointed.

He smiled. "Triangulation for the win."

"This is why I love science."

Their heading would take them across the base of the grassy hillside before returning to the trees.

"We need a plan for how to deal with that… thing," Evan said, turning serious.

"Yeah, as soon as it sees us heading this direction, it will probably move to intercept."

"It looks different than the other animal that scavenged the crate."

"Agreed. However, I don't think either one of them are what took out the Ranger-R during the survey."

His stomach twisted. "So, there's an even bigger predator out there."

"My best guess? Yes. But that doesn't mean it will have any interest in us."

"All right, let's take it one problem at a time. How do we make ourselves more unappetizing to this creature?"

"First, we need to start naming things."

"An Anyapanther," he jested.

"Absolutely not," she shot back while trying to hide a laugh. "But I agree, it is rather cat-like, so I'm good with 'panther' for now."

"And what about the other creature from last night?"

"Well, it scavenged a corpse, so I'm inclined to call it a 'vulture'—even though it's not a bird—until we can get a better look at it."

"Works for me," he agreed.

"Okay, so, the panther. Clearly, it prefers to be an ambush hunter. But when we spotted it, it made a move. We need to show it that it can't sneak up on us, so we're not worth it's time to pursue."

"How do we do that?"

"I'm not sure." She crossed her arms, thinking.

"I won't be able to contribute much to the brainstorming. My go-to is 'shoot the thing', and that was useless."

She pursed her lips. "That brings up another point. How was it able to dispel the energy charge?"

"The pistols are, effectively, a concentrated electrical charge. So, it must be able to control electrical energy to some extent."

"There is natural precedent for that. I've seen it in fish and lizards. Never a mammal like that, but why not?"

"I guess." Evan didn't know where to begin with the biology of such a creature.

"The first blast did temporarily take it down, when it wasn't expecting it. Hypothetically, a stronger charge could still do damage."

"Irrelevant since we don't have anything stronger with us. But…" He faded out as an idea came to him. "You know, I might have something, after all. If it can manipulate electrical energy, that means it probably has a charge itself, right?"

"Yes, most likely."

"That would give us a means to track it. We have the electricity sniffer from the supplies, right? Not great range, but we'll know if it's close, we could skewer it when it pounces."

She bit her lip. "Do you have experience spear-hunting?"

"No…"

"A lot of 'ifs' would need to go right to pull off a kill like that. It's risky."

"Well, it's hungry and it sees us as the easy target right now. I don't know what else to—"

"That's it!" Anya brightened.

"What is?"

"We need to give it an alternative. The weapon we have isn't effective against it, but it's the perfect tool to stun other prey animals. We can offer it an alternative meal."

Evan considered the proposal. "I suppose it's worth a shot."

"Which you will make, hopefully."

"Find me my target."

— — —

Guilt gnawed at Anya's heart as she pointed to a fuzzy herbivore she'd labeled as a goat. "That should work."

She looked away as Evan took the shot.

His shoulders rounded as he lowered the weapon. The animal was only stunned, but with the panther nearby, its fate was likely sealed. "I hope this works. I know it's to save our own hides, but still."

"Thank you for your sacrifice, little guy," Anya murmured.

They'd found the goat grazing at the far end of the field. It had wandered away from the rest of the herd, making it an easy target. With that kind of behavior, if they hadn't picked it off, another predator probably would have sooner than later. The knowledge didn't entirely assuage her guilt, but it helped. At least if the panther didn't take the bait, the goat would recover and be able to go about its life.

"Come on, let's get out of here." Evan holstered the weapon.

Anya followed him into the jungle. The only way to know that they'd been successful with the diversion was if they weren't attacked. That was hardly the most reassuring way to venture on the next stage of their journey.

"Assuming the whole cruiser wasn't destroyed in the crash, do you think we might be able to find a vehicle to get us back to camp?" Anya asked to keep her mind off a panther potentially stalking them. She also figured that the sound of their voices might be a deterrent to predators.

"A ground vehicle would be standard equipment for a military escort like this mission, so maybe," Evan replied. "But right now, my concern is making it to the crash site alive."

"Because jumping off cliffs is a *great* way to accomplish that."

"Hey, it's better than being eaten!" He flashed a smile. "And look, it worked."

She rolled her eyes and sighed. "Dumb luck."

When Evan didn't say anything more, Anya continued. "I don't mean to ramble, but talking might help keep that thing away."

"You lured it here so you'd have an excuse to get me talking, didn't you?"

"Darn, you've uncovered my devious plan!"

"If all of this was planned, I'm amazed that you could get so much to go wrong in the right way."

"That would be impressive." She paused. "We don't need to have a deep heart-to-heart about our hopes and dreams or anything."

"Good, because that wasn't going to happen."

"I'm not trying to interrogate you."

"I know, you're just making conversation. It's tough for me, after spending years in an environment where saying too much would get a person killed. It takes time for those guards to come down, and I'm not there yet."

"All right." Curiosity had Anya's mind racing about what Evan had done after leaving the military. He'd claimed to have joined the UPA Security Corps, but it was clear he'd been more than a generic beat cop—or at least not one who'd been aboveboard with his dealings. The mystery had drawn her in, despite her better judgment. Still, it didn't seem like he was playing her. When she met his gaze, he seemed genuine in his concern and commitment to their mission.

"What about you—what made you want to become a xenobiologist?" he asked.

Talking about herself might be a way to get him to open up, and it would keep the conversation going. "I loved animals as a kid. When I started to understand how big the universe was and how much different life could be out there, I wanted to learn about the creatures that might inhabit those places."

"Has it been everything you'd imagined it would be?"

She shook her head. "Not even close. It's so much better in some ways, but mostly, I've been left feeling… empty."

"Not a great way to describe your chosen career."

"There's no point being anything but one-hundred percent honest now. A panther could jump out and eat me at any second. And, truthfully, I'd be disappointed to not have more to show from my life."

Evan slowed his pace and turned to look at her. "Wow, I wasn't expecting that kind of deep introspection."

She shrugged. "I'm tired. I'm sore. I guess I get unfiltered under those conditions."

"Understandable."

"There's also no point in complaining. I can't change anything now."

"What would you have done differently?"

"Taken one less promotion so I would have remained a field researcher rather than spending my time analyzing data in my lab."

Evan eyed her. "Looks like you got your wish in a roundabout way."

"The irony is not lost on me."

"We can look at this experience as a major life derailment or an opportunity for a second chance. Since I was already hoping for a new life, I intend to take whatever surprising twists the planet throws at us in stride."

Anya nodded. "I'll try to do the same."

Evan picked up his pace again. "Good, because we have a long way to go. Anything could happen."

12

EVAN'S MUSCLES ACHED, especially his lower back. He dug his knuckles in and pivoted his hips to try to relieve the tension.

They had stopped for a break in a small clearing with a craggy rock formation with young saplings growing out from the cracks. Long shadows stretched from the surrounding trees. Gazing upward, he noticed the sun had dropped lower in the sky than he'd thought.

"Maybe we should make camp," he suggested.

Anya's face softened with relief. "Yes! I didn't want to call it a day first, but I'm exhausted."

He smiled. "You hid it well."

"All thanks to Vanessa."

Evan tilted his head. "Who's that?" He opened up his pack to remove the tent so they could begin the setup process.

"The bane of my existence for years." Anya began picking up small stones from an open area on the ground so there'd be a smooth place for the tent. "She was another field researcher when I was a newbie fresh out of school. Classic brownnoser—always sucking up to the senior scientists like they were a professor who'd decide her grade. Or maybe she was bucking for a promotion, I don't know. But *everything* was a competition with her. She had to be the first one up a hill, or the first to finish cataloging samples.

"I wasn't about to take her challenge lying down, so I pushed myself. And, naturally, I didn't want her to know when I was struggling. I'd push and push, sometimes to the point that I thought of quitting because I'd never be good enough. Eventually, though, I did improve in my weaker areas. I wound up being able to stand toe-to-toe with her in most things, much to her annoyance. She wasn't trying to help me, but I appreciate her for putting me through those trials. Without her, I wouldn't be as strong a person as I am today." Anya brushed off her hands after finishing the ground clearing.

"Did you ever tell her?" Evan unfolded the flattened tent and handed her one side.

She crouched down to place the tent corners. "No. I almost got it out one time, but then she told me that my hair was frizzy, and I decided in that moment that I had no interest in saying anything nice to her."

"I respect your petty vengeance."

"Hey, a person has to take the little wins, right?"

Evan activated the filament within the tent. As the fibers changed to their rigid structure, the flattened tent arched upward into a shoulder-height dome. It was approximately three by two meters, which wouldn't give them a lot of spare room but would be functional for the two of them.

Anya unzipped the door and poked her head inside. "Home sweet home."

"It's more than we had last night." Evan unpacked his bedroll and put it in place on the left side of the tent.

Anya positioned hers on the right. "This'll be cozy."

His mind went in multiple directions—first that the thin fabric would offer approximately zero protection against potential predators, followed by the pleasant thought of being close to her. Neither seemed wise to verbalize, so he settled on a nod in response.

With their sleeping arrangements handled, they turned their attention to the evening meal.

"I'll hunt around for some edibles," Anya said. "Can you get a fire going?"

"I'll see if I can find dry fuel. Everything we passed looked a little soggy from the rain."

"We can hunt around together." Anya grabbed her bioanalyzer and they set off into the trees around camp.

Staying within shouting distance of each other in case they ran into trouble, Evan searched for potential firewood. He focused on the base of trees where the ground was most protected by the canopy overhead. Even there, though, the fallen branches were damp. However, he eventually came across a dead tree. The outer bark was damp, but when Evan tried to break one of the limbs, it snapped off with a satisfying crack, indicating that its core was dry.

While Anya continued her search for fresh greens, Evan harvested as many broken branches as he could carry and hauled them back to camp. He took two more trips to collect the rest of the tree's branches that were small enough to break by hand.

By the time he returned, Anya was also back at camp and had two handfuls of a leafy plant. She was nibbling a piece.

"How is it?" Evan asked.

"Not bad. A little bitter, but pleasant enough. It's packed full of all the good stuff, so your doctor would be thrilled."

"Anything beats the MealPaks."

"Oh, they're not that bad." Anya pulled out two. She stared at them in her hands. "No, who am I kidding? They're barely edible."

"The worst thing is that they *could* make a reasonably delicious meal in this packaging. It's purely cost-driven decisions to make it the cheapest per-calorie delivery possible without being a straight-up nutrition cube."

"Better than starving."

"I can't argue with that."

Evan arranged a collection of smaller sticks from the tips of the branches and broke out the rotted interiors of some larger pieces to use as a tinder pile. Using a flint and steel from the emergency supplies, he tried to spark it. It took a dozen attempts before one of the sparks caught, but they worked together to nurture the small blaze and grow it into a pleasant campfire at the center of the clearing.

"This should help keep the animals away," Anya said as she leaned back, her arms propped behind her.

"I'll take whatever little measure of protection we can get. Seems like the trick with the goat worked."

"No telling when it may get hungry again. And we might not see it coming next time."

"I'm not going to worry about it," Evan said. "There's nothing else we can do right now, so there's no sense spending energy being upset."

Anya nodded. "That's the story of this entire experience. We have to take it moment by moment."

He smiled at her. "This moment isn't so bad."

Her cheeks flushed slightly as she gazed into the flames. "No, it's not."

They sat in silence for a minute before Evan spoke again. "Hey, this is a little strange to bring up now, but I just realized I don't know your full name—not that it matters."

"Ha! You're right. Anya Rojas."

"Is there a 'doctor' before that?"

"I do have a doctorate, but Anya is all you'll ever need to call me."

"Very well, Anya." He leaned forward and extended his hand. "Evan Taylor."

She grasped his hand and gave it a professionally firm shake. "Pleasure to meet you."

"Fancy meeting you like this. Come here often?"

"Most popular place, people are dying to get in!" She winced. "Sorry, too soon."

He laughed. "Dark."

"Yeah, slipped out." She held up her hand over her mouth.

They sat for a while longer, alternating between contemplative silence and small talk. Once they'd unwound a little more, they dug into the MealPaks and finished off with the fresh greens Anya had gathered. Though the leaves were more bitter than Evan would have preferred, there was a slightly minty aftertaste that worked well as a post-meal palette cleanser.

By the time they'd finished, the sun had dipped low into the sky, casting long shadows from the trees along the ridge. Every rustle in the foliage seemed louder now in the fading light—or, perhaps, the nighttime was when this world came alive, and now it was waking.

"Aside from the mystery monster, what do you know about the local ecology?" he asked, wanting to know what else might be lurking just out of sight.

"Enough that we can say the local plant and animal life are compatible with our digestive system. The entire *point* of this expedition was to conduct a survey of the specific species." She raised her gaze to him. "But you should *know* that."

He worked his mouth, not sure what to say. In the end, trying to lie would only dig a deeper hole. Better to come clean now. “I wasn’t exactly on the official expedition manifest.”

Anya studied him from across the fire. “Then why are you here?”

“That’s… a long story.”

“We’ve got nothing but time.”

He stared into the flames, debating how much to share. “They say that joining a new colony settlement is a ‘fresh start’, but it seems like there are some things you just can’t outrun.”

“Such as?”

He clicked his tongue against his teeth and then sighed. “Okay, fine. I’m here because this was the furthest, fastest I could get away from Constella.”

“Why?”

“The short version is that I found myself the target of some very bad people for trying to do the right thing. It was either wind up dead or hop on a ship that would bring me to a new life.”

“I probably would have made the same choice in your position.” Her brow furrowed. “Who did you cross?”

“Doesn’t matter.”

“It does. But if you’re not ready to talk about it yet, that’s okay.”

“Thank you.” His chest tightened every time he thought about the events that had led him here. *Was there anything I could have done differently?*

Doing it all again, there was a lot he’d change about his approach. Maybe it all would have led him to the same place, but he’d be a lot more informed about those choices and their consequences. In retrospect, he’d walked into a trap of his own design. Now, nothing about his ‘fresh start’ was turning out anything like he’d imagined.

— — —

Despite her statement that Evan could take his time to come clean about his background, Anya was annoyed that he hadn't taken the opening to break his silence. She respected a person's right to privacy and autonomy, but curiosity was driving her crazy.

Nonetheless, experience had taught her that pressing too much, too fast was more likely to make a person clam up. So, she'd decided to drop the topic—for now.

They stayed up chatting for a while longer before retiring to the tent for the night. Anya was exhausted, so she passed out within moments of hitting her bedroll.

After what felt like a couple hours of sleep, a sound just outside the tent snapped her fully awake. She tensed and raised her head, eyes wide. "What was that?"

Evan carefully propped himself up on his elbows, listening. "Some kind of creature, I think. The panther?"

Anya rose into a crouching position for easy movement. "That was a stalker. This sounds like it doesn't care about staying quiet."

Evan readied the pistol. "Should we try to scare it off?"

"No, startling it might make it worse."

Their packs were in the tent with them, which contained their rations. The MealPaks were vacuum packaged, so no scent should escape. However, they had a distinct scent as people—especially after the day's activity.

Please, leave, Anya willed the animal. She didn't want them to have to kill it unnecessarily. The goat from earlier that afternoon still weighed on her conscience, but she also didn't want to be eaten.

Through the opaque fabric of the tent's walls, they had no

way of knowing what type of animal it might be. They'd only seen a fraction of the planet's wildlife, and there were all manner of creatures that might be large and unafraid to wander into the camp. The only way to know for sure what it was would be to look outside, but opening the door might call attention to their presence. It might not know they were there, or at least not currently view them as a threat, so there was an argument to be made for staying still and quiet with the hope it would go away.

Anxious minutes passed. They tracked the animal's movements as it snuffled around the campsite. The footfalls stopped, followed by the sound of crinkling plastic.

Anya and Evan exchanged knowing looks. The animal had found the empty MealPak packaging. It spent the next few minutes licking off the remaining scraps. Based on the sounds of its actions, it seemed like it was stepping on the packages to hold it down. That meant it didn't have dexterous paws or fingers.

Smiling, Anya relaxed back onto her bedroll.

"It's still out there!" Evan whispered.

"I know, but it's a scavenger."

"So was the vulture."

"This one won't attack. Can't you hear the hooves?"

Evan listened. The tension slowly went out from his shoulders. "Good ears."

"All my field studies have come in handy."

"Invaluable." He kept the pistol in his hand but sat down from his crouch.

Eventually, the creature began moving again. The footfalls were heading directly for the tent.

Anya rose again, not wanting to be caught lying down in case it charged. Hooves said a lot about its style, but that didn't mean it couldn't ram them if it felt threatened. Her pulse quickened as she waited for it to make its next move.

The footfalls were right outside the door. Snuffles sounded—so close that the tent's fabric rustled from the breathing.

Anya clenched a fistful of her pants' cloth. *Stay calm. It's just curious. It's okay.*

Next to her, Evan slowly raised the pistol. His finger wasn't on the trigger, but he was ready if it made an aggressive move.

A ripple passed over the tent's front as the creature ran its nose over the wall. It then snuffled once and proceeded to walk around the tent. It stopped on Anya's side.

She slowly lay down, wanting to get out of the way in case Evan had to take a shot. Every muscle tense, she waited.

The creature stepped backward. A few moments later, it trotted into the trees. There was now only the wind and calm ambient calls of the jungle.

She released a relieved breath. "That was too close."

"You were right about it not attacking."

"You're never completely safe with a wild animal. We got lucky."

"I'm sure this won't be our last encounter." He reactivated the pistol's safety and set the weapon down within easy reach between them. "But we should get back to sleep while we can."

Anya's pulse was still elevated, but she took a series of slow breaths to calm herself. The steady chirp of insects in the background helped steady her nerves.

We're on an alien planet, surrounded by life. Despite the uncertainties and danger, she was living the dream of any xenobiologist. *All part of the adventure.*

13

EVAN CRACKED AN eye open to find light filtering through the tent's opaque walls. Though his head was fuzzy and his eyes itched from lack of sleep, the muscles in his shoulders and legs were significantly less sore than the night before.

Next to him, Anya was still fast asleep, with one arm flopped over her eyes and the other on her chest. Her mouth was hanging open as she breathed softly. He smiled at the candid pose, regretting that he needed to wake her.

"Anya, time to wake up," he said gently.

She snorted a little as she sucked in a breath. Stirring, she removed her arm from over her face and blinked in the morning light. "Wha—? Oh." She dug her fingers into her already mussed hair and scratched her scalp.

"You're not a morning person, I take it."

"Not after this many nights with interruptions." She stretched her arms above her head and then sat up. "What time is it?"

"Looks like it's been light for about an hour. We should probably get going," he said.

She pawed at her hair, doing little to smooth it. "I miss sleeping in."

"We can find you a stasis pod to take a year-long nap to make up for it."

She let out a melodramatic sigh as she rose to start packing her bed roll. "Very funny."

"It got you up, didn't it?"

She arched an eyebrow as she cast him a suspicious sidelong glance. "How do you know me so well already?"

"It's not you, specifically," he said.

She looked almost a little hurt at that, dropping her gaze as she finished bundling her bed roll.

"I just know how to read people," he clarified. "When your work depends on getting an accurate assessment of a situation—and when those scenarios sometimes involve weapons—you have to be a quick study."

"Understand people's motivations."

"Exactly."

"And what is it you've learned about me?"

"That you like to appear competent," he replied but instantly regretted blurting out an answer without appearing to give it any thought. The truth was, he'd thought about it considerably. But what had value as an assessment for his own use wasn't necessarily what he should have shared. The stress and lack of sleep were making him sloppy.

She jammed her gear into her pack. "Funny how a person can be reduced to simple traits that say everything about us."

"I don't believe that's all there is to you."

"Damn straight." She grabbed her pack and exited out the tent's front flap.

Evan drew a long, slow breath. *Definitely not a morning person.*

He finished packing up his own items, keeping out one MealPak for them to share as breakfast; hopefully, a little food would help improve her mood. His own nerves were on edge after the intense events of the last two days, coupled with the disruptive nights. With any luck, they'd be able to make more progress today without incident.

Outside the tent, there were prints and scrape marks on the ground where the animal had investigated their camp.

Anya was crouched down next to one of the disrupted patches of ground. "It does look like hooves," she said. "But three-prongs, which is unique."

"More stable on soft ground, I suppose."

"Good point. I'd guess it's around the size of a deer. It could have been one of them, but it was the middle of the night."

"Maybe there's a species that's nocturnal."

She nodded. "Might be. Maybe I'll be brave and sneak a peek next time."

"Not while I'm in the tent. I'm content to hide from the forest monsters."

"Oh, come on. If it's something cool, I promise to name it after you."

"Pass."

Anya smiled, her hostility from earlier nowhere to be seen. "Suit yourself."

They shared the morning meal and then packed up the tent. Once it was stowed in Evan's bag, they hefted their packs and cut a path into the jungle.

Energized from the food and with fresh legs after the night's rest, they made quick progress for the first hour. The route took them on a gentle downward trajectory. They came across an animal trail, which conveniently headed in the direction they needed to travel for half a kilometer.

When the path turned to the side, however, they needed to

return to bushwhacking. The undergrowth was becoming thicker, and they didn't have the proper equipment to clear the way. For lack of a long blade, they were reduced to using sticks to whack at vines crossing their path. Not only was it slow going, but the thicker foliage in the area made it difficult to track their shadows to maintain orientation.

"It would be too easy to get lost in here," Evan said as they continued bushwhacking their way through the jungle.

"We might need to use an old trick. It's not an exact science, but moss grows thickest on the side that gets the least sun. We know we have to head east, so since we're in the northern hemisphere, the thickest moss should always be to the north—our left."

Evan examined the nearby trees. There did, indeed, appear to be more moss on the left side of the trees and rocks. "Handy."

"None of our navigation has been precise. We'll need to find high ground out in the open where we can get eyes on the crash site."

"How close do you think we are now?"

"Maybe halfway. It's so difficult to tell."

It seemed like too little progress for two days on the trail. However, there was no escaping the fact that it was incredibly slow going through the thick trees. In retrospect, they wouldn't have been able to make it far in the rover even if they hadn't run into the swampy conditions. This part of the planet wasn't an environment for untrained people to travel.

Using a combination of shadow and moss tracking, they did their best to maintain a bearing in the right direction. Taking breaks when they needed and a longer lunch rest midday, they'd covered what felt like at least seven kilometers by late-afternoon. Evan couldn't help feeling frustrated knowing that they could have covered twice that, or more, over open ground in the same time. Yet there was no other route they could have taken. There was nothing but jungle between their plateau and the other crash site. Slow and steady was the only way forward.

They reached a particularly dense section of vegetation. Evan was still in the lead, doing his best to clear a path. Many of the vines bounced back into position as soon as he released them after pushing them out of the way.

"Gah! Damn it," Anya exclaimed behind him

Evan whipped around in time to see her quickly yanking her hand back from a vine. It was a lighter, brighter shade of green than the others, and it was moving on its own.

"Are you okay?" he asked.

She inspected her arm. There was a visible prick mark, even from a distance, and the area around a puncture on her bare forearm was already turning red. "Honestly, I'm not sure."

He went over to her, and she offered her arm for him to examine. The wound looked like it was infected, though it had only happened seconds before. "This really doesn't look good."

"It reached out and whacked me when I got close. I think those thorns might be poisonous."

"Then we need an antidote."

"It might be fine." Even as she spoke, Evan could see the concern in Anya's eyes. No injury started looking that inflamed so quickly unless it was serious.

"I need you to tell me what will help you," he said. 'While you still can' was implied.

He moved her away from the area with the attacking vine. She set down her backpack and began rummaging through it. It was clear that her injured right forearm was already starting to stiffen, based on her movements. After some searching, she pulled out the piece of electronic equipment she used to analyze biological samples.

"Use this on the vine," she said, holding out the device to him. "Be careful."

He looked at her with concern that she was having him do it. *Can she already not walk?*

She flashed a weak smile. "I just want to make sure you know how to use it when you go look for an antidote."

He nodded. "Right."

"Place the electrodes on a leaf or stem. Don't poke yourself on the thorns like my dumbass self."

He took the device and did as he was told. Within two seconds of holding the electrodes on one of the vine's spade-shaped leaves, the device's display updated with a readout of various chemical properties.

He jogged back to Anya. "Okay, I think I got it. What now?"

She looked over the results. "Good, that's a clean reading. And you're sure it's the right plant?"

"Yes."

"All right. Now, we need to run a genetic mapping of it and compare that to my blood."

He blinked at her. "I have no idea how to do that."

"Here." Her voice was growing weaker, likely from pain. She took a slow breath and then made several entries on the device using her good hand. The screen changed to 'Processing'. While it was working, she held the sample prong up to the wound on her arm. She selected 'Cross-Reference' from the menu.

Weakly, she handed the device back to Evan. "It's now looking at the genetic structure of the vine and isolating for the component that makes the toxin. That will offer a template to identify the inverse."

"A cure?"

"Right."

"That's a chemical structure, though. We can't… synthesize anything here."

"No, but poisonous plants and their antidotes typically grow close together. Test everything in the vicinity for something that matches the antidote's profile."

"Do you have any idea what I might be looking for?"

"It could be another vine, or a flower. Anything, really."

Great, that narrows it down. There had to be dozens of different species within an arm's reach. Testing everything would take time and focus—neither of which he had right now as he watched her become noticeably sicker by the minute.

"What do I do if I find a match?"

"Just put a sample in that compartment on the back. It'll crush it up and extract the right components to match the parameters."

"That's... it?"

She flashed a weak smile. "Technology doesn't always have to be complicated."

"Okay. Keep your heart rate low."

"That'll be easy once I'm not stressed about dying from this thing. Get going."

He rushed off. Being careful not to scratch himself, he began touching the sampling electrodes to various plants to test their chemical makeup.

The first six things he tried didn't come up with any matches. Those were the most obvious species in the vicinity, and he wasn't sure where to search from there.

Anya was slumped over and growing pale. There wasn't much time.

He resumed his search in earnest, placing the electrodes on every bit of biological matter he could spot. Nothing fit.

Then, he spotted a bit of red lichen growing under a decaying log. It was near a thicket of the poisonous bush, and he hadn't noticed it growing elsewhere. He was barely able to get his arm in to get the testing equipment in place.

At last, the screen lit up with a match.

"Finally!" He started grabbing fistfuls of the lichen and cramming it into the rear compartment. "I found it, Anya! Hang on."

Evan had no idea how much material the machine might need to synthesize an antidote, but he crammed it two-thirds of the way full and then sprinted back to where he'd left Anya.

When he arrived, her eyes were closed and her skin was pale, with red around her eyes and mouth. The puncture site was now turning dark purple, and a yellow-tinted discharge was flowing from the wound itself.

He kneeled next to her. "Anya, hey," he said while gently shaking her shoulder.

She moaned but didn't open her eyes.

"How do I give you the antidote?" With a sinking feeling, he realized that he hadn't asked about that part. It hadn't crossed his mind that she might not be conscious when it came time to administer it.

The bioanalyzer beeped, indicating that it had completed synthesis. A clear vial next to the rear collection compartment was now filled with a translucent liquid.

"Anya!" Evan tried to rouse her again. "What dose?"

She grunted and tried to pull away from him. Her skin was dangerously cool to the touch near her core but hot by the wound.

I need to guess. I can't let her die. Evan removed the vial from the device. He popped the cap and sprinkled a little of the liquid on the puncture. He then gently tilted back her head and opened her mouth to pour in the rest. Hoping it was the right thing to do, he carefully massaged her throat to encourage her to swallow. After a few seconds, she did.

He sat down with her, cradling her head and shoulders. “It’s going to be okay,” he murmured. “Hang in there.”

Excruciating minutes passed while he waited. Slowly, the color began to return to her face. In time, the redness around the wound diminished and her breathing came easier.

Evan brushed his fingers over her forehead. Her temperature was near normal. “You’re going to be okay.” *You have to be.*

14

ANYA WINCED AT the light filtering in through her eyelids. She didn't recall going to bed, but it must be morning. She cracked open her eyes, surprised to find a jungle canopy above her rather than a tent.

She bolted upright. "Wha...? Where?"

"Hey, take it easy." Evan applied gentle pressure to her shoulders to prevent her from sitting up completely. "You're still recovering." He was seated behind her, leaning his back against a tree.

She relaxed under his touch while she got her bearings. The incident with the vine came back to her in disjointed chunks, like the dream-like haze of being feverish. "You found an antidote?"

"Yes. It's a good thing you were able to tell me how to use that fancy device of yours."

"Really? I don't remember doing that." She looked around, squinting at the sky. "How long have I been out?"

"Half an hour, maybe a little longer. I figured I should let you sleep it off."

"I feel like I've been out for days, except not rested at all." She rubbed her eyes with the heels of her hands. Everything was itchy and ached.

He cracked a concerned smile. "I expect you'll sleep well tonight."

Anya examined her arm where she'd been pricked by the thorny vine. Her skin was still red and inflamed around the puncture, but the dark purple had faded, and her veins no longer stood out. More importantly, she could breathe without any pain and her heart rate had normalized. While she wasn't at one-hundred percent, she was well on her way to recovery.

"I can't believe how quickly that took me down," she murmured.

"Neither can I. I'll admit, you had me really worried there." His gaze softened as he searched her face.

She tried sitting up again, slower this time. "No way I was going to let it end that way for me. At least a panther attack would make for a good story. But 'she touched a plant' would be lame."

Evan laughed, a delightfully warm and comforting sound after the harrowing event. "I'm glad you're getting back to your usual self."

"I do feel much better." She flexed her arm, and a sharp pain shot through her wrist near the wound. "I nominate we call these 'assassin vines'."

"Very appropriate. I approve."

"What kind of plant was the antidote?"

"A lichen. This red stuff." Evan showed her a small sample.

She cradled it in her palms. "Thank you for saving my life, little plant."

Evan tilted his head, brows raised.

"And you, too," she added to him with a smile.

"My pleasure." He stood up and stretched his legs. "Not to rush you, but when do you think you'll be able to travel?"

"Now." Anya started to get up, and Evan held out his hand. She took it, grateful for the extra support as she found her footing. Her vision narrowed for a couple of seconds once she was upright, but the woozy sensation passed quickly. She took a few test steps, finding that her balance was acceptable. "I don't think I'll be at top speed, but I can move."

"Okay, then we should get going. I'd like to get to more open surroundings before we camp for the night."

They set out again. Evan initially took a quick pace, but he dropped back to match her slower movement when she didn't keep up. As much as she wanted to push herself, she recognized that her body was still recovering and she had to cut herself some slack.

After an hour, her balance had noticeably improved and her head was once again clear. Unfortunately, that left room for thoughts about everything else that could go wrong.

If this one plant had nearly killed her—and would have without quick intervention—how much else in this wilderness was a hidden hazard? She'd been so preoccupied with the obvious predator animals that she hadn't considered the other risks. Growing suspicious of everything, she kept her arms close to her body as she walked.

"Oh, I think we're coming out of it!" Evan said in front of her.

Anya had become so focused on her footing that she hadn't realized the trees were thinning ahead. After another dozen meters, the trees dropped away to brush and branches no taller than her waist. It wasn't until she stepped into the open area that tension released from her shoulders, which she hadn't realized she'd been carrying. Open skies above were a welcome sight.

Evan drew in a deep breath of the clean air. "It's good to be out of there."

"I second that." She savored the warm sun on her face. Sweat from the humid jungle began to dry out in the light breeze.

Evan checked the direction of his shadow on the ground. "Let's see, I'd guess it's about 15:00 now, so we should be heading that way." He held up his arm for direction. It was facing directly toward the mountain peak that had been serving as their directional marker. "How's that for navigating?"

Anya patted his shoulder. "You're good, can't argue."

The path took them through a kilometer of open field, and more trees were beyond. They began the slog through the grasses. Though the fine stalks offered little resistance, the long leaves were fine enough to slice when they brushed against bare skin at the right angle. Anya pulled her sleeves down to cover her hands as well as she could, holding out her elbows in front of her to part the stalks.

She sighed. "What I wouldn't give for some bare ground again."

"You just *had* to pick a lush paradise planet, didn't you?"

She laughed. "I know, so awful. I'll be sure to select flat, barren wastelands in the future."

"So much easier to travel."

A quarter of the way across the field, Anya picked up a new sound. At first, she thought it was a distant breeze. Then, it came to her. "Hey, is that water? A river or something?"

Evan listened for a few seconds before responding. "I think it might be. I guess we'll find out soon enough."

The rushing sound grew steadily louder as they continued to wade through the tall grasses. When it sounded like they were almost on top of it, the ground abruptly sloped down into a muddy bank.

Before them, a six-meter-wide river cut across the landscape. Each bank had a two-meter drop at a steep angle, which would make for a challenging entrance and exit. More concerning, though, was the swift, strong current. The water was too murky to see the bottom, so there was no way to know if it was shallow enough to wade across without getting washed downstream.

"Well, that's not ideal," Evan muttered.

"But this day was going so well!" She gripped her injured arm.

"All right, let's weigh the options," Evan began. "We can just go for it and try to wade or swim across here. We could walk the bank until we find a better crossing point. Or we could go back to the trees to gather up materials to help us across.

"You mean like a long tree trunk?"

"Yeah, something like that."

"I like the concept, but that's a lot of backtracking and work. We do have rope. Maybe there's a way to combine all those options."

"What do you have in mind?" he asked her.

"If we can locate a fixed object on the far bank, we might be able to hook a rope on it to help us across."

"Working on a ranch is one thing I haven't done in my life. Do you have some lasso skills you've been keeping secret?"

"No, but I understand basic physics. If we weight the rope with a rock and twirl it to build momentum, it should be easy enough to throw it across. Just need the right thing to hook it onto."

Evan's brows were raised with obvious skepticism, but he nodded. "I don't have a better suggestion right now. Let's see what we can find."

"Upstream or downstream?"

"You tell me, Miss Xenobiologist."

She considered the options. "Upstream is more likely to be narrower, and downstream is more likely to be wider, slower water."

Evan looked upstream, then downstream, and then over at the distant mountain peak in the direction they were heading.

"Upstream angles us closer to where we're going. Narrow and faster, it is."

"All right."

They stayed a couple of meters away from the top of the steep bank as they traced the river, keeping an eye on the far side for signs of any possible anchor point. After half a kilometer with no candidates, Anya was ready to suggest they try to ford the river.

"Maybe we—" she began.

Evan perked up. "Oh, wait, here we go!" He picked up his pace. Ahead, there was a tangle of bushes on the opposite bank. The trunks were thick and gnarled, and their partially exposed roots appeared to be deeply embedded in the ground.

"That might work," she assessed. "We just need something to tie to the end of the rope to weight it down and help it catch."

They had such limited tools with them that they didn't want to risk losing anything in their packs to the river if the rope-throw failed. So, they searched along the riverbank for an object heavy enough to serve their purposes. In the end, they settled on a combination of a rock and a sturdy, short stick. Working together, they wove the rope around the rock and then tied the stick to form a 'T' at the end. While a far cry from a real grappling hook, it wasn't terrible.

Evan gave the implement a few test swings in a loop. "Feels okay. There's only one way to find out if it will work for sure."

Since their packs were watertight, they kept them on with

the intention of simply walking across, using the rope for stability.

Evan wound up the grapple and made the toss. The hook sailed through the air… and plopped into the middle of the river. "Well, that wasn't supposed to happen."

"Just a first attempt," Anya encouraged.

He reeled the rope back in. Thankfully, the stick didn't catch on the riverbed.

Now wet, the rope sent out a spray of water as he twirled it for another toss attempt, building up more speed. This time, it landed just shy of the far riverbank and a little downstream of the bushes where he was aiming.

"Third time's the charm," Anya said.

As it turned out, it took eight attempts before the hook finally landed squarely inside the bush. They grinned at each other as it crashed down through the branches.

"Persistence pays off," Evan said through his broad smile.

"Nicely done."

"Moment of truth…" He gently tugged on the rope. It slid forward slightly and then stopped. The stick had successfully caught. "All right, now to get ourselves across."

"One at a time or together?" Anya asked. Both of them holding the rope at the same time would mean more force on it, but they'd also be able to help each other if something went wrong. She'd rather go together, but she was curious how Evan would approach it.

"Can you swim?" he asked.

"Well enough. You?"

"Same. I'm not convinced that anchor will hold both of us if we lose our footing. How about I stay on this side and hold the rope for you? Once you're across, you can hold it near the anchor to reinforce it when I come over."

She concurred with the logic of the plan. Wading alone into the murky water brought on a new wave of tension in her chest, but she nodded her agreement. "We've got this."

With more confidence than she felt, she grabbed the rope to help her slide down the bank. Evan held the top of it as she descended. A couple of steps from the bottom, she hit a particularly slick patch of mud and slipped the rest of the way down.

"Agh!" Her feet splashed into the cold water, sending a spray of mud into her open mouth. She tried to spit it out, but gritty particulates remained.

Evan was looking down at her with a mixture of amusement and sympathy.

"Was there something you wanted to say?" she asked.

"No comment."

Determined to make a better showing for the rest of her crossing, Anya repositioned her grip to face away from the bank, with her body on the upstream side of the rope for better bracing. Now that she was at river level with the chilly water eddying around her ankles, the distance across suddenly seemed much farther than it had from above. Not wanting to show any outward hesitation, she stepped deeper into the water.

The ground underfoot was slick with algae, making it difficult to keep her balance. She kept a firm grip on the rope to steady herself as she waded in. The water grew colder the deeper she went. When it was up to mid-thigh, the channel abruptly dropped away. She stretched out a toe, trying to feel for the bottom. Only open water met her probe.

"It gets deeper here," she called back to Evan. "I'm not sure how far down it goes."

"Are you doing okay?" he asked.

"Yeah, I'm fine." It wasn't entirely truthful, but close enough. "I'm going to go for it."

He tightened his grip on the rope. "I've got you."

Holding on to the rope with all her strength, Anya took the plunge. The water went up to nearly the top of her shoulders before her toes touched the bottom. Her pack offered a little buoyancy, keeping her from gaining traction. Without that footing, the river current pulled her downstream.

The rope went taut, shuddering as it caught her weight.

"Hang on!" Evan shouted from the bank.

another person than I do alone."

"I think it's more than that. Admit it, I'm kinda growing on you."

He cracked a smile. "There are worse people I could be stuck with, yes."

"Mm-hmm."

The truth was, he really had come to care about her. He'd known a lot of pretty faces in his life, but few had a good heart and intelligence to match. Were they back in the core worlds, she probably wouldn't have given a rogue like him two seconds in a random meeting, but he couldn't help noticing that her gaze occasionally lingered on him in the quiet moments of their journey. While the interest was definitely mutual, there was too much else going on right now to indulge those thoughts.

The moment of reflection drew on into an awkward silence. Anya cleared her throat and scraped the remnants from the bottom of her MealPak pouch. "What do you think is going on back home right now?" she asked.

"Define 'home'."

"Good point. I guess I just mean back in the rest of civilization. The election would have been today, right?"

"Yeah, that's right." That normally would have been a significant event, but time blurred in a strange way out in the woods. When surrounded by technology in a structured environment, there were constant reminders of routines and requirements. Out here, though, there were only the rhythms of the natural world. The rising of the sun, a storm passing through, the change of seasons. Days of the week became irrelevant. Moreover, every moment was about survival; political leaders on other planets were the last thing on his mind.

"That all feels so far away," Anya mused.

"Because it is. What matters most in life is what's right around us. Who we're with."

"Agreed. Home is a feeling of belonging, not a place."

"Maybe not even belonging. Just… familiarity."

She tilted her head, studying him in the firelight. "Did you move around a lot?"

"My parents owned a merchant freighter, so we were always on the move." The family ship was the only residence he'd known growing up. For that reason, the people he was with had always been more important than the physical surroundings. However, as he'd gotten older, the familiar faces had grown distant or passed away. Since his parents died when he was twenty-seven, he didn't have many people left from his younger years. Many friendships had long since fizzled, so leaving for Aethos hadn't meant leaving anyone behind. He was truly on his own now.

"No wonder you're such a loner. All the merchant brats I've met have been."

"Casualty of the trade."

"The origin of your flying skills."

He nodded. "That's one of the perks."

"Not a bad one. I'm not sure what I learned from my parents, exactly, but it wasn't anything that practical."

"What did they do?"

"Well, my mom was a doctor and my dad worked as a government consultant."

Evan was happy that the light was dim to hide his wide eyes and slack jaw. "Wow, so your family was loaded."

"I wouldn't say that…"

He eyed her. "I'm guessing that whenever you asked for something as a kid, your parents never told you 'no' because they couldn't afford it?"

"Well, yes, that's true."

"Not everyone has those kinds of advantages growing up."

"I suppose not."

He crossed his arms over his knees and stared at the fire. "I remember asking my parents for a toy one time—a simple toy they were advertising everywhere. It wasn't fancy or expensive. But they told me that it was either that toy or dinner for the rest of the week."

"I didn't realize finances were so tight on merchant ships."

"Depends on the ship. My parents had an ethical code that was, at times, in conflict with the best financial options."

"What do you mean?" she asked.

"I don't think you're naïve enough to believe that every shipping contract is above board."

"No."

"Well, when you make a point of ensuring that all your cargo has airtight records, you're bound to miss out on lucrative opportunities."

"No risk, low reward."

Evan nodded. "There you go." He paused. "I blamed myself, sometimes. If they hadn't had their kid with them, maybe they would have felt more comfortable taking on some of those jobs that would have allowed them to get ahead. But they were always so careful and made a show of setting a good example for me. What kind of example is it, though, seeing someone worked to the bone with no hope of breaking free from that grind?"

Anya's expression softened. "You broke free, didn't you?"

"I did, but leaving that ship meant I was nowhere to be found during the last two years of their lives. When we last spent any meaningful time together, I was complaining about feeling trapped. I never got around to thanking them for all the good things they did give me."

"I'm sorry."

He shrugged. "No sense living with regrets. I think they knew, even though I didn't say it."

"I'm sure they did."

Evan hadn't intended to share so much about his past, but it felt good to verbalize the thoughts. Rarely had he been in a position to talk about his youth so candidly. While far from a remarkable life, it was his story. Over the past few years, it had been easy to forget that.

"Where are you hoping to end up?" Anya asked.

"I don't know how to answer that question."

"Oh, come on. You have to have fantasized a little about your future."

"Oh, crash-landing on Aethos has been a dream come true!"

She eyed him from under raised brows. "Come on, I'm serious."

"I always dreamed of being able to set out and do my own thing."

"All right, so, the absolute dream scenario would be to get your own ship and be able to travel around as you please?"

"Yeah, something like that."

"Sounds lonely."

"I never said I'd want to do it alone—just that I'd want a say over where I went and when."

She nodded. "Okay, I can see that."

"Fat lot of chance that will ever happen now, though. What about you?"

Anya let out a long breath. "Honestly? Ever since my early teens, I've been fascinated by other planets and studying what makes life on them unique. This one is special, for sure, but the idea of being in one place for the rest of my life sounds pretty confining."

"You have an adventurer's heart."

"Sounds like you do, too."

"I guess we have that in common." He cracked a smile. *It took a new world to find the old me. Maybe I can find a way to live that dream, after all.*

16

"I REALIZE NOW how ridiculous it was to suggest walking this whole way," Anya said between labored breaths. Her limbs were tired from climbing a steep hillside, and her hands were covered in painful scuffs from gripping rough rocks.

"Hey." Evan caught her gaze. "We're in this together. We're going to make it, and we're going to find what we need."

"I appreciate your optimism."

"Anything else isn't going to get us there. Come on." He held out his hand to her.

She grasped it and he pulled her up to the next tier of the rockface they'd been scaling for the last half-hour. "Burning daylight, right? Back to it."

"Damn straight."

They'd gotten an early start on the day and had been making good progress on their eastward trek. Suspecting that they were nearing the crash site, they'd decided to detour to a nearby hill so they could get a higher vantage point. What they hadn't realized from the bottom was that the hillside was actually a mixture of grassy slopes and rock formations, and there was no way to get to the top without sections of climbing.

Having now been across several different types of terrain—

from steep hills to swamps to dense jungle—it was clear that traveling on foot was the only way to make it across the ground. But flying… she wished more than anything they had a shuttle to ferry them around.

They were nearing the crest of the hill. Already, the expansive landscape was opening before them. The river they'd crossed the day before formed a marbled blue-brown snake across a valley, surrounded by rolling hills covered in trees. In the distance to the west, the canopy was a different shade of green, which she suspected was the swampy area they'd walked around. Though it was impossible to trace their exact path, she had a new appreciation for how much ground they'd covered—especially given the challenging natural features.

Despite needing to scale rocky sections, the rest of the hillside was covered in grass no higher than her knees, which made for straightforward crossing. Nonetheless, her calves would no doubt be sore by that evening from walking up the steep angle.

"It may be tough to see the crash without a smoke plume," Evan said as they covered the final stretch to the top. No doubt, the statement was meant to head off Anya's own growing concern that they were nearing the highest vantage point for kilometers and they'd yet to spot any sign of their intended destination.

"It could be on the other side of this hill. We've been working in a general direction. That mountain we've been using might not have been quite the right path." The truth she hadn't wanted to admit was that they really had no idea where they were going. Their route had been an educated guess, at best. She'd be shocked if they stumbled into the crash on their first try.

They crossed the final grassy section to the top in short

order. Cresting the slope, Anya's breath caught in her throat as she took in the scene beyond.

A distinct scar of churned earth was carved into the landscape. Something that size visible from ten kilometers away could only mean one thing.

"The crash site," Anya said breathlessly beside him.

"Looks like our navigating was close enough." He smiled at her.

She beamed back. "We're almost there."

— — —

The crash skid was good news. It meant the ship had been in a big enough piece to carve out the strip when it touched down. However, that also meant it had been a hard landing and the ship hadn't had propulsion control. Hopefully, the core systems at the center of the vessel remained intact.

Evan judged the remaining distance against the height of the sun in the sky. "We can't make it there by nightfall. What do you think about camping near that clearing?" He pointed to a location midway between the wreckage and their current position.

Anya nodded. "I like the idea of getting there in the morning when we're fresh. No telling what we might find."

"All right, it's a plan."

She shook her head. "More than three days. I never would have guessed it would take this long."

"It was a lot farther away than it seemed." She began descending the far side of the hill.

Evan followed her. "This whole *planet* is a lot bigger than I'm used to. I've been living in space too long, apparently."

"Crossing this landscape is nothing like going from one

end of a space station to another, that's for sure."

"Terrible public transportation here! Making people walk everywhere? We may as well be back in the Dark Ages."

In a way, they were—so far removed from modern technology that they were navigating by celestial objects and using fire at night for protection and warmth. Yet, beneath his complaints and discomfort, he felt more alive and freer than he had in years.

Being out in the wilderness drove home just how sedentary his life had been recently. Sure, there were bursts of action, but for the most part he'd been in transit or sitting in meetings. Looking back on it, that had been no way to live. People were meant to go out and explore and be connected to their environment. Life in cities, where so many interactions were impersonal and there wasn't even a sky to see, was an extreme departure from humanity's roots. Even this short time on Aethos had awakened an inner yearning within him to connect with that part of himself.

"There's a power to this place," Evan mused as he walked down the verdant hillside with Anya. "Its raw, untapped potential. I've never felt anything like it on the settled worlds."

"Now you get it." She smiled, her brows raised in a knowing look.

"What do you mean?"

"Why colonists risk everything to travel to a new world. It's that pioneering spirit that's buried deep in all of us. It doesn't always awaken, but once it does, nothing short of an interstellar adventure can satisfy that yearning."

"I can relate to that."

She smiled wistfully. "It took me a while to realize, but xenobiology is just a convenient cover story for a much grander study of the meaning of life across the universe."

"Look at us! Three days in the wilderness and we've turned into wise philosophers."

"And not just that, but intrepid explorers," she pointed out.

"You know, on that note, I'm really impressed by your mountain climbing. First the day we crashed, and then again today."

"Oh, hah!" Anya laughed while sliding down a patch of loose rocks. "I guess my ruse has worked."

"How so?" Evan held out his arms to steady himself on the gravel.

"This entire time, I've had many moments where I wanted to fall over and never get up. But I didn't stop because I didn't want to look bad compared to you."

"Me?" He stared at her, incredulous. "Climbing up those hills, I could barely breathe! But you were doing so well, I made myself keep up."

She laughed. "Damn, so the only reason we've made such good time is because we were showing off to each other?"

"Sounds like it."

Anya's eyes sparkled with amusement. "Well, you put on a good show, yourself. Had me fooled."

"Me too."

A loose rock clattered by as it rolled from above. Evan whipped around. It could have been dislodged earlier, but—

He caught a glimpse of an animal crouching behind rocks above them, less than six meters away. Its silver, dappled fur was so well camouflaged with the rocks that he'd only spotted it when it moved. A similar size to the other panther they'd encountered, this one seemed equally adapted to a rocky hill as the other was to the forest.

Is it also resistant to a pulse shot? He reached for the

handgun. They'd gotten one useful shot on the other beast.

Anya picked up on his sudden shift in demeanor and whipped around to look behind her. After several seconds of searching, her muscles tensed. "What do we do?" she murmured, barely moving her lips.

"You tell me," Evan whispered back.

"Scare it. If it can't surprise us, it may go away. Now!" She waved her arms, shouting, "Get out of here!"

Evan joined her. "Go away! We see you!"

The silver panther froze in place, watching them. When Evan and Anya took steps toward it, the cat backed up and then spun on its haunches and fled. Its movements were silent as it dashed up the hillside, only dislodging an occasional loose pebble.

Anya let out a long, trembling breath. "If it hadn't bumped that rock..."

"Don't think like that," Evan said, as much for his own benefit.

"We've been really lucky here. These animals have no reason to fear humans."

"But they do. We'll keep watch, and we'll be fine."

"We should get out of its hunting grounds," she said, motioning him downhill.

After a check that it hadn't returned yet, he followed. "We could give it a gift meal like last time, but I haven't seen any prey animals."

"For this one, I don't think that's necessary."

"Why?"

"Its coat is camouflaged for the landscape up here—the gray rocks and gravel. I don't think it will stalk us in the valley."

Evan smiled. "Good sciencing."

Now motivated to get off the hillside as quickly as possible,

Evan and Anya slid and jumped their way to the bottom. It was only once they'd covered half a kilometer from the base through the valley that they slowed.

"We had a good run there between things trying to eat us," Evan jested.

"These bigger predators don't seem to like the mucky areas."

"They have good taste."

She sighed. "Let's keep moving."

Forested, gently rolling hills stood along the path to their intended campsite. Though less dense than the jungle they'd traversed before, the trees still limited visibility and made it difficult to follow a straight line.

As they walked in silence, Evan realized that their footfalls were sounding a little *too* loud. There were no birds singing or other creatures chattering, only the occasional buzz of insects. The back of his neck tingled with a warning that danger might be near.

Anya seemed to pick up on it at the same time, as she began swiveling her head to take in their surroundings.

Evan made his own assessment seeing little beyond the crushed groundcover from their path behind. However, a forest panther would easily blend into the shadows. He strained his ears, hoping to pick out the sound of pursuit.

A bush rustled to their left.

"Run!" Anya shouted.

Though Evan didn't see anything, he didn't hesitate to bolt through the trees after her.

In an all-out sprint, they dashed through the forest, weaving around trunks and hurdling over fallen branches. Evan was outside himself, barely registering the burn in his lungs and limbs as he pushed his body to its limit.

The ground dropped away in front of them to a fern-covered hillside. Carrying too much momentum, Evan was already over the edge before he had time to slow.

He skidded through the ferns, half-stepping, half-skiing his way to the bottom. Midway down, he missed a step and fell onto his backside. The wet leaves may as well have been a slide, continuing to carry him all the way to the bottom.

Eventually, he slid to a sloppy halt, struggling to get purchase on the thick groundcover of damp fallen leaves. The decomposing foliage left flakes on his hip and elbow.

It was quiet now. Whatever had been crashing along behind him had stopped, too. Quiet didn't mean it was gone. It might be watching him.

With a discontented grunt, Anya slid to a stop next to him. She rolled to her stomach and pushed up into a crouched position. Decaying leaf fragments clinging to her pants and shirt gave the garments the look of proper military fatigues. She was even moving more like a soldier now—calculated, deliberate, controlled. It was amazing how a few days of scraping by could toughen up a person.

"Are you okay?" he asked her.

She cautiously stood up, flexing her hands and then swinging her arms and shoulders to assess the range of motion. "Yeah, I think so." She placed a hand on the back of her neck and massaged it. "Definitely don't want to do that again!"

"You made it look stylish."

"Watch what you say, or I might push you down the hill to check out your moves."

Evan was pretty sure she was joking, but he knew it was best not to press his luck. He stood up and scanned the trees along the top of the hill. "Did you get a look at it?"

"No, didn't want to wait it out."

"It could have just been a bird."

"Maybe, but I'd rather not take the chance."

He couldn't argue with that. Not seeing any threat above, he returned his attention to navigating to their intended campsite. "I think the path is this way." He indicated the direction with the wave of a hand.

She nodded. "All right. Lead the way."

Whatever may have startled them, he had no intention of waiting around to meet it face to face.

17

EVAN TOSSED A branch on the campfire. The field they'd spotted from atop the hill had turned out to be a perfect campsite. Especially after their encounter earlier, the open area around the tent helped set him at ease that nothing could sneak up without their knowledge.

"Thank you for getting the fire going," Anya told him, as she'd said every night on their journey.

"Really, it's no problem."

She held out her hands to warm them near the flames. "I hate to admit it, but I'm useless without technology."

"You seem to be holding your own."

"Pure grit and determination. I'm freaking out on the inside."

He smiled. "You think I'm not?"

"Not as much as me."

"You might be surprised."

She sat in silence for several seconds, watching the flames. "It's a powerful experience to face your own mortality in such a visceral way. In life back in the settled worlds, we have so many comforts and conveniences. There's very little danger. Being out here like this is a return to our primal selves."

"We have a leg up on our ancestors."

"In some ways, yes. But they understood their environment. We're trespassers without a map." She smiled and hugged her legs to her chest.

"What?" he asked, curious what private thought had affected her mood in that way.

"Oh, I was just thinking about what you were saying earlier about the power of this place. I've spent my entire career studying ecology, biology, and all the interactions of natural environments. Yet, I've done most of that from within biodomes or from a ship in orbit. Even the field stuff, we were always in a big group with all the technological resources we needed to be safe and comfortable. I've never really *experienced* an environment before. Funny how you don't realize how out of touch you are until there's one situation that changes everything."

"I didn't expect it to be like this for me, either."

"You seem to have adapted fine."

He shrugged. "I do kinda like it. With people, you never know who's going to stab you in the back. But out here, the predators are obvious. It's refreshing."

She studied him in the firelight. "I take it you have experience with betrayal?"

"You could say that."

"Does that have something to do with how you unexpectedly found yourself on this expedition?"

"What landed me here was a lot of things."

"I'm going to get the story out of you one of these days."

"You're persistent, I'll give you that."

She tapped the side of her head. "Inquisitive scientific mind. Can't turn off the hypothesizing."

"Oh, I can't wait to hear your theories about me."

"Well, I'm thinking you probably did an initial enlistment term with the UPDF, maybe one re-up. But you realized that you could take the skills you'd learned and apply them in a more direct way, so you went over to the Security Corps instead. But working as a regular peace officer still wasn't getting to the heart of addressing what you saw as problems in society, so you wanted to do more. Maybe private investigator?"

Admittedly, she was close. He'd already given away more than he'd intended—not that there was any reason to keep it a secret. He just really wanted to be done with that life, and talking about it would make it all real. There was some comfort existing in the space between the parts of his life that had been fabricated as cover and the painful elements of his real past. Coming to this world was like starting a new assignment where he could write a persona to fit the needs of his situation. The person he had to become to survive here had no attachments, no past.

"All right, fine," Anya said with a little huff of annoyance when Evan didn't give her anything else.

"It's not because I don't trust you. It's just not something I want to get into."

"Maybe you're actually a con man." She met his gaze for a moment before looking away.

"I can assure you, the one thing I'm not is a criminal."

"I suppose I'll give you the benefit of the doubt. Not that I should."

"Anya." He stopped and looked into her eyes. "You can trust me. I promise you that."

She studied him for a long moment. "I do trust you. But I also know you're hiding things. What aren't you telling me?"

"I have my reasons for keeping some things secret."

"We all do, but these aren't normal circumstances."

"You're right. And our present situation makes what happened light years away from here even more irrelevant."

Her eyes narrowed. "Relevant or not, I'd like to know."

"It's complicated."

"Well, *un*-complicate it!" She crossed her arms. "Seriously, what's the point of keeping your past secret now? Did you kill someone or something?"

He flinched in spite of himself. He'd been on the receiving end of some epic ass-chewings, but there were few things more venomous than the glare of a frustrated woman. As much as he wanted to deflect, as was his custom, he couldn't bring himself to keep deceiving her. She might well be the one ally he had on this cursed world.

He swallowed and met her gaze. "I spent the last few years watching terrible people do awful things. But not as an accomplice. I was a deep undercover investigator for the UPA Security Corps."

She softened. "Why didn't you say so?"

"Like I said, it's complicated. I'm not used to putting faith in others."

"I can't imagine doing undercover work. I can barely keep my own life together, let alone manage a whole other persona."

He smiled. "If you make that persona someone who has their shit together, it makes it easier."

"How in the worlds did you go from doing that to here?"

"None of this was my choice. My cover was blown, and hopping on the colony ship was the escape plan I was given."

"What happened?"

"I can't talk about an ongoing investigation."

She raised an eyebrow. "How do you know it's still ongoing? We were in transit for months."

"Until I'm told otherwise, I need to follow protocol."

"Come on, what difference will it make? Seriously, who am I going to tell? That bird?" She pointed at a black and red bird the size of a crow perched in a nearby bush.

As if on cue, the bird squawked, fluttered its wings, and then took off while cawing loudly.

Evan threw up his hands. "Great, now the whole forest knows!"

Anya rolled her eyes but laughed. "Clearly, there are spies everywhere."

"You're right, everything that happened was worlds away and anything I could say here won't change any of it." He paused, having to fight against his training to speak openly about his experience. "I still shouldn't get into specifics, but in broad strokes, I got in deep with the Noche Syndicate."

Her eyes went wide. "Wow, *that* Syndicate?"

"The very one."

Understanding washed over her face. "Yikes, that must have been intense. How long were you under?"

"Almost three years."

"Oh, shit… I can see why you're touchy about some things."

He nodded slowly. "I haven't been out for long enough to break all the habits I needed to form in order to maintain my cover. There were some pretty twisted things going on inside the Syndicate. It felt like being in a cult. They even had these bizarre initiation rites."

"Wow."

Evan shook his head, wishing he could shake off the memory. "In this one ceremony, they gave an injection of… something. To this day, I don't know what it was. They said it would make us one of the 'chosen'."

Anya frowned. "Creepy much?"

"Right." Evan shuddered. "On my worst days, I felt like it was crawling under my skin. Fortunately, that hasn't happened since we got here."

"I'm sorry you had to go through that."

He shrugged. "It was part of the job, and I'd do it again. The main issue has been that because of how things went down at the end, I didn't get a proper transition back to normalcy."

"What happened?"

"Eh, that's…"

"In broad strokes."

Evan took a deep breath. "Basically, I was going about my usual business when I walked in on one of the Noche bosses talking to someone who definitely should not have been there. I can't say who, but suffice to say he's really high up in the Commonwealth government. The Syndicate must have snatched him in transit, or something. At that point, I decided I was his best chance at survival, so I broke cover and got us out."

"Very valiant."

"And also an impulsive move that threw three years of work out the airlock. It stirred up a shitstorm since it revealed that the organization had been infiltrated. And I was a dead man at that point, so that's how I got my express ticket on this colony expedition."

"That explains a whole lot."

"I still don't know if it was the right call to intervene."

"In all likelihood, you saved his life. I'm sure he and his loved ones are grateful, even if the authorities are annoyed about the blown op."

"I hope so. He didn't seem all that happy when I first rescued him, but the whole ordeal must have been a huge shock."

"I can only imagine."

They sat in silence for a few minutes, processing, as they stared into the fire.

"You could have told me earlier about what's going on with you, you know," Anya said at last.

"That would have spoiled the mystery."

She raised an eyebrow. "Does everything have to be a big show with you?"

"I didn't mean it that way." He leaned forward, resting his hands on his knees. "I'm sorry I wasn't upfront. I spent too long in positions where I couldn't trust anyone. It's difficult to let down those walls."

"I know how that can be."

"Still, of all the colony ships I could have escaped on, *this one*?" He let out a pained laugh.

"Yeah, same here, buddy. I finally decide to get back into the field, and now I'm potentially marooned forever."

"How was that supposed to work? Was this going to be a permanent assignment?"

"No, a science advisory team always accompanies a new colony expedition like this. The plan is for a two-year term to help get everything set up and address any unforeseen challenges on the world. We'd keep in touch with the core worlds, and they'd send a retrieval ship for us when our work was done. Then we could go on to the next."

"Not a bad system."

"When it works. But if we never make contact, they'll think we're dead and won't send help."

"You'd think they'd want to investigate what went wrong.'

"Unless it's disease, or solar flares, or who knows what. Any investigation would carry risk."

"Any *manned* investigation."

"What are you implying?"

"They might not send a *ship* to investigate, but wouldn't they at least send a probe—like what was sent here to do the initial surveys?"

She brightened. "That's a great point! I hadn't thought of that. So even if we can't get interstellar comms to work, we could still send a message from the surface to a probe in orbit."

"It'll be months before anything gets here, even if they sent it right away, but it is a good Plan B."

"I'm still not giving up hope on being able to send a proper long-range message."

"Me either. Just trying to be realistic."

She sighed. "I feel silly for not thinking of that sooner."

"Me too."

"I blame being hunted."

"It does make a person focus on the here and now, can't lie."

"And how the past doesn't matter when imminent survival is on the line," she added.

He nodded. "I didn't need to keep so much from you, I'm sorry."

"I understand why you did. And I appreciate you telling me now."

"If we're going to make it through the next several months, I know I need to learn how to trust others. A friendship with you seems like a good place to start."

"Friends, huh?" She smiled.

"Well, you did threaten to throw me down a hill just to mess with me. Seems like something a friend would do."

"Surviving a hostile alien world is a bonding experience, what can I say?"

"Teamwork makes the dream work."

"No. You didn't." She closed her eyes and groaned.

"Sorry."

"I might need to rescind friend status."

He grinned. "But you won't, because you secretly love corny catchphrases."

"You shouldn't know me this well already."

"But I do, and you wouldn't have it any other way."

18

WALKING THROUGH THE trees on the final approach to the crash site, Anya couldn't help looking at Evan with new perspective. She was surprised he'd opened up to her the night before, and the story hadn't been what she'd been expecting.

His evasiveness up to that point had led her to believe he'd done something wrong. Perhaps he'd abandoned his post and forged his credentials for the settlement expedition, or maybe he'd partnered with the criminals he was supposed to have been policing. Those things *were* true, in a sense, but not in the nefarious way she'd imagined. Granted, he could have been feeding her a made-up cover story to stop her questioning. However, she sensed the genuineness in his tone and the look in his eyes when he'd told her, and she had no reason to doubt him.

Now, if only she could be as honest about the strange circumstances in her own life that had led her here. She knew it was hypocritical of her, but she had nothing concrete to go on at this point, so any statement was more likely to come across as paranoia rather than well-intended openness. Consequently, she decided to temporarily keep those thoughts to herself until they'd had a chance to inspect the wreckage.

What they found there might reveal if her suspicions had any basis in reality.

They'd gotten an early start to the day and had already covered three kilometers. The crash site had to be close. For that matter, they might be almost on top of it but unable to see it through the trees. Hopefully, they'd find a sign to point them in the right direction for the final stretch.

"Hey, I think we're almost there!" Evan called from ahead of her.

She followed his sightline to a sheet of charred metal sticking out of the ground. It was nearly as tall as her and several centimeters thick. "A piece of heat shielding?" she asked.

"Probably." He looked around. "It may have come off on the final approach. Let's see if we can find more."

Feeling motivated now that the end was in sight, she followed Evan's quick pace through the trees. The lingering wetness from overnight rain had dampened sound as well as the ground, casting a blanket of quiet over the surrounding forest. She kept her ears open for potential threats.

A dozen meters ahead, they came across another piece of wreckage, smaller than the first but just as charred.

Evan inspected the piece. "I can't tell if this is burned from atmospheric entry or an explosion."

"We can figure that out later. It means we're on the right track." Anya continued forward. The only way they were going to find out what happened to the ship was if they could locate its flight recorder and figure out a way to access the data. Pieces of the ship and a giant crash path through the jungle meant that the bulk of the ship was intact. Answers were waiting for them—close.

They passed increasingly frequent debris as they hiked.

Eventually, they came across signs of broken branches that had rained down from the top of the canopy. They were almost there.

A sea of broken and burned trees opened up in front of them. The ground was still wet and soft along the crash path, dark soil spilling over the lip of the channel carved across the ground. At its terminus, the twisted metal form of the military ship rose upward fifty meters. The front third of its two-hundred-meter length was buried in the ground. Even through the dirt covering the ship, it was evident that the hull had been blackened in places and had large sections ripped away.

"All of that couldn't have happened in the crash," Evan said, reinforcing his previous assessment of the wreckage.

Anya was inclined to agree. The damage wasn't consistent with an accidental crash. It looked like it had been through an explosion—and not simply hit by shrapnel, but near a direct blast.

"What could have happened?"

"I don't know. Maybe there was some kind of system malfunction that caused an explosion. Or, it could have been… intentional."

"We don't know enough to speculate," she countered, even though her gut told her that Evan was correct in his assessment. Too much didn't add up about the strange circumstances of the expedition and subsequent crash. "We should get a closer look."

When Anya started to move forward, Evan remained at the tree line, assessing the ship from a distance. "What are you waiting for?" she asked.

"I'd really, really been hoping that I was wrong about seeing an explosion in space. Now that it's been confirmed, I don't know if it's safe to be here."

"Why wouldn't it be?"

"Because we found someone murdered in an escape pod. Clearly, something deeper is going on, and whoever is behind it probably wouldn't want witnesses."

"You mean, if there are survivors on that ship, they may be in on it—and not on our side?"

"Now that I'm here looking at the ship, the thought crossed my mind."

Anya shook her head. "That would have been helpful to realize days ago. If you don't want to check out the ship, then why did we come all this way?"

"I never said I didn't want to investigate it. If there are any answers to be found, they'll be on that ship. And I intend to get them."

"Okay, so…" She gestured toward the crashed vessel with both hands.

"I'm just saying, maybe running up to the ship and knocking on the door might not be the best approach."

"Maybe you're overthinking it. Could the hull damage have simply been from the crash?"

"Sure, it's possible. But we know someone was murdered."

He had her there. The clues had been adding up, and she'd already seen too much to believe that anything that had happened to them was a coincidence. "What are you thinking, then?"

"Surveillance."

"Looking for what?"

"Signs of life. That was a violent crash. It's possible everyone died. But if there were survivors, then what they've done in the past few days may give us clues."

Anya's heart sank as she grappled with the gravity of their situation. "This isn't going anything like how I'd envisioned. I thought making it here would be the hard part."

"We have an evolving understanding of the situation."

She side-eyed him. "Talking like that… you really were an investigator."

"I was. And this is a mystery I don't intend to leave unsolved." Evan set his jaw and sucked in a deep breath through his nose. "I *really* want to get a look at that flight recorder to see what happened in orbit."

"You said it: first, we need to see if there were any survivors."

"Yeah, let's scope it out. There has to be an opening somewhere."

Anya had figured they'd look for an airlock, but that became irrelevant when she realized that the hull damage included deep gashes that cut into the interior decking. Once they decided it was safe to approach, they'd be able to walk straight in.

— — —

Evan took another slow breath in an attempt to release the growing tension in his chest. The number of potential paths off the planet were diminishing with each new discovery, and confirmation that there'd been an explosion on the ship might be the most concerning yet.

While it was possible that whatever had happened was an accident, he knew enough about starships to understand that there were redundancies upon redundancies to prevent precisely that kind of catastrophic failure. Such an occurrence was especially unlikely on a military vessel, given rigorous operational and maintenance standards.

His question now wasn't if there had been sabotage, but

how widespread it had been. Were there attacks on both ships? Or did the explosion on this one accidentally strike the colony ship? Or vice versa?

The possible scenarios churned in his mind as they picked their way through the trees down the length of the ship.

There were large openings in the hull where the ship had been either blown open or broken on impact; he didn't have the technical expertise to say for certain, but the damage seemed too isolated in specific areas to be from the crash alone. Either way, the more they saw of the vessel, the less likely it seemed that anyone had survived. He also noted that there wasn't any sign of an encampment nearby, but any survivors would most likely use the ship for shelter, so that didn't mean much,

"All right, Anya," he said after they'd circled the buried nose of the vessel and walked the perimeter on the far side, "I'm not sure anyone's home. But just in case, let me approach first while you hang back."

"What? No way."

"Anya…"

"Don't give me that tone. What's your reasoning?"

"If there are hostiles inside, I wouldn't want to put you in danger."

"Then I should be the bait, because you know how to shoot and I don't."

"That's not—"

"Whatever you were going to say, don't. The only point that matters is that if you got captured, my biologist knowledge would not be the most useful skillset to mount a rescue."

He recognized the look in her eyes that the matter was not up for discussion. Moreover, she had a valid argument. "Fine. Take it slow and easy. Keep your hands visible."

"Just like approaching a wild animal."

"Sure, go with that."

Anya ventured from the cover of the trees, taking slow strides. She extended her arms to both sides for balance as she climbed over the fallen, burned trees piled around the crash site.

Evan scanned the ship, looking for any sign of movement through the viewports.

Nothing about the vessel indicated that anyone was around. He hated to think about the final moments of the crew. The initial explosion may have killed most on board, but the violent crash down to the planet very well could have doomed the rest. However, he couldn't rule out the possibility that some of the interior cabins may have been protected enough.

Anya had progressed to the halfway point between the trees and the ship. She stopped. "Hello?" Her shout rang out through the stillness.

She waited, listening. No reply came, so she continued forward.

When she reached the ship, she located one of the broken sections of the hull close enough to the ground to step inside. She poked her head in. "Hello?"

A few seconds later, she looked back in Evan's direction and shrugged. "Nothing."

Well, if there's someone here watching us, they're being crafty about it. With no indication that they were in immediate danger, Evan went over to join Anya by the ship.

The stench of singed metal permeated the air next to the fallen vessel. Flaked-off bits of the charred heat shielding and burned tree limbs crunched underfoot as he stepped up alongside Anya.

"How's it look in there?" he asked her.

“See for yourself.”

He stuck his head and shoulders inside the opening, careful not to touch the jagged metal around the perimeter. The gap led into a room approximately four meters square, and a hatch stood centered on the back wall. The door was ajar, and the corridor beyond appeared to be intact. There were no signs of the room’s former occupant, and the only furnishing that remained was a table bolted to the deck.

“In we go?” Evan questioned.

Anya fished out a flashlight from the top of her backpack. She clicked it on dramatically. “Adventure awaits!”

Evan retrieved his own flashlight. “Want me to take the lead?”

“Please.”

He took a cautious step inside, checking his weight on the decking. When it didn’t groan or shift, he continued inward.

The air was surprisingly clean inside the room. Evan shined the flashlight around, not seeing anything of note on the walls aside from singe marks around the gash in the outer wall. He continued forward across the awkwardly sloping floor to the inner hatch.

Evan braced himself for a gruesome scene in the corridor. However, there were no bodies to be seen. He had no doubt they’d encounter unfortunate crew members somewhere, but it was probably for the best that wasn’t the first thing they’d come across upon entering the ship.

They stepped into the corridor and shined their flashlights in both directions. The hall was lined with doors as far as they could see. Damage visible along the exterior of the craft extended inward in places. Evan’s stomach clenched as he inspected the wreckage, where one section of the hall appeared untouched and the next was a tangle of mangled metal. Even if someone had avoided the direct damage, the explosive decompression would have led to a swift end.

"Where would the communications equipment be?" Anya asked.

"In the Command Center, at the heart of the ship."

"And where is that relative to us?"

"I'm not familiar with this exact model. My guess would be a little forward from here and maybe up a few decks."

"So, this way?" Anya motioned toward the downslope, where the nose of the vessel was partially buried in the ground.

"That's my best guess. Assuming everything wasn't destroyed in the crash."

Steadying himself against the wall, he began working his way down the incline. Curled shards of metal poked into the walkway at dangerous angles, creating an even greater hazard in the already challenging conditions. The only saving grace was the rough texture of the decking, designed for maximum grip on combat boots. If this had been the colony ship wreckage, they would have been facing a slick slide down the glossy surface.

"The Command Center would be shielded, though, right?" Anya asked. "It's an important part of the ship."

"Yes, it's probably sturdier than some other areas. But a crash is a crash—not to mention the explosion. I'm not going to hold my breath for finding any functional equipment."

"I know that's the realist approach, but I'd hate to have come all this way for nothing."

"This was always a longshot," he reminded her.

"We'll see soon enough. No sense speculating now."

Twenty meters down the corridor, they reached a three-way intersection.

"Where now?" Anya shined her light down the two options.

Evan scanned the wall with his own light, looking for directional signs. He spotted the symbol denoting a stairwell pointing to the right. "This way. We need to go up—I think."

"What I wouldn't give for a directory right now."

"If the ship had power, we'd be able to pull it up on any of these screens. That's the problem with digital everything."

"The ship is large, but we can spend all day looking if we have to. There has to be more signage around here somewhere."

"Actually, the Command Center is one of the few places that *won't* be labeled," Evan countered.

"Why?"

"Think about a scenario of being boarded by an enemy force. You wouldn't want a sign pointing toward where to find your leaders, would you?"

She nodded. "Good point."

"Same thing with Engineering and weapons caches. You can easily pull up the locations with official credentials, but the map is designed to be hidden. One last chance to fight back."

"Is that kind of boarding really an issue?"

"That policy was implemented maybe twenty or so years back, based on what I've been told. Piracy was getting really bad."

Anya's eyes widened. "Even against military ships?"

"Some of these organizations have their own combat units to rival the government's. I got a glimpse into it when I was undercover, and… it's going to be interesting."

"What do you mean?"

"I think it's a matter of when, not if, their conflict comes to a head. Like, civil war style."

She sighed. "Great, that's all we need."

"Conflict is inevitable when you have this many people

competing for limited resources."

"That's why we're expanding to other planets."

"Too few, too slowly. This has been brewing for a long time."

She frowned. "Yeah, I guess it has."

"Hey, here we go." Evan pointed to a stairwell entrance ahead on their left.

The entrance was secured with a hatch, which was thankfully unlocked. With effort opening on a slope against gravity, Evan swung it upward and checked inside. Like the rest of the ship they'd encountered so far, it was empty.

He jogged up the stairs—closer to climbing on each switchback due to the slope of the ship. At each landing, he checked the symbols next to the door indicating the amenities that could be found nearby. Though their destination wouldn't be listed, he could use the process of elimination, knowing what *would* be listed and what would not be near the command hub. After passing several decks of crew berthing and social space, they got to a deck with few labels; one of the icons, though, Evan recognized as denoting the Officer's Mess.

"I think this is probably it."

"Lead the way." Anya motioned for him to go first.

They stepped through the hatch into another branching corridor. The interior finish was slightly more ornate than the other sections of the ship, confirming Evan's suspicion that they were in the correct place. He didn't understand why the officers' area should be nicer than any other part of a vessel, but he'd found that was a nearly universal trait.

He paused at the first intersection, trying to work out where the Command Center might be. He'd never been on a military vessel this large, so he wasn't sure how they might do things.

Heart of the ship. Where is most protected? He looked down the various corridors. "Let's try this way," he said, heading to the left on instinct alone.

His ankles and calves were getting tired from walking on the angled surfaces. They went down one more section before reaching a juncture near the mess. If his experience with smaller vessels held, they were very close.

"It might be down here." Evan headed down the side corridor toward the vessel's center.

The corridor terminated in a door, which was wedged halfway open. It was a strange way for it to have settled during the crash, but it worked to their advantage.

The space through the door was dark, so it hadn't been ripped open in the descent. That was good news.

"The comm controls may actually be intact," Anya commented as she made the same assessment.

"There's no way the exterior relays didn't get mangled, but I'll take any components we can get."

Evan wedged himself through the door opening, shining his flashlight inside. Everything that hadn't been bolted down was now upended and strewn about the room, but the most important components looked to be whole, aside from a few cracked screens.

And this is why they put the Command Center in the center of the ship rather than up top. He spotted the comm station and headed over.

Anya followed. "There's a lot to salvage here. There has to be someone among our group of survivors with engineering know-how."

"Let's see if the thing we came for is even in one piece before we make too many plans." Evan wedged his foot against the comm console's base to keep from sliding further down the room. He bent down to take a look underneath.

An empty cavity met his gaze. Not destroyed, but *gone.* Even stranger, the top panel had been removed. It bore a scratch mark along its surface from where one of the loose items in the room must have scraped it, and the scratch extended from the panel to the fixed console. That meant that the panel had to have been removed *after* the crash.

Evan swallowed. “Anya, things just got weirder again.”

19

ANYA'S STOMACH KNOTTED at Evan's concerned tone. "What's wrong?"

He motioned to a console in front of him. "The equipment is missing, but look." He held up a panel and showed her how it fit in, and that it had been damaged during the crash.

"So, someone took it," Anya surmised. "Which means people survived the crash. That explains the lack of dead bodies."

"But where did they go?" Evan's brows were pinched together. His hard gaze and downturned mouth were unusual to see after their jovial travels from the past few days. Furthermore, his open concern underscored the severity of the situation.

Anya swallowed. "Evan, what's going on?"

He shook his head faintly. "I wish I knew. None of this adds up."

Looking around the room, Evan settled on a console at the front, positioned near a fractured display screen. He went over to it and began fiddling with the front panel.

"What are you looking for?" Anya asked.

"I think this is where the black box should be stored. We

can find out what happened during the crash."

"What will we need to access it?"

"It's encrypted data, but from my undercover work I know a few generalized codes that will let us access some basic info," Evan said. "We'll need a screen that can operate under its own power in order to see it, though."

"All right, I'll look around for something."

Anya went out to search the nearby rooms for potentially useful equipment. She needed to find something with internal battery power. Worst case, they could hook the flight recorder up to their emergency pods back at base camp to review the information on the device, but it would be great to know what they were dealing with before going all the way back there.

The first three rooms she checked were a bust. Items were scattered around the spaces, though it was unclear if the disorder was from the turbulent landing, a hurried departure, or both. It appeared that most electronic systems were integrated into the ship itself, which wasn't helpful. Even if they could figure out how to turn the main power on, the ship was so badly damaged that activating the power would likely result in fires, or worse. Their options were limited.

She continued her search. Many of the doors and hatches had been left ajar, but eventually, she came across one near the end of the corridor that was closed and latched. It had the appearance of a storeroom, which seemed like a good place to look.

Trying the door, it didn't budge at first. She leaned against it with her shoulder. It popped open with a groan.

Her flashlight beam passed over a haphazard pile of fabric bags. A moment later, she realized the bags were actually bodies wearing jumpsuits.

Anya jumped backward. "Holy shit!" She covered her

mouth with her hands as a putrid stench of decay wafted into the corridor.

"You okay?" Evan called out.

She continued pinching her nose with one hand. "I found the bodies."

"What?" He jogged over to her. One glance inside the room and he recoiled, covering his own mouth. "Shit..."

The battered and burned corpses had been piled up in the room. The back section was a neater stack, devolving into a tangle of awkwardly angled limbs closer to the door.

Anya swallowed the bile rising in her throat. "Who would do this?"

"I don't know what to make of any of it." Evan's voice quavered slightly, a rare crack in his normally confident demeanor.

Seeing him struggle made her want to run back into the woods and take a gamble living off the land. However, the trying circumstances also awakened her scientific objectivity. This was a mystery that needed solving, in the same way she'd track down the beast responsible for a boneyard discovered in the jungle. She took a slow, deep breath to settle the queasiness in her stomach.

"This probably isn't the only room like this. Sealing them in a room is easier than burying." Anya risked taking a few steps forward to get a closer look at the bodies near the door. They were still wearing their IDs. "Maybe the idea was to keep them here for later cataloging and identification?"

"That's a good guess," Evan agreed. "But it's still strange that there weren't any signs of the survivors around the crash site. There are more resources on the ship, even if it's in ruins, than anywhere else on an unsettled world. Why would they leave this location?"

Anya's stomach dropped. "What if they did the same thing as us? I mean, they knew where we were supposed to put the settlement. Maybe they saw us come down. They could be on their way to the camp, and we missed them on our way here."

Evan sighed. "Bringing the comm equipment that we need with them." His fear from a minute before had transformed into exasperation. He didn't say it, but she could feel him swearing silently.

She wanted to let out a string of expletives of her own, but that wouldn't be helpful. "Did you find the black box?" she asked instead.

He nodded. "I did, and I was coming to find you."

"Good! I was starting to think maybe they would have taken that, too, along with the comm equipment."

"They lived through the crash—not a mystery to them."

"True."

"But we won't be able to learn anything if we can't view the drive. Any luck?"

"Not yet. I was going to look in here when…" She faded out with a glance toward the pile of bodies.

"We'll keep searching together, come on."

Anya's hands trembled as she resealed the hatch to the awful room. It was only as the latch clicked closed that she noticed a small, red diagonal slash near the handle. She couldn't recall seeing it before, but her brain had probably written it off as a paint smudge or something. Now, she realized it had been a deliberate indication about the horrors contained in the room.

"Evan, look." She pointed out the mark. "I suggest we keep any other doors with that closed."

He nodded solemnly. "Good idea."

They divided up the various rooms they encountered along

the corridor to search for the equipment they needed. Several officers' quarters initially seemed like strong contenders, but the only computer systems were those integrated into the vessel.

Then, they reached the medbay, and Anya's spirits lifted. "Oh, we're about to enter the diamond mine!"

"I hope you're right," Evan said without any enthusiasm.

Anya realized why as soon as she opened the door. The place had been completely looted. Cabinet doors were open, exposing empty shelves. A few random tools were on the deck or on surfaces, but they were nothing useful at first glance.

Her heart sank. "Of course, this is what people would take with them for survival."

"But we didn't come here for the meds." Evan flashed a weak but hopeful smile.

Anya began rechecking the space for anything valuable that may have been left behind. The medication cabinets had been completely stripped, as had medpacks, bandages, and most sets of tools. However, a cabinet at the back of the room still contained several medium-sized devices—probably deemed too cumbersome for travel.

A portable vitals monitoring unit caught her attention; it had various input connections and a screen. "Could this work?" she asked Evan.

He inspected the device. "You know, I think it would! Does it have power?"

Anya found the switch. With a pleasant hum, it sprang to life. The screen activated with 'No Input Detected' displayed at the center, but an icon in the upper right corner indicated that it had a full battery charge.

She grinned. "Now we're in business!"

Evan pulled out the black box drive from his pack. It was

only about twice the size of the MealPak packets and had a couple of hardline data cables sticking out of it. He identified one that was compatible with the medical monitor and plugged it in.

The screen lit up in a sea of random gibberish with a blinking prompt input at the bottom. Evan typed out a series of codes. After several attempts, he smiled as a root directory filled the display.

“Okay, we’re in,” he confirmed. “These lines of text indicate different segments of information. My codes won’t give us access to everything.” He scanned over the list. “Looks like we have the communication logs—timestamps but not the contents—and exterior camera feeds.”

“Where do we start?”

“I want to see what happened.” Evan navigated to the video library and scrubbed through to find the minutes leading up to the time of the emergency evacuation.

The initial video he brought up was a dark and highly pixelated feed showing floating debris against a starscape. He went back further. There was the flash of an explosion. He backed it up again. An object streaked through space, heading toward the ship, the video flashed from the subsequent explosion.

Anya’s heart leaped into her throat. “Wait, something hit the ship?”

“Looks like it.”

“A mini-asteroid?”

Evan replayed the video, squinting. After letting it loop three times, he located the playback settings and slowed it down. He paused on a frame a moment before impact. The object appeared cylindrical and smooth.

Anya eyed it suspiciously. “Is that just motion blur making

it look that way?"

Evan was frowning at the screen. "No, Anya, that's a missile."

Her heart skipped a beat. Their eyes met. "Does that mean...?" she began.

"None of this was an accident. The military escort ship was shot down, and the colony ship must have been taken out by the debris from the explosion," he finished for her.

Her brows drew together. "Who could have shot it?"

"I have no idea. But the liaison on the colony ship was murdered, and I suspect the events are connected."

When they'd ventured out to find this ship, Anya had approached it as a bid for survival. At no point in the process had she considered that coming here would be dangerous—aside from the trials of braving the jungle. But a sabotage to the expedition…

Her heart pounded in her ears. *Was this all a setup?*

She replayed everything in her mind leading up to this moment. How she'd pointed out the strange energy readings on the planet, and questioned them, and how two days later she'd been assigned to the expedition.

No, don't spiral. Not everything had to be a conspiracy. Sometimes, bad things happened. There was probably a much more straightforward explanation, and getting tied up in knots over wild hypotheticals wasn't going to help her situation.

Evan glanced over his shoulder. "I want to review the rest of this, but I don't think we should do it here. It's possible that whoever moved those bodies wasn't from this ship."

Her chest tightened. "What if they *are* going to our survivors' camp? It might not be to help."

Evan swore under his breath. "The two of us can't go up against people with access to missiles. If they have that, then what other resources?"

Anya's eyes stung as despair tightened her throat. She took a slow breath, forcing down the emotion. Breaking down now wouldn't keep her any safer. "This place was picked to colonize. That means it can support life. We'll die if we give up, but we can fight for survival."

Evan met her hard gaze, determination in his own eyes. "I'm with you."

She nodded. "Okay. Since we're here, we should see if there are any additional rations or weapons left on the ship. Once we've scavenged, we'll find somewhere to hole up and review the rest of these logs."

"That's the best plan I've heard all day."

20

A WEEK'S WORTH of food, a solar charger, another handgun, and a pulse rifle. It was a better position than they'd been in before their scavenging efforts, but Evan had no illusions about them being secure as he and Anya exited the crashed military ship.

He'd been slowly getting comfortable with the idea of going up against predatory animals and finding a way to live in the wilds. The primal thrill of it all had reignited a fire in him that he hadn't felt since his teens. But the recent revelations about an imminent human threat changed everything.

As Evan hopped over the fallen trees toward the cover of the forest, he mulled over their possible next moves. Anya's pensive silence suggested that she was also processing the discovery and mulling over her own possible scenarios.

The obvious answer was to head back to the main crash site camp. There'd be more safety in numbers, and the supplies from the drop pods would offer a foundation for eking out a new life on the planet.

Nonetheless, he couldn't discount the impact of their recent revelations. The military ship had been shot down. Granted, it wasn't a massive dreadnaught, but taking out a starship from orbit was no small feat. There was still a lot of data on the black box to go through, which might yield more information about where the shot had originated. Whether it had come from another ship or the surface, there was no doubt in Evan's mind that there were other people around Aethos. Considering that their actions had led to the deaths of thousands, he had no choice but to consider them the enemy.

Evan didn't see any way to stand against such a formidable adversary. They were out-gunned, and there were certainly more people than the two of them. That left one option.

"Anya, we can't go back to the original camp." Evan spoke the words without emotion—pure and factual.

She slowed her pace and looked over at him. "But we have to warn them about this threat. How can we do that without communications equipment, unless we go there?"

"Either the people on this planet have already gone to find them, or they don't know the other survivors are here. And if we go ourselves, we might lead trouble there." His gut lurched. "I hate to say it, but I think it might be better for them if we stay away."

"Is it possible we're being watched right now?"

"I haven't seen any indications of that, but I can't rule out anything at the moment."

Anya nodded solemnly. "I have a place in mind we could go, if you think we can travel without being followed."

He stepped closer to her, standing so he could whisper directly into her ear. "Where?"

"There are some caves we discovered during the survey, maybe another day or two walk from here," she whispered in reply. "It's in the opposite direction of the camp."

Evan stepped back and returned to his normal speaking volume, "That sounds like a good move for us. But the more I think about it, I don't see a way for the attackers *not* to know about the camp. It's impossible to target a missile without substantial visualization equipment. The two of us are small enough to have maybe gone undetected, but those pods are another thing. Not to mention, we told them to set a signal fire. Even though we weren't able to see it from the jungle, that doesn't mean they didn't light it after the rain."

She frowned. "Maybe we can find a way to help them from afar."

If there's anyone left... He shoved aside the thought. They still didn't know the attacker's motivations.

"We can hunt, I have the bioanalyzer to find edible plants and fruit," Anya continued. "We have the tent, bedrolls, and hopefully the shelter I just mentioned. It won't be glamorous, but we can make it work."

He smiled wearily. "An extended camping trip wasn't how I'd imagined life on Aethos."

"Me either. I suppose that's what I get for all of my complaints about needing a vacation."

Evan indicated for Anya to stop talking as they headed into the trees. There was so much cover that it'd be easy to follow someone without being seen, but moving silently through the brush would be next to impossible for a person. Evan stepped as lightly as he could, keeping a keen ear out for any signs of pursuit.

Anya oriented herself and set a course toward the region where the caves had been identified during the pre-colonization survey. Evan had no way to verify the information, but he was content to follow her lead. After everything they'd seen so far that day, having someone else take the lead was a relief.

As they walked, he continued to process the various clues

and try them on for size. Assembling a puzzle without being able to see the picture was a unique challenge and one he typically relished. This one felt decidedly different, though, knowing he couldn't call for an emergency extraction. It was either solve the mystery or die—no bowing out or second chances.

After a kilometer of walking in silence, Evan was satisfied that they weren't being followed. "All right, I think we're in the clear. But we should keep our voices down."

"This day has not gone how I'd anticipated," Anya replied softly.

Evan continued to keep watch on their surroundings. "I keep thinking about what could be behind the attack."

"Yeah, same. I've been replaying every conversation from my time at NovaTech to see if I missed a clue."

Evan nodded. "I also know that I might be overthinking it. My last assignment was really intense, and it made me question everyone and everything. I keep wondering if maybe there isn't some massive conspiracy here, and there's actually a super simple explanation."

"Which might be…?"

"That it's just a coincidence we both ended up here, like any number of twists life could have thrown us. And other people happened to get to this planet first."

She cast him a skeptical glance. "Okay," she said after a pause, "I can't refute the possibility. But it's *extremely* unlikely there were people here before us."

"About as unlikely as everything else we've encountered in our short time here."

"True. Look at us, beating the odds!"

"Right? But seriously, it's possible that some criminal element learned about the planned colony expedition and decided to come here in advance."

"I don't know *why* someone would do that, but I can't write it off."

"Lots of valuable materials are sent along with a colony ship," Evan pointed out. "That'd be a great prize."

"So, someone may have come all the way out here to rob us?"

"Think about it—anyone with the means to get out to a planet this remote would know that the expedition would come with an escort, so they'd be prepared to eliminate the military protection if they wanted to get away with stealing anything. That's what I would do if I wanted to pillage the colony ship. But the ambush went wrong, and our ship got blown up, too—probably a complete accident—and both vessels went down. We've already seen evidence of looting on the military ship, but it tracks that they were after supplies."

"That does make a lot more sense than a big conspiracy where NovaTech was in on it."

He nodded. "I still don't have an explanation for the shot liaison in the pod."

"Executed by a pirate infiltrator?" Anya speculated.

"Maybe."

She shook her head. "Still doesn't quite add up for me, but it does feel more plausible than where we started out with 'everything spontaneously went wrong all at once'."

"Murphy would be so disappointed in your lack of belief."

She smiled. "I think Murphy and I will be able to find common ground."

"This all goes to show how you can see enemies everywhere when you're on edge."

"Yeah, I was about ready to jump to 'they sent me here to die'."

Evan broke his stride. “Why would they do that, Anya?”

“Nothing.”

“Seriously?” He crossed his arms. “I finally opened up to you, but you want to keep secrets. What do you know that you haven’t told me?”

“You’re right.” She got a faraway look in her eyes and swallowed. “I should have said something sooner, but I think I inadvertently saw something I wasn’t supposed to, and it’s possible they sent me here as part of the coverup.”

“And by ‘they’ you mean NovaTech?”

She nodded. “But that’s insane. Right?”

“Nothing seems too crazy right now.”

“I hope it’s just in my head.”

He placed a hand gently on her shoulder. “Anya, where is this coming from? What did you see?”

“Remember I mentioned the strange energy surges we’d measured during the survey? Well, the whole thing was odd, but we’d written it off as natural electrical activity. Static charges can build up for a number of reasons. It’s not common, but there’s a lot of precedent so it didn’t raise too many flags. But seeing the image of a missile, I can’t help noting that the energy readings are somewhat like what you’d see from an underground base.”

His eyes widened. “Are you saying this planet might already have a colony?”

“Maybe. I don’t know.” She wiped the sweat from her forehead with the back of her hand. “Nothing makes sense anymore.”

“I’d assumed the missile was fired from another ship, but…” He gathered himself. “What if this planet has been serving as some sort of outpost for organized crime?”

“This is a *really* remote location. It’s no easy feat to get out this far from the core planets."

"Criminals have been operating in the fringes for decades—maybe longer. It's possible there's a base near here that no one outside the group knows about."

"Is that coming from your undercover experience or just general knowledge?"

"You learn all about the dark side of space-faring society when you grow up on a merchant ship. I've been hearing rumors about shadowy networks operating out in the fringes for as long as I can remember."

She pursed her lips in thought. "If this planet was claimed by some kind of crime group, they'd want it kept secret. And they'd want to defend it. I can see how we could have just gotten caught up in a bad way."

"It might not have been entirely coincidental. They could have operatives inside NovaTech."

Anya gaped at him. "Really?"

"Some of the organizations are extremely powerful—enough to rival the big corporations. The biggest difference is how much of their operations they're willing to share with the government."

"Honestly, I can see the appeal for going rogue."

Evan eyed her. "I'm surprised to hear that from you."

"Why? You think I'm a rigid rule-follower?"

"More than not."

She shrugged. "And it's because I abide by the rules that I understand how infuriatingly restrictive they can be at times. Not to mention, look where it got us! We go through years of planning and regulated checks, and our ship still crashed and left us stranded here. Coloring outside the lines is what's going to save us."

He smiled. "I like this side of you."

Anya grinned back. "You know, I do, too! Screw regulations, right? Just get the shit done!"

Evan laughed, catching himself to keep from being too loud. "Remind me never to get in between you and your objective."

"Good thing we're on the same side."

Their path through the trees intersected with a more defined animal trail heading in the correct direction, so they followed it. Glancing back where they'd come from, it looked like they might have been walking in parallel to it for a while.

"This organized crime angle is still only a guess," Evan said. "I don't want to assume anything about our opponents and find ourselves caught off-guard."

"Right." She nodded. "We need to be prepared for anything. It's so easy to get caught up in your own head."

"I know a lot about that," Evan admitted. "After the events that led me here, I'm prone to feeling betrayed and suspicious everywhere I look."

"I—" Anya cut off abruptly. "I think we're both looking for someone to blame," she said after a pause.

"Life tests us sometimes. I think this is one of those tests."

"I agree."

"And if I'm learning anything from the experience on Aethos, it's that we need to keep a level head and not jump to conclusions." Evan said it more for a reminder to himself than for Anya's benefit.

His time in the Noche Syndicate had unveiled a dark underbelly in society that had fundamentally changed his outlook. Corporate payoffs weren't unheard of, and he couldn't write off the possibility that there was a clandestine connection between players inside NovaTech and whatever crime organization could potentially be operating on Aethos.

Even one well-placed contact could have positioned the expedition as a target. However, until he knew for sure who might be involved, he didn't want to stoke the fire of suspicion in Anya's mind.

The truth was, they were facing an imperfect data set under terrible conditions. His training told him that they needed to take a breath, study the facts, and regroup. The priority was finding a safe place to review the rest of the flight log, and then they could make a more informed decision about what to do next.

Evan had just resolved to follow that approach when a print on the ground caught his eye. "Wait." He crouched down to get a closer look.

The indentations he'd noticed were too distinct to be natural remnants from the recent rain. They were tracks. Boot marks.

He met Anya's eyes. "This might not be just an animal path. Question is, was it survivors or the people who shot down the escort?"

Her face scrunched up, and she glanced in the direction of the crumbled skeleton of the ship. "You saw the state of the bodies in there. Do you really think anyone could have survived?"

"If someone was strapped in, maybe. But I do think it's more likely that these prints belong to whoever else might already be on this world."

"In that case, do you think these lead back to their base?"

The marks led into the thick brush, and much of the ground was covered in springy moss that hid all signs of travel. It was impossible to tell how many people may have passed by and when.

"Very possibly. Which brings us to a big decision. Do we

try to find out who it is? Or do we stick with the plan and go into hiding?" Logic told him that hiding was still the correct choice, but curiosity was threatening to override reason.

Anya took several seconds to respond. "If we hide, we could be hiding forever. There's an old saying about 'going down swinging', right?

"Yeah, there is." He was drawn in by the fire in her eyes. It filled him, as well. They'd been attacked, and he wanted to know why. Hiding would never get them answers. "Forget about the safe plan. Let's see where these prints lead."

21

"IS IT BAD that I'm feeling excited by danger?" Anya asked as she hiked through the lush trees with Evan.

"Probably, but I'm feeling it, too," he said with a smile next to her.

"I don't know who these guys are, but they're clearly awful. Only a bad person would attack colonists."

"Agreed."

All of the frustration and fear Anya had been trying to keep at bay for the past several days had been bubbling up inside her and coalescing into steaming anger. She'd been robbed of her future, and she wouldn't rest until she put a face to her enemy.

When she'd thought that the crash was an accident, she had been content to accept a life being marooned on Aethos, in whatever form that took. The place was beautiful, and she'd never run out of exotic plants and animals to study; really, she couldn't ask for more as a xenobiologist. But that was before she'd learned that her fate had been sealed by the selfish acts of rogues.

Whether it was pirates, or mercenaries, or whatever else they might call themselves, the fact remained that Anya and her people had been targeted, and she was pissed. There'd been a terrible, senseless loss of life, and now those who'd survived the initial assault would continue to suffer. The people behind that couldn't be allowed to continue operating unchecked.

She almost laughed out loud at the absurdity of her attitude. *Who am I? I couldn't even stand up to my boss when he saddled me with this assignment, let alone take on an interstellar crime network!*

Still, her anger had replaced fear, and she vastly preferred that feeling of empowerment over weakness. Maybe she'd be able to find the strength to transform her vengeful ambition into reality.

Before any plans could come to fruition, they first needed to track down the people responsible and get a read on their capabilities. Anya would have felt out of her depth to take on that task on her own, but covert data-gathering was Evan's specialty. She could handle the print-tracking and he could take over as soon as they acquired a target.

She smiled to herself. *I'm already thinking more like an investigator.*

The ground underfoot transitioned from muddy grass to moss. Anya stopped, unable to see any further tracks on the springy surface.

"Where's the trail?" Panic edged her tone. *We can't lose the lead now. We're so close!*

"It's got to pick up around here somewhere." Evan continued forward along the travel path they'd been following.

Anya took a steadying breath. Evan was right—the trail had to continue. All they needed to do was walk the perimeter of the mossy area and they'd invariably find prints somewhere on the other side.

While Evan searched straight ahead, Anya headed to the left where the trees were more open for a natural pathway.

Animals liked to take the least resistive route, so it would make sense that people would do the same.

After a couple minutes of searching, she came across a patch where the moss gave way to dirt with fine grass. The wet ground held several boot imprints leading further into the trees.

"Hey, we have a trail again!" Anya called out with an excited grin.

Evan bushwhacked his way to her location. "Nice work."

"Turns out people are a lot easier to track than tiny rabbits—at least when they aren't trying to hide their path."

"That's right, and we don't want to let them know we're here following them. The element of surprise is about the only thing we have going for us."

"Hey, we have wit and charm in spades. Don't sell our underdog duo short."

He smiled. "Forgive me."

"This time," she jested back.

Evan's smile abruptly dropped and he froze, listening while his eyes scanned the trees.

Anya immediately followed his example. She didn't see or hear anything but remained still all the same.

After a minute, Evan relaxed. "For a second there, I thought I heard voices."

"We may be getting close."

"We should limit the chatter from here on," he said quietly. "Not that I don't enjoy our conversations."

"Stealth before socializing. It will be my new motto."

Walking the talk—or lack thereof—they continued through the trees along the newly identified path. After another twenty minutes, the trees thinned into a meadow.

Evan motioned for Anya to slow down and step off the

sparse trail they'd been following. They continued forward, creeping behind trees and bushes for cover on their approach.

At the meadow's edge, with a clear line of sight across the open area, there were no signs of people present. The meadow would have been unremarkable were it not for a mound covered in a camo tarp.

"Oh, I really want to see what's under there," Anya whispered.

"Me too."

"Do you think it's safe to check it out? I don't see anyone."

Birds sang and insects hummed, but no voices carried on the warm breeze. If there was a guard, they were well-hidden and remaining silent.

"Let's check for security," Evan said. He located an arm-sized stick and hurled it into the center of the clearing. It soared through the air and landed with an audible *crack* as the rotted wood flaked apart.

Anya and Evan remained silent and motionless while they watched for a reaction. None came.

After two minutes, Evan stood up. "I'm going in. Wait here."

"Not this again. Let me go—same rationale as last time."

He hesitated.

"Don't fight it." Anya slinked from their hiding place and popped up into clear view four meters away.

She casually strolled into the meadow, wanting to appear unassuming in the event she *was* being watched. All the same, she was reassured by the weight of the newly acquired handgun scavenged from the ship now tucked into her waistband. Evan's thirty seconds of instruction wouldn't make her a good shot, but it was a wonderful confidence booster.

Anya stopped in the center of the meadow. "Hey, what's

this?" she asked loudly enough for anyone nearby to hear. Playing bait was pointless if she didn't draw out potential watchers.

When no one appeared, Anya tossed back one corner of the tarp. She was greeted by the sight of several mud-smeared crates with military markings. Most likely, they were materials salvaged from the crashed ship.

"I don't know who would leave this here, but they don't seem to be around now," Anya said loud enough for Evan.

He appeared out of the trees, in a completely different location than she'd left him. "But we have no way of knowing when they might be back." He assessed the pile from afar. "Wow, that's a lot of stuff."

"Either a dozen people or more carried all of this here, or someone took a lot of trips. We're about an hour from the crash site, right?"

"Something like that. It's too far for multiple trips. I think we're looking at a sizable group to have moved it."

"Not to mention, there weren't any footprints going in the opposite direction," Anya pointed out.

"And there's that. Which also means that either the people who brought this here arrived on the crashed ship, or they're taking a different route back to their base than the path they took there."

"In either case, why leave this *here*?"

— — —

Evan couldn't deny that finding a stash of supplies would be immensely helpful for their own long-term survival, but that was the problem—it was entirely *too* convenient that someone had left them out here in the open with very little disguise.

Either they'd walked into a trap, or their opponents were so confident in their position that they hadn't bothered taking any precautions. That level of hubris could only mean one thing.

"This isn't the work of pirates—they're all about secret stashes. A supply cache like this is military M.O., where it's easy to locate again. I think whoever brought it here crashed with the ship, and for whatever reason, they had to leave it behind."

"That would suggest a larger objective. Moving slowly is a worthwhile tradeoff for this many supplies."

"Unless there are extenuating circumstances, like you said." Evan could think of a dozen reasons off the top of his head where speed would be prioritized over ferrying additional supplies. The assumption would be that they could always come back for it. The tarp covering the items was for protection from the elements, not camouflage.

"I really wish we knew who'd fired that missile," Anya murmured.

"Me too." That was the most frustrating piece for Evan. He didn't know how many players they were dealing with, so trying to figure out motivations and actions was next to impossible.

He wanted to think that any surviving soldiers from the escort ship would help them and the other colonists, but that was the kind of assumption that would get someone killed. For all he knew, they could have been in on the scheme. After all, most of the people on the ship died; the fact that they survived was either dumb luck, or they knew to prepare for a rough crash. This could have been the plan.

Now who's the one letting conspiracy theories run wild? The truth was, he didn't know enough to draw any conclusions. He didn't even know enough to speculate.

"Do we stay here and wait for whoever left this stuff to come back for it, or do we press on?" Evan asked.

"What do you think?"

"I'm asking you," he countered. "Gut instinct—what's it telling you?"

"I don't think you want to know what I'm really thinking."

"I do, however crazy it may sound."

Anya sighed. "Okay. The conspiratorial thought that keeps running through my mind is, what if we weren't meant to survive the crash? We've been assuming that it was an accident that the colony ship was destroyed in the explosion, but what if that wasn't the case? What if it was targeted, too?"

He nodded faintly. "I haven't wanted to admit that possibility, but you may be right."

"I knew in my gut something reeked about this whole situation." She shook her head. "I've tried to rationalize it away or find alternatives, like the pirate theory, but I keep coming back to the entire expedition being a massive setup."

There were too many pieces for there to have not been some level of grand orchestration, Evan had to agree. He didn't want it to be the case, but he couldn't deny the mounting evidence that there was much more to this planet than it being an untouched world ready to house the next human settlement.

"Play out your theory," Evan said. "Say the expedition *was* a setup. Why?"

"I don't know... Maybe they were using the colonization as cover to get a military ship here for some other sort of exercise."

"Given that missile, there does appear to be a hostile force here. You may be onto something with that."

"The malfunctions on our colony ship were caused by

more than the cruiser's explosion. I still think there was some kind of sabotage that caused the botched evacuation. I feel like whoever was behind this didn't want *any* survivors, either military or civilian. Witnesses would be loose ends."

Evan looked at Anya. "Forget the naïve bravery from before. Hiding is our only option."

"Evan—"

"What else can I say, Anya? My best guess right now is that there's *something* on this planet that multiple factions want to control, and we somehow stepped into the middle of that power struggle. I don't know *who* those factions are, but they're the kind of people who have both the capability and willingness to blow up ships and indiscriminately kill thousands of people to accomplish their goals. Is that really who you want to go up against right now?"

"No, you're right."

He trusted her. As far as he could tell, she trusted him, too. However, that left them two people against the world—or, more likely, adversaries with ties all the way back to the core worlds. The more he thought about it, there was no way a military escort ship to a colony expedition would be destroyed without being a part of a much larger conspiracy.

I never should have agreed to go on this expedition. The exit plan had seemed like the best move at the time, with the Noche Syndicate on his trail. Now, though, they seemed like the least of his worries. *What in the planets did I stumble into?*

22

EVAN'S HEAD WAS spinning from the multiple shifts in direction. Questions about who and why still pestered the back of his mind, but his survival instinct had surged to the forefront. They were in over their heads, and holing up in a cave remained their best option.

Before they'd reach that safety, they still had days of travel through potential enemy territory.

Anya's demeanor had also darkened since their last conversation. Having finally shared with each other the thoughts that had seemed too outlandish to voice, it was alarming to realize that they shared the same suspicions. Either they were more alike than they'd realized, or the clues were truly too obvious to ignore.

The one reassurance amidst the uncertainty was that he was going through it with a friend. Going to hide alone in a cave would have been too bleak a thought to bear, but Anya would make for great company. Part of him was even happy about the prospect of setting up a camp with her and having the opportunity to grow closer.

"It would be super messed up if NovaTech were in on it," Anya commented while they walked.

"Call me cynical, but I wouldn't be that surprised."

"Really?"

"Sure. Lying to the public to gain power and profit is as old as human civilization."

"True." She sighed. "Some things never change."

"But also throughout history, there have been the brave souls who expose the corruption to make things better for their fellow citizens—even though those gains are often short-lived."

"Are you changing your mind again about us going to hide?"

"I never said we'd be the brave souls in this scenario."

"I still kinda want to be," Anya admitted.

He couldn't help admiring her thirst for uncovering the truth. He shared that passion, and it was easy to recognize their kindred spirits. "Staying alive is the priority. We can't help anyone if we're dead."

"Yeah, trying to do the right thing when you're out of your depth is a fool's errand. Been there, done that."

"What do you mean?" he asked.

"I can't talk about it."

What happened to being honest with each other? He cast her an accusatory sidelong glance. "Can't or won't?"

"NDA."

He held his arms wide. "Come on, you're worried about violating an NDA? Who am I going to tell? I trusted you and that bird with my secret. I promise, it'll stay between us."

She sighed. "Let's just say that I learned some less than savory things about my employer's business practices, and they found appropriate means to make sure we saw eye-to-eye about the issues."

"They paid you off to stay quiet?"

"I didn't say that." But there was confirmation in her eyes.

He nodded his understanding. "I'm guessing your concerns were of an ethical nature?"

"Everyone has topics that are near and dear to their heart."

"Was it related to this expedition?"

"No, it was years ago. But my career never fully recovered, and I'd blamed that incident for landing me on this assignment. Now, I'm not so sure."

"Tell me what happened."

"Seriously, I can't talk about it." Her eyes narrowed. "It's not like you've been completely forthcoming about your past, either."

"If I bare mine, will you do the same?"

"Why does it matter?"

"Because you worked for the very organization that may have royally screwed us over, and I suspect that there's some pretty damn critical information that you're keeping to yourself."

"It's not related."

He threw up his hands. "Fine, whatever! Keep your secrets and we'll die a slow death out here."

She smirked. "Dramatic much?"

I really thought we were getting somewhere. Maybe he'd overestimated her trust in him, after all. "I've got nothing left," he said. "This aimless 'investigation' of ours has gone nowhere. There might be pirates or mercenaries or worse stalking us. And the wildlife on this planet wants to kill us the first chance it gets. So, forgive me if I'm grasping at the smallest sliver of hope to understand what might be going on!"

"Fine." Her eyes narrowed. "Tell me, why did you decide to leave the military?"

"There were a lot of converging factors. My reup was shortly after the change in administration, and I didn't like the way the new policies were going."

Her demeanor softened. "Oh. Yeah, I think a lot of people preferred Chancellor Conroy." She shook her head. "Shame what happened to him."

"We pretend space travel is safe, but bad things happen."

Anya flourished her hands to encompass the surroundings. "Clearly."

"You know what I mean."

"I do. And they certainly took full advantage of that accident to lock everything down that only made life more difficult for most people."

Evan reflected on the dark days following the chancellor's shuttle crash. Conroy had been a beloved leader, and the accident was a reminder that even those in power weren't invincible. The following civil unrest and policy changes in reaction to the incident had changed the Commonwealth's culture in a way that hadn't yet recovered in the five years since. "I'm glad it didn't happen while my parents were still around. The new policies would have destroyed our little family business."

"I've heard about that happening. Sad."

He nodded. "Naturally, the tightening of legal restrictions led to a crime surge. Worked out for me, though I probably wouldn't have been able to go undercover as easily if they hadn't been ramping up their operations so much."

"And they probably wouldn't have needed you to go undercover in the first place without that increase in activity."

"True."

"Do you think they ever wrapped up your last case and brought them down?" Anya asked.

"I wish." Evan scoffed. "But realistically, there's no way to stop them now without collapsing the whole system. They'll bring in a few token people to prosecute here and there so they can claim they're being 'tough on crime', that'll all be for show."

"Ah, classic."

"One advantage to getting stuck here is that I don't have to deal with *that* anymore, so that's a plus."

"That sounds frustrating. And speaking of frustrations, I suppose there really isn't any reason to keep my past work situation from you."

He looked over at her. "I'm listening."

"Well, it started when—"

A bush to the left rustled, prompting them both to freeze.

Evan started to reach for his handgun when a firm, male voice stopped him.

"Don't even think about it. No reason to bring weapons into your domestic spat." A muscular, dark-skinned man wearing fatigues stepped out from the bushes. He had a rifle trained on Evan.

He was joined by three other men of similarly substantial build, each with weapons of their own pointed at Evan and Anya.

"How long have you been following us?" Evan asked.

"Long enough to tell you that whatever you think is going on here, you haven't begun to scratch the surface," the first man replied.

Evan glared at him. "Who are you?"

"My name isn't important."

"Because you're going to kill us?"

"That depends on you."

Evan scanned his surroundings for a possible escape. Four-on-two wasn't great odds, especially since the soldiers already had their weapons in hand. There was no way he'd be able to draw before they could pull their triggers, and there weren't many improvised weapon options handy.

Keep them talking. He took a calming breath.

"Let's slow this down and get to know each other," Evan said, holding up his hands. "How about we all put down our guns and have a chat?"

"I can be reasonable" the man said. "Set down your weapons slowly, and we'll do the same."

Evan and Anya each reached for their guns and set them down on the ground. As they lowered them, the soldiers set down their own rifles.

"Okay, that's better," Evan said, drawing on every part of his training to remain calm and charming when staring potential death in the face. "Let's start over. I'm Evan, and this is Anya."

"Last names?"

"Evan Taylor."

"Anya Rojas."

"Is that so?" The lead man studied them with what almost seemed like recognition in his dark eyes. "Well, you can call me Samor. You two are a long way from where the escape pods came down."

"And it's a long story of how we got here."

"Give me the highlights."

"We were hoping to find a working comm system on the escort ship to call for help," Anya chimed in. "But it was taken. Did you do that?"

"Our highlight reel is a lot longer than that."

"Care to share?" Evan asked.

"Nah, not my place."

"Then what's the plan here?"

"We're going to take you in," Samor said.

“Take us where?”

“That’s classified.”

Evan exchanged a glance with Anya. Terror filled her eyes. He shared her concern. *If we go with these men, we may never get out.*

This was their best opportunity to mount an escape, while the soldiers had their weapons down.

Evan dropped down to reach for his handgun. Samor was faster, sweeping the weapon away with his feet. But Evan was ready for the move. He instead curled his fingers around a stick. It would make a terrible weapon, but it was better than being empty-handed.

His heart pounding in his ears, he swung the stick upward, smacking Samor in his face.

“Gah, damn it!” the man exclaimed.

The other soldiers rushed in. Evan kicked at them, but one tackled his shoulders while the other grappled his legs. The third soldier grabbed Anya and pinned her arms behind her back.

Evan struggled against the men, to no avail. *Well, that didn’t work.*

Samor sneered down at him. “You don’t know when to give up, do you?”

Evan tasted blood. He ran his tongue over his lower lip and found that it had been split. “Can’t fault a guy for wanting to live.”

“We’re not here to kill you.”

“Sure.” He couldn’t believe anything these men said.

“I’m sure you have a lot of questions—like why your ship exploded.”

“It’s been on my mind.”

“There are powerful people who didn’t want settlers on

this planet," Samor revealed.

That wasn't what Evan had expected to hear from him. He paused his struggle against the soldiers' grip. "Why?"

"I'm not the right person to explain."

"Then who is?"

"That's who you're about to meet." Samor held up two dark cloth sacks.

Anya rolled her eyes. "A hood, really?"

"We're not going to hurt you, I promise. We had plenty of opportunities to shoot you, if that's what we wanted."

The soldiers released Evan, and Samor handed him a hood.

Evan took it but didn't put it on yet. "Where are you taking us?"

"You'll find out soon enough."

He looked over at Anya, who'd been handed the other hood. She nodded to him and slipped the fabric over her head.

"You know, we'd be able to walk a lot better if we could see," Evan pointed out.

Samor smiled. "Nice try. We'll make it work."

"It was worth a shot." Reluctantly, Evan slipped on the hood.

23

EVAN SQUINTED AGAINST the sting of sudden, harsh light. He sucked in the cool air, refreshing after the hot humidity inside the hood. Strangely, the air had the same crisp quality as the filtered environment of a spacecraft.

That's not possible. He strained to identify his surroundings and the people present.

He'd been tied to a chair in front of what he now realized was a metal table. Unless the furniture had been salvaged from the ship's wreckage, the objects shouldn't exist on this planet. But moreover, he was clearly inside a *room.*

He had no idea where he might be. His sense of direction had been completely shattered after walking for an hour through the jungle blindfolded. Initially, he'd tripped over himself without being able to see, but eventually, he'd learned to interpret the prods of the man guiding him so he could step over obstacles and navigate slopes.

His next surprise had come when they'd arrived at a vehicle. Evan couldn't tell how large it was, but it had seemed much more substantial than their little rover. At that point, noise-canceling earmuffs had been placed on his head, and he'd lost all orientation and sense of time. Now, sitting in what he could only assume was an interrogation room, he had no idea what to expect next.

"Who are you and what is this place?" Evan called out. He'd intended to sound firm and demanding, but his confusion softened his tone.

A metal door creaked open behind Evan and slammed shut, a deadbolt thudding into place. Slow footfalls approached, and a man with close-cropped dark hair and piercing blue eyes came into Evan's periphery. He wore a military jumpsuit similar to the soldiers that had captured Evan in the jungle, except this outfit included gold bands around his sleeves and a chevron insignia on his upper arm, identifying him as an officer.

The officer tossed a tablet down on the table. It displayed a document with numerous bullet points, and from the looks of it, it was only one page of many in the file.

"You have quite the history, Evan," the man said, sitting down in a metal chair across from him. "Or should I say 'Alex'?"

"How do you know that name?" Evan asked.

"We have our sources. Your face came back an indent match to multiple aliases. Alex's exploits are quite a read. Theft, extortion, fraud, black market dealings…" He let out a whistle through his teeth. "You're quite the criminal."

"I engaged in criminal activities, but I'm not a criminal," Evan corrected.

"That seems like a minor semantic difference."

"No, there's a big distinction. When I participated in all those things, I was working undercover."

"Who were you working for?" the man prompted.

"The Commonwealth. I was an investigator with the UPA."

The soldier pursed his lips in thought. "That does seem like the story Evan would tell. The problem is, I'm not sure which version of you is the real one."

"My cover was good, but if you have as much on me as you claim, you'll see that Alex and the others get fuzzy with the history more than five or ten years back. I'm Evan, even though I had to set myself aside for each of those ops."

"Why should I believe you?"

Evan scoffed. "That's really something coming from a man with a bunker on a supposedly unoccupied planet."

The officer evaluated him from across the table. "Why did you come here?"

"It wasn't by choice."

"Stowed away on the wrong ship?"

Evan glared at him. "I'll keep saying it until you get it through your thick skull: I'm not a criminal. I was assigned passage on the ship after my undercover alias was blown by rescuing Alven Shah—the Deputy of Economic Development."

The man's flippant demeanor turned serious in an instant. "What happened to Shah?"

"He was apparently captured by the Noche Syndicate, and I happened to walk in on them interrogating him. I broke cover to get him free. But helping him escape put a target on my back, so he made sure I could get far away by joining this expedition—a chance to start over."

"Are you saying that he personally arranged for you to be on the colony ship?"

"I don't know who handled the logistics, but he was the one to tell me about it."

The officer had grown distinctly uncomfortable. "I need to check on some things." He abruptly stood up and left.

What was that about? Evan was once again alone in the small room, still semi-blinded by the interrogation light.

He'd been through a training exercise once about what to do under those exact circumstances, but all of those techniques were fuzzy, distant notions. All he could think about now was how he was going to get out of the chair, and whether or not Anya was going through the same thing.

Evan continued to sit there for what felt like close to an hour. His back and shoulders were sore from having his hands bound behind him for so long, not to mention the lack of padding on the metal chair.

Finally, the door opened again. A figure stepped forward. Evan could only make out booted feet, everything higher still obscured by the blinding light directed at his eyes.

"Why aren't you with the other survivors?" a deep voice asked.

At this point, Evan saw no point in resisting. Being truthful would be his best hope of getting released from the chair. "Anya and I went looking for communications equipment to call for help."

"Thank you for cooperating. She wasn't very forthcoming when I spoke with her."

Evan's pulse spiked. "You'd better not have hurt her!"

"Oh, she's fine," the man said casually. "Our enemies are the only ones who need to worry."

"And who is your enemy?"

The man let out a gruff, humorless laugh. "Evan, I'm sorry to tell you that you've stumbled into the middle of a war."

He sat in confused shock for several seconds. "Pardon?"

"I'm truly sorry for this mess."

The light abruptly extinguished. As Evan's eyes adjusted, the speaker came into focus. The face was unmistakably familiar, except his presence made even less sense than everything else from the last several days.

"Chancellor Conroy?"

The gray-haired man nodded wearily. "Surprise! Yes, I'm still very much alive, contrary to the reports."

Evan worked his mouth, unsure how best to direct his shock. The man had been reported dead in a shuttle accident five years ago, but he was somehow alive on a supposedly unoccupied, remote planet. "Am I hallucinating?"

"No. And I can't imagine how crazy this must seem."

"How…?"

"Through a strange twist of fate, not unlike how you found yourself here."

"I'm going to need a lot more than that. How are you here? Clearly, you faked your death."

"Not exactly." Conroy's shoulders rounded and he stared into space. "There's a funny thing about power. When you get into a high enough position, you start to think of yourself as invincible. You're surrounded by staff who'll make you look good even when you mess up, and you're protected by guards who'd lay down their life for you without hesitation. But even with all those things, you can fail. And you can be hurt. As I came to understand the true reality of my position and what was unfolding around me, I realized that I'd have a lot more leverage as a ghost."

Evan took in the words, not understanding the deeper meaning of the statements. "Leverage to do what?"

Conroy sighed. "That's difficult to explain. The most concise way I can put it is that there was a coup. The current government was not legitimately elected, despite what the public believes."

"That…" Evan faded out, unsure what he could possibly

say in response to the bold claim. On its surface, the assertion was absurd. However, he was also on an alien planet talking to a man whom he'd spent the last five years believing was dead.

"You don't have to take my word for it," Conroy continued. "I'll show you."

The chancellor held up his hand. A soldier entered the room and released the bindings on Evan's wrists.

Evan massaged his hands. "Thank you. I'll hear you out, because there's frankly been too many weird coincidences for it to all be chance. But may I speak bluntly?"

Conroy inclined his head. "Please do."

"Why would you share information that sensitive with *me*—just a random guy who happened to be in the wrong place at the wrong time?"

"Was it random coincidence, though?"

Evan started to chuckle, but Conroy's gaze was intently serious. "I didn't make my own plans to join this colony expedition. It was given to me as an extraction plan. I don't know how those arrangements were made."

"And what if I were to tell you that many arrangements were made on behalf of the other passengers? There was no lottery for this expedition—not a genuine one, anyway. Everyone was selected to come here because that was the easiest way to get rid of two thousand people without there being too many questions."

"All right, we're going to need to back up, like, ten steps. What are you talking about?"

Conroy drew a slow breath and let it out. "Evan, Alven Shah was never captured by the Noche Syndicate. He was working for them."

Evan gaped at him. "What?"

"That meeting you saw—it wasn't a kidnapping

interrogation or anything like that. It was a planned meeting, and you disrupted the whole operation when you broke cover to 'rescue' him. But he couldn't very well tell you that without exposing himself as a traitor, so he had to play along. And he wanted to make for damned sure that you didn't put the pieces together after the fact and expose him, so he sent you away on a doomed mission with all the other people who knew too much from their various roles in the master plan. Just another poor soul caught up as collateral damage."

Not for the first time that day, Evan found himself floating as his sense of reality dropped out from beneath him. "I don't understand."

Conroy stood up. "As I said, I'll explain everything. Why don't you get cleaned up, and then we can have a proper chat."

24

FOR SOME REASON, Anya was more nervous stepping into the tiny residential quarters than she had been in the interrogation room. Part of it was that she was now only wearing an ill-fitting jumpsuit with nothing underneath—with the promise of her clothes being laundered while she bathed. It didn't help matters that she hadn't seen Evan since they'd been blindfolded and transported to wherever this place was. And it really didn't set her at ease to discover that the former leader of the Commonwealth, whom she'd spent the last five years thinking was dead, was, in fact, alive.

The revelations were too much to take in all at once, and she was still missing critical details. Those were actually ideal conditions for taking a refreshing shower to wash away some of the drama from the last several days. She had a feeling, though, that everything was about to get way crazier.

She found a compact washroom at the back of the quarters, equipped with a sink, shower, and toilet. Using proper indoor facilities to relieve herself was an unexpected delight after roughing it since the crash. But the shower that followed proved to be one of the most satisfying in her life. To her disgust, the water runoff started off cloudy and brown; it was no wonder they'd sent her to bathe before sitting down for a debrief.

With her skin clean, she also got her first good look in the past half-day at the wound on her forearm from the vine. It was still a little red and tender, but it had scabbed over and appeared to be healing well.

A second jumpsuit was hung on the back of the bathroom door, and she put it on. There were no electronics anywhere, so she sat down on the lower bunk to wait.

Within five minutes, there was a knock at the door.

Anya tried the handle, only to concerningly find it locked. "Come in," she called out.

The door unbolted and swung inward. A middle-aged female soldier stood in the hall, holding a nicely stacked pile of Anya's formerly soiled clothes. She also had Anya's backpack slung over one shoulder. "Here are your things," she said with a warm smile.

"Thanks." Anya took the clothes first and set them on the bed, then took the pack. Somehow, despite having less equipment inside, it was still heavier than she remembered. *I really walked all that way with this?* Her heart swelled with pride in herself.

"Would you like to change?"

Considering she was still wearing no undergarments, that was an easy answer. "Yes, that would be great."

"All right. I'll wait here for you, and then I'll take you to meet with the chancellor."

Anya closed the door and quickly got dressed back in her own clothes. Before letting the soldier know she was ready, though, she checked through her bag to see if anything was missing. Annoyingly, her bioanalyzer was gone, as was the handgun she'd acquired from the crashed ship—no surprise there. Swallowing her frustration, she called out to the guard. "Okay, ready."

The soldier escorted Anya from the quarters and along a series of metal corridors. Even without a blindfold this time, she quickly lost all sense of orientation.

Coming around a corner, the tension went out of Anya's shoulders when she saw Evan approaching with his own escort. His hair was still slightly damp, and his clothes had been laundered, like hers. She smiled. "Evan, it's good to see you."

"Likewise. You okay?" Genuine concern filled his eyes.

"Yeah. My head is still spinning."

"You aren't alone in that."

Everything Anya had seen and been told since being captured in the jungle had left her with more questions than answers. None of it made any sense and just seemed like a surreal dream—or, more accurately, a waking nightmare. Not only were her outlandish suspicions of an interstellar conspiracy unfolding before her eyes, but the depth of that web was shaping up to be far more complex and ran deeper than she could have ever imagined.

"Conroy said he'd explain everything once we got cleaned up. I intend to hold him to that," Evan said.

"Good. Let's go get the grand tour and find out what in the planets is going on here."

The two soldiers continued leading Anya and Evan down the corridor. They stepped through a large hatch, where they found Chancellor Conroy was waiting for them.

Conroy beamed and gave them a little wave. The old man had a more casual demeanor than Anya would have expected from a former statesman, but perhaps that had come from his time in hiding. "Good. Now that you've been able to get cleaned up and are reunited, I hope you'll see that I mean you no harm," he said.

That's exactly how someone who wanted us to let our guard down would act. Anya gave him a polite nod. "Feeling much better, thank you."

"Now, if you don't mind, I have questions of my own," Evan stated.

"And I will answer what I can, in time. First, there are a few matters I'd like to go over with both of you, as that information will no doubt change the conversation."

Evan crossed his arms. "Meaning, you want to find out what we know before deciding how much to share?"

"I shouldn't be surprised that someone with your background knows exactly how this works. So, you'll also know that the more honest you can be with me, the easier this will be for all of us."

Evan bristled. "We're not here to cause trouble."

Conroy shook his head. "That's not what I meant. I'm hoping for your help."

"*Our* help?" Anya asked incredulously. They weren't in a position to offer much. "What can we do?"

"Hopefully, solve a mystery."

"What kind of mystery?"

"The sort with the potential to change everything."

His grand, vague statements were grating on her nerves. "Before getting into that, we need to talk about the other colony ship survivors," Anya said.

Conroy looked over at her as he guided them down the hallway. "I respect that you're thinking of them even now."

"Well, our goal from the start was to help as many people live as possible. If you've survived for five years out here, then you must have decent resources. At least, you don't look like you're sick or starving."

"We've done well enough. We have already offered aid to the other members of your group, not to worry. They mentioned that you two had gone to scout out the crashed escort ship, which is how we found you."

"Are they getting the same offer about helping to solve the mystery?" Evan asked.

"No. Because none of them are pilots who worked for the Noche Syndicate."

Evan blinked at the former Chancellor with confusion. "What does that have to do with anything?"

"Because, Evan, we are currently trapped on this world. And we may have one, singular way off the planet, and I'm hoping that the two people who were resourceful enough to make it this far against incredible odds will have the skills and fortitude to pull off the impossible."

Anya's mouth went dry. "With all due respect, Chancellor, you must have way more qualified people here with you. Speaking for myself, anyway," she hastily added. "Evan has a much broader skillset than mine. Unless you need plants analyzed—and assuming you'd give me my equipment back."

He smiled at her. "If the first part is successful, you'll have a lot more than just plants to study."

"What do you mean?" Anya asked.

"One thing at a time."

"Well, I hope the explaining starts soon, because right now I'm hearing a lot of promises for answers without any delivery," Evan grumbled.

Anya gave him an appreciative nod. She shared his frustration and was antsy to understand the specifics of their new circumstances.

"I'm getting to that." Conroy led them a little further down the hall to a thick metal door with a spinning locking wheel. It resembled a pressure hatch on a military starship.

"Hey, how did you build this place?" Evan asked, eyeing it.

Conroy smiled. "We disassembled our ship and basically reconstructed it under ground."

Anya gaped at him. "That's a *huge* undertaking."

"It was, but we didn't have a lot of choice. We needed to hide the ship, and we needed somewhere secure to live. We had heavy equipment to help—it's not like we were digging with hand shovels."

"Still."

Conroy shrugged. "You do what you must to survive." He gripped the locking wheel and gave it a firm spin. The bolt unlocked with a clang.

The heavy door swung open to reveal the repurposed interior of the former ship's Command Center. An illuminated table served as the centerpiece, and a dozen workers were positioned at various stations around the room.

Anya recognized a dark-skinned man standing next to the table as the soldier who'd captured—or rescued—them in the jungle. She hadn't decided yet if it was a good thing they'd been brought here. Samor, she recalled his name being, had a purple-red mark on his forehead where Evan had gotten in a whack with a stick.

Evan evaluated the man from across the room. "Hello again. Sorry about the…" He pointed to his own temple and then Samor's.

"No hard feelings." Samor stepped around a table in the center of the room. "Sir." He inclined his head deferentially to Conroy.

Only then did Anya realize that she'd been speaking with a former chancellor and hadn't once used any kind of honorific. Her cheeks burned, recognizing her oversight.

"Now, you're probably wondering what happened to your colony ship," the chancellor said before Anya could correct her mistake.

Evan fixed him in a level gaze. "We saw a missile on the flight recorder."

Conroy nodded. "I know what you're probably thinking."

"And?"

"You're right. It was ours."

Anya shifted on her feet. *Did he just readily admit to murdering all of those people?*

Evan asked the next pressing question. "Why?"

Conroy released a long breath. "That's part of a much larger discussion, but the short answer is that they were here to kill me and every one of my people, so proactive defense was our only option."

"The colonists did nothing wrong!" Anya exclaimed, finding her voice.

"No, and we had nothing to do with the destruction of the colony ship. Your escort took care of that."

Evan's brows knitted. "Wait, what?"

"The escort ship fired on the colony ship's propulsion. The ship was going down regardless of our actions."

Anya worked her mouth, struggling to find the right words. "Why would the military escort shoot down the colony ship it was sent to protect?"

Conroy winced. "I know this is difficult to hear. The truth is, the entire expedition was pretense to launch a military assault on this world. Everyone on that ship was selected because they had a hand in a much larger plan, and the powers that be didn't want to risk the wrong person putting together the pieces. We knew it was always the intention for the colony ship and its passengers to be a sacrifice in service to greater ambitions, but we'd never dreamed they'd destroy the ship while it was still in orbit."

The air may as well have gone out of the room. Anya gripped the table to steady herself. "Who would do something so awful?"

"The current leaders. The same people who tried to have me killed." Conroy's face darkened. "We'd been waiting to fire on the escort until it was farther away from the colony ship. I will forever regret not taking action the moment the warship arrived."

"Some of your people were on board the colony ship?" Evan asked.

The chancellor nodded. "Several dozen, whom I'd been counting on to help us through the next phase of our plans. They were bringing the supplies and materials we sorely need. All of that was lost in the explosion."

"The other survivors from our camp... None of them?"

"Unwitting bystanders."

"Like me," Anya said, looking down.

"This was supposed to have been our chance to resupply and bring more people to our cause. It's a rare moment when your interests align with your enemy's, but this expedition was one of those instances. We'd wanted the colony ship to bring us supplies and personnel, and the opposition wanted an excuse to deploy a warship to wipe us out. We each almost got what we wanted, but we destroyed each other instead." His face twisted into a pained grimace.

"I'm sorry you lost your friends, but why are Anya and I getting special treatment?" Evan asked.

"Because our mission hasn't changed. Of those who survived the crash, you are our best opportunity to get back on track."

"Sir, I don't mean to be flippant, but I'm exhausted and feel like my sense of reality has shattered. So can you stop talking in riddles and just tell us what in the planets is going on?" Evan demanded.

Samor went rigid, and several of the other workers around the room glanced over their shoulders at Evan. Everything grew quieter in the sudden tension of the moment. Anya braced for a tongue-lashing.

However, Conroy tilted his head and raised an eyebrow. "I'm not used to people speaking to me so bluntly, but I have to say it's rather refreshing."

Anya relaxed. "It's been a trying few days, sir. We can't help being on edge."

The chancellor nodded. "This is a leap of faith on both our parts. You have no reason to trust me, nor I you. Frankly, you were not my first choice to bring into the fold, but you're who I have. So, let me show you what all those people died to protect, and maybe then you'll understand why it's important enough that it could change the entire face of our civilization." He turned his focus to the tabletop. After he made a few inputs, a holographic display illuminated in midair. It appeared to be a topographical map of the region. "Do you recognize this location, Anya?" he asked, indicating a valley toward the center of the image.

Anya manipulated the projection with her hand to examine it from another angle. "Maybe. I'm not sure."

"All of our surveys point to that site, and your research independently corroborated it as a location of interest."

"How do you know what I was researching?" Anya asked.

Conroy raised an eyebrow. "What, you don't think we haven't been keeping tabs on what's happening back in the core worlds?"

Evan's green eyes brightened. "You have interstellar comms?"

"We have a lot more than that. There are those still loyal to me in key strategic positions. And all of their information confirmed that this site is the best lead we have."

"Lead for what?" Evan asked.

Samor let out a slow breath. "An express shuttle to crazy-town." He caught himself and shot an apologetic look at the chancellor. "Sir."

The older man smiled. "No, that's a fair characterization. Let me get them up to speed."

Samor bobbed his head and went over to another station, leaving the three of them at the holographic display.

Conroy spread his hands on the tabletop and leaned forward. "We had reasons for selecting this planet to be our place of exile, and what we hope we've located will justify every action we've taken. When this planet was originally surveyed, they found some… anomalies—energy readings where there shouldn't be any."

Anya's eyes widened. "I'd seen that, too. We'd written it off as natural, but then I figured it was you—this base—here, as soon as I learned about this place."

"No, these anomalies predate our arrival."

Anya and Evan exchanged glances. "What are they, then?" Anya asked.

"Research was conducted separately from an investigation my administration undertook seven years ago. We had reason to believe that this planet was originally colonized by non-human intelligent beings."

"Sentient aliens?" Anya couldn't keep the skepticism out of her tone. Though there was plenty of *life* on numerous planets, that wasn't the same thing. Sure, humans had been talking about intelligent extraterrestrial life since before venturing into the stars many centuries before, but there'd yet to be any close encounters with another sentient species.

"We'd come across old inscriptions pointing to this world—and, specifically, that it held ancient, powerful technology."

"And you think that location on the map is where it's hidden?" Evan asked, sounding equally skeptical.

"We believe it is one piece in a large, complex puzzle we've been trying to solve for years," Conroy replied. "I could use your help putting those pieces together."

"I'm not sure I'm qualified to go on an alien treasure hunt," Evan said, echoing Anya's inner thoughts on the subject.

"You made it this far," Conroy countered, "which means you can navigate the jungle out there. My team has been here for years and still has difficulty. But, Evan, your unique background is what we need now."

Evan seemed caught off-guard. "How do you know so much about me?"

Anya took a step back from the table and crossed her arms. She looked at Conroy expectantly. She'd been wondering about the background research, herself, since she'd first had a detailed file about her own professional and personal history presented in the interrogation room an hour prior.

"We've been listening to everything back in the core worlds," Conroy revealed. "Well, not *everything*, obviously—but the important things. You might not have realized it, but the last case you were working on was connected to a much larger conspiracy."

"That case doesn't matter anymore. I was burned. Coming here was supposed to be my retirement in the pasture."

"No, that case was everything. They'd sent you here to get

you out of the way. When one of my insiders back home first told me you were unexpectedly on board the colony ship as a last-minute addition, we weren't sure what to think—if you could be a potential ally. But all of our plans were interrupted when we discovered that the military escort ship had been compromised. We sent a warning to one of our people on your colony ship, but clearly they didn't have a chance to act on that message."

Anya exchanged another glance with Evan. "Was one of your contacts the expedition liaison?" she asked Conroy.

"Yes, why?"

"We found him in an escape pod—shot," Evan revealed.

Conroy hung his head and shook it slowly. "If he was murdered over that information, it's probably because he moved it up the command chain."

"Which means someone even higher up was in on it," Evan said.

Conroy nodded solemnly. "We have a manifest of the colony ship's crew. It's a short list for who he might have told about our warning. And, whoever it is, I suspect was one of the first to escape in a pod."

"Could the killer be one of the survivors in our group?" Evan asked.

"More likely, they went to meet up with the saboteurs from the military ship. Finding me is their primary mission."

"What about the surviving colonists at our camp?" Anya questioned.

"We sent a team days ago. Your people are now safe at one of our outposts," Conroy replied. "We saw the pods come down, and a signal fire led us right to them. You'd left already by the time our envoy arrived, and we'd been trying to find you since then."

If we'd only stayed put... Anya couldn't help second-guessing every decision she'd made up to that point. Though they'd had no way of knowing that there were already other people on the planet, the benefit of hindsight had a way of making smart choices feel wrong.

"You still haven't explained why you wanted to recruit *me*?" Evan said. "What does my undercover work with the Noche Syndicate have to do with anything?"

Conroy smiled. "Because one of the things we lost in the crash was an important sample, but you already have that very substance in your blood. You, Evan, can give us a chance to recover from this terrible setback before the enemy finds us."

25

THE PLANET'S GRAVITY was wrong. Roman Santano couldn't pinpoint *what* was wrong, exactly, but it'd taken less than a week for him to decide that he couldn't stand anything about Aethos. Given that general disdain, it wasn't surprising that he'd detest something as fundamental as its perfectly normal gravitational pull, too.

He let his rifle hang on its shoulder straps so he could use both hands to swat at a particularly persistent bug dive-bombing his face. "Anything?" he asked his scouting partner, Sten.

The other man wiped sweat from his flushed forehead with the back of his gloved hand. The red in his face made his white-blond hair and brows seem even paler. "No. We may as well be trying to find a grain of sugar in a pile of salt."

Locating people on a planet should be easier than that. People left an imprint. "There are clues somewhere," Roman said. "We just have to look at this the right way."

They knew their quarry was buried somewhere on the planet—somewhere close, from what the remote surveys had determined. Regretfully, their long-range survey equipment had been destroyed in the crash, so they only had vague directions indicating a handful of different search areas. While not an insurmountable effort, manually searching still meant time and labor that would be better spent tracking down and destroying the traitors who'd caused this mess.

He'd been pretending to straddle both sides for so long that it felt like a lie to be his real self. When he'd slipped away in an escape pod while the colonists on the ship panicked, he'd been able to shed the façade he'd kept up for over a year. Pretending to be an officer excited about helping people start a new life on the planet had been exhausting, knowing every one of those poor saps was going to die. Shooting the meddlesome liaison had been a cathartic release of his pent-up annoyance. At least they were finally through that stage and he could focus on the real work.

Since landing, Roman had been put in charge of tracking down the alien ruins. A second team from the military ship had been tasked with tracking down the disgraced chancellor who'd previously fled to the planet after faking his death. The Syndicate had been working for years to get operatives into the necessary positions to make their move, and both teams would need to be successful in order for the larger plan to come to fruition.

The humidity of Aethos' too thick air added even more pressure to Roman's chest. Not only was this mission critical to the larger plans for the Noche Syndicate, but it was also an opportunity to finally step out from his brother's shadow to stand on his own. A stumble now would be an unthinkable setback.

He really couldn't be off to a much worse start. They'd been wandering around for days now and had absolutely nothing to show for it.

"How much longer are we going to keep at this?" Sten

asked as he smacked an insect on his forearm.

"As long as it takes."

"Which will be forever if we keep aimlessly wandering," Sten insisted. "We need a better plan."

He's acting like that approach was my idea. I should have never agreed. Roman sighed. "The search area didn't seem this large when looking at it on the map."

"Yeah, geography is funny like that."

The comment sent a wave of heat through Roman's core. He let out a long, deliberate breath through his nose to release his annoyance. Even the little things were grating on his nerves. He didn't want to be here, and that was coloring his perception of everything.

Marcus better keep his promise. Roman regretted not standing up to his brother when he'd directed him to go to Aethos. He'd let Marcus get into his head by believing that he was here as a trusted insider to ensure that the job was done right. But the more time he spent on Aethos and realized what was really going on, he'd come to the conclusion that Marcus had just wanted him out of the way. The big moves would all happen back in the core worlds, regardless of how things shook out here. He'd fallen in line, just like Marcus had planned. But after what they'd been through, he owed Marcus that much.

Thinking about his brother sent another surge of annoyance through Roman. He wiped his nose and sniffed loudly to cover his frustration. "A plan. Right."

They'd been following a grid search pattern of the jungle, using past survey data to prioritize the zones with identified 'areas of interest'. However, the energy readings that had been observed in the original survey had not been replicated since they'd landed on the planet. Roman didn't know what that meant for their chances of success, but it was clear that they'd need to change tactics.

"I think we've been looking at this all wrong," Roman said, an idea forming. "We approached it knowing what we know. But the people here on Aethos don't have our perspective. They shot down the ship, so they'd want to verify their kill. We were so anxious to start the search that we didn't stop to think about how we could use them to our advantage."

"What are you saying?"

"That our ship crashing is the most significant thing to happen on this planet in half a decade, and there's no way that they wouldn't have gone to scope it out."

Sten caught on. "So, if we can locate their trail around the ship, we can follow it back to their base and find out what they know about the alien ruins."

"Precisely."

Sten gazed out into the trees. "It's not far from here."

"We're as close as we're going to get within the search grid. I figure it's worth a detour to scope it out rather than continuing to wander around here hoping to stumble upon an ancient alien shipwreck."

"The other team won't like us snooping around."

"I don't care. Besides, they're probably long gone—and I doubt they had this same idea to wait for the enemy to come to them. If this strategy works, just think of what it would do for our standing if we locate Conroy's base first! And if anyone knows where to find the alien ruins, it's them. Stars know they had to have been doing *something* productive while on this planet for all those years."

"You might be giving them too much credit."

Roman sniffed and wiped his running nose. "Probably, but I'll take the risk if it means we can get ahead."

Sten considered the suggestion for a long moment. "All

right, let's do it."

The two men set a brisk pace through the trees. After days of wandering, they'd gotten efficient picking the path of least resistance through the foliage. But when the plants got too thick, he didn't hesitate to use the machete hanging from his belt.

They made good time on the hike. Roman tracked their progress using a map on his wrist communicator, heading to the destination of the military ship's emergency beacon he'd noted before the other team had disabled the signal. The escort ship had managed to launch a navigational satellite before it was shot down, which was the only way to cut through the electromagnetic interference that made most systems unreliable—yet another strike against the planet. He was fortunate to have the satellite's access credentials; it may as well not exist otherwise.

Regrettably, the colony ship and its escort had been destroyed before they'd gotten to the stage of their plan to eliminate Conroy's own interstellar comm system. The intention had been for the Noche Syndicate to be the single entity controlling messaging on and off the planet. That was still achievable, but now they'd need to eliminate the ground-level units instead of the satellite.

We've had setbacks, but the mission isn't lost, he reminded himself.

While his navigational map was a great start, Roman would be a lot happier if they also had a shuttle or some other form of transportation. Slogging through the jungle was so inefficient and primitive.

He wiped another drip from his nose. Something in the air of the confounded planet had kicked his sinuses into overdrive. The sooner they completed their mission, the faster he'd be back in civilization with filtered air and environmental controls.

Sten swatted at his arm. "These damn bugs. They won't stop!"

"Everything on this planet either wants to kill me or I want to kill it."

"This is why humans went to live in space."

"Believe me, I can't wait to get back."

Like many kids, Roman had spent part of his childhood on an orbital station and other times planetside. The station years had been his favorite, by far. But his previous time spent on-world had been nothing like this. He'd been in cities, surrounded by shops and restaurants and transportation. All things that he enjoyed having easily in reach.

Were it not for the critical importance of this mission, he'd have left the bushwhacking to others and stayed in the core worlds where civilized people spent their days. Anyone who'd willingly spend their time in this sort of primitive environment was clearly deranged. But the inhospitable nature of the world was also what made it a perfect hiding place.

The tracker on Roman's wrist beeped, indicating that they were within fifty meters of the target. He and Sten crept up to the tree line around where the forest had been flattened and burned around the crashed ship.

"Wow, they came down hard," Sten commented.

"They're lucky they didn't end up vaporized at the bottom of a crater after that kind of landing." That would have thrown a massive wrench in their plans. As it was, they were already onto the contingency actions, but there were still ways to salvage the operation. "Let's try to find a trail."

They made a slow sweep of the crash site's perimeter, keeping watch for footprints or broken branches that might indicate someone passed by.

After twenty minutes of searching, Sten called out. "Hey, Roman, I've got something!" Sten waved him over to where he was crouched down, inspecting the ground.

Roman went over to him. There were several overlapping footprints exposed on a patch of dirt. The surrounding grass had returned to upright, so the prints were a few hours old, at least. "Those definitely aren't ours. This is what we were hoping to find."

"Should we tell the others?" Sten asked.

Roman hesitated. The prints may well lead back to Conroy's stronghold, which would make them heroes if they found it. Conversely, following these prints now took them away from their primary objective of securing the most critical alien artifact. If the trail was a dead end, it'd be difficult to recover from the setback.

Is a delay worth it?

One simple fact drove him onward: If they could gain access to Conroy's search records, it would make his team's work that much easier—not to mention that if they killed Conroy and his people now, then they wouldn't need to constantly be looking over their shoulders while retrieving the alien tech.

"Not yet. Let's follow the trail and see what we find," Roman told Sten with a nod. He set off to find his redemption.

26

WHAT MISSING PIECE could Evan have? Anya wondered as she looked between the former chancellor and her new friend.

Evan was glowering at Conroy. "I'm not special."

"That's relative."

"No," Evan shook his head, "you don't find two random people wandering in the jungle and then name them the center of your interstellar political plot."

The chancellor remained calm and measured. "Finding you in the jungle wasn't how we wanted this to go. We never dreamed they'd destroy the colony ship, killing all of our people and destroying our supplies. And we definitely didn't expect you to wander away from the other survivors. We've been adapting our plan at every stage, so here we are."

"You know, it doesn't matter." Evan held up his hands. "I didn't sign up for this."

Anya met his gaze. "Evan, I think we should hear him out." Her insistence surprised her. Part of it was curiosity, but she also remembered looking at those original planetary surveys. She'd wondered about how something like that could exist naturally, and it was now looking like it *wasn't* possible. *Could those energy signatures really be signs of alien tech?*

Evan scowled. "All I wanted to do was to get help so the other survivors didn't die a slow, horrible death in the jungle. Since it sounds like you're already taking care of them, I'm done." He turned and walked back toward the door.

"Evan!" Anya ran after him. She gripped his arm and pulled him aside to an unoccupied corner of the room.

"Please, don't fight me on this," he said, barely above a whisper.

"We haven't even heard close to the whole story. How can you walk away now?"

"Because how am I supposed to believe a single word he says? Don't forget, the man was teetering on the edge of public disgrace before his alleged death. All of this is absolutely insane."

"I know, it really does sound crazy. But I don't know." She crossed her arms. "There's something about all this that feels… real. More real than anything else I've heard recently. I can't explain it, it's just a feeling."

Some of his bluster faded. "What makes you believe that any of this is legit?"

"I can't speak to all of it, but I know those energy readings are real, if nothing else. I've seen enough weird stuff that I want to know more."

He sighed. "I came to a whole new star system, and they still find a way to put me to work."

She smiled and placed her hand on his arm. "Why don't we give him half an hour? If you're still not on board, I'll walk out of here with you."

Competing impulses warred within her. If Evan was convinced, there was a strong chance she would be, too. Though they'd only been traveling together for a short time, Evan had proven himself to be virtuous and well-reasoned in his decisions. If he determined that Conroy's mission was worth undertaking, then that was a journey she'd gladly take with him. But by then, they'd be committed. Walking away now might be the only hope to break free.

But I want to see this through, she realized. *I've always known there was something different about this world. I didn't let myself see it back then, but now I want to know the whole story.*

"Half an hour," Evan yielded, to her relief.

"Okay," she nudged him back toward the holotable, "let's find out what's really going on."

— — —

"All right," Evan said to Conroy, "no more evasion. Why is this alleged alien tech so damned important?" Beyond the obvious fascination factor of finding proof of intelligent alien life, he didn't see how that connected to the larger political situation Conroy had mentioned, let alone the dealings of an interstellar crime ring. *If they're willing to kill for it, there has to be more going on.*

Chancellor Conroy tilted his head thoughtfully. "Let me ask you, Evan—and I promise this relates to your question—what's been the greatest limitation for the development of our civilization?"

"Resources to support everyone, I guess?"

"Not exactly," Conroy replied. "Resources are a part of it—but not in the sense that there's a limit, but rather getting them where and when they are needed."

"Same thing."

"But it's not. We have plentiful production abilities, but transportation is the hangup. The transit time between worlds.

We are limited by the capacity and placement of our jump gates."

"Okay. What about it?"

"Imagine the economic impact of near-instantaneous travel to anywhere."

Evan raised an eyebrow, unable to hide his skepticism of the outlandish concept. "It would change everything. A limited group in possession of that technology would dominate. But if everyone had it, the current system would collapse."

"Precisely. Which is why those in power could never let it come to light."

"That's all hypothetical, though… right?"

Conroy cracked a smile. "That's what we're here to find out."

Evan crossed his arms. "You're still avoiding the heart of the issue. Please stop dancing around whatever it is."

"All right." Conroy nodded. "We found clues pointing to an alien shipwreck on this planet, and we have reason to believe that it has a jump drive that our engineers back home might be able to reverse-engineer."

Anya gaped at him. "So, that 'alien presence' you hinted at before isn't ancient city ruins or whatever. It's a ship?"

"There may be much more. We don't know for sure. It's possible this planet was some kind of outpost."

"Any clues about where the alien race is from?" Anya asked, excitement filling her eyes. No doubt, alien life was a topic of great interest for a xenobiologist.

"No," Conroy replied. "But if we get that ship…"

Evan saw where the suggestion was leading, and he didn't like it one bit. "That could open up trade… or war."

"Two very different but very real possible paths. Which direction it goes may come down to who controls the technology and is directing the exploration."

Evan studied the man. "You want to be the one to lead it. Your big return to the political stage—offering something too monumental for anyone to deny your leadership claim." He'd witnessed the kind of ambition he now saw in Conroy's eyes, and it never ended well.

"This isn't about me reclaiming power. It's about stopping the people who would use this technology to terrible ends."

"What makes you think the current administration would mishandle it like that?"

"Because they were willing to kill me to keep it secret. When I first learned that the alien tech might exist, I proposed researching it in the open, for the betterment of all. The opposition decided that keeping that discovery confined to an inner circle was worth eliminating me. When their fabricated smear campaign failed to remove me as a political obstacle, they took more drastic action."

Evan wasn't sure he could take Conroy's word for it. After all, he was one man presenting his own perspective. Regardless of the following he'd seemed to garner, there were still a lot of unknowns. To align himself with Conroy would no doubt place a target on Evan's own back—assuming anything he'd been told was true. That wasn't a situation he wanted to sign up for without serious consideration.

"I'm going to need more to go on," Evan said after a pause. "How is the Noche Syndicate involved?"

"They have been covertly working with the current government administration and NovaTech, but I'm not at liberty to disclose all of the details at this time."

Evan's eyes narrowed. "Then I'm not the person to help you with whatever it is you want to accomplish. I'm done being a pawn for other people, blindly following orders without understanding the bigger picture. I didn't like how that ended last time, and I'm not about to make that mistake again."

"We're angry with the same people, Evan. This is a chance to reclaim everything that was taken from you."

"At this point, I don't want it. What life would I even be getting back? I've been someone else for longer than I've been myself." It was difficult for him to admit, but saying it out loud acknowledged a deep loneliness he'd tried hard to ignore.

"Then consider this an opportunity to make whatever life you want, *wherever* you want," Conroy said. "Is Aethos honestly where you want to spend the rest of your life?"

Evan let out a long breath. "No, this wouldn't be my first pick. Being able to go outside without having something trying to kill me would be nice."

"Leaving hadn't seemed like an option before now," Anya chimed in. "Are you saying that you intend to fly the alien ship out of here?"

"It's a scenario we've considered," Conroy said. "The feasibility is yet to be determined."

Evan scoffed at the absurd suggestion. Were they in almost any other circumstance, he would have walked away again, and this time never come back. However, the fact remained that they were trapped on this alien world. They *could* try running and hiding, but wars had a way of finding reluctant participants all the same. In all likelihood, he'd eventually have to pick a side. He may as well hear this one's sales pitch. "What's your plan?"

"First, we need to get the ship," Conroy continued. "There's no telling what state it might be in, assuming it does exist."

"All right, so, if I understand you correctly, you want the two of us," Anya motioned to Evan and herself, "to track down a ship that all of your people have been unable to find in the last five years?" She raised an eyebrow.

"You have something we don't."

"Which is?" Evan asked.

"A primer." Conroy hesitated. "The Noche Syndicate has been dealing with other pieces of alien tech for a couple of decades now. That's what enabled them to rise to power so quickly. And they discovered that the tech is genetically keyed. They developed a serum to enable compatibility with humans—something they only give to their trusted inside people."

Evan's eyes went wide. *No. No way!*

The skepticism that he'd been fighting faltered. He itched everywhere, thinking about what may actually have been in the shot he'd been given two years into his undercover assignment. "Holy shit, are you saying that weird 'initiation' shit they gave me is actually this alien interface 'primer'?"

"Yes, we believe so. After years of trying, we'd secured a vial of that serum and were intending to experiment with it here. But it was blown up in orbit, like so much else. There's no way for us to get more of the serum here anytime soon, but we do have you. Which means that you are now our only reasonable chance of accessing that ship. We need you to secure it before the others do."

"Which others?" Evan's voice trembled more than he'd like.

"The insiders with the colony expedition who were sent to stop us. They're somewhere on the surface now, and they're hunting for the ship—and for us."

Anya eyed him. "You pulled us in from the jungle. How do you know that *we're* not working for them?"

"We vetted you with our contacts back in the core worlds."

"How is that reliable?" Evan found it difficult to believe that they'd rely on information relayed from light years away.

"It's only a start. You need to look someone in the eye. And after speaking with you, I know you're not yet fully with me, but I am also certain that you're not working with my enemies."

"So, all those interrogation questions when we first got here… you were testing us?" Evan asked. *How big of a setup was this?*

"Yes, that was a necessary step to verify the information in your profiles."

"I still can't get over that you've been pulling strings in the core worlds all this time," Anya said.

"Observing more than manipulating anything," Conroy replied. "However, we've never been fully removed from the rest of civilization."

Anya's brows pinched together. "The survey didn't indicate any satellites, or—"

"It's not difficult to hide such things when you have an ally who's programming those systems."

"Just how many connections *do* you have back to the core worlds?" Anya asked.

Evan had also been wondering how far the web spread. Clearly, Aethos was far from the remote, untouched colony world they'd thought.

"Political tensions had been building for years," Conroy explained. "People had been picking sides since early on, and I didn't have an insignificant following. When I needed to disappear, there were people who helped and supported me in the process. Some of them came here to Aethos, and others remained behind as liaisons. They have all kept my secret, and they will help me reveal the truth once the pieces are in place for my return."

His return for what? Evan decided against voicing the question. Based on Anya's concerned expression, her mind had also gone down a darker path.

"Sir," Anya began tentatively, "what's the endgame here?"

"To maintain the balance of power so that humanity doesn't destroy itself."

Anya's brow scrunched up. "I'm still missing something."

"Have you ever been around someone with true power?" Conroy asked.

"In what sense?"

"The kind of person whose word is law. They can't just change a life, but the course of an entire civilization."

Anya shook her head.

"I can't say I have," Evan replied. "Though, I'm no stranger to people at the life-ending level." The leaders of the Noche Syndicate were powerful within their domain, but they didn't hold interstellar civilization-altering sway. They'd been terrifying enough.

"Well, that's not a surprise, because there are few positions that afford that level of influence. Being Chancellor was one of them—to a degree. I still answered to the people, and knowing that I could be forcibly removed at any time helps keep you honest."

Evan struggled to keep a straight face. *Honesty isn't what comes to mind when thinking about politicians.*

"But consider what would happen if there was a fundamental shift in the power structure," Conroy continued. "If a new jump drive technology were to be introduced, so there were no longer the current limitations that have constrained our civilization's development, then whoever controlled that technology would dictate everything. They could control trade, resources—everything that would decide who thrived and who suffered."

"And you believe that ship on Aethos is the pivotal discovery for that future?" Evan asked.

"Yes, or at least a major stepping stone." The chancellor paused. "I'm sure you're thinking that I can't be trusted with the power of that technology, either, and you'd be right. No single person should be able to dictate the course of so many lives. But what I can tell you is that I'm aware of that. That's why I was so adamant about making the discovery public and sharing the benefits of the technology with all. However, the people we're up against want to maintain complete control, without regard for the harm it would no doubt cause to common citizens. We must prevent the technology from falling into *their* hands, as I firmly believe that isolated power would doom our civilization. And you'll just have to believe me when I promise you—as I have to everyone else here—that I will not use this discovery for my own gain. I only wish to do what's best for my people."

It was a lovely sentiment, but Evan couldn't put any stock in the words. "Let's set all of that aside for now," he said. "I want to understand how the colony mission even moved forward if all of this was happening behind the scenes."

"No, Evan, the expedition happened *because* of those things. Founding a new world was all pretense."

Evan tried to assemble a mental map of the events. "What you said earlier about the current government wanting to send a military ship here—the colonization efforts were a good cover."

"Yes, with the express purpose of quietly wiping us out. And assigning people they deemed 'loose ends' to the colonist manifest was a great way to tie off those lingering threads."

Anya frowned. "Not everyone on the manifest worked for NovaTech."

"No, and they were viewed as sacrifices. That's the level of evil we're dealing with in the opposition."

"Chancellor Rostov is in on this, seriously? And he's coordinating with the Noche Syndicate?" Evan asked, finding the entire story ridiculous. Sure, the Commonwealth's sitting leader had his issues, but so did every politician. Victor Rostov didn't seem worse than any other. *Isn't it more likely that the person who faked his death and started camping on a planet in the middle of nowhere is the crazy one?*

"I know how it must sound, Evan, but I swear I'm telling the truth," Conroy insisted. "Find that ship, and that will be the verification you need."

No, it won't be. Evan didn't want to get into an argument with the man, but he'd seen enough cover stories to know how people could distort the truth. Finding an alien ship would only prove that there was an alien presence on Aethos. It would offer no insight into which side was fighting for a greater good versus personal gain—or do anything to refute that *both* parties weren't in a power struggle for totalitarian control.

However, that made Evan's path clear. *I can't trust Conroy, and I can't trust Rostov. I can only trust myself.*

He needed to find the alien ship—not for Conroy, but to keep it out of everyone's hands until he'd had an opportunity to verify the other facts of the case. He *would* need to pick a side, but one speech from Conroy wasn't going to convince him that this was the right team to back.

There was a lot to process. Evan wished he and Anya could go somewhere private to chat, but there was no polite way to extract himself from the present conversation. Instead, he decided to keep Conroy talking while he was in a forthcoming mood.

"So, let me see if I understand," Evan began. "The people

in NovaTech who organized this expedition knew it was all a sham, and they were fine with letting thousands of people die because it made for good cover to get a warship to this planet. And that warship was supposed to destroy you, but you shot it down first. And the colony ship was *supposed* to have been sabotaged, but your attack on the warship messed up those plans, and civilians survived even though it was planned for everyone on the expedition to die. Do I have that right?"

The chancellor nodded. "With the exception that there were a few enemy collaborators on both the colony ship and warship, and the plan was always for them to evacuate and survive—which they have, as far as we know."

Anya crossed her arms. "Which means that you want Evan and me to go back out in the jungle to look for an ancient alien ship that may or may not be there while we're being hunted by homicidal insurrectionist saboteurs?"

Conroy hesitated. "That's not the most flattering characterization, but yes."

She pursed her lips. "Is *everyone* at NovaTech crooked? Because it's a massive expense and time commitment to send a colony ship out here. There had to have been a more efficient way to get people out here without that much waste."

"There aren't many ways to commit mass murder without drawing a lot of questions," Conroy countered. "But send a colony ship to a new world, where no one can see what happens… Well, it's easy enough to say that there was an unexpected weather phenomenon or something that caused everyone to die while landing. Not only would it explain the deaths of all the witnesses they wanted eliminated, but it would also make other people want to avoid the planet in the future. That leaves them free to continue the investigation into the alien tech unchecked."

Evan frowned. "That all seems a little… extreme."

"Once you accept that they are willing to lie—to say or do anything necessary to accomplish their goals—then you'll see that there is no measure too extreme."

Evan couldn't argue with that. He'd seen people do some awful things to accomplish their goals, and the stakes weren't nearly as high as this. Destroying two interstellar ships and killing a few thousand people was a minimal sacrifice when considering civilization-altering motives.

Conroy changed the holographic map to a larger view of the surrounding territory. "Let me finish going over what I know, and then you can decide if you're willing to help. I think there's a way for us to come to a mutually beneficial understanding that gets me what I need and will get you off this deathtrap."

27

ANYA HAD BEEN through some serious debriefs in her career, but the presentation from Chancellor Conroy had shaken her entire perception of reality. Now, waiting in a small room with Evan, she kept running over the information in her mind and applying the new context to her past experiences.

"I should have realized they were up to something big," she murmured.

"I think it's fair to say that most people wouldn't have seen any of this coming," Evan replied.

"But there were signs."

"And what would you have done about it?"

"Well, I…" She faded out. "I suppose I would have tried to stop the colony expedition, and if I couldn't, I would have bowed out."

"So, I would have been stuck here on my own," Evan said.

"That wouldn't have been very fun for you."

"It's true. Selfish as it is, I'm glad you're here."

Anya nodded. "Perhaps destiny brought us here."

"I don't believe in that stuff."

"I don't either, really. I like to think I have control over my life. But there are times I wonder…"

"Recent events have made me reevaluate my stance," Evan admitted.

Anya stepped closer to him. "Well, let's say fate did bring us together here. How about we make a pact that wherever this crazy journey leads next, we're a team?"

He looked her over thoughtfully. "Are you sure you want to attach yourself to a walking disaster?"

"You're really good at getting yourself out of trouble, though. You've looked out for me since we've been here, and I hope you feel the same way about me. We work well together."

"I agree. It's been nice having a friendly face out there in the jungle."

She smiled. "All right. Then it's a deal." She offered her hand.

Evan shook it. "Partners."

Anya leaned back against the metal wall. "Well, partner, it feels pretty good to know we weren't going crazy this whole time, right?"

Evan laughed. "Yeah, though the reality is far wilder than I ever could have imagined."

"It really is."

He drew a slow breath. "I'm not sure if it's for better or worse that it wasn't just in our heads. I have a feeling now that whatever we find buried on this planet, I'll wish it's something I didn't know."

"Once you see, you can't unsee. But I think we passed the point of no return a long time ago."

"You're probably right about that."

"On a positive note," he continued, "we're not alone on a planet without any infrastructure, after all."

"Yeah, but accepting their help comes at a steep price. I'm not sure I want to get involved in this conflict."

"Is there really much choice?"

He shook his head. "It figures."

"What does?"

"That I'd travel across star systems to a whole new planet only to get pulled into a messy conspiracy."

"It is pretty miserable luck, no way around it."

"We could still bail and try to go it alone out there, like we'd planned."

"What's the point?" she asked. "We're fighting to live, but what kind of life can we have here?"

"Anything we want."

"No, that's the lie they sold to hopeful colonists. This planet was never going to be a utopia. Just like every other world, it was a well-planned scheme to exploit resources. I'd said we could run and find a little cave to call home, but that was before I knew what was coming. The way I see it now, we need to pick a side."

"These people certainly want us to think they're the good guys."

"Do you trust them?"

He shrugged. "I'm not sure."

"I don't know, either. But I can say that we're ill-equipped to survive here without them. That's the irony of it all. Damned with them and damned without. So, I ask again, what's the point in running away?"

Evan was silent for several seconds before responding. "The point is to live the best life we can."

"Hiding doesn't seem like the best way to do that. Are things stacked against us? Yeah. But the only sure path to defeat is to give up. I'm not a quitter, and I don't think you are, either."

"It's never too late to try something new."

She side-eyed him. "Taking up 'quitting' as a new hobby. That's a novel approach."

He let out a pained chuckle. "Obviously, I don't mean it. This is all just..."

"It's a lot."

"Yeah."

She looked him in the eye. "We're in it together, though. Sucks a little less when you're not alone."

"Very true." He sighed. "I suppose fighting for *a* cause is better than running."

A knock sounded at the door, and it swung open without waiting for a response. Samor stood in the open doorframe. "Hey, are you hungry?"

Anya's stomach rumbled on cue. "I can't even remember my last meal."

"Breakfast, and that was a long time ago," Evan said.

The soldier smiled. "Well, we can fix that."

— — —

Evan took in the buffet lining one wall of the Mess. While far from glamorous, it was a huge step up from the MealPaks and bitter greens they'd been subsisting on for the past several days.

His brief one-on-one chat with Anya had settled some of his concerns, but he still had major misgivings about taking Conroy's statements at face value. Though he'd been a fine leader of the Commonwealth during most of his tenure, at least according to the news reports, politicians were notorious for talking a good game on the surface while working an ulterior motive. And there'd been rumors of corruption swirling in the media shortly before his supposed death. Evan didn't believe for a second that the former chancellor had told them everything, or that he'd been honest in what he had shared.

When their plates were full, they took a seat at one of the tables in the back corner of the room.

"Oh, real food!" Anya ripped her roll apart and stuffed an overly large chunk into her mouth. She closed her eyes with satisfaction as she chewed. "Old me would have thought of this as boring cafeteria food, but it's amazing how a few days in the woods can change your perspective."

Evan took a more reserved bite of his own roll. "As long as it fills the empty spot, I'll take whatever I can get."

Ravenous, they didn't speak again until they'd both eaten their fill.

Evan pushed his empty tray forward. "That might be the most satisfying meal I've ever had."

"Agreed."

They fell silent again in contemplation.

"Has it started to sink in for you yet?" Evan asked.

Anya nodded. "Yeah. All of this…" She faded out, shaking her head. "There have been so many things that didn't add up. It's kind of a relief to hear that there really is something deeper going on, right?"

Evan chuckled. "I never thought I'd say it, but yes."

"But it's so messed up—all of us being sent on this expedition to get us out of the way because they thought we knew too much."

"I went from thinking that we were so unlucky to have crashed, but really, it's miraculous that we made it out alive."

The crash was only the start of it, though. If what Conroy had said was true, that meant NovaTech was in on the conspiracy. Evan couldn't begin to wrap his head around taking on an interstellar organization of that size. Even a few bad actors would be too much to stand against, considering that the company would want to prevent an unsavory incident from coming to light.

His shoulders slumped under the weight of the realization. "A person can only take so much."

Anya's eyes softened with genuine compassion. "We have had a lot thrown at us recently."

"It's not just that." He sighed. "I've spent my entire life being what others have wanted, or expected, me to be. This was supposed to be my chance to live my own life."

She shrugged. "Fine, screw 'em. They can figure out how to fight their war without us."

Evan shook his head. "No, we talked it out and decided to see this through. I'd be wondering 'what if' forever if I walked away now. I was deluding myself before to think it might be possible to stop caring. But a sense of duty isn't something I can switch off, as much as I want to, sometimes. "

"Caring isn't a reason to beat yourself up."

"No, I'm not frustrated with myself. Just annoyed with the universe, in general, for not having its shit together."

"I'm afraid you're setting yourself up for a lifetime of annoyance, then. The universe isn't likely to get any more orderly. In fact, its whole thing is kinda 'controlled chaos'."

"Thanks, Anya. That makes me feel much better."

She smiled at his thick sarcasm. "Happy to help."

"You're right, though. The universe can throw us for crazy loops, and the only aspect we can control is how we react. We have to be true to ourselves. And we both knew in our gut that there was something bigger going on than just an accident in space. Oh, were we ever right!"

She chuckled. "Admittedly, there were moments when I doubted my own perceptions."

"You science types... always analyzing the data and forming hypotheses."

She eyed him. "You just admitted you do the same."

"Fair enough." He paused. "We can't kid ourselves, though, Anya. Eventually, we have to face the reality that we've been conscripted into a civil war."

"That's a little dramatic."

"Come on, you know how this will play out."

She pursed her lips in quiet contemplation. "All right, yes. If we do what they've asked of us, we will be in the thick of it."

Evan crossed his arms and leaned back in his chair. "The most annoying thing is that deep down, I'm not that upset. It's actually a little exciting."

Anya laughed. "I know, right? Hearing about the mission, I felt like a super-spy."

"We should probably be careful about how loudly we say that, or they'll give us more assignments."

"Would that be so bad?"

"Not if I was going with you."

Their eyes met.

"Hey, how are you two settling in?"

Startled, Evan looked up to see Samor approaching their table. "Far from settled, and mind going a thousand different directions," he replied.

The soldier nodded. "I can only imagine how overwhelming it is coming into this cold."

Evan lowered his voice to a whisper. "Did you know what you were getting into when you came here? I mean, this whole thing isn't exactly inside the normal scope of duty."

"To the contrary, what could be more important than fighting for the future of humankind?"

"Well, I'm not sure I would have had it in me to follow

Conroy into exile," Evan admitted.

"I have no regrets. I think once you've had time to process everything about what we're doing here, you'll see that committing to the cause is the only way forward."

"I'm trying to keep an open mind," Evan told him. It was all hearsay at this point about the Commonwealth's political leadership and what sort of coup may or may not have transpired. Samor had clearly picked a leader to back, but Evan would need to see how it played out. Just because he'd decided not to run away from the brewing war didn't mean he'd settled on what part to play in the fight.

"Good, because when I show you what we've learned so far about the alien ruins, it's going to take things to a whole new level of weird."

"How much stranger can it possibly get?"

Samor flashed a rueful smile. "That's what I thought, too. Follow me."

28

ROMAN DROPPED TO his stomach and brought his binoculars to his eyes, granting him a zoomed-in view with a thermal view overlay. The bunker's entrance was camouflaged enough that it'd easily be overlooked by a casual observer. However, the heat signatures around the hatch unmistakably belonged to guards. No one would be posted outside something that wasn't worth protecting.

"I think we've found ourselves a stronghold," Roman whispered to Sten.

The other man nodded as he set down his own binoculars. "I count six guards. Four at ground-level and another two up in those trees—probably snipers."

"That's what I spotted, too. As much as I'd love to play hero, we can't take that many alone, not to mention however many soldiers inside. We have to call it in."

"They're going to take all the credit, you know."

"We don't have a choice. The mission comes first." Roman smiled. "But they'll know this was us."

They silently retreated to a grove of trees where they'd be out of visual range from the enemy.

The established protocols said they were supposed to

maintain radio silence unless there were extenuating circumstances, but this seemed like a worthwhile exception. Roman tuned into the other team's comm frequency and hit the alert tone in his identification pattern.

The radio crackled, and a woman's voice spoke, "This better be important."

"I'm staring at the entrance to Conroy's bunker. Wanna know where it is?"

"Why are you off-mission?"

"I'm not. Change of tactics."

"Well, you're about to blow our cover. We're casing it now."

Roman exchanged glances with Sten. "You're… here?"

"Do I have to repeat everything?" She let out an exasperated sigh. "Don't screw this up for us. Meet at this location."

Roman's wrist map updated with a point seventy meters to the northwest of their present location. "On our way." He ended the call.

"So much for glory," Sten said.

Roman resisted the urge to punch the smirk off his face. "Let's move."

They cut through the trees to the meetup location. Soldiers were waiting for them, rifles at the ready.

"Great to see you, too," Roman greeted with a sneer.

A tall woman swaggered forward with an expression that suggested she'd like to grind his face into the ground. "You're not supposed to be here."

"Well, we thought of a different search tactic, and it involves gathering intel from inside that facility."

"This is a military operation."

"And you wouldn't be here if it wasn't for us. We're

supposed to be working together, remember?" Roman was fuzzy on the details of the arrangement his brother had struck for the Syndicate to help the government, but they had to be getting something valuable in return. Marcus never made a deal that didn't benefit their organization—and, especially, him personally.

The soldier didn't seem interested in the arrangement. "Do what you're told and stay out of our way. We're here for Conroy, but you can do whatever other research you want after we accomplish our objective."

"Fine with me. Do you have a name?"

"Yes."

So, that's how she wants to play it. He stared at her, unwavering.

She rolled her eyes. "Call me Red." Nothing about her dark, almond eyes and black hair contrasting pale skin suggested how the name might have originated.

"I'm Roman and that's Sten," he introduced.

"I know who you are."

"Then you should also know not to mess with me."

"Why do you think you aren't dead right now?" Red hefted her rifle and walked back to talk with a burly man keeping watch.

"Off to a great start," Roman mumbled.

"At least they know we're on the same side," Sten replied. He eyed the soldiers' weapons.

Roman had considered himself well-armed for his part in the mission, but this other group made it look like he was playing toy soldier. Not wanting to show any weakness, he confidently walked up to Red and the rest of her group. "When are we going in?"

"Waiting for twilight," the burly man next to Red replied.

"Sounds like a plan." Roman stood in awkward silence for a few seconds.

"It's sure convenient that your ship came down so close to this base."

Red raised an eyebrow. "Seriously? You think that was by chance?"

"I—"

"Wow. Did it not occur to you that we knew where the base was all along and aimed for it?"

Roman's brows knitted. "We had no record of its location."

She scoffed. "Well, we did."

"Why didn't you tell us?"

"Because we don't trust you! Make no mistake, this is a temporary marriage of convenience, nothing more."

"That works two ways."

"Sure does. And don't you forget that you're the ones outgunned right now."

Roman was acutely aware of that fact already, but it occurred to him that there should be a lot more soldiers than those within his field of view. "Where are the rest of your people?"

Red grimaced. "We lost a lot in the initial explosion, and then more in the crash. We were already on our drop ship in the cruiser's hangar getting ready to come down when they fired on us, so we made it out okay. Others weren't so lucky."

"We're down in numbers, then."

"Doesn't matter. We have enough to get our job done. You'd better do the same."

"We will," Roman assured her. "You handle the breach, and we'll take it from there."

— — —

Evan hadn't felt full or comfortable for days, and the decompression time over a hearty meal with Anya had been exactly what he'd needed. As he followed Samor through the strange subterranean facility constructed from a former ship, he couldn't help wondering if the short relaxation had simply been the calm before a much bigger storm.

Conroy hadn't overtly *said* that time was of the essence, but all of his statements did suggest urgency. They were being hunted by an unknown number of soldiers from the crashed military escort, as well as any Syndicate conspirators from on board the colony ship. If Evan and Anya had found their trail, then other trained soldiers certainly could, too.

"Hey, Samor," Evan ventured, "you'll probably say it's none of my business, but what kind of defenses do you have set up for this place?"

"You're right, that's not your concern."

"Except it is, considering I'm here, and you've straight-up said that there are other people on this planet who want you dead. That doesn't bode well for us."

The other man raised an eyebrow. "Are you a security expert now, too?"

"No, just a regular guy looking for some reassurance so I can sleep well tonight."

"If you're going to lose sleep, let it be over how to access the alien ship."

"I imagine you'll want us to head out first thing in the morning?" Anya asked.

Samor nodded. "I think Conroy would have preferred you left immediately, but there are too many benefits to a night in a real bed after what you've been through. A small team of guards will be ready to head out with you at dawn."

The persistent aches in Evan's back agreed that a mattress sounded a lot better than a thin bedroll for the night. "Whatever you wanted to show us, let's make it quick so we can go pass out."

Samor led them into large room that looked like it may have been a repurposed cargo hold. With crates stacked in various piles around half the space, it seemed to still be serving that purpose. However, there were also several objects resting on top of other crates that made it clear this wasn't any old storeroom.

The strange objects were made of a dark metal with a slightly pearlescent quality. Even more striking were their curved forms and highly detailed texture, which resembled lizard skin more than anything he'd seen come off a manufacturing line. There were five such objects, ranging in size from half a meter to two meters wide. The larger piece had a distinct jagged edge where it had been broken.

"What is this?" Anya asked, eyeing the pieces.

Evan knew the answer before Samor spoke.

"We recovered these from a dig site in that valley we've been investigating. The metal composition is unlike anything in the Commonwealth. It's alien," Samor stated.

Even having his suspicions confirmed, Evan had difficulty accepting the objects. He'd seen a lot of seemingly unbelievable things that day, but discovering that a man he'd thought was dead had been living on a remote planet for the last five years was an easy truth compared to physical evidence of intelligent alien life. And not just *intelligent*, but incredibly advanced life, at that.

"What is it?" Evan asked. That wasn't the most elegant or insightful question, but those were the only words Evan could form in his overwhelmed state.

"We think it's remnants from a former outpost. These were just the pieces that were small enough to transport, but there were much larger components buried underground. Our imaging shows what looks like a network of rooms and corridors."

"Built underground?"

"No, more likely, just old enough that they've been covered in dirt and vegetation over time. It's relatively low ground. I'm sure you've witnessed the weather."

"Yeah, a little too up close," Evan said while he approached one of the mid-sized objects closest to him. "I can't imagine putting this much detail work into a simple building."

Samor nodded. "That's been a point of contention for us, too. One working theory is that the metal is actually a programmable nanomesh."

Anya perked up. "Meaning, the structures could be... grown?"

"In a sense, yes. But whatever control mechanism might make that possible is long gone. There is a faint energy signature coming from it, but it's no longer active, as far as we can tell."

"How much more is buried there?" Anya asked.

"Difficult to know, since we haven't been able to finish excavating the area—just picking away at it bit by bit over the years. Our last attempt was interrupted with your colony expedition's arrival. But, that's not where the ship is."

Standing a mere meter from one of the alien objects now, Evan was filled with a warm glow. The sensation was most concentrated in his core, but it extended down his limbs to his fingertips and toes. He had a sudden compulsion to reach out toward the object.

As he extended his hand toward it, the metal surface

shimmered—almost like it was rising up to greet him. "Whoa, did you see—"

A concussive force echoed through the walls, raining a fine cloud of dust.

Anya ducked down. "What was that?"

"Wait here." Samor headed for the hallway door.

"It sounded like an explosion," Evan said just loud enough for Anya to hear.

"I thought so, too." Her brows were pinched with concern and her eyes wide.

Evan's chest constricted. Based on everything he'd been told in the last few hours, there was only one group that might be leading an attack. And, by all accounts, they'd be well-armed. Not only was Evan not mentally prepared for a firefight, but he was in about as unfamiliar surroundings as a person could get.

Samor had paused at the doorway and was peeking into the hall. He shook his head to indicate that he hadn't detected anything.

Evan motioned for Anya to follow him. "Whatever else you were going to tell us will have to wait," he told Samor. "I don't want to be trapped in a place with one way out."

Samor nodded. He ran back into the room and grabbed a hand-sized device from one of the consoles and slipped it into his pocket. "I need to get to a radio. We'll talk on the way." The group really *must* be tight on resources if they didn't all have personal communication devices on hand.

"So much for a restful night in a bed," Anya grumbled.

"We don't know what's going on. You still might get that." Samor cautiously entered the hallway, listening. "Follow me."

Evan and Anya jogged after Samor down the corridor.

Another concussive wave passed through the structure,

rattling the metal walls and making the floor tremble. Evan wasn't sure if he should be relieved or alarmed that he didn't hear any signs of fighting in the distance.

"I want our weapons back. Or new ones—whatever," Evan demanded.

"That's…"

"You want us to work with you, right? If this is an attack, I don't want to wait for the fight to reach us before arming up."

While the soldier didn't look pleased with the prospect, he nodded. "Okay, let me check in with Command and we'll take it from there."

After several turns through the maze of corridors, Samor motioned to a door ahead. "In here," He opened it and ducked inside.

The compact space was filled with electronics equipment, and it was loud from multiple fans running. Evan guessed it was a server room.

Supporting that assessment, Samor went to a console and made several entries. "Command, this is Sergeant Samor. What's our status?"

"Sergeant, be advised that enemy targets are attempting a breach of the main entrance. Prepare for emergency evacuation. All available units to defensive positions."

"Roger that." He ended the comm link. "You heard him. Let's get your things prepped to leave."

"What about our escort?" Evan asked.

"I'll see what we can do."

The group continued down the corridor to a weapons locker where there was a flurry of activity while several other soldiers were gearing up.

"What have you heard?" Samor asked them.

"Enemy found us. Haven't gotten a good count, but they

have explosives. We're trying to hold the main door," one soldier replied. "We need everyone."

Samor swore under his breath. "I need to get these two out the back way. We can't send them out alone."

"General's orders are to hold off the enemy. We can't spare anyone."

"What about you?" Evan asked Samor.

"My responsibility is to the chancellor."

"We did okay before on our own, Evan," Anya said.

"That was before we had people shooting at us!"

Samor handed Evan a rifle and a handgun, and then gave a handgun to Anya, as well. "Let's get your gear. I'll see if I can find someone to go with you."

As a precaution, Evan also grabbed a recharger; while he'd have a finite number of shots from each weapon in combat, the recharger would allow him to indefinitely restore the firing capacity. He preferred kinetic weapons as a rule, but not needing to worry about ammo inventory was a distinct advantage to energy weapons.

With the guns in hand, Samor led Evan and Anya back to the residential area of the facility. There were no other soldiers around, with everyone likely already in defensible positions. At the intersection where they should have turned right toward Evan's room, they instead went left.

"Hey, isn't—"

"This is mine," Anya cut in.

Two doors down, Samor unlocked the entrance, and Anya ran inside to gather her things. "I want my bioanalyzer back, too," she said as she reemerged.

"No time. Just the essentials," Samor countered.

"It *is* essential. If we encounter any biological material at the ruins, I need to know what we're dealing with."

"My quarters, then the rest." Evan ran back in the direction of his lodging with Samor and Anya close behind.

As soon as Samor reached the door, he unlocked it. Evan rushed inside and grabbed his pack. He still had the tent, bedroll, and other basic supplies. However, they weren't equipped for another extended stay in the wilds.

"We need that bioanalyzer and some rations," Evan said once back in the hall.

"Analyzer first. We can feed ourselves if it comes to it," Anya stated.

Agreeing with her logic, Evan let Samor lead the way through the empty corridors. After several turns, they arrived at a room set up as a rudimentary science lab. Anya quickly spotted her device and crammed it into her pack.

"Food," Evan said.

"There's a provisions locker on the way to the back exit." Samor took off down the hall.

"There are probably armed maniacs surrounding this base! How are we supposed to get away without getting shot?"

"There's a back exit tunnel that will take you half a kilometer from here," Samor revealed. "We used a natural cave system to construct this place, and that tunnel was part of it."

"Let's assume we do get away and find the ship," Evan began in a more optimistic tone than he felt. "What in the planets are we supposed to do with it then?"

"Keep it from falling into enemy hands. Nothing is more important."

"But—"

Samor glanced over at him as he ran. "I don't know. Conroy told me to brief you on current status, but he didn't specify what to do beyond that."

Kinetic weapons fire rang out in the distance. Samor

glanced in the direction of the fighting. "They're inside. I need to get you out *now*."

"An escort—"

"It's too late," Samor cut off Evan's protest. "It'll be up to you to find the ship."

Evan shook his head. "Sending the two of us out there alone with a couple of guns is not a solid plan to save the Commonwealth."

Samor motioned him down the hall. "This attack has changed everything. You can either stay here and hope we win this fight, or you can get out now and try to secure our future."

"We'll do our best," Anya said, flashing a determined look to Evan. "Is there some kind of radio we can take with us to get in touch with you?"

"There might be one with the provisions," Samor replied. "Using it would be risky, because it could give away your location."

"We'll only use it if we have to," Evan told him.

"This is insane," Anya muttered as they jogged after the soldier.

Evan exchanged glances with her, silently relaying that her assertion of insanity was the understatement of the century.

They reached the provisions locker and loaded up as many MealPaks as they could fit in their bags. There was no telling when they might get back to a place where they'd be able to resupply, so they had to assume that whatever they were carrying would need to last. Hopefully, with Anya's bioanalyzer, they'd be able to forage enough that they could keep the MealPaks for emergencies. Well, *more* of an emergency. Their lives were turning into one persistent crisis.

"I'm sorry you've been put in this position," Samor told them as they left the locker. "The rest of us had a choice when we came here."

"Being conscripted into a secret rebellion isn't how I thought this day would go," Evan said. "I can't make any promises about what we're going to do."

Samor nodded his understanding. "All I can do is give you information and hope you'll choose to do the right thing." He pulled out the small device he'd previously placed in his pocket. After pressing a series of three buttons, a low-resolution holographic map appeared above it. "We established a research outpost here. Copies of all our survey files are stored there."

"A trip to the library isn't going to help us right now," Evan retorted.

"No, but there's no way the enemy will know about this site, so it'll give you a safehouse." He handed the device to Evan, revealing that it had straps for equipping it like a wristwatch. "And it also has all the details you'll need about how to access the ruins with the alien ship."

Evan secured the device to his left wrist and deactivated the map.

"What do you mean by 'access'?" Anya asked. "Don't you mean 'find it'?"

"No, we're pretty sure where the ship is. A team of us located the site about a year after we got to Aethos. There's an entrance in the mountains near the other ruins, but it was locked. We're hoping that the Syndicate's 'initiation' serum is what's needed to *un*-lock it."

Anya frowned. "What about me? Any reason to think it would be dangerous to enter after it's open?"

"I honestly don't know, Anya. We've only just started to study the serum's properties based on our analysis of Evan's blood."

"That's why you took my bioanalyzer."

"Yes, sorry. We're very short on scientific equipment here.

Those of us who came to Aethos with the chancellor were either security or political aides—not an ideal bunch for discovering the deep secrets of an unexplored world."

"I'm guessing you weren't able to complete a new serum this afternoon?"

Samor shook his head. "Not even close."

"Well, I'll see if I can figure it out." Anya reached over her shoulder to pat her pack containing the bioanalyzer.

"That map I gave you is a static representation of the topography. It won't show you where you are, but there should be enough landmarks to orient yourselves."

"You don't have a nav satellite?" Evan asked.

"I wouldn't trust any of our orbital systems right now, given the enemy presence," Samor replied. "And to that end, be careful. Don't trust anyone you may meet, regardless of who they say they are."

"Assuming we find the ship, how do we relay a message?" Evan asked.

"That'll be the time to break radio silence. Our identifier will be 'Phoenix'."

It was an on-the-nose reference to Conroy's reemergence, no doubt, but simple enough to remember and an unlikely guess. "Okay. We'll be 'Trailblazer'."

"I'll make sure others know." Samor continued to lead them down the hall to a hatchway, larger and thicker than the others.

Half scraped-off lettering printed in the center of the hatch read 'Airlock'. Samor spun the locking wheel, and it unbolted. He swung it open to reveal rough, tan stone.

Evan fished out a flashlight from his pack. "I guess it's time to go spelunking."

29

ANYA WASN'T FOND of dark enclosed spaces, but this was the wrong time to bring that up to Evan. She took a slow, deep breath in a vain attempt to settle her nerves and followed him into the stone passageway. As soon as she passed through the threshold, the metal hatch swung closed behind her and the bolt clanged into place.

Evan fanned his flashlight beam around the space, but there wasn't anything to see beyond the natural stone walls. "We need to move fast. That door wasn't hidden, so if they take the facility, they'll be able to trace our path."

"How in the planets are we supposed to do even a fraction of what they're asking of us, Evan?"

He shook his head, made more dramatic by the large shadow cast from his flashlight. "Acting agreeable was the only way we were going to get out of there, but without an escort, we aren't beholden to anything. I don't know how we can trust a word they told us."

"I have no idea what to believe."

"Neither do I, which is why I say we *do* go find that ship, and then *we* determine what to do with it. Personally, I don't think we should hand it over to either group until we understand what it can do."

"Agreed. First, we need to get to that research outpost."

"It didn't look too far from here. But I have no idea what time it is. You think it's dark out?"

"Feels like we were there for several hours at least. Might be."

"Once we get out of this tunnel, we can figure out our next move."

— — —

"I would have thought they'd bring better explosives," Roman whispered to Sten as they watched the soldiers attempt to breach the facility.

The other man kept his mouth shut but pinched his brows to indicate that he agreed.

So far, very little in the raid of Aethos was going as planned. As if getting shot down wasn't enough, losing people in the crash had left them shorthanded, and Roman wasn't convinced that the survivors hadn't been the bottom-tier unit. Red's tough act was seeming more and more like a cover for incompetence, though Roman hadn't yet seen enough to be certain.

What he did know for sure was that the breach was shaping up to be messy business. As much as he wanted to get information from the facility, he had no interest in waiting around all night for the pleasure of getting shot at.

"Let's get out of here," Roman said.

Sten eyed him. "What about the plan?"

"Let them worry about Conroy. There's another way to get what we want." Roman slinked away from their vantage point.

"Where do you think you're going?" Red snapped.

“Change of plan,” Roman replied. “It occurred to me that we don’t need to go inside to get what we need. If something is important, they’ll bring it out to us.”

“What are you talking about?”

“They’ll be running scared. We don’t need to figure out the important information, because whatever they value most, they’ll try to preserve by getting it as far away from this threat as possible.”

“We checked. There’s no other exit.”

“That you’ve found,” Roman pointed out. “These people may be traitors, but they aren’t stupid. There’ll be a back way out.”

Red nodded pensively. “Come to think of it, there were some cave mouths half a klick north of here. We scoped out a few of them and they were all dead ends, but it’s possible one of the others goes deeper, and might connect. That might be a good place to start.”

“Thanks. Good luck with the breach.”

She grinned. “We’ve got ’em right where we want ’em.”

It didn’t seem that way to Roman, but he’d be the first to admit this wasn’t his area of expertise. Stakeouts, on the other hand, were right up his alley.

He led Sten northward, navigating solely by the moonlight. Once they’d been away from the bright flashes of the assault for several minutes, his eyes had adjusted to the point where he had no difficulty picking out the details of his surroundings. He wanted to be used to the dark so that any artificial light would stand out, in case any escapees were dumb enough to use flashlights. More likely, though, they’d take a stealth approach, and Roman didn’t want to give away his own position.

They carefully slipped through the trees and ground

foliage, moving as silently as possible. The sounds of explosions faded into the wind as they moved away from the bunker's front entrance. Roman kept track of the distance covered using his watch. As they neared the half-kilometer mark, he started the search for possible cave entrances.

Sten tapped his shoulder and pointed.

Following the line of his arm, Roman spotted a dark recess at the base of a low hill. Other similar dark spots started to jump out at him across the hillside as his eyes further adjusted.

Roman found a nearby boulder that would make decent cover and positioned himself behind it, taking in the wide view of the caves. There was no telling which one might lead back to the traitor's hideout, but this would give them a perfect vantage to spot anyone fleeing. No doubt, those people would be carrying anything deemed valuable enough to get to safety.

He swatted away the nighttime insects as he scanned the hillside, poised to act. *Now all we have to do is wait.*

— — —

Everything about the day was a complete disaster. Samor raced back through the corridors toward Central Command. He needed to check in with Conroy and relay the codeword he'd agreed upon with Evan and Anya.

That ship is everything. Without it, we've lost.

Putting so many plans on an item they didn't have in hand—and might not exist—was a strategy of desperation. But they *were* desperate. People in control didn't run away to distant planets or recruit random strangers to help. But they'd lost so many people along the way and were backed so far into the corner that they had no choice other than to make one final bid for survival.

Had he known they'd arrive at this point, Samor wondered if he would have made the same decision to join Conroy. He'd been in the first lead role of his career, overseeing the third unit of the chancellor's personal security detail. They were the transportation specialists responsible for getting him from Point A to Point B, while the two other details would handle security at the origin and destination locations.

Then, on that fateful day in the shuttle, they realized they had failed. The shuttle's guidance system had been compromised, and the craft was on a collision course with a mountain.

Samor still remembered the panicked pounding of his heart in his chest. He wasn't a pilot, or an engineer, and that sensation of helplessness had threatened to freeze him. But he was a soldier, and he wouldn't give up under any circumstances.

Within thirty seconds, he'd donned an emergency parachute and grappled Conroy in a tandem harness. Bailing out had meant blowing the emergency hatch and dooming everyone else on board, but it was what his protection mandate had demanded.

The insane blur that had followed remained a dizzying memory of whooshing wind and sheer terror during the initial freefall to the planet's surface. Within seconds of deploying the parachute, he'd witnessed the shuttle crash into the rocky mountain and explode into a ball of flame. Only once his feet had touched the ground did he process how close he'd come to death.

But then Conroy had told him that it would be better if they *had* died in that crash. And now they'd have to disappear.

In the weeks and years that followed, he'd learned the shadowy truths that had driven Conroy's decision to die in the public's eye that day. The machinations of interstellar politics had been well beyond the scope of his responsibilities, and many of the moves stretched the limits of his understanding. But he was confident that he'd saved an important life that fateful day. The Commonwealth was approaching a critical juncture, and Conroy would play a central role in guiding its future.

But all of those hard-fought plans would collapse if their operation fell today. This was another decisive moment, and he would do anything to fulfill his duty.

Driven by that purpose, he raced along the corridor, ready to fight.

Another concussive thud reverberated down the hallway. Gunfire sounded in the distance. But any distance was too close.

They're coming deeper inside. Samor's stomach clenched at the thought. *After all this time, is this how it ends for us?*

He refused to give up.

As much as he wanted to head to the entrance to help hold back the invading forces, he had a more pressing mission. Conroy needed to be brought to safety, and Samor needed to relay his information about Evan and Anya. There was still hope to turn around the fight as long as that ship made it into the right hands.

Assuming it exists… He had to believe it did. Otherwise, all of his sacrifices would be for nothing.

Samor ran for Central Command, knowing that's where Conroy would hole up in an emergency. The room had access to all the surveillance feeds and was the most fortified part of the structure. And what he hadn't told Evan and Anya was that it, too, had an escape route. They'd repurposed a former maintenance crawlspace from the ship as an emergency egress—slower and more awkward than the back cave tunnel, but survival was more important than dignity. He hoped it wouldn't come to using it tonight.

As Samor rounded the corner leading to the final corridor on his route, loud scuffling and shouts sounded nearby. He heard a metallic object clink across the metal flooring and roll in his direction.

He knew that sound. *Grenade!*

Samor ran back the way he'd come and ducked around the corner. No sooner had he rounded the bend than an explosive flash and smoke filled the corridor. Gunfire erupted in the chaos.

He was so close to his destination, but that route was no longer an option. To make it inside Central Command, he'd need to approach it from the other side and hope he could beat the invaders there.

Samor backtracked to a previous branch in the corridor and headed left. One advantage to living in the same, small facility for the past several years was that he knew every hallway by heart and every possible route. It was his one advantage over the invaders.

Evasion was his best chance right now. The moment he got in a firefight, that would likely be the end of his chances to make it inside the room, and he may as well die here in the hallway.

No, I'm not dead yet. This fight isn't lost.

Even as he ran down the corridor along the back route, he couldn't keep worry from darkening his thoughts. This facility was never meant to hold off an invading force. Most of the people here weren't trained fighters, and even the soldiers were out of practice. *He* was out of practice. The entire point of coming here had been to be far away from violence. They'd been seeking a technological and diplomatic solution.

"Samor!" a voice hissed in front of him. Erik peeked around a corner ahead, rifle in hand.

"What the hell happened?" Samor whispered back.

"They threw too much at us to stop." Erik motioned him into hiding. The side corridor wasn't the path Samor needed to reach Central Command. "Colonel Walthers is dead."

Samor grimaced. Walthers had been a colleague and friend for years, and it was a huge blow to lose their most senior military officer. But there wasn't time to mourn. "I need to get to Conroy."

"What you need to do is get him out of here. We can't hold them."

"Are they uniformed?"

His friend nodded solemnly.

They'd always known that it was a possibility they'd eventually come face to face with their former comrades. Lines had been drawn the moment they'd decided to back Conroy and depart the Commonwealth's established territory. He hadn't expected that today he would finally reconcile those past decisions.

"All the more reason I have to get to him," Samor said. He swore as he released a long breath to release the tension welling in his chest. There was no more time to waste. "Are you coming with me?"

Erik hesitated. "I'll try to hold them off."

A pained twinge struck Samor's heart, knowing this might be goodbye. "You're a good soldier, my friend."

Erik gave him a resolute nod. "Keep our leader safe."

The two men ran in opposite directions. Samor was tantalizingly close now to the Command Center. Shouts and gunfire still carried down the hall, but they weren't yet on his heels.

Samor reached the door. Pressing his palm to the biometric lock, the device responded with an angry beep and red light. He spotted the security camera and stared up at it, waving his arms.

A couple seconds later, the door clanged unlocked. The security wheel spun, and the door swung inward.

"Quickly!" a woman's voice urged.

Samor ducked inside. Stepping over the threshold, he saw that the speaker was Rebeka. He knew her well from their many years working together. She was a political analyst by trade, but the years on Aethos had broadened her skillset significantly. Based on the rifle in her hand, she'd graduated from administrative expert to honorary guard.

The second Samor had both feet inside the room, Rebeca relocked the door behind him. "Is it as bad out there as it seems?"

"Afraid so."

Conroy was working on the other side of the room, studying security feeds displayed on various screens.

"Sir!" Samor called out.

Conroy looked up, his shoulders rounding at the sight of Samor. "Did you get them out?"

"Yes." Samor jogged over to him.

"Did they agree?" Conroy asked, his eyes pleading.

"I think so. It was difficult to get a read on them. I wish we'd had more time to share our side and make them understand."

"We'll need to trust," the chancellor said.

"If they find it, the verification will be—"

An explosion blasted out the main door, accompanied by a plume of smoke. Both kinetic rounds and pulsefire sliced through the smokey veil, indiscriminately sweeping across the room.

Without thinking, Samor tackled Conroy and threw him to the ground. As they fell, searing pain ignited in Samor's right shoulder, followed by sharp burning in his lower left back.

Shouts around him grew fainter with each passing moment. Darkness closed around the edges of his vision. His pain was no more than a distant warmth.

"Sam—"

Gunfire faded into the blackness.

30

EVAN CHECKED OVER his shoulder again. He knew that he'd be able to hear someone coming up from behind due to the tunnel's acoustics, but he couldn't stop the compulsion.

It wasn't supposed to be like this. Evan had done a lot of unsavory things in his life, no doubt, but he'd never dreamed the recent chain of events would lead him here.

It still astounded him that a place could be such a colossal nightmare and liberating at the same time. Somehow, even though it seemed like everything on Aethos was trying to kill him, it still felt safer than the core worlds, where material pursuits were treated as a matter of life and death. Dying here would have a certain poetry to it—being returned to the ground, becoming a permanent part of the place. Though he had no intention of meeting his end here, at least if it did happen, that was a lot better way to go out than becoming meat-popsicle space debris.

Anya had been quiet and stoic through their dash down the rock tunnel. He caught occasional glimpses of the fear in her eyes, but she seemed determined to present a tough exterior. And she was tough—he had no doubt about that. They wouldn't have gotten this far without her refusal to give up in the face of adversity, and that attitude would continue to carry them through the challenges to come.

Their shadows danced along the stone walls as they ran across the uneven surface. Evan came close to rolling his ankle a few times in his haste, but the last few days hiking along challenging terrain had improved his reflexes. Hopefully, those quick recovery instincts would help get them to safety.

After a long, monotonous journey through the dark tunnel, Evan finally spotted faint light ahead. He slowed his pace and covered his flashlight's beam to verify that it wasn't just his eyes playing tricks on him. Sure enough, there was a portal of weak, blue-tinted light straight ahead, and several smaller slats along the left wall and ceiling.

"Must be the exit," he whispered, not knowing how far his voice might carry in the strange acoustics of the tunnel.

"I can't wait to get out of here!" Anya muttered.

"Go slow." He left the reason unspoken, not wanting to invite a scenario where enemies were waiting outside to ambush them. Yet, it was a real possibility. Samor had no way of knowing that this exit was sufficiently hidden to have avoided detection, and Evan didn't want to walk into a trap.

Even knowing there could be ambushers, he didn't know the best way to proceed. They'd be exposed the moment they stepped outside the cave, yet they couldn't see what was out there until they left. *I really wished we'd asked to take a surveillance drone,* he thought with a pang of regret.

Determined to puzzle his way out of the situation, Evan turned off his flashlight and proceeded to feel his way forward, keeping one hand on the wall for spatial reference. Anya followed him, mimicking his movements.

The indistinct light ahead took on more definition as they neared the cave's mouth. They'd swung past dusk to full nighttime lighting, with the moon hanging low in the sky. Occasional animal calls broke the silence, adding to the eeriness of the night.

Evan couldn't explain it, but his subconscious told him that it wasn't safe outside. Over the close calls throughout his life, he'd learned to listen to those impulses. He dropped to a low crouch and crept to the opening, wanting to look for any signs of danger that would solidify his worries.

At first glance, the surrounding jungle was relatively still and quiet, as it should be. The moonlight made it easy to pick out details, and there definitely weren't dozens of soldiers openly staking out the cave. That didn't mean there weren't hidden threats.

Evan scanned the trees for any shapes that might be out of place. An unnatural shine drew his eye, near a rock formation halfway up the slope to the left. He immediately ducked back to full cover.

Anya was already moving forward. "Come on, let's—"

Evan held up his arm to stop her. He pressed his index finger to his lips and drew her back into the shadow within the cave.

"What is it?" Anya whispered.

"I think I caught a glint. I'm not positive."

"Glint?"

"Off something reflective. Like metal. I haven't seen anything naturally shiny around here."

Her brows drew together with concern. "Could they know about this back exit after all?"

"Anything is possible."

She swore under her breath. "What are we supposed to do?"

"We can't stay in here and give them a chance to close in on us. We need a distraction."

"Like what?"

"That's what I'm trying to figure out."

The day had somehow managed to keep going downhill. Even adrenaline was becoming less effective in keeping weariness from seeping into Evan's bones. If going back to his prison cell-like quarters in Conroy's camp had been an option, he'd have been there in a heartbeat. But resting was out of the question now. He needed to focus, and he needed a feasible plan.

"We have to shoot and make it look like it's coming from somewhere else," Evan said.

"Doesn't that require *being* in another location?"

"With what we have, pretty much yeah." A remote firing array would have been super handy, and finding one in the cave was about as unlikely as stumbling into a luxury resort in the middle of the jungle.

Anya glanced up. "What about one of those skylights? I think I could squeeze out, and then I could swing around and make a distraction shot."

The openings in the side wall did, indeed, look large enough for Anya to fit through. However, he didn't like the idea of her drawing fire. In the scenario he was playing out in his mind, a distraction shot would get all hidden shooters to reveal themselves by firing back. Meanwhile, Evan would make note of their positions and then use the rifle to eliminate as many as possible. The glint he'd spotted was a good place to start, but others might be out there and better hidden. Giving all of them something to shoot at might draw them out.

"They could have thermal imaging, Anya. It's risky."

"I'll find cover."

He looked at the openings again. "Maybe I can fit through."

"And how are you going to get up there? Come on, boost me." Anya set down her pack and then went to size up the rock wall. She stuck her handgun in her waist band. "What are you waiting for?"

For this to be a good idea. Reluctantly, Evan cupped his hands for Anya to use as a step.

She placed her foot on his hands, and he boosted her up. She found handholds on the wall and hauled herself up to the opening. Seeing her right next to it, he wasn't sure she could fit through, after all.

"Can you make it?" he asked.

Anya lined up her head and chest. "It'll be tight, but yes."

"What can you see up there? Is there cover?"

"Yeah, I'm good." She shimmied through the opening.

As much as Evan had grown to trust Anya, he'd also learned that she was also reluctant to share when things were not going to plan. "Anya, please be careful."

She stuck her head back down through the hole and smiled. "Yeah, I've got this. Hand me my pack."

He passed the heavy bag up to her, and she squeezed it through the opening.

"There could be snipers," Evan warned.

She turned solemn. "I know. I'll keep cover, don't worry. I'm going to swing around above to keep the high ground. I've got a plan." She held up her deactivated flashlight and shook it with a flourish.

"What are you—"

Anya smiled again. "A distraction from a safe distance. As I said, I've got this. Now go get into position so you can spot whoever is stalking us." She disappeared into the dark night above.

Evan silently jogged back to the cave's opening and pressed

his back against the worn rock. He risked a peek toward where he'd seen the glint before, and the same metallic form was still catching the moonlight. It shifted slightly.

Worried he may have been spotted, Evan ducked out of view again. He dropped to his belly and crawled forward, hugging the wall. Nestling behind some loose, torso-sized rocks at the entrance, he was able to feed his rifle through a gap while keeping complete cover.

He waited.

A beam of light illuminated the hillside, shining over from above Evan. A flash of kinetic muzzle flare came a moment later—originating from next to the glint location. Evan aimed for the muzzle flare, and he took a shot of his own.

An indistinct shout rang out. The glint flashed, and Evan shot at it again.

The moonlight caught the reflective object tumbling to the ground. Evan scanned the hillside and surrounding area for signs of additional adversaries but none came.

Cautiously, he rose up, keeping his rifle trained on the place where the enemy shots had originated. He couldn't detect any further movement.

"You got them," Anya said from above.

Evan glanced upward in time to see her sliding down a rock outcropping above the cave mouth. He held up a finger to his lips, indicating for her to stay quiet.

She took one more look at the enemy location and then dropped down from the ledge, appearing extremely pleased with herself.

Evan jogged over to meet her, keeping his rifle raised and pointed toward the jungle. "There might still be others out there," he whispered, continuing to scan for potential threats.

"I only saw those two," she replied softly. "I think one of

them might be dead, and the other guy dropped his rifle and ran off. Your first shot hit his gun."

"'How did you see all that?"

"It was easy to keep watch once I rigged up the misdirect." Her eyes sparkled.

"Anya, what did you do?"

"Well, I realized that the flashlights are operated with a pressure switch, right? So, I wedged the flashlight between some branches and tied some cloth around it in a noose knot. That way, I could pull to activate the light from a couple meters away. It did work, but the light came loose after turning on, so that's why it was flashing all over the place."

"That was brilliant thinking."

She grinned. "I have my moments."

It was a lot more than occasional highlights, but Evan kept the thought to himself. "Stay vigilant. The other guy might still be out there."

Anya drew her handgun from her waistband. "Let's see who we're dealing with."

— — —

Roman clutched his wounded hand as he blindly ran through the trees. He'd expected to catch the escapees by surprise, not been the one to be ambushed himself. Clearly, he was dealing with skilled soldiers on Conroy's team.

He couldn't go back to Red and her company to admit he'd been wrong to strike out on his own. His best bet would be to regroup, find out who he was dealing with, and then make a move where he could regain the upper hand.

And do it all one-handed, he realized, cradling his right hand to his chest.

A well-placed shot had struck his rifle, searing the weapon and his hand in the process. His opponent had been close enough that any halfway decent shooter could have made the shot, but what had surprised Roman was that he hadn't seen them coming. A flash of light above the caves had drawn his eye, and he'd fallen for the bait. It'd been a rookie mistake, and he should have known better. If only the infernal bugs hadn't been buzzing around his head to make him antsy.

Roman spotted a small recess in the hillside that may have been an animal burrow. He ducked inside for cover and to assess his injury.

Using a beam of moonlight streaming into the entrance for illumination, Roman peeled back his shirt sleeve from his wounded hand. He gritted his teeth to keep from crying out from the pain as he separated the fabric from drying blood and burned flesh. His hand trembled from the shock and pain, but he made a concerted effort to keep his breath slow and steady through his nose.

Getting his first good look at the injury, his fingers were all intact, so that was a good thing. There were severe burns along the back and outer side of his hand, but skin could heal.

Using his good hand, he rooted around in his pack for his medkit. He opened it up and pulled out the emergency spray for open wounds—a handy catchall treatment for anything from gunshots to scrapes or burns. It sprayed on as foam, the searing pain darkening the edges of his vision. Soon, the agony gave way to cool numbness as the foam dried into a flexible bandage. While not as good as the care he could get in a proper medical center, the emergency treatment should keep infection at bay and allow his hand to heal enough to regain function.

Roman returned the medkit to his pack and crawled out of the burrow. He listened for signs of the enemy.

Hushed voices came from nearby.

"It was a good shot," a woman said.

"Would have been nice to question him," a man responded.

With a twinge in his chest, Roman thought of the horrific moment when a lethal pulse blast had struck Sten. A moment later, his own rifle had been hit, prompting him to flee. Had he been trained as a soldier, he might not have left his friend without checking. However, his self-preservation instinct had prevailed. Just like when a firefight broke out back home between rival gangs, in the heat of the moment it was every man for himself. Only now that he'd tended to his wound did he have the headspace to consider his fallen comrade.

No wonder the real soldiers didn't want us around. What a shitty way to treat another person. Even with the realization, he felt no guilt. There was only the fear of being on his own, and being hunted. He'd liked it much better when he was the one on the offensive. *I need to get back in control.*

How to go about doing that was a more complex matter. He was now effectively operating alone, and he didn't know how many opponents he was up against. That meant he needed more information before he could formulate a logical plan.

Surveillance. He inched from his hiding place to pinpoint the speakers he'd overheard. They'd clearly been near Sten's body, but Roman hadn't paid close attention to his location when he'd fled earlier.

"Should we try to track down the other guy?" the woman asked.

Roman remained still, not wanting to give away his location.

"I'd rather put as much distance as we can between us and them," the man replied.

Good, let them think they're alone. Wilderness tracking wasn't Roman's strongest skill, but he felt confident in his ability to gather information about his opposition from a distance. All he needed to do was figure out how to shoot them all without getting shot himself. His remaining handgun should be sufficient for that task.

The people started to move away from Sten's body. No one else had spoken.

Maybe it's just two of them. This may be even easier than Roman had realized. He followed them at a distance, waiting for the right moment to make his move.

31

ANYA DETESTED VIOLENCE, as a rule. Worse, she hated that her time on Aethos was beginning to make her see it as a necessity.

A week ago, her stomach would have turned over at the sight of the corpse crumpled by the rocks. Now, she viewed the dead man as an eliminated threat—relief tinged with a hint of regret for not being able to ask him questions. The shift in mentality scared her.

Evan walked alongside Anya, his rifle slung over his shoulder. They'd opted not to take the weapons from the dead man with them, since they were already encumbered, but they had hidden them away from the body. He checked the time on his new wrist device containing the map. "We should find a place to camp for the night."

"Not anywhere close to here," Anya replied.

"At least we have a full moon to make nighttime travel easier."

She nodded. "But being in bed would be a whole lot better right now!"

Evan stopped and looked behind him.

"What is it?" Anya whispered.

He didn't reply at first. After ten seconds, he relaxed.

"Thought I heard something following us."

The back of Anya's neck prickled with the thought. She was tired enough that her senses had dimmed, and it concerned her that she hadn't detected anything herself. *First feeling numb staring down a dead body, and now not having situational awareness. I really do need sleep.*

However, settling down for the night was the last thing on her mind, knowing that there were armed attackers less than a kilometer away. They needed to just focus on putting one foot in front of the other to get to relative safety.

"Should we make a push to get to the outpost tonight?" she asked.

Evan considered the suggestion, glancing behind him again. "No, a tent is fine. No reason to go to an empty shell of a place."

She flashed him a quizzical look. Everything they'd heard made it sound like a fully outfitted facility, and Evan knew that. *Does he think someone might be listening to us?* She took a steadying breath. "Shame this planet never got built up. It could have made a nice colony."

"Pretty, but a whole lot of nothing." Evan was definitely misdirecting.

Anya tensed and started to reach for the handgun in her waistband. Evan gently gripped her wrist to stop her.

"No sudden moves," he whispered, barely audible and with almost no movement to his lips. "More non-information. Keep them listening."

Shit! Her pulse spiked. And, naturally, her mind went blank right when she needed to think of something that sounded useful and worth keeping her alive to learn more without actually giving away anything real and useful.

"I don't see any clouds coming in," Anya finally said.

Weather was always safe smalltalk.

"I'd be happy to never experience another storm."

"Yeah, good luck with that." Keeping her tone light and casual was difficult, but she figured it was best to make the conversation sound as natural as possible.

"I think we could make it to the canyon by morning," Evan said.

Canyon? In her tired state, it took Anya a moment to realize he was making up a fake destination for the benefit of their stalker. "Do you think it's a good idea to push through the night?"

Evan took her opening to vocalize a plan. "You know, making camp to get a little shuteye would be better. That way, we can still have daylight to work in when we arrive."

"I hope we won't have to dig much."

"We'll scope out the site and make sure what we want is there. It's exciting to think the search might be over tomorrow."

Despite the anxiety of knowing that they were being pursued, genuine excitement did warm Anya's core. They were getting close to uncovering a major mystery on Aethos—albeit a different target than their current cover conversation. But once they did find the real thing, everything could change for them.

First, they needed to shake their shadow. Evan seemed to be forming a plan, and she'd be ready to do her part.

— — —

The hyperawareness that often made it difficult for Evan to sleep at night at least came in handy when danger was nearby. He'd known they were being followed almost immediately, and he was thankful to have detected the threat before he and Anya found themselves in a compromised situation. Though they were far from safe at the moment, being aware of a risk was the first step toward mitigation.

Evan motioned for Anya to take the lead, wanting to keep himself closer to the unseen stalker. He had no doubt it was the other shooter. Based on the dribbles of blood he'd seen in the moonlight, the man was at least slightly injured. That would be helpful should they come to blows.

They continued through the moonlit trees, making occasional comments to keep up the appearance of being relaxed and unaware. All the while, Evan was looking for the right place to make a move.

His foremost concern was to not get injured or captured. The attackers had already demonstrated that they had no qualms about violence. Couple that with anger about an ally getting killed, and Evan had no doubt that their pursuer was out for blood. Most likely, the only reason they hadn't been shot yet was because the stalker wanted to see if they had any more useful information to share. That's what Evan would have done, were the roles reversed. So, he wanted to put on a show.

"According to the survey, we should be able to find an entrance at the southwest corner of the canyon," he began, making up the story as he went along. "I have the map with the exact location in my pack. I'll pull it out when we get to camp so we can plan our approach." He hoped the statement would plant the seed for a distraction.

True to form, Anya played along perfectly. "It was such a relief to get actual instructions about what to do after we've been stumbling around in the forest for days."

"I'd love to fly out of here on a spaceship."

She grinned—definitely a genuine emotion and not just acting. "I would happily join you."

Ahead, Evan spotted a location with the right characteristics to fit the plan he'd been plotting. It was a small clearing with a formation of chest-height rocks on one side that would make excellent cover. A dense grove of saplings on two other sides would make it difficult for anyone to sneak up around back, meaning that their pursuer would only have one reasonable approach.

Having established that there was valuable information stored in his pack, Evan intended to leave it near that approach path. However, he still needed to hedge their bets to avoid getting shot.

"I hope the two-part encryption works. Conroy's people didn't strike me as tech whizzes."

Anya tried to hide her confusion. "I think they've got it figured out."

"It is a smart idea to give us each a password and need both of us to unlock the map together."

She nodded, catching on. "They're no strangers to betrayal. I don't blame them for taking precautions."

"This is as good a spot as any to set up for the night," Evan said as they reached the clearing.

In line with his plan, he set his pack near the natural funnel leading into the shelter, but far enough in that no one could sneak up to it without being noticed.

"Let's clear a spot for the tent." Evan motioned Anya toward the rocks. He made a show of setting down his rifle. As he passed close to Anya, he whispered, "When our backs are turned, slip me your gun. I want him to think I'm unarmed."

They began stomping down grass and small brush to make a spot for a tent. On one of the passes as they circled each other,

Anya deftly passed her handgun behind her back to Evan. He tucked it into his waistband under his jacket, using every bit of the slight of hands skills he'd picked up while working undercover. All the while, he kept an eye on his pack and rifle.

"Stop," a deep male voice called out.

Evan froze in place, his right hand partially behind his back.

A man wearing dark, camouflaged body armor stepped from the trees, holding a handgun. Though the weapon was pointed at Anya, he was looking at Evan. "Don't think about trying anything," the man said.

As if statements like that ever work. Evan kept his posture relaxed. "You're the one with the gun, I've got it." He made a regretful glance toward his rifle to play it up.

"And your other one?" the man prompted.

Evan sighed and fished out his own handgun to set down, keeping Anya's hidden.

The man nodded to Anya. "What about you?"

She cocked her head. "Do I look like a soldier?"

That seemed to satisfy him. Keeping his weapon leveled on Anya, the man crouched down next to Evan's pack. "Where is the device?"

"It's in there, toward the bottom," Evan replied. There *was* no device in there, since it was actually strapped to his wrist, so he anticipated a lot of digging and building of frustration, which was the distraction he wanted.

"Do you want any help—"

"No," the man cut Evan off as he opened the backpack.

It was awkward work, holding a weapon while trying to look two places at once, and his right hand also appeared to be injured. After several seconds of cumbersome rooting around, the man grabbed the bottom of the pack and inverted it, dumping out the contents on the ground.

Evan held in a groan, annoyed that everything was going to get dirty and disorganized; he hadn't considered that part.

"Where is it?" the man demanded.

"Oh, *right*!" Anya exclaimed. "Did we actually put it in mine?"

Evan sighed dramatically. "You know, you're right. We did."

She motioned toward her pack, which was resting against the rocks close to them. "Should I…?"

"Back up," the man instructed, approaching them. He was wise to keep his distance from them, having a ranged weapon. Too many people made the mistake of getting within grappling distance.

Even if he could get close enough to make a move, Evan recognized that a fistfight was unlikely to go well for him, given that the other man was wearing armor. So, Evan continued walking slowly backward until the man told him to stop.

"What's the plan here?" Evan asked. "You're in control. We don't want any trouble."

"If you don't want trouble, then tell me where I can find that damned ship."

"The crash—?"

"Don't play stupid!" the man snapped. "You know I mean the alien ship. I know you have the coordinates."

"We know a general location, but the specific coordinates are on that device we mentioned, and we haven't looked at them yet. It's encrypted, and each of us has half of the key to unlock."

"Then do it." The man shifted the aim of his handgun to Evan. "Where is the device? Now!"

Evan exchanged glances with Anya. He hoped his

expression communicated for her to stay calm and continue to follow his lead.

Heading slowly toward Anya's pack, Evan kept his left arm, facing the aggressor, outstretched at his side while his right hand remained bent backward within easy reach of the hidden pistol.

He reached the pack and knelt down. Moving to open it, he feigned difficulty. "The clasp is stuck."

"Yeah, it's tricky," Anya replied. "Here, I'll get it." She headed toward Evan, passing close to the man.

"Stay back!" He kicked her chest, sending her tumbling to the ground.

Anya clutched her ribs where his foot had made impact, coughing. She started to crawl further away behind him.

While the man's head was turned to look at her, Evan lunged for his rifle.

"Don't!" the man shouted, whipping back to face him. He made a warning shot into the ground between Evan and the weapon, sending up a plume of dirt and grass fragments.

Evan froze. "Sorry. We're good."

Behind the man, Anya was getting to her feet. She had something in her hands. Without hesitation, she ran forward and whacked the man in the back of his head with what appeared to be a rock.

The man stood motionless for a moment. A trickle of blood dribbled down his left temple. He tried to take a step forward but dropped to the ground, unconscious. He was still breathing.

Anya dropped the heavy rock to the ground. Her hands were shaking and her breath was ragged. She clutched an arm around her midsection.

"Are you okay?" Evan asked her.

"Yeah. Is he...?"

Evan nudged him with his foot. There was no response, but he was definitely alive. "Out cold. That was a gutsy move—"

Anya ran to Evan and threw her arms around his neck. Caught off-guard, he took an awkward step backward before steadying himself.

"It's all right," he soothed while hugging her back. Her breath was warm against his skin, and she pressed against him in the embrace. Part of him wanted to pull her even closer, but he resisted. "We should secure him before he wakes up..."

She cleared her throat and dropped her arms to her sides. "Right." She was still trembling.

"Hey, what's wrong?"

She took a ragged breath. "I... I've never had to hurt someone like that before."

"Are *you* hurt?"

She rubbed her bruised ribs. "Nothing serious, but—"

"Then be happy the roles aren't reversed." Evan went to dig out a rope from his pack. "He'll recover."

"His friend from earlier won't."

"That one's on me. What's one more sleepless night weighing the value of life?" Evan had already had enough of those nights that he'd stopped keeping track. "We did what we had to do to make it out of there."

Anya nodded, though her brows were still knitted.

Evan set about binding the man's wrists. He was still unconscious and only let out a faint moan as Evan rolled him on his side. When Evan pushed up his sleeves, he almost recoiled. On the underside of the man's right wrist was a tattooed symbol he never thought he'd see again.

The three interlocking rings were a mark of the Noche Syndicate. Evan had never been up high enough in the organization's leadership to receive the mark himself. He was actually surprised to see someone as young as this man branded with the emblem. It was normally reserved for people with decades of service, or—

Family. Evan's pulse spiked. *If he's one of the family…* That meant that the Syndicate was even more embedded in the plot than he'd realized, if they'd risk sending one of their own here to Aethos. There'd been enough people on the colony ship that they wouldn't necessarily have run into each other. It was possible. But he didn't like any of it.

"Everything okay, Evan?" Anya asked, apparently picking up on his shift in mood.

"Yeah." He didn't want to go over the details here, in case the man was more lucid than he appeared. "I was just debating whether or not we should try to interrogate him, but that could take hours or days. I think it's more important that we get out of here before we become a check on someone else's kill scorecard."

"Why keep him alive?" Her face twisted with pained disgust with herself for asking.

"It's a risk, but I hoped that by sparing him his people might show us some mercy, if we're unlucky enough to get captured ourselves." While *not* getting captured was the goal, he'd rather hedge his bets should a worst-case scenario come to pass. If he was, indeed, one of the family, then they wouldn't be safe anywhere in the galaxy if they took his life. He saw no need to worry Anya with that detail at the moment.

Anya nodded her understanding. "Not killing is good by me."

Searching the unconscious man's pockets, Evan found two blades and took them, as well as the handgun. The man wouldn't be in great shape when he woke up, but being without weapons should encourage him to go back to his people rather than pursue them. To further dissuade his pursuit, Evan also took the man's boots.

"Oh, he's really going to hate us," Anya said with a grimace when she saw what Evan was doing.

"Well, he should be grateful he's alive." Evan went to pick up his own things off the ground. Thankfully, they'd landed in an area with a mixture of grass and moss that had prevented them from getting too soiled.

When Evan had finished repacking, Anya picked up her backpack from where she'd dropped it. "And here I thought the planet's wildlife was bad."

"Humans have always been the most dangerous enemy to each other." Evan slung his pack over his shoulders. "Let's go."

32

ROMAN HATED TO admit defeat, but he also recognized when he needed to call for backup. However, that backup was worlds away. And he'd have to get his wrists free before he could call them.

Whoever had tied the knot had known what they were doing. Cutting the rope would have been easy business with his combat knife, but of course they'd taken that, along with his boots. Bastards. And with his legs bound, he couldn't even have walked back to Red's company right now if he wanted to.

A sharp rock might be his best bet to get free. He could saw through his wrist bindings and then hike back to Red in his socks. He quickly rejected that idea. He'd be the laughing stock of the unit if the others knew how easily he'd been bested. No, it was better to free himself, take Sten's boots—assuming they hadn't stolen those, too—and then bring back an embellished story.

He'd learned that they were heading for a canyon. Vague, but it would narrow down potential locations when combined with the map of the energy signatures they'd been investigating. Hopefully, that information would be enough to distract the others from everything else.

Roman's head throbbed. The left side of his face itched. He rubbed his face on his shoulder, and there was a smear of drying blood on the fabric.

Great. That explains the headache. The woman must have hit him from behind. Apparently, she was feistier than he'd anticipated.

He winced, staring upward at the night sky. The two visible moons were still in a similar position to when he'd last seen them, so he couldn't have been unconscious for too long.

There was no gear left in the clearing, so the two people had moved on. It might have been possible to catch up with them if he could get going right away, but that'd be next to impossible between his bindings and lack of proper footwear.

He wriggled his hands and bent his elbows to reach his hip pocket. Patting the fabric, he wasn't surprised to find that his utility knife was also gone.

Sharp rock, it is. Roman looked around for a suitable candidate.

He'd only crawled a short distance when he spotted a rock a little smaller than his head with a bloody smudge on one side. His blood boiled at the sight of it, more from embarrassment than anger. If he'd been in top form without the infernal allergies he'd been suffering on the planet, he never would have been tricked so easily.

The rock itself had no sharp edges—a blessing, considering that could have been deadly for him—so he squirmed on across the grassy clearing toward the rock formation. At the base of the boulders, he spotted several smaller fragments that had flaked off. He found one that had a relatively smooth side that would make a nice grip paired with a sharp edge along a fracture on the other side.

Positioning it and going by feel behind his back, he started the slow process of sawing through the ropes. He'd have plenty of time to plan his next move.

— — —

Anya's heart didn't stop pounding in her ears until they were a least a kilometer from the clearing where they'd left the man tied up.

She wasn't sure what about the encounter had rattled her so much. What she'd told Evan about it being the first time she'd had to hurt someone in such a hands-on way was true, but there was more to it than that. Her nerves were fraying. She hadn't realized that the feeling had progressed to this point. It had snuck up on her in the last few hours. After thinking that she was finally back in a safe place, that security had been ripped out from under her, and she was now in a worse place than before they'd met Conroy.

Maybe we should have run off to that cave, after all. Hiding did have a strong allure now. All the talk of finding a secret ancient ship that could turn the tide in a brewing civil war was way out of her comfort zone. She'd put up a strong front when Evan had said he wanted to walk away, and now she regretted not following him out the door. At the time, she'd been taken in by the idea of being part of a team with a lifeline back to the core worlds.

None of that mattered now—they were on the run through the jungle, and an ancient alien ship that might not even exist was their only potential salvation. It was pure insanity, any way she looked at it.

"Evan, what are we doing?" she asked, breaking the longtime silence.

"In what sense?"

"Everything."

He let out a long breath. "I think we do need to try to find the ruins."

"What's the point? Could there really be a functional ship buried there?"

"Your guess is as good as mine. But I do know that we don't have any other way off the planet right now, so we need to do *something*."

"In other words, go on a mythical treasure hunt because we have nothing better to do?"

He cracked a smile. "When you put it like that, how could we *not*?"

Anya chuckled. "Yeah, I guess so."

"For the record, I'm highly skeptical about finding an intact ship that could still fly," Evan said after a pause.

"That does sound highly unlikely."

"In my experience, though, there's often a kernel of truth to rumors. So, I'm hoping that we can still find something of value. Anything tangible that we can get in our hands will put us in a better position for negotiation."

"Meaning, we might be able to barter for our lives, if not a way off this rock."

"Exactly."

"I am all for that plan."

Evan shook his head. "I don't think I've ever lived with this much uncertainty—and that's saying something."

"Yeah, I know what you mean."

He side-eyed her.

"What, you think everything has been easy for me?"

"I didn't say that."

"But you were thinking it."

Evan hesitated. "I don't doubt that you've had challenges.

We've just had very different experiences."

"You've definitely faced down danger and death more than I have—more than a lot of people. Still, it wasn't all peace and harmony for me, you know." Her chest tightened. She hadn't thought about the painful parts of her childhood for a long time, but something about the night's events had dredged up those feelings of being unsafe.

Evan seemed to pick up on her shift in mood. "I didn't mean to upset you."

"You aren't the first to pass superficial judgement."

"Whoa, hey." He caught her gaze, looking genuinely remorseful. "I'm sorry for whatever I said. Where is this coming from?"

She smoothed her hair. "This is me overthinking things, like I often do. I'm tired and cranky."

"That may have brought it out, but there's still a reason. I'd rather talk it out than let it fester."

Anya studied him in the moonlight. She had passed some snap-judgements of her own about him as an ex-soldier, but his empathy and consideration had been a pleasant surprise. Wrestling with her own issues wasn't a reason to dump on him.

"A few days ago, when I mentioned my parents, it sounded like you thought I had it easy because we had money."

He tilted his head, eyes narrowed slightly. "Money does make things easier."

"In some ways, yes. And I do appreciate the security and opportunities wealth offered me while growing up. But, there *is* a dark side to it. When you don't need to worry about putting food on the table, it leaves room for vices." That caught his attention. "My dad used to drink a lot," she continued. "He wasn't violent, exactly, but he'd yell. If I'd done anything wrong that day, or gotten less than perfect marks in school, he'd tell me how I'd never amount to anything. My mom would try to walk it back and explain it was just the alcohol talking, but there were times it really got to me."

"I can imagine."

"They never addressed it as any kind of problem. You seem like less of a drunk when it's a classy booze like wine rather than whiskey or vodka, right?"

Evan's expression softened with compassion. "I'm sorry, Anya. It must have been difficult."

"Everyone has something shitty about their childhood, right?" She shook her head. "I know I got off easy compared to a lot of people."

He reached over and gave her hand a supportive squeeze. "Thank you for telling me. That can't be easy to talk about."

She shrugged. "You've opened up, so I figured I should do the same."

"I realized that keeping things to myself was all a twisted self-delusion. I've spent so much time pretending to be someone else that I can no longer tell the difference between my real experiences and the fiction I invented for backstory."

"I imagine there were bits of truth in there."

He looked down at his hands. "Lie to yourself enough and you can never be sure."

"I think I rewrote a lot of experiences with my parents in my own mind. The days Dad was really out of it, I'd tell myself he was just tired or sick or something."

"I am thankful my parents never made me feel unsafe. We may not have had a lot of money, but we always had each other."

"That sounds really nice. And I don't mean to make it sound like it was all bad. I do have a lot of happy memories. Like, when I was little, my dad used to take me outside at night to look at the stars. He'd put me up on his shoulders where I could get the best view. I remember thinking I could reach out and touch them."

Evan nodded. "And then we grow up and learn they'll always be just out of our reach."

She scrunched her nose. "I don't think of it that way. We're here on a different planet, aren't we? We're now covered in little bits of stardust from the star warming this world. Every planet we go to, we take a little bit of it with us."

"I'm surprised to hear such a romanticized perspective coming from a scientist."

"You're not giving us science types enough credit. We can be very complex."

"Clearly."

"I also suspect you're not as cynical as you'd have me think."

"I'm just a realist."

"I haven't known you for long, but I know you're also a dreamer. The two states can coexist. I'm proof."

He sighed. "All right, yes, I have been known to think aspirationally on occasion."

"Good, because we have a lot of aspiring still to do. There's a ship to find, right?"

"I grew up reading about treasure hunters seeking out ancient ruins, so why not live the dream!"

She smiled. "Exactly. I mean, what else is there to do around here?"

"Not get eaten."

"Oh, right." She swallowed. "Speaking of which, there is something I should mention."

"What's that?"

"The place we're going, where Conroy said to find the cave

entrance. That's near where the Ranger-R was mangled."

Evan let out a humorless chuckle. "Oh, great!"

"Yeah."

"What about the research outpost?"

"It's at the edge."

"Then we're better off approaching in daylight."

She nodded. "And that's still several kilometers from here. We'll need that navigation of yours to get us the rest of the way there."

Evan smiled down at the device strapped to his wrist. "We really pulled one over with that guy pretending that the map was on something else."

"You're quick on your feet."

"I had to be in my line of work. You were fantastic playing along."

"Have to be pretty nimble when dealing with wild animals, in all fairness."

"Very true."

Anya looked up at the night sky. "What should we do about camp for tonight?"

Evan glanced behind them. "I don't think we're being followed, but I'd still like to put a couple more kilometers between us and the last place we saw anyone. We can find a private spot to pitch the tent. No fire."

"Sounds like a plan."

33

"SAMOR! HEY!"

Samor startled awake. He bolted upright, only to experience shooting pain through his right shoulder. He shifted his weight to his left arm to prop himself up, finding that his lower back on that side was tender, too.

He was on the ground, and Rebeka hovered over him. "Thank the planets you're okay!" she exclaimed.

"Mostly." Samor winced as he flexed his shoulder.

The air had a damp musty quality to it. The space wasn't well-lit, but Samor could make out natural rock forms. They must have evacuated to one of the caves. The recent events started coming back to him in flashes.

"Conroy! Is he—?"

"He's fine." Rebeka soothed. "You took a shot for him, but we got you out. We bought ourselves enough time to evac."

"Why haven't they followed us?"

Her face pinched. "We blew Central Command. Collapsed the tunnel."

Samor laid back down. "All that tech…"

"I can't think about it right now. I'm just thankful we got as many people out as we did."

His stomach twisted. "How many did we lose?"

"We're not sure yet. People are scattered. There are only eight of us in this group, but we know there are others. And there's the whole team with the colonists at Echo Falls."

But what if it is only the eight of us against the world? He had to believe that there were many more than that out there.

Despite his pain, he propped himself up on his left elbow again. "Tell me what I can do to help."

"Right now, rest and recover." She checked the dressing on his shoulder injury. "You're in no shape to do anything else."

"I need to talk to Conroy."

"He's busy."

"It's important."

She glanced across the dark space to something unseen. "All right, I'll tell him you're alert. Try to get some rest until he comes by."

Samor had been ready to ignore her instruction, but his heavy eyelids got the better of him. He wasn't sure how long he was out, but a familiar voice roused him.

"How are you feeling?"

Samor smiled as he opened his eyes. "About as good as you after that night out on Candelin."

The chancellor laughed. "We weren't supposed to talk about that night ever again."

"You said 'not in this lifetime', and I nearly died, so I figure I get a pass."

Conroy patted Samor's good shoulder. "I'll grant you that." He turned serious. "Rebeka said you wanted to talk?"

Samor propped himself up with some effort, careful to hide his pain from the chancellor. "I was about to tell you before they broke in. Evan and Anya will identify themselves as 'Trailblazer', and our confirmation is 'Phoenix'."

"That is very important information, indeed. Thank you."

"Sir…" Samor searched for the words. "What do we do now?"

The chancellor slumped—an unfamiliar show of vulnerability from a man so many revered as an unflappable beacon of strength. "I'm still trying to figure that out."

"We can fight back."

"And we will. But this isn't a fight to be won with sheer firepower. That has never been our strategy, and we must be even more careful with our approach now."

"I'm here for you, sir. Whatever you need."

"Thank you, Samor. I'm glad you're on the mend. If you hadn't pulled me down when you did, I'm not sure I would have fared so well."

Samor nodded, a swell of gratitude in his chest. "Just doing my job, sir."

The chancellor chuckled. "It stopped being that a long time ago. The pay is too terrible for that to be the only reason you stick around."

"Come to think of it, I haven't received a deposit in going on five years now—"

"You just focus on healing." Conroy smiled. "I don't want to do this without you."

"I'm not going anywhere."

"Well, hopefully soon, you might have to. I still hope we can find a ride off this planet, and then the real work can begin."

— — —

Roman picked the final rope strands from his ankles. Cutting through his wrist binding had taken a solid twenty minutes, and the knots securing his legs had been a pain to untie with only one fully functional hand. He'd let his frustration fuel him, and he was anxious to get back to Red's team so he could implement his new strategy.

The painstaking task of freeing himself had given him time to strategize. He knew the general location of where the two people were going to find the ship, which significantly narrowed down the search area. He *had* been successful in that aspect of his mission.

Now, though, they needed to *capture* that ship. And hold it. For that, he needed an army.

Though he'd only encountered two people in the jungle, he had no reason to believe that they didn't have backup of their own. He refused to be bested again in their next encounter.

Roman set as brisk a pace as he could through the jungle given he was only wearing socks. Every rock fragment jabbed his feet, but the leaves and dirt were comfortable enough to walk on. The primary moon was still high and bright enough to offer ample illumination.

Before heading back to find Red, Roman returned to the overlook to locate Sten's body. The unfortunate man was still sprawled where he'd fallen. The headshot had dropped him instantly, and Roman was thankful that at least he hadn't suffered. Having been through a firefight where a couple of the victims had received gut wounds, he wouldn't wish that kind of slow, painful death on any colleague.

Sten's weapons were missing, but he appeared otherwise untouched, including his boots. Roman breathed a sigh of relief at that. Sizing them up, they were a little big for Roman, but not unreasonably so.

Once he'd finished paying his respects and lacing up his newly acquired boots, Roman set out to find Red. He was thankful for having had the good sense to mark his path from the facility entrance, so it was easy to navigate back from the overlook.

He took as quick a pace as he dared over the uneven terrain, striking a balance between speed and stealth. While he didn't think any of Conroy's other associates were likely in the area, he'd rather not make his presence known.

On the final approach, he slowed to listen for indications of where Red's team might be. He overheard the cadence of conversation with the speakers making no effort to muffle their voices. The tone was upbeat and joyful, though he couldn't make out the specifics of the words from that distance.

He announced himself as he stepped from the trees, knowing that the soldiers might be the 'shoot first' sort.

"What took you so long?" one of the men asked, not quite lowering his weapon all the way.

"Where's Red?" Roman countered.

"Wondering what took you so long."

"I have information, and she's probably also wondering why you're delaying me from telling her."

The man's eyes narrowed, but he stepped aside. "She's down by the entrance."

Roman could feel the eyes on him as he stepped from the trees into the clearing. Much of the grass was now singed, and there were several small craters where it appeared munitions had exploded.

Red was talking to a small group of soldiers near the entrance. The door was ajar and the area around it was pitted and blackened. She dismissed the people when she noticed Roman approaching.

She stared at him expectantly. "Well?"

"They got away, but I know where they're going."

"What happened?"

"They ambushed us—killed Sten. I was able to track them to a camp, where I overheard them strategizing."

"Where?"

"They're going to a canyon, about fifteen kilometers north of here." The location was an educated guess, in reality, but he figured it best to state it as certainty in order to ensure assistance.

Red didn't look happy with the news. "That's in the red zone."

"I know, but the prize is worth the risk."

"You shouldn't have let them get away. They can't be allowed to discover this world's secrets."

"Which is why I came straight back to you as soon as I learned their intentions."

"We'll send a team. We can't let them share the truth about this place."

"I'll go with whoever you send."

Red whistled and motioned to one of her soldiers. He jogged over. "Ansen, get the drop ship ready. We've got hostiles on the move and need to head them off."

Drop ship? Roman's spirits lifted. He had figured they'd need to walk all the way there, but he wasn't about to turn down a ride—especially given the alleged monster roaming the area. The craft would be capable of reaching orbit, but it lacked interstellar capabilities as well as any weaponry of its own. So, while it was better to have a vessel than none, it was far from a game-changer longer term. There was only one way he would leave the planet. "We're close to our target, I know it. Securing that alien ship is my top priority."

"And you'd better take care of this loose end while you're at it."

The two survivors really had become a major annoyance. "I will. But it's not like they could do anything with the information, even if they do stumble across the truth. They're isolated on this planet."

"Even still, it's not a risk we're willing to take."

"They've been surprisingly elusive. I recognized the man from the ship's manifest, but his actions didn't seem to match the background on his roster."

"If he booked passage under an alias, he could be anyone."

Roman nodded. "There's someone that disappeared right around the time the ship departed. I never met him, myself, but if he's the traitor..."

"How could that be possible? I thought they vetted everyone."

Roman shrugged. "I don't know, but it's all the more reason to track them down and make sure they can't talk."

She glared. "Yes, and you were supposed to have intercepted them—not let them get away."

"Well, it's not the first aspect of this mission that didn't go to plan."

Based on her livid expression, that had been the wrong thing to say. "Just find them."

"I will." If he didn't, he'd have bigger problems than Red's wrath.

— — —

Evan shivered. The temperature had noticeably dropped, and the wind had picked up. Tree limbs creaked overhead as they swayed with each wind swell.

Anya frowned at the clouds rolling across the sky. "This expedition keeps getting better and better."

"The activity director sure took 'endless adventure' to heart."

She rolled her eyes. "Good one."

"I'm not sure we should keep walking around with a storm blowing in," Evan suggested. "Maybe we should find a sheltered spot to pitch the tent for the night."

"I could really use some rest. Let's do it."

After a little scouting, they identified a site where they could anchor the tent against a large rock where there wouldn't be any trees overhead that might fall. With its orientation, the rock even blocked the worst of the wind.

As soon as the tent was assembled, they dove inside to warm up.

To his surprise, Anya sat right next to him and leaned over so her shoulder and head were against his chest. "I miss being able to have a fire," she said.

Admittedly, if he'd known a lack of fire would get him closer to such an attractive woman, he'd have come up with a reason for not having a nighttime fire much sooner. "Hey, at least this means we don't need to spend time looking for firewood."

"How else are we supposed to spend the time?"

The question, coming while she was so close to him, seemed a little flirtatious, but he wasn't confident she'd meant it that way. "We can always plan our next move," he said instead, figuring that could be taken multiple ways.

"Right now, I'm just happy to be in the moment." She snuggled a little closer.

"Me too." He wasn't about to complain, but the close contact caught him by surprise. Sure, they'd been a little playful over the past few days, but this was a definite escalation from where things had been.

Still, he was all too aware of the reality of their situation. Not dying from one of the numerous hazards in the environment or at the hand of the people now chasing them was the priority. A romantic entanglement would only be a distraction from their goals. Yet, despite knowing all that, it felt nice to have her close to him. It'd been a long time since he'd felt able to let his guard down around anyone and allow himself to be contented. So, despite the dangers lurking just outside the tent, he found himself at peace.

He reclined on his bedroll, propping one arm behind his head as a pillow. She lay down next to him, positioning herself in the crook of his arm. With the encroaching cold, he was happy for the warm contact.

Just as Evan was beginning to drift off to sleep, he bolted awake to an approaching thunderous roar. At first, he thought it was the stormfront rolling in. However, the sound was soon unmistakable.

"That's a shuttle."

"What?!" Anya's face twisted with confusion. "How?"

"Must have come down with the escort ship."

"That's not good."

"They're probably heading for the canyon where we said we were going."

She frowned. "We have to go through there to get to the actual ruins."

"This just got a whole lot more complicated."

34

ANYA HAD BEEN restless for the remainder of the night after the ship passed by overhead. There was no telling where the enemy soldiers may set up, and there was already the concern about the unknown monster. Sometimes, she really wished she didn't know anything about the dangers on the planet and could just take each problem as it came.

It'd been a cold night in the storm, but at least being close to Evan had offered some warmth and comfort. He'd been a perfect gentleman about it, which was for the better in their present circumstances.

Stress had a strange way of messing with one's priorities. Feeling so isolated here in the wilderness, she found herself wanting to latch on to whatever human connection she could find. Evan, by far, had been the most consistent presence in her life for the past week. In that context, it was no surprise that she'd grown attached. Once they were somewhere with more security, though, she wouldn't mind seeing what more they could potentially have together.

Stop it! she chastised herself. *That should be the last thing on my mind right now.*

The next couple of hours would be critical as they headed

into dangerous territory with a known predator as well as hostile enemy forces. About the only good news was that the overnight storm had passed. Wet ground would make them trackable, but it would also mean they could see if other people had passed by. All in all, she'd rather have that indicator than not.

"I say we head for the research outpost, and we can bail if it looks like it's been discovered," Anya said as she walked alongside Evan through the forest. There was less undergrowth but lots of springy moss groundcover in the area, making for a comfortable hike.

"I don't suppose you know what time of day the Ranger-R was attacked during the survey?" Evan asked.

"I don't."

His brows were pinched with concern.

"I'm not going to worry about things we can't control," Anya said. "We need to pass through that canyon, so let's do it and be done with it."

"Agreed."

Despite trying to sound confident, she did have genuine concerns about what they were up against. Still, to Evan's point the night before, humans could be far crueler to each other than any animal. Ultimately, she'd rather take her chances with the mystery predator than cross paths with the enemy soldiers.

Using the map on Evan's wrist device was tricky without a helpful 'you are here' indicator, but they were able to identify a couple of mountain peaks and a stream that allowed them to get oriented. Once they had that figured out, they were able to set a course to their destination.

They kept close watch on the ground and foliage for any signs of humans passing through, but everything appeared pristine and untouched, aside from the occasional small animal trail.

"I think we're getting close," Evan said after consulting the map. "But we're coming up on an area shaded in red."

"We didn't have any zone shading in the surveys I saw," Anya said. "I wonder where that came from?"

"Red is often an indication of danger."

"Or high activity," she pointed out. "Any other shades elsewhere?"

"Not that I've seen."

"Hmm." She wasn't sure what to make of it, but the more detailed information allegedly contained inside the facility might yield some insights.

They continued for a while longer, reaching a section of the forest where the vegetation was thicker again. She couldn't see more than a dozen meters ahead. It'd be easy to walk right into an ambush under those conditions.

Evan seemed to be thinking along similar lines, because he had begun taking a lighter touch with his footsteps, moving quietly and minimizing the disturbance to branches. Anya did the same, calling on her experience hunting down small animals to tag for research.

Abruptly, they stepped from the thick vegetation into an open area. However, it wasn't a natural clearing. The underbrush had been flattened to the ground and branches had been snapped off overhead. A curving path disappeared around bends in both directions.

Anya and Evan stopped in the middle of the path, exchanging confused glances.

"Did someone drive through here?" Anya asked, thinking of no other possible explanation.

"I don't see tread marks," Evan replied after inspecting the ground.

The pathway was too large for a game trail. However, the

breakage pattern on the plants did resemble animal passage. "I don't know what could have made this."

"Should we follow it?"

"It's not going the right direction," she observed. "And I'm not sure I want to meet whatever made it."

"I second that."

They continued forward, and she did her best to shake the uneasy feeling in her gut that there was something large lurking just out of view.

At last, a welcome sight stood out from the surrounding trees ahead. Straight lines rarely formed in nature, and the thing ahead had multiple.

"Hey, that must be it up there!" she whispered excitedly while pointing at the partially obscured form ahead.

The outpost appeared to have been unattended for years, or perhaps the jungle had been faster at reclaiming the structure than she would have anticipated. It was approximately twenty-five meters long and ten wide, designed to be air-lifted into position. The exterior of the facility had the look of a standard prefab field unit, with gray exterior metal sheeting and uniform, tinted windows on two sides. Moss and vines now covered half the structure, including a portion of the entry door centered on the building's front side.

She started to head for it, but Evan grabbed her arm to stop her.

"Wait," he said. "Regardless of what Samor said, they might be watching this place."

"How do we test that? We can't wait in hiding forever. We need to get inside."

"Same as we did before. One person goes first," Evan replied.

"And as we agreed before, I'll be the bait and you can play

soldier to rescue me." She cast him a stern look to drive home that it wasn't up for discussion.

He took a step back and nodded. "Be alert."

"Always."

Anya continued forward toward the structure. There was absolutely no movement in the surrounding vegetation—not even birds rustling.

"There's no one here, Evan. Come on!" she urged. It was too quiet. Though it might be nothing, she couldn't shake a creepy feeling rising on the back of her neck.

He jogged toward her, no longer in stealth mode after her shout. "This wasn't the plan."

She didn't wait for him to reach her before continuing to the door. "It's too quiet. Something else might be stalking us. I'm not worried about soldiers right now."

The two of them jogged the rest of the way to the building's entrance. Evan tried the door, finding it unlocked. On an uninhabited planet, there really wasn't a reason to lock anything hidden in the middle of nowhere.

Stepping inside, Anya waved her hand in front of her face to clear the musty air. She blinked as her eyes adjusted to the dimmer light.

Long work surfaces lined the walls, as well as several standing-height tables in the middle of the space. Most surfaces were covered in plasheets and scattered equipment. It appeared someone had taken everything from the shelves, thrown it on the worktables to sort through, and then left in a hurry.

Evan closed the door. "This isn't what I was expecting."

"Me either." Anya stepped further into the room, walking over to one of the tables to investigate the contents. "I'm surprised there's so much printed material."

"Yeah, I'd thought there'd be a couple of computers and

some equipment for analyzing rock and plant samples, or whatever."

"That's what most research outposts are, for sure." Anya picked up one of the printouts. The very presence of the plasheet was unusual, but the contents were even stranger.

The semitranslucent plasheet had a series of curved lines with tiny numbers next to each; it reminded her of a topographical survey. There were other sheets below it, and she arranged them into a neat stack to look at them together.

The dark elevation lines lined up with each other, and each layer had a cluster of dots, which formed red blobs, collectively.

Evan was looking over her shoulder as she pieced it together. "That looks an awful lot like a red zone."

"But what does it *mean*?" Anya set down the stack so she could examine other materials. It was more than a little unnerving that was the first thing she'd come across.

"NovaTech was up to something." His gaze swept around the room and landed back on her. "Did you know anything about this?"

"No."

"I really want to believe you, Anya, but how could they have kept this much secret from the team?"

Her cheeks flushed with annoyance at the accusation. "After everything we've been through, you think I've been hiding secrets all this time?" She looked directly into his eyes.

He stared back levelly, evaluating. "I've known too many people who can lie to someone's face without flinching."

"Am I doing that to you now?" She couldn't deny that she'd withheld details here and there, but she hadn't lied. And she didn't believe she'd done anything to warrant an accusation now. She'd opened up to him more than anyone else in recent memory, and it hurt that his trust might not run as deeply as she'd thought.

Evan continued to stare into her eyes. There was something subtle in his expression that she'd missed initially—a sense of concern that wasn't directed toward her. He shifted his gaze up slightly and past her head. The change was so minute that it wouldn't be noticeable by an outside observer.

She crossed her arms and spun around with a feigned huff of frustration. As she turned, she followed Evan's eyeline. There was a security camera mounted to the ceiling, and its recording indicator light was on.

Her pulse quickened. *That doesn't mean anyone is watching this feed. And why does he want us to seem like we're at odds with each other?*

— — —

Evan almost dropped his show accusation when he saw the genuine hurt and confusion in Anya's eyes. Their recent heart-to-hearts had forged a real bond between them, and questioning her honesty had cut deep.

However, now that he knew for certain that the Noche Syndicate was working with the people who'd sabotaged the colony expedition, he had to be extra careful. If they were captured, he'd rather they not know that Anya meant anything to him, or she'd be in even greater danger. Evan had no doubt that they'd be out for vengeance against him, and he didn't want any of that coming back on her.

While it was possible that the cameras were simply motion-activated and no one was watching the feed, he was unwilling to take the risk. He needed to sell a story that Anya was nothing to him.

"I just want to know the truth," Evan said. "You might not

be the one to help me do that." It pained him to tell the lie, but it was necessary.

"If you want to do this alone, fine," Anya shot back.

"I need to clear my head." Evan headed for the door. Once again, Anya had intuitively played her part perfectly, and this gave Evan a reason to do a perimeter sweep of the building—all under the guise of a cool-down walk.

He went outside and began walking a clockwise circuit of the pre-fab building. He wanted to look for any outside equipment that could indicate the feed was being transmitted to a remote observer.

Evan took a slow circuit around the structure, pretending to focus on his feet while stealing glances to the exterior finishes. He saw no signs of equipment installed after the building was in place—however, surveillance hardware could be smaller than a grain of rice, so there were no guarantees. Nonetheless, not seeing obvious signs of the enemy forces coming by was a good thing. They'd need to gather information quickly and get out of here to stay ahead.

As Evan was rounding the final corner to complete his circuit, something large crashed through the trees. It sounded like it was coming straight for him.

Without hesitation, Evan ran back to the building's entrance. He yanked open the door and dashed inside. The door slammed shut just as the nearby tree branches began shaking violently.

He stared out the window in the door at the thrashing limbs, looking for some sign of what had disturbed them. His heart pounded in his ears, and he shook slightly from the sudden adrenaline surge.

"Back already?" Anya asked.

"There's something out there." Evan didn't take his eyes off the window.

She came up next to him and peered out. "*The* something?"

"Possibly. I didn't get a look at it, but..." He motioned toward the branches that were still swinging from momentum. Whatever had caused it appeared to have moved away.

Anya frowned. "We can't stay in here forever."

"I'd rather move in daylight. Let's finish looking through here."

"Back on my team?" she asked, raising an eyebrow.

"I'm just doing what I need to do," he replied.

Her brows knitted with confusion, but she played it off as annoyance. "Whatever."

They headed to opposite sides of the room to conduct a more systematic search.

Evan started with a storage shelf on the left wall. He sorted through the items, not finding many things of interest. He did come across another flashlight and a range-finder, so he added those to his pack.

He was about to try one of the computer terminals when Anya called to him from across the room. She was holding what appeared to be a printed map.

"What is it?" he prompted when she hadn't spoken for a minute, still studying the document.

"I'm trying to figure that out. I..." She tilted her head. "I believe this is a plot map for a xenoarchaeological survey."

"That would imply there was evidence of civilization, right?"

"Non-natural structures, anyway. It supports what we were told."

Evan walked over to her. "Is it dated?"

She pointed to the upper right corner. "Two years ago."

"Which means this information was known well before

our colony ship departed. At least, Conroy's people knew. Tough to know how much was relayed back to the core worlds."

"Doesn't do much to dispel the conspiracy," she whispered.

"Only supports it." Evan sighed. "I still don't understand why they would send a whole colony ship here when they had no intention to let it land. Yeah, I know what Conroy said about using the cover to tie up loose ends, but it still feels like there must be something more."

"Doesn't matter right now," Anya said. "We need to learn more about what they discovered at this site."

"And anything else about where to find other things," he said, keeping the statement intentionally vague. While he was now less concerned about the opposition listening in, he didn't want to give too many details just in case.

"Hey, I think this is part of a bigger survey," Anya said, noting a number sequence on the page's footer.

"Do you think the rest could include…?"

She nodded. "Very possibly." She rifled through a stack of printouts. "I don't see it here, though."

"Maybe it wasn't printed?" Evan suggested.

With a search of the physical printouts exhausted, they turned their attention to the digital files. Evan and Anya each took a workstation and divided the directory so they didn't duplicate efforts. Feeling pressure to depart as soon as possible, Evan didn't conduct a thorough review—just scanned through file and folder names for anything that might be connected to maps and surveys.

"I think I've got something!" Anya called out.

Evan went over to her workstation. Her screen displayed a series of pictures featuring the objects they'd seen in the storage room just before the evacuation. "That looks familiar."

She smiled. "And the best part? It's geotagged."

They loaded the coordinate data into Evan's wrist navigation to see where it was relative to their current location. The site was approximately four kilometers to the northeast. There was still the matter of the cave allegedly hiding the ship.

"We still need to locate the entrance," Evan said.

Anya nodded. "Working on it."

They continued looking through the computer files in silence.

Evan came across a directory with mention of what seemed like energy readings. That was promising. However, when he opened it, there were only a handful of datasheets measuring atmospheric ionization.

Abruptly, Anya pushed back from her workstation. "There's nothing here. Forget it." She powered down the computer. "I'm leaving. Come with me, or don't." She flashed a glare in his direction and then headed for the door.

Taken aback, Evan remained at his computer. *Was that an act or is she actually angry with me?* Either way, splitting up was a bad idea. He powered down his own workstation, grabbed his stuff, and followed her out.

They headed into the trees. Evan followed Anya's purposeful stride.

"I got the cave location," she said as soon as they were beyond earshot of the building.

"I was really hoping that's why you wanted to leave."

She glanced over at him. "Did I appear sufficiently mad at you?"

"The dagger eyes were boring into my soul."

"Good. Now, what was all that earlier?" Anya asked, her eyes narrowed slightly.

"I didn't mean any of those things," Evan said hastily. "I do trust you."

She placed her hands on her hips. "Was it about the camera?"

"Yes. On the off-chance someone was watching us, I don't want them to think we have a good relationship."

"Why not?"

"Because I've seen how bad people will prey on others' concern for one another, and I wouldn't want them using you to get to me."

"Why would they care about either of us?"

Evan couldn't help checking around again to make sure there was no one else nearby. "Remember how I said I was undercover with the Noche Syndicate?"

"Yeah. And it seems like they were working with NovaTech to take over this colony expedition."

"Right, which means if they ID me, they're going to be out for blood because I tricked them. And on top of that, the guy that we fought… as I was tying his wrists, I saw that he had an insignia reserved for only the Noche leadership."

"Meaning, they didn't just help organize this sabotage—they're actually hands-on *here*."

Evan nodded. "That's why I didn't want to try interrogating him."

"Shit, Evan, that's…"

"I can't say enough times how scary-bad these people are. They won't hesitate for a second to kill someone they even suspect of daydreaming about crossing them."

"It's amazing you made it out alive."

"I surely wouldn't have if they weren't convinced that I would die here. In those terms, my death here is a lot simpler than if I'd been murdered back in the core worlds."

Anya crossed her arms. "I don't like that that guy can ID you."

"Trust me, I don't, either. But I can guarantee you we're still a lot better off than if we'd killed him. Anyone marked like that is inner circle—like family, whether blood relation or not. Any vengeance that would rain down would be tenfold if one of them were harmed."

"We need to get off this planet and disappear."

"For that, we need a ship. And the only possible ship with interstellar capabilities is an ancient alien vessel that may or may not fly. I don't think we're going to be disappearing, but departing… remains to be seen."

"One step at a time."

"Now that we're away from potential eavesdroppers again, any more you can share about those survey maps you found?" Evan asked.

"Not really."

"No mention of unusual survey results?"

"Well, we did know about the energy readings. That, combined with some locked files in the project directory made me suspect there was something going on."

"What else? Any and every detail is important now."

She shrugged. "There's not much to tell. I only heard vague references to some kind of 'significant discovery'. That could have been anything. I'd figured it was a natural resource of some sort—you know, a mineral or plant with far-reaching manufacturing or biotech applications."

"That does often go hand-in-hand with a new colonization effort."

"Right. But the secrecy around this one was very unusual. Normally, they brag about the new discovery and make it clear who'll own it."

"Why keep this one secret, then?"

"The only explanation I can think of is that it's something

so different and valuable that they were worried about someone stealing it."

"Not many companies would have the resources to send a ship over here."

"No, but they do exist. And anyone with those resources wouldn't hesitate to take extreme measures to secure supremacy over a pivotal discovery—especially if it's what Conroy thinks it is."

She looked at him, eyes imploring. "I know neither of us came on this expedition expecting a treasure hunt, but after everything we've already faced, maybe we can find out why we've been stranded here."

"I suppose solving the mystery is a worthwhile consolation prize."

"At best, maybe it will be something useful to make our stay here more viable."

Anya pulled out a rolled-up plasheet from under her jacket. "There may be another prize."

He raised an eyebrow. "Is that so?"

"You were being so shifty that I figured there was a reason you didn't want to talk openly inside. So I slipped this out. It's got an 'X' marks the spot, and it's not far from here. Something other than the vessel we're after."

"I'm intrigued."

"I thought you would be." She pointed to the location. "I believe this is referencing an open dig site—possibly what they were investigating when they were interrupted by our arrival."

Evan perked up. "You game for a detour?"

35

THE PAIN IN Samor's shoulder and back had diminished to a manageable ache after his latest round of medical nanites. The technology may as well be wizardry in terms of his limited understanding of the science, but he couldn't argue with the results.

Against doctor's orders, he got up to go see who else was among their group of evacuees—and moreover, find out the plan. They couldn't stay in the cave for too long without risking detection. Getting to one of the emergency evacuation shelters needed to be a priority.

He found Rebeka and Conroy along with five other people from Central Command in the midst of a heated discussion.

"North is the best option," Rebeka was insisting.

"It would mean an extra hour of exposure. It's risky. I still say East," Wes, one of the analysts, countered.

Samor surmised that they were debating which evacuation site made the most strategic sense for them to go to. The various outposts had been set up inside caves in the surrounding area. They were different distances away and not equally stocked, due to their limited supplies. The site to the east, Echo Falls, was one of the closest and considered the default fallback point if anything were to ever happen to their main base; it was also where they had set up the survivors of the crashed colony ship, and none of them knew about Conroy yet. The outpost wasn't as well hidden, and though it was stocked with emergency rations, there weren't as many natural resources readily available for long-term survival in that area. The northern site, nicknamed Hidden Grotto, was farther away and had less equipment and rations stocked, but there were ample fruit trees and animal life nearby to make for a strong position long-term. It was also exceptionally difficult to locate for anyone unfamiliar with the area, so they had a better chance of remaining undetected. As far as Samor was concerned, that was the priority.

"I vote for Hidden Grotto, too," he said, joining the group.

"You're not supposed to be on your feet," Rebeka chastised.

"The shitty hospital bed has no ergonomic support. I'll take my chances being vertical." He eased down onto a rock mound that was as close to a chair to be found in the old lava tube.

"I agree that we need to think long-term," Conroy said after a few moments of deliberation. "We can exchange supplies with Echo Falls later, after we've regrouped."

"Any word from other survivors?" Samor asked.

The chancellor shook his head. "No, but I'm not assuming the worst yet. Staying hidden and quiet is the smart move for everyone until we know more about our enemy's capabilities."

Their capabilities are that they could wipe us out in a matter of minutes if they catch us again. They'd been extremely lucky to escape the initial assault, but they weren't likely to repeat that good fortune in another encounter.

"All right," Wes yielded. "We'll go north. I suppose Echo

Falls already has their hands full."

Once Conroy made a decision about anything, that was the end of the discussion. They'd followed him this far, and no one would question his word now. The war they had been preparing to wage for years had now come to their door, and it was time to fight.

— — —

Organized crime was at the top of the list of things that Anya didn't like. The seedy underbelly of society was an unpleasant fact of life, but she'd been able to steer clear from its influence for the most part. Now, knowing that Noche Syndicate associates were actively pursuing her was a new kind of nightmare.

If running away was an option, she'd already be long gone. However, she was in the thick of it now—and it was a matter of life and death. She couldn't help being a little amused that it was fact rather than hyperbole.

They'd been walking for hours and were nearly to the destination she'd identified on the survey maps. Her chest was tight with anticipation about what they might discover, excited about the possibility of getting an initial view into the scale of former alien activity on the planet. As a scientist, she was skeptical of information until she'd verified it through her own study and analysis. She suspected that Evan had similar inclinations. Other people could tell them about aliens and ancient technology all day, but none of it would be *real* until they were actually staring at it with their own eyes.

In the back of her mind, she'd wondered if there was actually just a big psyop in play and there was nothing of value on the planet. In some ways, that would be a relief. Yet, her adventurous spirit yearned for incontrovertible truth that humanity was not the only space-faring race in the galaxy. There *had* to be more out there. It was a 'when', not 'if', in her mind—and what a thrill it would be if she found herself on the leading edge of that discovery.

Evan checked the navigation on his wrist display. "I think it should be on the other side of this rise."

"Finally!" Her back and legs were sore from keeping a brisk pace.

They scaled the final hill. As the view on the other side opened up through the trees, her heart sank. A drop ship was parked in a clearing at the center of the valley.

Evan sighed. "I was afraid of that."

Anya had almost forgotten about the ship that had passed by overhead the night before, but seeing it now sent a surge of anxiety through her. "What do we do?"

Evan remained silent for nearly a minute, referencing information on his navigation unit and checking it against the ship's location in the landscape. "We told them we were going to a valley, and they picked this one. They must know something is here. The place we're *actually* going is on the other side, which means we either take the long way or just risk it."

"They know we know they're here. They'll be looking for us."

"So, maybe we buck all expectations and just brazenly walk through the middle of the action?"

Anya raised her eyebrows. "That's crazy."

"Maybe. But I have a plan for how it might work."

—

It turned out that Evan's plan was, indeed, insane, but his

approach to be bold did have merit.

Like many good but risky plans, this strategy was contingent on the enemy falling for a distraction. The trick would be to appear they were in multiple places at once to divide the enemy's attention and resources. In short, they'd construct time-delay fires to send up smoke. Any self-respecting soldier would be compelled to investigate, even suspecting a trap, which would draw at least some of the eyes away from where they would actually be. *How* to set a time-delayed fire with their limited resources was a part of the plan Evan had yet to explain.

Anya stood with her arms crossed, observing Evan as he assembled a pile of sticks. With his intense focus, there had to be more to it than that, but Anya had no clue where the exercise was headed. "I don't get it."

Evan glanced up at her before refocusing on his work. "Burnable material is a key part of a fire."

"Sure. But… that?"

He finished balancing the sticks and slowly pulled back his hands, gauging the stability. The pile held. "I intend to use the flares to ignite several fires in different places. We'll set the flares at different distances from the burn piles so the main fuel piles will—hopefully—ignite around the same time even though we'll light the 'fuse' at different times."

"And how do you know how to time everything?"

"Good old-fashioned guestimation."

"How scientific."

"Do you have a better idea?"

"No," she admitted.

"I have no illusions that this will work perfectly. In fact, if things light up in a random order and not at the same time, it doesn't really matter because we won't be in any of those places. We just need to buy ourselves a little time at your X-marks-the-spot location, and this should serve as a distraction."

"How do we know that they won't leave people there?"

"Oh, I imagine they will. That's where the shooting comes in."

Her stomach knotted. Despite the knowledge that any of the enemy soldiers would readily shoot *her* without hesitation, she wasn't fond of taking lives. She hoped that would *never* become an easy choice.

Watching Evan's meticulous work was making her anxious, so Anya wandered away, leaving her pack near Evan's worksite. She began slowly pacing with the hope of settling her nerves.

Her roaming took her to a curious patch of purple-blue flowers. She'd passed by similar clusters on their hikes, but there'd never been time to admire them. They had a slight sparkle to the petals, making them seem almost bioluminescent. When a gust of wind rustled the flowers, electrical energy arched between the plants.

Fascinated, Anya bent to get a closer look. As she crouched down, she noticed a pair of large amber eyes staring at her from the nearby underbrush. Her stomach dropped. *Oh, shit.*

Evan was beyond her immediate line of sight, and shouting for help might provoke the creature. She began slowly backing away.

The creature continued watching her. When Anya had gone five steps, the animal started slinking forward. As it came into full view, Anya realized that it was the same panther species they'd encountered a couple of days before. While she'd rather be face-to-face with it than whatever mystery monster had taken out the scout Ranger-R, the panther still ignited every primal instinct of terror.

Anya willed herself to remain calm, knowing that most predators had a knack for sensing fear. Running scared was likely to get her killed, and she doubted her pulse handgun would have any effect on the animal.

The panther continued to advance, its movements smooth and silent through the underbrush. When its forefoot touched the strange plants, an electrical charge of miniature lightning danced up its leg. The energy seemed to be absorbed by the time it reached the animal's chest. The panther began pawing the ground, much like a cat's kneading.

Anya's fear was pushed aside as her analytic science-mind took over. She began an internal debate about the relationship between the plants and panther. Did the panther absorb and store energy from the plants, which could then be used to actively defuse weapons fire? Or had the panther simply evolved the means to avoid being shocked by the plants, and that adaptation enabled it to cope with energy weapons, as well? She was leaning toward the latter option when Evan spoke in a low voice behind her.

"Come to me." He was holding the pulse rifle, but he didn't have it raised.

"It's all right," Anya whispered back. "I don't think it wants to hurt us."

The panther was still standing contentedly in the middle of the flower patch. Energy crackled up its legs, and static shocks arced across its shoulders and ran down its tail.

"What is it doing?" Evan whispered.

"I'm not sure." Anya pursed her lips in thought. "I can't decide if it's charging up or simply using those plants as defense. It seems relaxed."

"Either way, we shouldn't hang around. We were chased before."

As much as her scientific curiosity begged her to observe, Evan was obviously right. She'd been lucky to not have immediately become its dinner. "I wonder why it hasn't attacked?"

"Come on," Evan urged, backing away.

Anya followed him, continuing to face the panther. It made no motion to pursue.

As soon as they'd returned to where Evan had set the signal fire, Anya shouldered her pack. "Why did you come after me?"

"I'm finished here, and shouting for you seems like it would only bring unwanted attention."

She nodded. "Well, thanks for showing up when you did." She was confident that she could have gotten away from the panther on her own, but reinforcing their partnership seemed more important. There were a lot of unknowns in their future, and she wanted to know that he would always have her back, whether she needed help or not.

"Anytime." Evan lit the flare. It sent up a little sparking flame but was too far from his stick pile to catch immediately. "Clock is ticking now." He glanced over his shoulder in the direction of the panther before jogging away.

Seeing no further signs of the creature, Anya followed him, looping her thumbs over her backpack's straps to keep the bag from bouncing as she ran.

The panther encounter had been one of the strangest of her career, and she continued to ponder it as she followed Evan to the next distraction site. *Why didn't it attack us? What's the relationship between the wildlife and the energy pockets on this planet?*

The more she learned, the more questions she had about the strange world. But with any luck, they'd have answers soon.

36

A ONE-SHOT MISSION was a terrible time to experiment, but Evan was low on ideas and feeling desperate.

He'd set three time-delay fires and was working on the fourth. If his guesses were even halfway accurate, he wouldn't have time for more. It'd been a relief that none of the others had ignited already—or equally possible that he'd miscalculated and *none* of them would catch because the flare was too far away. That was why experimentation didn't belong in the field.

Nothing I can do about it now. He'd committed to the crazy idea, so now he needed to see it through. They just had to get closer to the archaeological site so they'd be ready to move in when the fires ignited. They'd be a good distance away from any of them, so hopefully that would thin the soldiers' numbers while they dispersed to investigate.

Evan led Anya through the forest to what he hoped would be a good waiting place near their destination. There was a clearing barely visible through the trees ahead. Though there was no sign of human activity nearby, that meant nothing since their pursuers may well have set an ambush.

"How long until showtime?" Anya asked in a whisper.

"Should be soon," Evan replied, not wanting to admit just how much of a guess his work had been.

They waited.

Evan tried not to over-analyze the situation and just let it unfold. The planned distraction was a longshot, at best. Not only was he counting on the fires igniting, but the activity also needed to draw their adversaries away from the dig site.

His heart leaped as the first fire ignited. Gray smoke rose into the sky.

"Hey, up there," a male voice said in the distance. Evan spotted movement behind a bush a dozen meters away.

"Think that's them?" someone else asked.

"Does look like a campfire," the first person replied.

The next fire ignited.

"Wait, what's that one, then?" the second person questioned.

"Not sure. Could be other survivors from Conroy's group."

"What do we do?"

"Wait it out until we get orders otherwise," the first person said.

Evan's heart sank. *We did the hard part of getting the fires to work, and the distraction part totally fails.* He glanced at Anya, seeing her disappointment.

A few minutes passed, and a third plume of smoke began to rise.

"This is really weird," the second man stated.

A radio crackled. "We're seeing some strange fire activity and need to check it out. Viko and Lawrence, keep on watch duty at that dig site."

"We've got our coordinates. It's not too bad a hike from here," the first man said. "Move out."

The brush rustled as they headed away.

Evan and Anya remained still and quiet until the men were well past them. He kept an eye on the sky, anxiously waiting for the fourth fire to ignite. After two more minutes, Evan decided to call it. Three out of four wasn't bad, considering. The smoke rising from those other sites would have to be good enough.

"Come on, we won't have much time before they figure out we're not in any of those places," Evan said. He ran from their cover.

— — —

Anya jogged toward the dig site after Evan. There were two guards trying to remain hidden at the tree line, watching.

Evan motioned for Anya to loop around. They got behind the two men, and Evan fired a rapid shot from his rifle at each. The guards collapsed to the ground.

"Others will come," Evan said. "See what you can find." He hopped down into the pit.

Anya slid down into the work pit after him. She hadn't conducted any archaeological surveys, herself, but she'd had a couple of friends while attending her science-focused university who'd worked in a related xenoarchaeological field. They'd stressed the importance of minimizing disturbances, since details always mattered. From the looks of it, this site was already disrupted enough to not matter. Aside from the original dig activity, there was also significant weather erosion.

"Do you feel that?" Evan asked suddenly.

"What do you mean?"

"Like a… pull." He was staring at the ground.

"No, definitely not." She walked over to him. "Can you be more specific?"

"I don't know… it's like a pulse. Sorta like when you can feel the vibrations of a ship engine even when you're wearing noise-cancelling headphones and you can't hear it."

She understood the analogy, but she was experiencing nothing like that. "Where is it pulling you to?"

"That's what I'm trying to figure out." He turned in a slow circle. "I think it's deeper underground."

Evan began kicking away dirt with the toe of his boot. After several kicks, he uncovered an eroded channel where the rain had drained deeper underground. "That's strange."

"One sec." Anya hopped out of the pit and scavenged a couple of sturdy sticks to use for digging. She returned to the pit and handed one to Evan.

Using the sticks, they made quick progress carving away the soft ground. It was unclear if the soil had fallen back into place after a previous excavation or if they were going deeper than the previous dig.

Evan's stick hit something hard, letting out a metallic *thunk*. That was definitely not a normal thing to encounter in the middle of the jungle on an unpopulated world. Their eyes met with excitement.

They set down the sticks and switched to digging by hand, not wanting to accidentally damage whatever it was.

They slowly pulled up the damp soil, water starting to pool at the bottom of their digging area. With the view obscured under the soupy mess, they relied on feel to carve out around the edges of the metal object.

It was relatively smooth and seemed to be about the length of Anya's arm. One side was rounded into a sphere.

"I think I can get it now..." Evan reached elbow-deep into the water and gave it a firm tug. The mud sucked it back, and he tried again. This time, the sphere side rose up.

Anya grabbed the end and helped Evan pull it free the rest of the way. Together, they dragged it partway up the sloped wall to a dry area.

"What the...?" Anya scanned the object, noticing fine carving details in the metallic surface. The material had a slightly golden sheen unlike anything she'd seen back in the core worlds. It shared some aesthetic attributes with the artifacts in the storeroom Samor had shown them, but this metal was a different shade, and the carvings were distinctly more ornate. Its level of detail was rarely seen outside fine art.

"I don't have the slightest clue what this could be," Evan said, sounding equally mystified. He brushed his hand along the long edge to wipe off the mud. Golden lights illuminated in the recesses of the carved details. He yanked his hand away. "Whoa!"

Anya's heart skipped a beat and her eyes opened wide. "How is that possible?" She reached out to try to replicate the effect.

When she ran her fingers over the object, nothing happened. "Why?"

Evan touched it again to confirm. Sure enough, it responded to him.

He frowned. "When Conroy said that the Syndicate's injection had something to do with the alien tech, I didn't believe it."

"I really wish I had a full lab to study you," Anya murmured.

"Gee, thanks."

She snapped out of her scientist mindset. "Sorry, I didn't mean for that to sound so creepy. Come on, let's get it out of this pit."

They each took a side and shoved it the rest of the way up

the slope. It was shockingly heavy for being relatively small.

"We should bring this somewhere more private where we can study it," Evan said.

"I want to know if there's anything else down there."

Evan glanced into the hole. "Me too, but this took a while to get out. I don't think our distraction will last for much longer."

Running into the soldiers would be a disaster, especially with the alien tech now in hand. Really, they already had what they needed—confirmation that there *was* an alien presence on the planet. While the device was a far cry from a ship, it did offer physical evidence to support the other stories they'd been told. Given that they had a much bigger prize to find, remaining free was more important than conducting an exhaustive search.

"All right," Anya yielded. "Let's move."

Even on level ground, it took the two of them to move the object. Ripples of golden light passed along the textured surface where Evan was holding it, which made for a mesmerizing distraction in its own right. Anya had seen various technologies with a bioelectronic interface, but those were nothing like this. She couldn't begin to guess at this object's purpose or what kind of injection had enabled it to respond to Evan's touch.

They jogged through the trees lugging the heavy object. After they'd gone half a kilometer, Anya was panting and needed a break.

"Rest for a minute?" she asked.

Evan stopped. "Yeah." On his mark, they set down the object.

"What the heck is this thing?" Anya placed her hands on her hips, breathing heavily.

"Not sure, but I'm super weirded out by it," Evan said. He ran his hand along its edge again to illustrate the point.

"Do you feel anything?" Anya asked.

"There's kinda an electrical tingle where I touch it. That 'pull' from earlier is still there, too."

"It wants you to use it?"

"Seems that way, though I'm not sure what it *does*."

"This isn't a good place to experiment."

"No, it's not." He crouched down to get a closer look at the etchings. "This sort of reminds me of circuitry."

"That's a strange thing to have on the surface where it's so exposed."

"Unless this is actually an interior component."

"True. I wonder what's powering it?"

"It might be this." He pointed to the sphere.

"What makes you say that?"

"The same thing that told me it was buried underground."

Anya squatted to examine the device with him. "That's so strange."

"Any weirder than half the other stuff we've encountered here?"

"No, that's true."

"Well, you're clearly linked to this thing." She motioned to the device. "Figure out what it can do."

— — —

Evan was completely mystified by the alien technology before him. The materials alone were fascinating, but its responsiveness to his touch was beyond anything he'd ever encountered. Sure, there was plenty of touch-activated tech in the Commonwealth, but he didn't *feel* those in the same way.

This one was somehow a part of him.

The tingle that ran up his arm each time he touched the device radiated into his core, accompanied by a tickle in the back of his mind. He couldn't make out its purpose, but it was beckoning to him.

He concentrated on the feeling, willing it to tell him more. Images of warmth and heat filled his mind. When he tried to read more, he only saw an orb of light explode into a cloud of tiny sparks.

"Getting anything?" Anya prompted.

"I think it might be some kind of weapon," Evan replied. "I'm not sure. It just feels… hot."

"Well, we don't want to accidentally set it off."

"I wish it was smaller so we could take it with us."

In response to his statement, the sphere dropped out of the device and plunked onto the ground. The main rectangular body stopped glowing, but little golden pathways continued to trace through the grooves along the sphere.

"Whoa." He stared at the newly separated sphere. "Did I do that?"

"Seems like it."

"I'm not sure how."

"This is an amazing find, Evan. It's beautiful," Anya said through an awed breath.

While Evan agreed with her assessment, he also found himself feeling terrified by the device. Something about how the mental image had shown the light exploding gave him the impression that this was meant for destruction. "It might be dangerous," he said abruptly.

"Maybe. How do we figure out what it does?"

"I don't know. But I don't want anything to do with it."

"Well, we can't very well leave it here to fall into enemy

hands. What happens if they find this and then go looking for more?"

Evan's heart sank, knowing she was right. "This is all getting a lot more 'real'."

"You can say that again. But our roles have already been decided. Given the alternatives, I can't walk away now. I don't think you can, either."

Evan let out a long breath and stared at the device. He touched the rectangular portion and got no response. "All right, I think the sphere is the important part. It's a lot more mobile than the rest of it. What do you think about just taking that?"

"Seems like a reasonable compromise. Though, I think we should hide the other piece."

They stashed the rectangular housing behind some bushes. While not an optimum hiding place, the likelihood of someone randomly coming across it was extremely low. Regardless, Evan was still more concerned about *them* getting found than the inert part of the device.

With the big piece stowed and the sphere in-hand—too large to fit in Evan's already full backpack—they set out through the forest again. Now, the race was on to reach the caves where they could allegedly find an alien ship.

Evan no longer doubted that there was an important artifact waiting to be unearthed. However, he remained dubious about any craft's space-worthiness, as well as his ability to pilot it. But those were future worries. The caves would offer shelter from the people that were pursuing them, so that was a good enough reason to get there as quickly as possible.

As they walked, Anya kept glancing over at the sphere. "Can I hold it?"

He frowned at the device but handed it over. "I'm telling you, there's something not right about it."

Anya cradled the object in her palms. Her brows furrowed as she concentrated on it. The sphere remained dark. "I've got nothing." She handed it back.

The moment Evan touched it again, the golden lights reignited. "What in the planets did the Noche Syndicate give me?"

"I want to know where they got their hands on other alien tech that enabled them to engineer that serum of theirs," Anya said.

"I hadn't heard anything about an alien discovery. But if they were giving those injections, then they must have been planning on some larger rollout of the technology within the Syndicate."

"There does seem to be something big going on in the shadows. With what we've seen here, it's looking like Conroy was being honest about Rostov's government collaborating with the Syndicate."

"If that's true, then the side we need to take is clear," Evan said. "No one who'd work with the Syndicate has good intentions."

"You'd know better than most."

"I wish I didn't." He watched the golden light ripple across the sphere. "I'll do whatever I can to keep this power out of their hands."

Evan and Anya fell silent as they continued their hike toward the mountains. They were making good progress through a fairly sparse section of forest when the trees abruptly opened into a clearing. Waiting for them in the center of the field was a panther. Evan couldn't be certain it was the same animal they'd recently encountered, but he guessed it was.

"Wait. Stay back." Evan held out his arm to prevent Anya from stepping into the clearing.

Her breath caught when she noticed the large animal. "Has it been following us?"

"Or leading us."

The panther paced in front of Evan, but not in an aggressive way. It seemed to be transfixed by the device in his hand. He moved the sphere side-to-side, and the panther's eyes followed its movement. Evan tossed the sphere on the ground a couple of meters in front of him. The creature laid down, watching the device.

"It's acting submissive to it…" Anya said, sounding genuinely confused by what she was witnessing.

"What possibly would make it do that?" Evan asked.

"I have no clue. In all my years of research, I've never seen a creature respond to an object like that without extensive training."

They watched the large animal calmly resting in front of them, its front paws outstretched and its tail slowly swishing.

"What do we do?" Evan asked. He wanted to pick up the sphere and go, but that seemed like a surefire way to break the dangerous predator from its trance.

"Samor said the alien structures were grown. What if some of that tech made it into the native animal life?" Anya mused.

"Meaning, they're alien hybrids?"

"It wouldn't be the craziest thing."

"I suppose it's not." Evan wasn't convinced, but it ultimately didn't matter. Regardless of how the creature came to be, the fact remained that it was an imminent threat.

"Well, if it *is* connected to the tech somehow, maybe you can communicate with it in the same way you can with the sphere," Anya continued.

"What, like… telepathy?" He stared at the creature. Its attention was still on the device rather than them, but its ears pivoted each time Evan shifted on his feet.

"There's no harm in trying."

He drew a slow breath as he bit back a retort. A person didn't just spontaneously develop telepathy. Then again, there was a piece of advanced alien technology involved, and there were plenty of direct neural link technologies out there. Who was to say this device didn't have those same capabilities and could serve as an intermediary?

Evan formed a mental image of peace and friendliness with the panther, willing it to understand that they meant it no harm. He held the intention in his mind.

Slowly, the panther's attention shifted from the sphere to Evan. It stared at him, unblinkingly with its brilliant amber eyes.

We need to take that device and go. Please don't hurt us, he said in his mind to the creature.

Evan's breath caught in his throat as the panther abruptly rose to its feet. It stood there, tail swishing, for several seconds. Then, it turned around and loped away, disappearing into the underbrush on the opposite side of the clearing.

Anya let out an incredulous laugh. "Did that really just happen?"

Evan shook his head, mystified. "Yeah, it did. I…" He didn't have the words. The whole interaction had felt as natural as breathing.

"This place keeps getting stranger and stranger."

"You're telling me." Evan picked up the sphere. He knew it would take time to process the encounter, so he didn't bother trying to wrap his head around it in the moment. Everything about his interactions with the alien device was unnerving and wonderful at the same time. Even now, his blood felt warmer in his veins following the interaction.

He was about to continue their hike through the clearing when the sound of kinetic weapons fire rang out. Two men came into view across the field, running and shooting behind them.

Evan scrambled backward and crouched down behind a bush, pulling Anya with him. He had no doubt that the men had encountered the panther.

More shots sounded followed by a thud.

With a twist of his stomach, Evan peeked around the bush. The men gathered around something on the ground.

Anya looked down at her hands when she saw Evan's expression. "We need to kill them," she murmured.

Not long ago, Evan would have been relieved to know the panther was dead. His brief encounter had changed his entire perception. Now, he didn't see the animal as a threat. The problem was those men. Anya was right.

The sphere warmed in Evan's palm, lights radiating from the pressure points along his fingers. He'd need to keep it hidden while he dealt with the men.

"Don't." The deep male voice coming from behind him was accompanied by the distinct whine of a pulse weapon priming.

Evan tensed, and Anya cast a worried glance next to him as she raised her arms. The sphere warmed in Evan's palm. "What do you want?"

"You two have been a major pain in our collective asses. Boss wants to talk with you. And wants *that*." There was no question he meant the device.

Evan halfway raised his arms to give the impression he was cooperating. "We never wanted a part in this."

"Then you should have no trouble handing that over and telling us everything you know."

Evan slowly turned around to face the man. He was confronted with a large soldier half a head taller with broad shoulders. The man had a pulse handgun trained on Evan, and a kinetic rifle was slung over his shoulder. His brow was furrowed above hard, bloodshot eyes.

"Look, I'm sorry you've been up all night chasing us around," Evan began. "We don't know what this thing is, or—"

"Put it down!" another man bellowed behind Evan.

Two sets of footfalls rapidly approached from the direction of the field. Knowing both of those men had rifles, Evan recognized that they were surrounded and outgunned. Were he alone, he might try something stupid to get out of it. But with Anya there, he didn't want to risk her getting shot.

This is it. There's no way out.

They'd been running for so long now that it was almost a relief for it to be over. However, he knew in his core that he couldn't simply hand over this powerful alien tech to people who were so willing to indiscriminately kill. Yet, he didn't see another choice.

He started to lower his arm holding the device. An electric tingle began in his fingertips and quickly moved up his arm. As it traveled, his skin felt like it was on fire. It took a second for him to realize the sensation was originating from where he was gripping the device.

Reflexively, he tried to drop it. But it was already too late.

A pulse of energy shot out from the sphere. It struck the enemy soldiers, almost instantaneously reducing them to red mist.

Their gear dropped to the ground, empty and unharmed.

The red residue in the air and on the items was the only indication that there had been people there only moments before.

"My god…" Evan sucked in a sharp breath, trying not to gag. He shook the device free from his hand and quickly backed away. "What the…?"

His stomach lurched. He hadn't pulled any trigger. What kind of weapon fired of its own accord?

37

ANYA STARED AT the space where men had been standing a moment before, her mouth agape.

"I didn't mean to..." Evan's wide eyes passed from the device to the men's gear piled on the ground.

Anya found her voice. "I know you didn't."

His brows pinched with disgust. "We have to get rid of that thing."

"No." She surprised herself with how calmly she spoke, and even more by how quickly her horror had turned to acceptance.

"What? But it—"

"It's the most incredible thing I've ever seen," she completed for him. "Terrifying and awful in its power, but amazing. We can't get rid of it."

"Because they could get it."

"And then we wouldn't have it. We needed something to give us an edge."

He took an unsteady breath. "I don't know how to control it, Anya. I'm worried about what else it could do unintentionally. That something could happen to *you*."

She met his gaze. "Did you want those men to die before

they could hurt us?"

"Yes," he admitted.

"Do you want me eliminated?"

"Of course not."

"Then I don't think there's anything to worry about. The device seems to be linked to you on a subconscious level. It didn't do what you told it to do, but it did what you *needed* it to do."

"That's an even more frightening prospect."

A radio crackled on the ground, followed by a woman's voice. "Bravo Team, come in."

Evan located the device in one of the gear piles. "There's no way they'll buy it if we try to fake a response," he said to Anya.

"Bravo Team, come in," the woman on the radio repeated.

She nodded her agreement. "Do you think the radio has a GPS locator?"

"On a normal planet, yes. It's a tossup for if it would be functional here."

"Better not to risk it, then," she assessed.

While taking the radio would potentially give them an advantage to track the enemy's movements, it could also be turned back on them through false communications or tracking the signal. The downsides outweighed the benefits in her mind, and Evan didn't disagree.

Evan pulled out a spare shirt from his pack and used it to pick up the sphere. Anya couldn't blame him for not wanting direct contact with it after what had just happened. She'd heard that molecular destabilizing weapons capable of vaporizing a person had been used in historical wars, but nothing like that was currently used in any corners of human civilization, as far as she knew. While efficient, the technology was horrifying.

Given the Noche Syndicate's brutal reputation, she couldn't imagine the terror they could rain down with such a tool at their disposal.

Anya's chest tightened with renewed urgency about their mission. *We need to get to the caves. We need to get somewhere safe.*

They stepped out into the field. In the distance, a drop ship rose above the trees. It headed straight for them.

— — —

Roman waited in anticipation of a response, but none came.

"Something is wrong," Red said, ending the communication on her radio.

One of the teams of three who'd been sent out to investigate the fires had failed to report in. Roman wasn't sure how the multiple fires had been ignited, but the missing team indicated where their quarry might be. "I'll go," Roman volunteered.

"There's more than one kind of monster out there. It's dangerous," Red told him.

"No more dangerous than staying here." Roman ran toward the drop ship without another word.

He couldn't go another day empty-handed before reporting in. His brother was neither patient nor forgiving. What had happened to the team was a clue to advance his mission, and he'd go anywhere or do anything to find the technology he desperately needed. Those confounded people who'd bested him before had critical information, and he suspected they were behind this disappearance.

He boarded the drop ship with a team of five soldiers—the

only people who could be spared. Still, six on two were good odds.

The ship took off and glided low above the treetops. As it approached a clearing, Roman spotted two people at the tree line.

"Land here," Roman instructed the pilot.

As soon as the craft was on the ground, he ran out through the back hatch. The two people were running for the trees. Roman fired a warning shot in front of them. The man and woman skidded to a halt.

The man was the first to turn around. He had a bundle in his hands, wrapped in cloth.

Roman's heart leaped in his throat. Even from a distance, he was pulled to the object. His blood ran warm in his veins, calling for him to get closer and claim the power.

"You've been busy," Roman said, walking up to the pair. He was focused on the man holding the mysterious bundle, but the woman caught his attention at the edge of his vision. She had one hand behind her back and a hard look in her eyes that told him she was going to be trouble.

These two have been a real pain in my ass. Roman swept his gun's aim from the man to the woman. "Don't even think about it."

Her pretty mouth twisted with annoyance, but she dropped her arms to her sides. "Why are you doing this?"

"Why do you think?" Everything always boiled down to the pursuit of money and power. If these two dolts couldn't figure that out, they weren't worth the air they breathed. "Show me," he instructed the man.

Reluctantly, the man peeled back the cloth covering the object. An intricately carved sphere was revealed.

"Set it down."

The man set it on the ground.

Roman was drawn to the object's power. It tickled the edge of his mind. *What are you?*

Trees in the distance began shaking violently. Something large was running toward them.

— — —

Evan felt the creature approaching before he saw it. Whatever strange energy resonance in his core that connected him to the alien tech ignited in his veins. But this wasn't in response to a device—this was *alive.*

A violent, thrashing wave swept through the trees as it approached. Over the cacophony of shaking branches, a piercing roar rang out that reverberated in Evan's chest.

This is how it ends. The thought unbiddenly entered his mind. But he saw no way around the beast's power. Even without laying eyes on it, there was no doubt that the thing coming for them now had been what took out the Ranger-R. Jaws that could mangle metal would make quick work of human flesh.

He braced for its attack.

The beast burst through the final wall of trees. Everyone pivoted to face it, forgetting the interpersonal dispute in light of the threat.

Evan's heart caught in his throat. The creature stood nearly three meters tall, supported on four primary limbs with another six appendages fanned out like tentacles from its sides and back. Its skin was covered in dark, interlocking scales that reminded him more of armor plating on a vehicle than anything biological. Each of its ten limbs ended in a three-point pincher, and the top two framing its elongated head were snapping. Four blue eyes stared at the humans, each glowing slightly.

The soldiers opened fire, sending a barrage of kinetic rounds. The beast curled its tentacle-like arms around itself and spun into a ball, sending up a cloud of dust. The action seemed to deflect the weapons fire, and it also explained the strange tunnel through the forest Evan and Anya had encountered earlier that day.

When the men stopped shooting, the creature stopped spinning. It quickly darted side to side, showing incredible speed and dexterity.

“Kill it!” a man shouted, and the soldiers launched another volley of kinetic rounds.

In response, the creature snatched one of the men from where he stood and threw him across the field. He shrieked as he sailed through the air, landing hard on the ground at an awkward angle in the distance.

“Shit! Don’t stop,” another man shouted as he kept firing.

Evan stood still, deciding it was better to appear non-threatening rather than try to fight it.

He tuned out the gunfire and shouts. Anya was creeping backward, making a slow retreat to safety.

I need to make sure she gets away. Evan took a slow step to the side to place himself between the beast and her.

The beast curled itself into a ball again. Faster than he could track, its tentacles lashed out and knocked everyone in the vicinity to the ground.

Evan landed hard on his back, forcing the air from his lungs. In the blink of an eye, the beast was standing over him.

The creature sniffed, slitted nostrils flaring at the end of its intense face. The scales covering its body flexed, sending a metallic shimmer down its length. A warm air breezed over

Evan's face with each exhale, carrying an unexpected aroma of copper and salt. With its metallic armor and pincher-like hands, the creature had seemed almost more machine than animal. But it *was* clearly alive.

A living weapon… or maybe a protector? He didn't know what to make of it, aside from it being beyond his capabilities to fight.

All he could do was lie there on the ground with its mouth hovering less than a meter over him. He could be swallowed whole before he knew what was happening—

Images abruptly flooded his mind. A cave, dark and desolate, with brown stone walls that were too smooth to be entirely natural. It was *more* than a cave… A former stronghold, long since abandoned. Technology had been merged into the stone itself—as though the material had been reshuffled to the desired shape and the computer technology had been grown in place. But even more incredible than the underground facility was an ancient craft resting on the floor of a back chamber. Sleek and wonderous, the ship beckoned to Evan.

Evan's senses returned to the present. The beast snuffled and backed away, giving him one final glance before turning to the other human attackers.

What the…? Did it just give me a telepathic message? Evan scrambled backward.

With a lurch of his stomach, he realized he'd dropped the sphere. He jumped to his feet.

The beast was engaged in a complex dance with the soldiers. Every time they fired their weapons, it wound into a writhing ball and evaded their assault. At this rate, their weapons wouldn't last.

That wasn't Evan's concern. The beast had spared him, and

Anya had put good distance between herself and the action. This was their opportunity to run.

Evan caught Anya's attention and pointed toward the trees. She hesitated.

"Go!" he mouthed. Without waiting for a response, he dove forward to scoop up the sphere from where he'd dropped it.

When he straightened, Anya was already halfway to cover. He dashed after her, cradling the sphere to his chest with one arm. His pack banged uncomfortably against his back with each stride, but nothing mattered except getting the sphere to a secure place.

Anya paused just inside the tree line to wait for him to catch up. As soon as he was close, she forged a path ahead, nimbly jumping over fallen trees and ducking under overhead branches.

Evan focused on keeping up with her, only glancing occasionally behind him to check for pursuit. There were no signs of either the soldiers or the beast.

They must have run for close to a kilometer before Anya finally dropped to a walk. She was breathing heavily, as was Evan. Only once he'd slowed did he realize how much his chest was burning and how hard his heart was beating in his chest. He dropped his pack on the ground to air out his back and help him cool down.

Anya did the same. She took in several deep breaths before speaking. "Before you ask, no, I've never seen anything like that."

"It was connected to the alien tech somehow. I could sense it. And it showed me some images, but I'm not sure what to make of them."

Her eyes widened. "I'm stumped."

“Me too.” He wiped sweat from his brow with the back of his hand. “I wish we’d never found this thing,” he said with a glare toward the sphere.

“Well, we have it now, and we need to keep those people from getting it.”

“I know. I just…” He sighed. “I wanted to live out my days in a quiet corner of the galaxy. This situation is feeling very ‘the fate of humanity is in our hands’, and that’s a lot.”

“You might be blowing it a *little* out of proportion.”

“I don’t know.” He studied the sphere. “There’s power here that we haven’t yet begun to understand. If this one, small device can do what it does, what kind of capabilities might an entire ship possess?”

“There’s only one way to find out.”

38

SWEAT STUNG ROMAN'S eyes. His rifle was down to its final rounds, and the beast hadn't slowed. *What is this thing?!*

The shifting scales reminded him of nanotech armor used by Special Forces soldiers. Only, that was a suit. This seemed to be integrated into the creature itself.

His gut told him it wasn't from this world. Everything on the planet was alien, but this was *alien* alien. But there wasn't supposed to be any active alien life on the planet, just the remnants of their technology. He had no explanation for what the creature might be.

The beast tossed another member of Red's squad across the field; he screamed as he flew through the air, falling silent after a hard landing.

Roman set his jaw. He didn't have enough ammunition to keep up the fight for long. With what he had left, there was a better target.

The two troublemakers were making an opportunistic getaway. Smart on their part, and also helpful for Roman. They clearly knew where to find the alien prize, and they could lead him right to it.

Roman held up his rifle to look like he was shooting but

didn't pull the trigger. He began working his way around the side of the beast to block him from view of the other members of his alleged team. Should any of them make it out of this encounter alive, he didn't want them to think he gave up and deserted them—better to believe he was incapacitated and got separated from the group.

When he was certain that they didn't have eyes on him, Roman ducked and made a run for the trees.

His feet were knocked out from under him. As he fell, a tentacle passed through the corner of his vision. Its pinchers snapped at him.

He rolled to the side, barely avoiding the claws wrapping around his leg. Letting his rifle hang from its strap around his shoulder, he drew his knife.

The pinchers came at him again, and he drove the blade into the tentacle. Rather than blood pouring out from the wound, the skin around the incision shuddered. A ripple passed over the scales, and the blade was forced out, leaving no sign of damage. The entire process only took two seconds. *No wonder our bullets aren't doing anything!*

Roman remained seated and began scootching backward across the grass. With his weapon down, the beast ignored him.

What will happen if the others surrender? For a moment, he thought about shouting his observation. However, that would give away his intentions. He needed to get away quietly, lest his prey be tipped off about his pursuit.

He reached the tree line and slipped behind a trunk. Though he ached in several places from various blows and falls, he was mostly unscathed.

Where did they go? Quietly, he rose to his feet and then crept through the trees to search for the two escapees.

Sounds of fighting in the field faded into the distance as

Roman worked his way around to where he'd seen the man run for cover. He and the woman couldn't have gotten far in the short time it had taken him to give chase.

Footfalls crunching over dried leaves caught his attention. He paused to listen, swiveling his head to track the direction. They were in a hurry, leaving an obvious trail in their wake. It would be easy to follow from a distance.

Beyond the disturbed branches and tracks on the ground, Roman knew the trail to follow because he sensed the pull of the alien sphere. It now resonated with the primer coursing through his bloodstream. The people carrying it couldn't possibly know the power they possessed. Only a handful of humans had been conditioned to interface with it. As one of those select few, Roman yearned to claim its power. And he would—as soon as these people led him to the greatest prize of them all.

Until then, he needed to be patient.

— — —

Conroy surveyed his new home. The space was anything but cozy. However, it was secure. He'd take security over just about anything else at the moment.

They'd made excellent progress moving their gear and getting items grouped according to function. Now, they needed to get it all operational.

"We need to set up a communications hub ASAP," he instructed. His team immediately got to work.

With any luck, he'd be hearing from Evan and Anya soon. *How did those two become our lifeline off this planet?*

Strange circumstances had led them to this place, and the stakes grew more dire with every trip down the rabbit hole. He still remembered the first time he'd heard mention of an ancient alien discovery. As preposterousness had given way to verified wonder, he'd allowed himself to dream of a new Golden Age for humanity. Those aspirations had quickly been dashed when he realized that those holding the most power across the interstellar Commonwealth wanted no part in expanding prosperity to common citizens. As long as they maintained complete control, they could share technological developments when they saw fit and keep the rest within their inner circle.

Their already significant power would become absolute if they had the ability to travel across the galaxy in a fraction of the time it took with conventional space travel. Not to mention advances in medical science to extend lives, eliminate common health concerns—anything that would stoke their self-image of godlike power among regular men. They viewed themselves as the chosen few to advance humanity, and there was no interest in bringing civilization as a whole along for that journey.

Common citizens were useful for tasks automation or artificial intelligence had yet to take over, but there was little regard for individual lives from the thirty-five-thousand-kilometer view from which they observed society. 'Ants pushing dirt' is how one of Conroy's campaign donors had referred to commoners during casual conversation at a fundraiser. Too many others shared that sentiment.

Conroy had endeavored to model an alternative path through his leadership. And when enough people caught on to his challenge of the status quo, his former donors chose their own self-interest.

Disgust for that selfishness had driven Conroy forward in the moments when the path ahead seemed too steep and hopeless, in moments like this when what little he had salvaged was once again ripped away. And then he'd see hope in the eyes of his remaining followers—their commitment to never give up, to fight the good fight until they could no longer stand. For them, he would push through. He'd keep taking one more step forward, even if he was constantly getting pushed back two.

Evan and Anya's hunt for the alien ship was a chance to finally take a giant leap. With that, Conroy could be back in the game. It was the grim reality of his situation. Those two strangers were now his best play to avoid a slow death in exile. He wouldn't admit that to another living soul, but it was the truth.

To keep his mind off his fate being out of his hands, Conroy set about organizing the MealPaks by flavor. He'd be in the way while his capable specialists did their own jobs, and he knew everyone would appreciate being able to quickly find their preferred meal after a busy and stressful day. The little things made all the difference with morale.

"Sir, we have a problem," Samor said as he approached Conroy, carrying an electronic component in his hands. Based on his grim expression, it wasn't a minor setback.

Conroy turned away from his freshly organized crate of noodle soup packets. "Tell it to me straight."

"The amplifier for our comm relay is blown. We've got basic walkies for short-range, but we're completely cut off from the orbital array."

"As well as the sat phone Evan and Anya would use to call us."

"Correct."

"Where can we get a replacement?"

Samor winced. "That's the thing… the only other one I know about is with the Echo Falls team."

"Which means taking it would leave the rest of our people

and the crash survivors in the dark."

The soldier nodded. "How do you want to proceed?"

"Can we rig up a relay so they'd be in standard walkie range?"

"Yes, that should be possible."

"All right, let's get the amplifier over here and make whatever other modifications so we can stay in contact with them. I know everyone is busy, so I can make the run to get the part."

"No, sir, you should stay here," Samor said. "I'll go."

"You were half-dead a day ago—"

"And now I'm back on my feet."

"I didn't come all this way to have others fight my battles for me. I need to be involved."

"And you can be involved from here," the soldier stated. "We've got it covered."

Conroy wanted to protest, but he knew Samor was right. Everything they'd battled for so far would be lost if he died. People were counting on him as a leader. He wanted to be in the center of the action, but he needed to think about his best chances of survival.

"All right, I'll finish getting everything set up here. Report back as soon as you can."

"Yes, sir. Keep your head down and don't come looking if I'm not back by tonight. Lots of unknowns out there."

"Please, be careful. I already came too close to losing you once today."

"That was yesterday now. My lives have replenished."

"See that it stays that way."

As Samor ran off to prep for his mission, Conroy returned to organizing the MealPaks. *Control what you can, and trust your people for everything you can't.*

It was easier said than done for someone who'd been backstabbed, but the only way was forward.

— — —

Samor appreciated that Conroy was the kind of leader who was willing to get his hands dirty, but the mission at hand was far too dangerous to risk him. Though the mission would have been straightforward under other circumstances, the current presence of enemy forces meant any venture from cover bore significant risk.

Having come face-to-face with his own mortality more times than he could count, Samor no longer feared danger. Nor would he show any indication that his injured shoulder burned like fire every time he raised his left arm more than ninety degrees. He had a job to do, and physical discomfort wouldn't prevent him from completing that mission.

He quickly gathered the communication materials he'd need to set up the walkie relay, grabbed food and water, and loaded his weapons. Anything else would be extra weight and slow him down. Besides, he'd have the amplifier to carry on the way back.

Rebeka came up to him while he was placing the final items into his pack. "You're going out alone?"

"Quicker and quieter to travel solo," he replied.

"But no extra eyes."

"I'll be fine."

She reached out to his left arm. "Samor—"

He shrugged her off, trying to hide a grimace from rolling his injured shoulder. "Don't worry about me."

Rebeka pursed her lips, eyeing him with silent protest. After a few tense seconds, she nodded. "I can't stop myself from worrying, but I know you've got this. Be careful out there." She'd come a long way in the last five years. It'd been difficult for someone who'd never known life outside a desk job to understand that facing danger was part of a soldier's life. It wasn't long ago that she would have continued to press the issue.

"I'll be back before you know it," he told her with a smile.

Once he'd finished packing, he left through the back access tunnel, since that would let him out closer to the other outpost. All access points were well hidden inside one of the numerous cave systems on the planet. On his way out, he passed through the most notable feature of this new headquarters—a completely walled-off section of jungle, which functioned as a private daylight atrium for the otherwise underground facility. The structure had led them to nickname that outpost Hidden Grotto.

Echo Falls, where he was headed, had an interior waterfall that became its namesake. Though beautiful in its own right, Hidden Grotto was the superior location, in his mind. Water was important for life, but greenery… that's what enlivened the soul. There weren't many colony worlds like Aethos with so much natural plant life.

We can never take what we have here for granted, he reminded himself.

They were fighting for not only this planet, but a way of life. A life where everyone could experience the beauty and bounty of lush worlds, not only those with the wealth to pay for access.

To fight for them, he would push through the pain. He wouldn't surrender.

39

ROCKS SLIPPED UNDER Evan's feet as he scaled the latest section of treacherous mountainside. He and Anya had been climbing and hiking upward for what felt like hours. They were in a particularly exposed section of the hill now, though large rocks and trees had offered ample cover for most of their trek. He'd yet to see any sign of the drop ship, so he hoped they weren't under long-range surveillance.

"We must be getting close," Anya said through labored breaths.

The steep terrain was taking a toll on Evan, but he refused to give any indication. With every step, however, it was becoming more difficult not to double over and wheeze. "Must be," he managed to get out without gasping.

At last, the terrain started to level out. Anya stopped to catch her breath, and Evan was happy to pause alongside her. He placed his hands on his hips and looked back at the hillside they'd just ascended. From the top, seeing the elevation gain and steep slope, he felt better about his burning lungs and legs; it really was a serious climb.

When his heart rate had started to normalize, he turned his attention to a rock cliff face rising behind them. "What kind of entrance do you think we're looking for?"

"The kind that opens." She flashed a smile, which looked even more charming with her flushed cheeks.

"I suspect we'll know it when we see it."

"If it's anything like the other alien tech, you'll be able to feel it when we're getting close."

Evan nodded. "I have been noticing a change in the sphere. It's had a sort of hum since I first picked it up. And now it's getting faster, or more intense. I'm not sure how to describe it."

"I'm going to take it as a good thing."

"Well, at least a sign that we're headed in the right direction. Whether finding the ship turns out to be a 'good' thing remains to be seen."

"True. It could assimilate us and use our memories to destroy everything we love."

Evan gaped at her. "What twisted things are going on in your mind?"

She laughed and flashed another disarming smile. "I'm joking. Mostly. Come on, daylight's burning." She continued along the animal trail they'd been following up the hill.

Still taken aback but amused by her dark humor, Evan followed her.

After another half-hour, the energy hum Evan had noticed had intensified into a constant whine. Anya was unable to hear it, so it must be related to the shot he'd been given. It was clear through that connection to the alien tech that they were getting close to something large and powerful. He could only hope it was the ship.

They came over a rise to a mostly level area with an abrupt cliff edge dropping off on the right, forest ahead, and a rock wall to their left. The wall was mostly smooth stone, but a portion of it at the base was broken. Evan was drawn to the damaged section.

As he walked past it, he realized that there was an optical illusion with the striations in the rock, and what he'd thought was a minor protrusion was actually a bigger piece with an opening behind it. The hole continued deeper than the natural sunlight shone.

"There's a tunnel!" he called to Anya.

She came over to evaluate it with him. "Obviously, a starship wouldn't fit through here. Unless the aliens are really tiny."

He chuckled. "That would be something. We go to all this trouble, and it turns out that it's a starship made for ants."

She smiled as she pulled out her flashlight. "Aww, little space ants sound kinda cute."

"Until they shoot you with their space lasers."

"Now who has the twisted mind?" Anya clicked on her flashlight. Intricate carvings along the tunnel walls became visible with the shadows cast from the beam. She grinned. "Hey, I think this is it!"

"Yeah, I sense something in there." Evan got out his own flashlight and then led the way down the stone corridor.

As they continued down the tunnel, Evan ran his hand along the rock wall. It was smoother than he would have expected, like the texture of river stones worn away by a steady current. Except, the surface was too perfectly vertical.

Nature doesn't make straight lines. Alien planet or not, that was a universal truth.

The place had to be man-made—well, probably not *human*, but by some kind of sentient being. The same designers that had made the sphere capable of disintegrating a person with a single telepathic command. His stomach dropped with the thought.

Ten meters in, it opened into a roughly six-by-six-meter chamber, flanked by a pair of meter-wide columns at the entrance—too square to be natural. Directly across from the entrance was a carved three-meter-tall panel, which struck Evan as a doorway.

"Through there," he said.

"How do we open it?"

Evan ran his hand along the stone surface. Touching it, he realized that it wasn't actually rock, but rather a metal similar to the sphere and covered in a thick layer of dust. He brushed it off.

Anya reached out to help him.

"No," he stopped her. "Better if you don't touch it. We were told there's something in my blood that should enable me to open it. We don't know what it might do to someone who *doesn't* have that."

She nodded and stepped back.

Evan located a hole in the door, which was roughly the size of his fist. That also made it about the same diameter as the sphere. "I wonder…"

He unwrapped the device.

"Don't move," a male voice called out into the chamber, echoing in the enclosed space. The voice was familiar.

Evan swiveled his head as a man stepped out from behind one of the columns at the chamber's entrance. He was wearing dark camo, and his face was unmistakable. "You."

— — —

Roman kept his gun leveled on the man. "Why didn't you kill me?"

The man and woman looked shocked to see him. They

raised their hands to show that they weren't holding weapons, though Roman spotted two handguns and a rifle between them, plus a strange object in the man's left hand.

"Like we said before, we didn't want any trouble," the man told him. "Killing you seemed like it would make more for us."

"You're right about that." Roman gestured to his wrist. "I take it you saw my brand?"

The man nodded.

"You're well-informed to recognize it."

"How about you put the gun down and we talk this out?" the man said. "I'm Evan. This is Anya. What's your name?"

"We're not doing names. Set that thing down."

"I—"

"No!" Roman moved his finger to the trigger.

Evan set down the sphere, as requested.

"Out." Roman nosed his gun to direct them toward the exit.

As they looped around the far wall of the chamber, he mirrored them on the other to keep his distance. When they were in front of the tunnel, he stepped forward to force them out. Roman stopped to pick up the sphere and then continued directing them back out of the tunnel.

He needed to get them outside. Sending them over the cliff would be the easiest and cleanest option. No shots fired, and plausible deniability on his part. His brother wanted them brought in alive for questioning, but the headache wasn't worth it to Roman. This way, it would seem like they simply fell to their deaths while trying to get up here.

The group reached the daylight. Roman kept backing up Evan and Anya until their heels were at the edge of the cliff.

The two people were surprisingly calm, given their mortal peril. Heat rose in Roman's chest. "Why aren't you begging for your lives?"

“Would it change your mind?” Evan asked.

“No.”

“There’s your answer.”

“With that attitude, you deserve to die.”

“If you really felt that way, we’d already be over that cliff. Yet, you’re still talking to us.”

Roman faltered. He really *should* have killed them by now, but something was holding him back. *Should I go against Marcus’s wishes?*

He’d seen what happened when others had defied his brother’s orders. These people might be able to offer useful information. There was no coming back from death.

“I do appreciate you sparing my life. Why should I do the same for you?” He lowered his weapon slightly.

Anya finally spoke up, “That door in there is still sealed. How do you know that you can open it?”

“Do you?” Roman countered.

“Well, I’m a research scientist by trade,” she said. “Experience has taught me that when you have a puzzle, it’s better to have multiple tools at your disposal. Do you want to risk going it alone?”

She did bring up a valid point. They could prove to be a valuable human resource, but keeping them around also came with risks—risks he couldn’t afford to take.

Roman raised his pistol again. “I don’t need you.”

“Then end this,” Evan told him, meeting his gaze.

“All you need to do is step back.”

“No. If you want us dead, you’ll have to shoot us.”

Roman noticed that the man kept glancing at the sphere in his hand. He was also moving his feet ever so slightly to inch away from the cliff’s edge. There were dozens of ways this encounter could play out, and none of them made it worthwhile for him to listen to these two for a moment longer—or for them to continue drawing breath.

"We're finished here." Roman fired into the ground at the man's feet, hoping to surprise him into falling backward.

However, Evan stood his ground and Anya dove to the ground away from the cliff.

Roman tracked her with his pistol, preparing to fire again. He was about to pull the trigger when sharp pain erupted at his right bicep. A knife handle was sticking out the side. Evan must have thrown it. His muscles spasmed, threatening to drop his pistol.

The sphere he'd picked up started to feel warm in his left palm. Energy coursed through him.

— — —

The attacker had the alien sphere in his palm. Anya had witnessed what happened when the device was wielded as a weapon, and she didn't want to be on the receiving end.

The man fired his pistol at her. She dodged to the side and it breezed past her. She barreled into the attacker.

He fell on his side and rolled toward the edge of the cliff. As he rolled, he held firmly onto the alien sphere, but his pistol came loose from his hand.

Evan tackled him. The two men wrestled on the ground, vying for the sphere. With limbs flying, Anya didn't know how best to help.

She spotted the attacker's pistol on the ground and grabbed it. Evan was still tussling for the sphere, so she didn't have a clean shot.

The attacker kicked Evan, causing him to double over on the ground. The man got to his feet, holding the sphere. Anya lined up a shot with his hand. If she could hit his wrist and make him drop it…

She fired.

The shot struck closer to his elbow than hand. His fingers remained firmly curved around the alien device as he teetered back.

"No!" Evan shouted, reaching out to keep the man from falling.

But the attacker plummeted over the edge.

"Shit! I…" Anya faded out.

Evan's eyes narrowed, but his expression softened as soon as he looked at her. "I know that's not what you meant to happen. It's okay."

She cautiously approached the cliff and peered down. It was so tall that she couldn't make out details on the ground below to see where he'd landed. She let out a long, shaky breath. "I'm sorry. I can't imagine he survived that fall."

Evan crawled over and checked over the edge. "Unlikely, but there's no way to tell from here." He sat up and checked a scrape on his palm. "If we go after the sphere, we might not make it back up here again before more of his people arrive."

"But they'll also go looking for him, and they'll find it."

"It'd be a whole lot worse if they get the ship. As far as we know, there's only one of those. But there might be more of these sphere devices. I mean, we didn't need to look around for long before we found it, so they'll probably get their hands on others, anyway."

She crouched down to be eye-level with him, resting her forearms on her knees. "I feel awful."

"There were a lot worse ways that could have gone, Anya. I'd rather have you than that device."

"Likewise."

He cracked a tired smile. "If they wanted perfection, they shouldn't have put the fate of the galaxy in the hands of a couple of nobodies."

"I think we're doing pretty well for bumbling our way through."

Evan stood up and dusted off his pants. "Damn straight. Now let's go get ourselves a starship."

40

SAMOR BRUSHED FLAKES of moss from his hair and shoulders. He'd forgotten how dense the vegetation was leading up to Echo Falls.

He was almost to the entrance. As he'd walked, he'd done his best to mask his presence, not wanting to give away their hiding place. They'd moved the group of survivors from the crashed colony ship to the cave, so there were no doubt signs of human transit in the area, but he wanted to avoid drawing a direct line back to Conroy's new hiding place.

Midway along his journey, he'd placed the walkie relay far away from the standard path. Roughly equidistant between the two outposts, it should provide reliable communications between them. Then, once the amplifier was installed at Hidden Grotto, they could relay relevant information to the other camp.

The Echo Falls entrance was hidden behind vines, which hung down over a rock wall undercut from ancient water erosion. The hollow looked like a dead end upon initial inspection, but it curved around into a tunnel that descended deep underground. A handful of shafts too narrow to crawl through provided light and air to the larger chambers below.

As he descended the tunnel, the characteristic thunder of falling water rumbled in the background, growing louder the further he got.

His brows knitted. *That's* too *loud.*

He picked up his pace. Voices were urgently shouting at each other in the distance.

Samor's boots splashed in water. *There shouldn't be water here!*

He continued forward slower, checking his footing before committing to each step.

"Rogers!" he called out over the roaring water.

The voices fell silent.

"Who's there?" a man replied after several seconds.

"It's Samor." He held out his arms, anticipating that his old friend would come verify it was him.

Sure enough, the soldier's familiar face peeked around a rock archway, illuminated by one of the natural skylights. "What are you doing here?"

"Helping your asses, apparently. Why is it flooded?"

Rogers' shoulders rounded. "It started out as a trickle, but a wall fully gave way a few hours ago—the rains last night must have been the final straw in a weak point we didn't see before. We've been moving everything to one of the higher chambers. The colonists were a big help. I didn't think I'd say it, but I'm glad we have them."

There'd been a lot of mixed feelings from the ranks when Conroy had announced the plan to bring in the colony expedition survivors. It'd been of paramount importance to keep Conroy a secret, so everyone had been relocated to Echo Falls and fed a cover story about there being members of a survey crew left behind on the planet after crashing themselves. The explanation wouldn't hold up long-term, but it'd done what it needed to do for now. Apparently, though, there were new problems.

"Is everyone okay?" Samor asked.

"Yes, just wet and cranky. We're lucky there were people here to start pulling out the supplies before the wall crumbled completely."

"Is the equipment...?"

"Most of it was in sealed crates, fortunately. It's actually good that this happened when it did. We hadn't unpacked yet."

"Yeah, wow."

Rogers glanced over his shoulder. "Look, we've got our hands full. What brings you here? Is something wrong?"

"Our amplifier is toast. I'm here to get yours."

Rogers glowered. "Why are we even here, then?"

"We need to have more than one stronghold, and we can't tell your guests everything yet. You know that."

"Well, clearly we're not in a position to offer much assistance to you at the moment." There was more than a touch of bitterness in his friend's tone.

Samor felt for the soldier. He knew that he'd requested to be with Conroy's team at Hidden Grotto, but they'd needed his leadership here. The fact that the gear and everyone was safe confirmed that the personnel assignment had been the right call.

"As soon as we have everything squared away, we can send you help to see what can be done about repairing that wall."

Rogers shook his head. "Don't bother. We've found an alternative spot on higher ground that will work. We're just writing off the lower levels. It'll be a nice swimming hole on hot days."

Samor smiled. "You've always had a knack for finding the silver linings."

"Yeah, yeah. Just take your damn amplifier so I can get back to work."

While they waded through knee-high water to go retrieve the device, Samor explained the relay setup. It wasn't ideal, but at least Rogers kept his annoyed quips to a minimum.

The amplifier was still installed in the outpost's comm unit, so it took a bit of work to extract it. There were no signs of charring like on the damaged one. Samor carefully wrapped it up and stowed it in his padded pack.

Before leaving, they did a quick communication check with the walkies, finding that the relay had done the trick.

"See, I'd never leave you high and dry," Samor said with a smile.

Rogers squished his wet boots on the ground for effect. "Definitely not dry."

"Thank you for this, seriously." Samor gave his friend an appreciative nod.

"Anything for the bossman, right?"

"For the Commonwealth."

Rogers nodded. "For the Commonwealth."

— — —

Losing the sphere was a big blow. Evan could tell how badly Anya felt about the situation, so saying anything more to her about it wouldn't accomplish anything. She'd been trying to end the fight and keep him safe, and he couldn't fault her for that.

The simple facts of their situation were that there were an unknown number of people after them, likely with lots of guns, and it would be too great a risk to go after the sphere. They needed to prioritize getting control of the alien ship, if it indeed existed. And it was likely through the door inside this cave.

Once we have the ship, we could fly it down to get the sphere, he rationalized. He didn't fully believe they were going to find a flightworthy craft sealed away underground, but telling himself it would be there was better than admitting that they'd lost a verified piece of alien tech. A *dangerous* piece of technology that would be disastrous for their enemy to possess. Yet, he couldn't think of a scenario where it would be smart to go after it and risk being cut off from access to this site. *We need to get inside. We need to end this, one way or another.*

Having dusted himself off from his fistfight on the ground, Evan headed back inside the cave. His and Anya's backpacks were on the ground at the back of the chamber where they'd set them down, and the ancient door was still sealed. While it would have been convenient to find that pathway open upon their return, it was for the best that it didn't randomly unseal with no explanation.

"All right, let's figure out how to unlock this," Evan said. He blew on the door to finish removing the layer of dust that had settled into the intricate carvings.

The design style was the same as the sphere, with an ornate web of carved channels. The lines seemed to originate from the hole at chest-height into the middle of the slab. Evan pushed down a wave of regret that they didn't have the sphere to try as a key. However, that might not be the answer.

"They said that only I could open it, because of what's in my blood. So…" He eyed the mysterious opening in the door.

"Can you telepathically control it, like with the sphere?"

"No, it's not beckoning me in the same way. I think this is more of a physical thing."

Anya frowned. "You're thinking of reaching in there?"

"I don't have any other ideas."

"This seems dangerous. What if it chops off your arm?"

"What if we don't get the door open and an army shows up outside?"

She frowned. "All right. Do it."

Evan took a deep breath. "Here goes nothing..." He braced for a hidden guillotine.

Heat spread from his hand to his wrist, similar to what he'd experienced when handling the sphere. Then, a sharp pain shot through his forearm. He tried to yank his arm out but found that it was stuck.

Anya gasped. "Evan, what—"

He tried to remain still, since struggling only made it worse. Taking a shaky breath, he closed his eyes to center himself. *It'll be okay.*

The hidden vise released. Evan withdrew his arm, finding three blood pinpricks on his shirt sleeve.

Golden light illuminated in a ring around the hole and then traveled along the channels across the slab. When the light reached the perimeter, it traced the edge until the entire outline was glowing. Segments of the slab then began folding outward from the center hole, disappearing section by section along the channels. The glowing extinguished as soon as the final segments were gone.

A dark tunnel now stood before them.

"Wow," Anya whispered.

Evan rubbed the pricks on his arm. "Yeah, you can say that again." He stepped forward and cautiously stuck his arm over the threshold. It was only open air. "In we go, I guess."

They hoisted their packs from the floor and stepped into the corridor. Two meters in, Evan spotted a blue stone embedded in the natural rock wall. He waved his hand over it. Behind them, the passageway started to reseal.

"It didn't take a lot to figure out how to open it, but better to not make it too easy for anyone following us," Evan said.

Anya nodded. "And not everyone will have that fancy whatever-they-gave you."

The man who was now at the bottom of the cliff certainly had received the same treatment, but he wouldn't be any help now. Hopefully, there weren't others.

The tunnel walls began as natural-looking rock but soon transitioned into the same smooth, vertical surface as the corridor leading into the antechamber. The deeper they went, the more carvings appeared along its surface. Evan slowed his pace to admire the carvings, realizing that they appeared to tell a story. There were stars and what appeared to be outlines of city skylines, and there were also figures that could have been representations of the alien race, with multiple arms and elongated heads reminiscent of the beast they'd encountered before climbing the mountain.

By the time the walls were completely covered in an elaborate scene of ships leaving the planet—as far as Evan interpreted the images, anyway—the tunnel ended in darkness.

Evan's flashlight shone into the void before them, but the beam didn't reach a ceiling or walls.

"Wow, this place must be huge!" Anya exclaimed.

"Let's see if we can find a way to get more light in here," Evan said.

Stepping into the cavernous dark was a bit like piloting a ship into the blackness of space, only there weren't even the distant reference points of pinprick stars. Evan swept his flashlight beam around with the hope of catching an object that would help orient them.

At last, he noticed something resembling a table at the outer limits of his flashlight beam. "Anya, over here."

She joined him as he walked over to inspect it closer.

The table turned out to be more of a console, with a slightly curved upper portion, a flat desktop, and stone pillars supporting it on either side.

Evan sensed power deep within the console. His blood hummed with it, calling to him. *How could it still work after being dormant all these years?* But the sphere had come to life, so it was possible. And he felt that same potential here—only more powerful.

He reached out his hand to the console.

Anya grabbed his wrist. "Wait. What are you doing?"

"Seeing if it will turn on."

She raised her eyebrows. "We don't know what it might do!"

"And how else are we supposed to find out if it *does* work unless we try?" he countered, pulling his wrist free from her grasp.

"And what if it works and we don't like what it does?"

"Obviously, that would be bad. But, how much worse could it be than what we're facing now? We can either look for a possible escape, or we can die here."

She crossed her arms. "Dying doesn't sound great."

"Agreed." He waved his arm in an all-encompassing gesture for the room. "That leaves us with what's here—which we can't even see yet. But maybe this thing will turn on the lights. What do you say?"

Her arms dropped to her sides. "Okay, but be careful."

"I couldn't begin to guess at how to do that."

"Yeah... Well, just take it one thing at a time."

"All right." He took a deep breath.

The console was completely blank, but it had a smooth finish not unlike a touchscreen. Such controls had won out for most interfaces in human society because of their modularity and multifunctionality. It would make sense that an alien race would have arrived at a similar design preference for the same reasons. A few days ago while they'd been hiking, Anya had called that principle 'convergent evolution' during one of her tangential explanations about how life on so many different planets often shared many similarities.

An instruction manual would be really nice right now... Unfortunately, no such guide popped into his head telepathically. For lack of a better approach, he placed his palm flat on the table.

Nothing outwardly happened, but warmth spread through his hand along with a subtle electrical zap. He picked up his hand and waited.

A barely perceptible vibration started underfoot, which Evan interpreted as a power system activating.

Anya shifted on her feet. "Something is definitely happening."

"Who knows how long this equipment has been dormant."

In spite of his low expectations, the console illuminated. It wasn't a full-screen touch interface in the way he'd envisioned, but there were rather lighted golden symbols set against the dark, matte backdrop. None of the symbols made sense at first glance.

What had initially seemed like chaos started to look more orderly the longer Evan stared at it. In particular, a symbol on the middle-right of the console reminded him of a light; it was two concentric circles with little dots around the outside. Another reminiscent of a satellite dish suggested communications, and three wavy lines appeared to be water. Many others related to various utilities and other functions started to stand out to him.

It couldn't be that easy, could it? he wondered. While there was no ignoring the potential influence of his telepathic connection to the technology, it was still a big leap. "What do you think of this one?" he decided to ask Anya.

"Which one what?"

He pointed. "The symbol."

Her brows shot up. "Wait, you see something on here?" She motioned to the console.

"Yeah, there are all sorts of golden symbols covering it. You don't see that?"

"No, I felt the floor start to vibrate, but everything else is dark."

"What about in the chamber out there? Or with the alien device? Did you see any lights?"

She nodded. "Yeah, with those. But whatever you're seeing now on this slab must only be in your mind. Maybe that's what the injection enabled."

Evan's skin crawled. "It was bad enough thinking about it being in my blood, but if it's done something to my brain..."

"I'm sorry, I wish I could help," she said. Her eyes were wide and sincere as she met his gaze.

"All right, if this is only in my head, then I need to go with my gut about what I'm seeing." Perhaps the images made sense to him because the alien tech was translating to symbols he would understand. Visual representations were simpler than trying to figure out words in an unfamiliar language.

He pressed the light symbol.

Soft, blue-white light illuminated along the distant seam between the floor and walls. It swept upward along the wall, growing brighter the higher it got, as though the chamber was awakening at dawn. As the light traveled upward, it backlit the outline of smaller structures within the cavern.

Anya's jaw slackened. "What is this place?"

"I don't know." He looked around with wonder. "If I didn't know better, I'd say it was a city."

"*Do* we know better?"

"No, I guess we don't." The notion that there was an ancient, alien city inside the mountain was far-fetched and borderline insane, but the evidence was right there in front of his eyes. It was the same place he'd seen during his brief telepathic exchange with the beast.

"It makes sense though, in a way," she said cautiously. "We chose to colonize this planet because it can support life like ours, and we've found many other planets compatible with our biology. There might be another intelligent race out there that needs a similar temperature range and nitrogen-oxygen mix atmosphere. What's to say they didn't have their own plans to form a colony here?"

"A whole community of alien life." Evan slowly shook his head. "I don't know where to begin."

"I want to get a closer look at one of the buildings," Anya said. "Its design might give us clues about what the beings look like."

"Yeah, I'm curious about that, too." If the aliens were anything like the beast they'd fought, they might be absolutely terrifying to meet. However, he wouldn't judge all humans based on an encounter with a soldier in a mech battle suit, so he tried to keep an open mind about what they might be.

The lighting was now bright enough for them to no longer need their flashlights. They crossed the cavern to a walkway between the buildings, making it seem like the historical videos he'd seen of an old-timey Main Street through a quaint ghost town.

Up close, the strangest thing about the structures was that

they appeared to come right out of the stone floor.

"Do these buildings look… 'grown' to you?" Evan asked.

"They do. Like Samor suggested, I think these aliens must have some kind of nanotechnology that self-replicates using whatever material is nearby. Hypothetically, an entire mountain could be disassembled and then remade in whatever shape the designers wanted."

"Could that work on living materials, too?"

"Not in exactly the same way, but yes."

"Kind of like some of the strange plant and animal life we encountered that seems to have the same properties as this alien tech?"

She nodded slowly. "Yeah. Very much like that."

They came around a corner in the road, and the ground sloped downward. More buildings were arranged in tiered levels all the way down.

Evan took it in, struggling to grasp the scope of the discovery. "There must have been tens of thousands of people living here at one point."

"Just because it could hold that many, it doesn't mean that they ever moved in." Something caught Anya's attention in the distance, and her eyes went wide. "Evan, look!" She pointed to a part of the cavern that was still masked in shadow. "Is that a… ship?"

— — —

Dark-green blurred into blue. High-pitched ringing consumed everything.

Roman blinked. The dark-green smudges began to solidify into trees, and white clouds came into focus in the sky above. The piercing hum filling his ears retreated.

What...? Where...? He rolled his head to the side as he tried to get his bearings.

The fight came rushing back to him.

I fell. He spotted the cliff. *What I need is up there.*

It was much taller than he remembered. High enough that he was uncertain how he was still breathing.

He tried to raise his head. Stars in his vision and sharp throbbing told him that was a terrible idea.

Instead, he remained on his back and closed his eyes until the dizziness subsided.

When he opened his eyes again, he instead tried rolling onto his side. There was again a disorienting change to his sight, but it passed quickly.

To his good fortune, Roman recognized a cluster of boulders at the cliff's base. He'd passed by this place on his way up to the trail, which meant he had a rough sense of how to get back to the drop ship.

But the alien ship... He tried to elevate his head again. This time, he was able to prop his elbows behind him without feeling like he was about to pass out. However, he realized he was in no condition to be scaling cliffs or navigating a tricky trail. *I somehow survived this fall, but I doubt I'd be that lucky again.*

Staying alive was important. To die performing a great service would be one thing, but a pointless death from tripping and falling would be a waste—not to mention an embarrassment to his family.

And I'm not empty-handed. He was still gripping the alien sphere.

Unfurling his fingers, he was shocked to find that a portion of the sphere had pressed into his palm. Golden energy was flowing through complex grooves on the sphere's surface, and the lines extended into his skin.

Roman gasped and tried to flick the sphere away. It held on for two sharp snaps of his wrist and then popped free. It plunked into the dirt, and the lights extinguished.

What the…? He cradled his hand and massaged his palm. There was no visible sign of the energy. Yet, he could still sense the warmth of it on his skin and traveling up his arm.

And then he understood. *It saved me.*

He stared at the sphere with new appreciation. The technology had chosen to open itself to him. To grant him its power. While not the ship, it was still an important alien artifact. It might be enough to hold off the full force of his brother's fury.

Roman hauled himself to his feet. He bent down to pick up the sphere. With it in his palm once more, the energizing heat spread through him again. His aches began to fade.

He set off toward the drop ship. With each step, he grew stronger and more confident.

This is only one. How many others are buried here? He intended to find and deliver every piece of that treasure.

41

ANYA WAS ANXIOUS to get to the alien ship, but she couldn't pass up the opportunity to study the ancient city as they passed through.

After the realization that the city had likely been grown using some kind of nanotechnology, she couldn't help looking at it with new eyes. The forms were surprisingly organic, seeming to follow natural contours in the foundational rock rather than being built along a set grid. There were places along the structures where doors and windows should be, but they were covered in lines much like the door leading into the cavern. Either the whole place had been shuttered, or the city had never been occupied.

"I really want to see inside one of these places," she commented to Evan. He seemed singularly focused on getting to the ship, and she was shocked by his lack of curiosity about the rest of the place.

"We came here to—"

"To learn everything we can about this alien technology," she cut in. "And a whole city seems like an even bigger discovery than a ship."

"A city can't fly us out of here."

"And that ship might not fly at all." Anya picked one of the buildings and pointed at it. "See if that door will open for you."

Evan sighed, but he walked over to the door and placed his hand on it. Lines of golden light spread out through the carved grooves, and the door material folded into itself like the main entrance.

Anya stepped up to the doorway, and lights came on inside, running in strips along the ceiling. The interior space was almost completely bare, with only a few cutouts in the otherwise smooth walls. There were also several blobs sticking out of the floor in one room, which looked like they may be intended as some kind of seating.

"I've got nothing," Evan said.

"Yeah, this wasn't very helpful." However, at least in the case of this structure, it didn't look the least bit 'lived in'. "I don't think anyone ever resided here."

"I'm getting that impression, too. Let's check a few others."

They investigated another four buildings, and none of them showed any sign of prior habitation.

"Why build an underground city at all, and why wasn't it used?" Anya wondered aloud.

"Too many possibilities," Evan said. "All I can tell from here is that they seem a little taller than us, and the limb configuration is different."

"Agreed."

He headed back out to the street. "Come on. I bet the ship's control interfaces will tell us more."

— — —

The empty city exuded a strange energy that set Evan on edge. The place had clearly been intended for larger-scale plans, and *something* had happened to prevent the creators from following through. *Did they never make it to the planet, or did they crash like our expedition?*

It was impossible to date any of the structures or modifications to the cave. Since it was sealed, it could have been like that for tens or hundreds or thousands of years. Or it could have been recent history. The more he saw of Aethos, Evan's questions continued to multiply. Now that there was irrefutable evidence of other intelligent life having visited the planet, he wanted to know more about the beings—where they came from, if they were still alive somewhere, and why they were no longer on Aethos.

His investigative nature would make him question those things normally, but spending time around Anya with her exceptionally scientifically minded outlook on life had made any mystery too enticing to ignore. The ship was his best hope to get answers.

They hurried the remaining distance to the alien craft. It was smoother and more organic in form than the blockier ships he was used to seeing for human use. Any craft designed to land in atmosphere had more aerodynamic styling, but the space-only ships were known for putting utility over beauty. This alien ship was as elegant as they came. It was only a hundred-fifty-meters-long or so, indicating that it was probably a scout ship rather than a vessel meant for transporting a large number of people or lots of cargo.

However, it was probably large enough to house all the survivors of the crashed colony ship. It could be a ticket off this planet for everyone who'd been dragged into the nightmare—if only he had any clue about where Conroy had taken the colonists.

They made the final approach to the ship. There was a

slightly golden sheen to its metal hull.

"I can't believe this is real," Anya murmured.

"Neither can I. But unless there's a giant hatch, I don't see how we can fly out of here."

"Not with that attitude!" Anya urged him toward the craft.

He followed her, filled with a combination of excitement and nerves. He hadn't actually believed that they'd find a ship—despite the telepathic message from the beast—so confronting it now had upended his sense of reality. Nonetheless, the chance to explore a real alien ship was too huge an opportunity to pass up.

There was no obvious way onto the vessel. But when they were a dozen meters away, a beam of golden light appeared on the side. The light fanned outward, morphing into a line that traced out an opening in the side hull. The light continued downward as a ramp formed out of small blocks—much like the doorways. When the ramp reached the ground, the lights extinguished.

Anya looked at him, brows raised. "That's an invitation if I ever saw one."

"Aboard we go." Evan tentatively ascended the ramp to the open doorway.

The moment Evan passed through the hatch, his skin began to tingle. No lights or other systems were visible, but it distinctly seemed like there was power on the ship.

"Whoa," Anya said as she stepped into the vessel after him. "Do you feel that vibration?"

"For sure. But… how?"

"I'm guessing this thing isn't as dormant as it looks."

"Let's find its flight deck, I guess."

"At the front?" Anya asked.

"Front, top, or middle are the standard configurations for

our craft, but there's no telling how aliens may have thought about it."

"Well, it's not that big. May as well start our way at the top front and work our way down and back."

Evan and Anya set off down the passageway toward what he had taken to be the bow of the vessel. There were doors along its length at irregular intervals. Curiously, they were only a little larger than standard human doors.

"What I wouldn't give to see a photograph of one of these aliens…" Anya murmured.

"From everything we've seen, it seems like they have a few extra limbs, but they don't seem all that different from us in the grand scheme of things."

"At least in terms of their built structures," Anya replied. "Like you said, once we get eyes on the controls, we'll have a few more clues about their biology. How a being would interact with an object can tell you a lot about them."

"Everything else has been telepathic. I'm not sure what that means."

"I can't be any help with that."

"Unless it magically responds to my thoughts, my plan is to start mashing buttons until something happens."

She cast him a sidelong glance. "That's a terrible plan."

"I'm working on the fly here, cut me some slack. Do *you* want to try to fly the ship?"

"All right, I can't offer a better strategy than button-mashing. But you can do it *systematically*."

"Naturally."

They reached the flight deck. It was filled with various consoles that could have been at home on most human vessels.

"More convergent evolution?" Evan asked.

Anya looked around the room, visibly unnerved. "I don't

know. It's all a lot more... familiar than I would have expected."

"That makes two of us."

"We should try to radio Conroy that we found the ship," Anya said. She set down her pack and dug around for the radio.

"Getting a signal out through this rock might be difficult. I wonder if the ship's comm system might be able to send out a compatible signal?"

"Do you think you can get this old hulk to even turn on?"

"I was about to try." Evan went to one of the consoles and poked at it. Nothing happened.

Anya raised an eyebrow. "Flipping random controls for something written in an alien language is a terrible idea."

"Oh, there aren't any visible labels." He continued his efforts, working his way from console to console. After no results from four, he was beginning to think that maybe the ship was simply too old and its power reserves too low to start up.

But then on the fifth console, a pleasant electrical buzz responded to his touch.

Several components around the flight deck suddenly sprang to life, including a screen at the front of the room. A progress bar appeared along the bottom of the viewing space.

"What is that indicating?" Anya asked.

Evan shrugged. "No clue. Startup sequence, maybe?"

The bar inched toward completion at a frustratingly slow pace.

"Ugh, why is this taking so long?" Anya groaned.

"The boot sequence on ships can take hours. So many system checks."

"I just want to know if this thing can fly."

"It's a great sign that it's even powering on. Honestly, I had expected we'd find a few rusty pieces of heat shielding if we found anything at all."

"Well, since we do have a ship, we should probably figure out what we're doing," Anya said.

"That's a big question. We don't have more than a few days' worth of food and water left, so we're not in a position to go back to the core worlds for help."

"Not to mention, people back there tried to get us killed—if Conroy is to be believed."

"We could make a run for another colony."

"And how do we explain this ship? What do we do with it?"

"Also a terrible option," Evan admitted. "Honestly, the only thing that makes sense is to get ourselves out of *immediate* danger by going to the other side of the planet away from these Noche goons. We can hide out there and stock up on foraged supplies, then we can take it from there."

"Sounds good. Let's let Conroy know our plan, if we can get through."

They tried the radio but were unable to make contact.

"It's probably these cave walls," Evan said. "We can try again once we launch—if I can find a way out of here." The ship had gotten into the cavern, so there was a way to get it out, presumably.

At last, the progress bar finished its slow crawl and faded from the screen. New images loaded on the various consoles.

Evan resumed his hunt around the flight deck and tried various things. Eventually, he identified a control that showed an outline of the ship and several features in the outside environment. One of the notations was a horizontal line above the ship. He selected it.

A message popped up in an unreadable alien language. The

back of Evan's mind tickled, and his gut told him that it was asking for confirmation to open. He pressed it.

Loud rumbling started outside. The graphic on the console changed to show the line moving aside.

Anya went to one of the ship's viewports and stuck her face up to it. "Wow!" she exclaimed. "The whole ceiling is folding back!"

"I guess that nanotech isn't inactive, after all."

"No, this place is still very much functional," Anya agreed. "I just wish I knew why it was built and why it's abandoned now."

When the hatch had fully opened, Evan used another console to activate the ship's propulsion system. Against all odds, it started up.

Excitement swelled in his chest. *I should be terrified right now.*

Perhaps it was the strange telepathic connection with the alien technology or just his inner sense of adventure, but there wasn't fear. This ship was the embodiment of opportunity. He could no longer be forced to bend to the will of others—this was his chance to seize control and write his own story.

"Anya, if we're going to do this, there's no going back," Evan said.

"Interesting twist of fate, since that's what we said when we left for Aethos."

"This is a different kind of no return. The limitations we thought were laws will no longer apply."

"I already know too much to turn back," she said.

Evan had already made up his mind to proceed a long time ago. The mystery called to him, begging to be solved. He needed to do this—not only for the future of humanity, but to satisfy his own curiosity. Even without the monumental stakes, he'd be at the ship's helm all the same.

"Okay." He activated the launch sequence. The ship responded to his commands, its power calling to him.

Anya gave a nod of approval, a smile spreading across her face and into her eyes.

The ship rumbled and took off. It rose through the ceiling hatch, just barely clearing. Evan laid in a course for the other side of the planet.

The course cleared from the navigation display.

Evan input it again, and the course cleared once more, replaced with a destination outside the planet's atmosphere.

"What's happening?" Anya asked.

Evan tried to fight back his growing panic. "It keeps overriding me."

The ship headed toward space.

— — —

By the time Roman reached the field where his drop ship was parked, he was nearly healed. Only the snags and bloody smudges on his clothing offered any evidence of his once severe injuries.

The sphere had almost fully absorbed into his left palm. The golden metal had spread out, and only a slight dome remained in the center. Light flowed down his fingertips and up his forearm.

He shoved his left hand into his pocket to avoid any unwanted questions. That was, assuming there were still people at the ship.

As it turned out, there were only two: the pilot and Red.

Red had a bloody smear on her right temple, partially covered by her dark hair. When she noticed Roman approaching, she rolled her eyes and sighed. "Where've you been?"

"I got knocked out," Roman replied. It was true, even though he was taking creative liberties with the timeline. "Where is everyone?"

"They're all dead."

"That sucks."

She stared at him with disbelief. "That's all you have to say?"

"Sorry you weren't good enough fighters to take on one animal."

"You asshole!" Red ran at him with her knife bared.

Roman pulled back his right sleeve to bare his trefoil tattoo. "Are you sure you want to hurt me?"

Red stopped, her face twisting with anger and anguish. "Make their deaths mean something."

"Oh, they will." He brushed past her. *If you don't mess this up for us.*

The interior of the drop ship was hot and humid after baking in the sun all day. He kept the hatch open to help air it out while he went to the flight deck to access the comms.

He dialed home to his brother. Thanks to the interstellar comm relays, they'd be able to speak in real-time. There'd been too many developments to not update him on the mission status.

Marcus picked up. "You'd better have the ship."

"No, but I have something nearly as good." Roman filled him in on the recent events, and he showed him his palm.

"It's a part of you now?" Marcus asked, keeping his emotions guarded. But Roman knew him well enough to recognize that he was pleased.

"And it's amazing what it can do. If there are others, I'll

find them. But even with this one, we have a template. Once we replicate it, we'll be unstoppable."

Roman was about to get into the details of the plan he'd formulated during his walk over, but he became distracted by a strange energy reading on the screen. It was registering as a vessel.

"Shit, they must have found the ship! It's headed for space."

Marcus glowered. "Can you stop them?"

"All I have is this drop ship, and it doesn't have any weapons. But I can re-task one of our orbital probes to follow them."

As the data flowed in from the probe racing after their target, Roman noticed something strange. Another energy source had appeared, but this one was in high orbit near Aethos' smallest moon. "What is that?"

— — —

Samor kept a swift pace through the trees as soon as he was far enough away from the Echo Falls outpost entrance to no longer worry about minimizing his tracks. He needed to get the communications equipment back to Conroy as soon as possible.

A roar sounded in the distance.

What could that be? He couldn't see anything from the ground.

Samor climbed up on some rocks to get a better vantage. Still unable to see anything, he began scaling a tree. Pulling himself up the branches with his injured shoulder sent searing pain to his fingertips, but curiosity drove him onward.

He reached a point where the foliage opened up, and he caught a clear line of sight to a ship rising from the mountainside. It was at least a hundred meters long—though difficult to judge from that distance. But he knew one thing for certain: it wasn't the enemy drop ship.

They found it! They actually found it! A smile split his face. *We're still in the fight.*

His euphoria faded, remembering that the amplifier was still in his pack.

If they called us and we didn't answer, where will they go?

He scrambled down from the tree. It might already be too late.

42

EVAN'S HANDS FLEW over the controls as he desperately tried to regain command of the ship.

"Evan, what's happening…?" Anya asked, panic sharpening her tone.

"I don't know why it isn't responding. It's like it's on some kind of autopilot."

"To where?"

"I have no idea!"

Heading into space would be a disaster. They were weeks from the nearest colony and months back to anywhere he'd consider civilization. Worse, the autopilot probably wouldn't even take them toward any of those places. After everything they'd been through, their salvation ship was now going to be the death of them. They'd be dead within days after they ran out of water. Best case, there was water on board so they could instead starve to death in the coming weeks. Assuming there was enough oxygen that they didn't suffocate first.

"Evan, focus!" Anya shouted at him.

He realized that he was breathing heavily and had gone fully into his own head. *Focus. Get control of the ship.* He tried to clear his thoughts.

Feeling a little more centered, he once again tried the controls. Instead of allowing him to enter new coordinates on the planet, this time he was completely locked out from making changes. "What the…?"

Anya tried the radio again to call Conroy, but it wouldn't connect. "We might already be out of range." She braced herself on the console. "We were just supposed to go to the other side of the planet. How could this happen?"

"I don't know! I'm not in control."

"If you're not in control, then what is?"

The question had been tickling the back of Evan's mind. Hearing it articulated aloud now awakened another presence in his head.

It began as a nonsensical whisper and grew to a full voice. The sounds were chaotic and overlapping gibberish. Slowly, the patterns became recognizable, though still meaningless. And then there were words.

"Had… Ho… Her… Hello."

Evan froze. *"Who are you? Are you in my mind?"* he directed the questions toward the foreign presence.

"I am the ship."

Anya's brows knitted. "Evan, are you okay?"

He rubbed his eyes with the heels of his hands. "I don't know. I think the ship is telepathically talking to me."

Her eyes widened. "Wow…"

"Would it be easier if I spoke?" a voice said over unseen speakers, filling the room.

Evan and Anya both jumped at its sudden appearance.

"You're the ship?" Anya asked tentatively.

"My local processing systems are integrated into this vessel, yes."

"How do you know our language?" Evan asked.

"In short, I read your mind. It was not difficult to map the syntax of your spoken word."

"Well, ship, it's great to meet you, but we would really like to go to the coordinates I entered," Evan said firmly.

"I saw your goals in your mind, and I know what you need to accomplish those objectives. Landing this ship on the other side of the planet would not achieve your desired outcomes."

Evan frowned. "Well, that's what we want to do. You don't know all of the variables."

"Neither do you organics. Unlike you, I have run a comprehensive analysis of three-hundred-thousand variations using the known factors, and I have determined that the destination I have set is the best course to accomplish your goals."

"And where is that?"

"My homeworld."

The ship rose through the final layers of atmosphere, and the view outside changed to the darkness of space.

"We'll die on a journey over. We don't have supplies," Evan tried to explain to the ship. He didn't expect the artificial intelligence to understand the fragility of human life, but hopefully its makers had similar biological limitations.

"How long can you survive with what you have?" the ship asked.

"A couple of days."

"That will be sufficient for our journey."

"But how…?" Evan faded out when he noticed an incredible scene unfolding on the front screen.

The ship was approaching the smallest of Aethos' three moons. A swarm of metal-like components were rising from its surface, swirling around each other like a swarm of insects. They formed a writhing stream on a direct course for the ship.

Evan braced for an attack, his heart racing. *We're going to be ripped apart!*

The swarm broke moments before reaching the ship, instead fanning out to encircle it. The individual components began to link up to create a latticework around the vessel.

"What's happening?" Evan asked, mesmerized.

"We are becoming whole again," the ship replied.

"You'll have to be more specific."

"We need to travel to a distant system, and this is the component we need to enable interstellar travel."

"Like an auxiliary jump drive?"

"That is a good way to characterize it within your frame of reference."

Anya's eyes went wide. "I thought jump travel without a fixed gate was only theoretical?"

"Not to my makers," the ship stated. "I will take you to my home."

"And what will we find there?"

"The answers you seek."

Anya took Evan's hand, offering grounding and reassurance that no matter what happened next, they'd face it together. "No going back," she said.

He nodded. "We're ready."

— — —

A small number of people had made life exceptionally annoying for Marcus Santano, and his brother was at the top of the list. Losing the alien ship was yet another setback in a string of failures.

The latest sequence of blunders had begun when it was discovered that an undercover cop had infiltrated their organization. Him witnessing a discussion between a Noche lieutenant and the sitting chancellor's Deputy of Economic Development had really thrown a wrench in things. Marcus had wanted to kill the witness, but his sister had talked him into sending the man on the doomed Aethos colony mission instead. It was a ship filled with all the loose ends left over from their decade of planning, so it'd made sense to agree at the time. However, knowing now that a number of the people had survived on Aethos threatened to expose their secrets. Worse, Conroy had an opportunity to get his hooks into them.

The entire situation was a disaster, and there was little he could do from afar. The one saving grace was that Roman had been able to send a probe through the spatial distortion when the alien ship had jumped away, so they had coordinates to where the ship had gone. Unfortunately, they didn't know who was on board, and it would take months to get their own ship to the destination using their available technology.

Marcus needed to fill in his collaborator. He called up Chancellor Rostov.

The chancellor answered. "This better be urgent, contacting me on this line."

"It is." Marcus jumped right to it, knowing that was the chancellor's preferred style. "Good news and bad. There *is* a ship. We don't have possession of it at the moment, but we know where it is." He forwarded the probe's scan data.

The chancellor reviewed the readings. "Interesting."

"Do you know it?"

"It's a world that's come up before. One of many—too many to have known where to focus our efforts. Now we do."

"And I'll see that it gets done right," Marcus assured him "I gave my brother a chance, and he failed. Marta will make sure the job is finished."

"We can't afford any more mistakes. Nor can we let Conroy get control of that ship or any of the other tech."

"I won't let that happen."

"Consider this your final warning. If you can't deliver, I'll find someone who will." The chancellor ended the call.

Marcus leaned back in his chair. This opportunity was likely the Noche Syndicate's only chance to get a real seat at the table. He wouldn't let it go to waste.

He opened a comm channel with his sister. "Marta, I have a new job for you."

— — —

The orbital scan data had Conroy and his team perplexed. There was a new energy signature by the moon, and no one could figure out what it might be or where it had come from.

"Did the enemy send reinforcements while we were in the communications blackout?" Samor pondered.

Conroy shook his head. "These readings aren't like any known ship in our fleet or private sector. It's something else." Frankly, they didn't have enough data to draw any conclusions.

"Well, we know a ship got off the ground. I can only hope it was them," Samor said.

"I believe it was," Conroy replied. "Without comms at the time, they wouldn't have been able to reach us. They left to get the ship to safety when we missed contact. It's what I'd hoped they'd do."

"And now we need to hope they'll come back for us."

"They will."

Conroy couldn't know that for certain, but he had a good feeling about those two. He'd been around enough people in his political career to get a sense for who was trustworthy and who wasn't, and Evan and Anya both struck him as genuine people who'd do the right thing. Hopefully, he'd made his case that he was on the side worth fighting for.

"Sir, a message just came through for you," Rebeka said. Her face dropped. "It's from Chancellor Rostov."

Conroy kept his expression composed for the sake of his team, while inside he was swearing at the mention of the traitor. The backstabber wasn't worth the air he breathed. "Let me see it."

Rebeka stepped aside to allow Conroy to open the message without others seeing the contents.

As it turned out, it was nothing he wouldn't want the trusted members of his team to see. "He hasn't changed a bit." Conroy left the text on display for others to read.

The message simply read: 'Check.' It was a reference to their time playing chess together, back when they considered each other friends. Rostov wanted to send the message that he was closing in for the kill. Nonetheless, there were still moves. It wasn't over yet.

"What does this mean for us?" Samor asked after seeing the message.

Conroy stared at the star map showing where the message had originated from the capital planet—the world that was his once and future home. "It means that we're back in this war. And we're going to win."

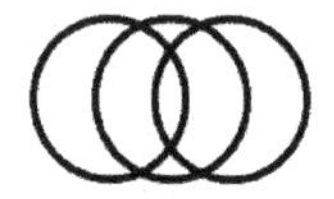

THE STORY CONTINUES IN *LOST PLANET…*

Lost Planet (Starship of the Ancients Book 2)

Powerful players scheming from the shadows. An ancient alien starship. Who can be trusted with the most coveted technology in the Commonwealth?

Evan and Anya have escaped Aethos, but there's no evading the new target on their backs. Everyone wants the ancient alien starship now under Evan's command, and they'll claim it at any cost. As they embark on an ambitious investigation to track down the ship's builders, Evan and Anya soon discover that the interstellar plot to transform the Commonwealth with alien tech runs much deeper than they'd ever imagined. With opposing factions vying for control of the alien tech, Evan and Anya will need to pick a side. Can they keep the ship from falling into the wrong hands?

ADDITIONAL READING

Cadicle Space Opera Series
Book 1: Shadows of Empire (Vol. 1-3)
Book 2: Web of Truth (Vol. 4)
Book 3: Crossroads of Fate (Vol. 5)
Book 4: Path of Justice (Vol. 6)
Book 5: Scions of Change (Vol. 7)

Mindspace Series
Book 1: Infiltration
Book 2: Conspiracy
Book 3: Offensive
Book 4: Endgame

Taran Empire Saga
Book 1: Empire Reborn
Book 2: Empire Uprising
Book 3: Empire Defied
Book 4: Empire United

Dark Stars Trilogy
Book 1: Crystalline Space
Book 2: A Light in the Dark
Book 3: Masters of Fate

See a complete list at www.akduboff.com

AUTHORS' NOTES

Thank you for reading *Stranded*! I hope you enjoyed this first installment in the Starship of the Ancients series.

The early concepts for this story first came to me several years ago, and I spent some time letting them percolate before putting any words to paper. It began roughly as "*Lost* in space", but being me, I knew I'd need to flesh out a broader interstellar conspiracy of some sort. Figuring out how to put the various pieces together took a long time, but I'm really pleased with how this book came together in the end.

From the outset, I'd envisioned a survival story about crash survivors on an alien world. They were on the *right* world, but not precisely where they were supposed to be and without most of the resources that they should have had as part of the colony expedition. I wanted to work toward a significant midpoint in the story where the straightforward survival plot took a big turn, and suddenly a much bigger story opens up with a larger cast of character POVs (points-of-view, i.e. perspective characters). That was the goal, anyway, so I'll leave it up to you to say whether I was successful in that mission!

The story will continue to widen over the course of the series. I'm planning a trilogy arc that will culminate in a satisfying conclusion, but I will continue the series beyond that with a new story arc if it proves to be a world and characters my readers would like to explore further.

I appreciate you not only reading the book but also taking the time to look at these notes, and I want you to know how much it means to me to be able to share my stories with an audience around the world. I couldn't do this as a job without readers like you, thank you!

I also could not produce books without the ongoing support of my wonderful beta readers and proofing team. They have so many great insights, and I'm forever indebted to them catching issues so I can correct them before books ever go to press. My heartfelt thanks to John, Gil, Leo, Mike, Manie, Doug, David F, Charlie, David B, Kurt, Eric, Jim, Liz, Bryan, and Steve for their invaluable feedback. And thank you to my amazing Propellers and other author friends for your support and encouragement all these years! The sci-fi indie author community is truly one of the coolest groups of people.

There's much more to come in the Starship of the Ancients series, and I hope you'll come along for the ride. Until the next installment, happy reading!

ABOUT THE AUTHOR

A.K. (Amy) DuBoff has always loved science fiction in all its forms—books, movies, shows, and games. If it involves outer space, even better! She is a Nebula Award finalist and USA Today bestselling author most known for her Cadicle Universe, but she's also written a variety of sci-fi and fantasy books, short fiction, and screenplays. Amy can frequently be found traveling the world, and when she's not writing, she enjoys wine tasting, binge-watching TV series, and playing epic strategy board games.

www.akduboff.com

Made in United States
Orlando, FL
11 September 2025

64897726R00243